YOU, WITH YOUR WAITING

A NOVEL

LESLIE LACIN

WRITE THE WAY HOME PRESS

 Formatted with Vellum

CONTENTS

For my children's children — with all my love forever.

PART I SORROW
JUNE-DECEMBER 1941

Wait for me, and I'll return, only wait very hard.
Wait, when you are filled with sorrow as you watch the yellow
*   rain;*
Wait, when the winds sweep the snowdrifts,
Wait in the sweltering heat,
Wait when others have stopped waiting, forgetting their
*   yesterdays.*

K. Simonov - translated by Alexander Werth - 1964

Inset (top right):

RUSSIAN S.F.S.R.

Zheleznovodsk • Mineralnye Vody

Mt. Beshtau △• Pyatigorsk
• Malka   Terek

Zayukova •   • Malgobek
Nalchik •   Furthest German
Mt. Elbrus △   Urukh advance, Nov 1942
                        • Ordzhonikidze
                        • Mt. Kazbek

GEORGIAN
S.F.S.R.   Aragvi
                        Georgian
50 miles   Kura   Military Road
                        • Tbilisi

Main map:

SWEDEN

FINLAND

BALTIC SEA

LENINGRAD

ESTONIAN
S.S.R.

LATVIAN S.S.R.

RUSSIAN
S.F.S.R.

LITHUANIAN
S.S.R.

Volga   Kama

NAZI
GERMANY

BYELORUSSIAN
S.S.R.

■ MOSCOW

S O V I E T   U N I O N

Furthest German
advance, Nov 1942

Poland

General
Government

• Voronezh

• Saratov

• KIEV

KAZAKH
STEPPE

Kharkov •

Don   Volga

UKRAINIAN
S.S.R.   Barvenkovo • Krasny Lyman
Dnieper   • Stalingrad   KAZAKH
                                                    S.S.R.

HUNGARY   Krammatorsk
Dnepropetrovsk   Donets

MOLDAVIAN   Stalino •
S.S.R.

Taganrog
Batays k • Rostov-on-Don

ROMANIA   SEA OF
            Crimea   AZOV   Slavyansk • Solsk

                        Kuban   • Tikhoretsk

                        • Stavropol

                        SEE INSET

BLACK   SEA   C   Terek
                        A U C   • Malgobek
BULGARIA   U   C

                        GEORGIAN   A
                        S.S.R.   • Tbilisi   S
                                    Kura   U
                                            S   CASPIAN
                                                SEA

                        AZERBAIJAN
                        S.S.R.
            ARMENIAN
            S.S.R.

GERMAN OCCUPIED
TERRITORY OF THE
SOVIET UNION, 1941-42

TURKEY

- - - - - National border
- - - - - Internal border   } May 1941

■   Capital city
• • •   City or town
△   Mountain peak

SCALE: 300 miles

IRAN

CHAPTER 1
ROSTOV-ON-DON, JUNE 1941

IT WAS JUST AVSEY'S LUCK. HE'D LOST HIS POCKETKNIFE AT THE moment he needed it most. The knife wasn't in the birch treasure box he kept hidden under his bed. It wasn't on the balcony where he'd opened it the day before to admire its shiny blade. He didn't dare ask Bronya if she'd seen it, because he wasn't supposed to own a pocketknife. Papa had been adamant: *Not until you're thirteen.* Avsey knew his sister would disapprove; she disapproved of rule breaking in general. He could hear her now, her tone condescending: *You are only eleven, Avseyka. Have you forgotten what Papa told you about playing with knives?* On top of everything, if Bronya found out that he was a thief, he'd be in *real* trouble.

Dima, the bully who shared Avsey's desk at school and deserved every bad thing that ever happened to him, had finally made a stupid mistake. He'd left his pocketknife under the diary on his desk when he was called to the board for a math problem. Avsey, who'd made a career of waiting for Dima to make stupid mistakes, took full advantage of the situation. As Dima hesitated in front of the numbers, chalk in hand, Avsey slid his fingers under the diary, fingered the knife, and slowly slid it into his schoolbag. Seconds later, Dima, chastised by the teacher for his lack of preparation, slunk angrily back into his chair. Turning to the back of the room to roll his eyes, he grabbed his diary and stuffed it into his schoolbag. In his humiliation, Dima had failed to notice the absence of his prized possession, stolen by the desk mate he loathed.

As Avsey lay in bed later that night, sleepless with good fortune, it dawned on him: The knife was the perfect thing to take to Artek, the youth camp on the Black Sea, where he would spend the summer. A pocketknife would certainly impress the other boys at camp. He'd make friends and command respect. For the first time in his life, he'd be popular. And all the bullying at school, the endless insults, the gratuitous punches, would fade and disappear. Somehow, fortune had smiled on him.

Until fortune stopped smiling and the pocketknife disappeared.

Avsey opened the bedroom door. Bronya continued to play her scales without looking at him. He wasn't allowed in their shared bedroom when Bronya was practicing her violin, but she'd been at it a long time and he'd run out of patience. Avsey waited for her to stop, and when she didn't, he blurted out, "Maybe I shouldn't go. You'll be here alone when I leave."

Bronya stopped playing, her bow hovering above the strings. Without looking at him, she said, "We'll talk about it later, Avseyka."

Avsey backed out of the room and Bronya pushed the door shut with her foot. He heard the soft click of the lock and her slow inhale before she resumed her scales. Avsey shouted into the closed door, "You don't care!"

The music stopped. For a moment, the silence hung heavy in the air. Avsey worried he'd pushed his sister too far. He felt the muscles tighten in his neck. She opened the door a crack and with a stiff smile said, "Avsey, I need ten more minutes. Please."

"I'm not going to Artek."

Bronya stood and opened the door wide. Her gaze traveled down the length of his dirty uniform, past his bloody leg, to his dusty shoes. He'd been pushed on the street next to the school and his knee had taken the brunt of the fall. *Dima's friends*. He pushed the damp hair from his forehead and tucked his shirt into his shorts, trying in vain to appear composed.

"What happened, Avseyka? Did you fall off the bike again?" Bronya put the violin and bow on the bed and led Avsey to the living room.

"You can't make me go. The boys there will know. And I won't let them say things about Mama."

Bronya kissed the top of his head. "Artek is the best place on earth. No one will know anything about you. And if they do, it won't matter. You'll learn to sail and swim, you'll go to Kherson, and most of all, you won't be here. It will be good for you." Bronya walked into the kitchen and returned with a cloth and a bottle of zelyonka for Avsey's knee.

"I want to stay with you and Papa. What if Mama comes home and I'm not here?"

Bronya wiped the blood from Avsey's leg. "I won't be here to take care of you. I'll be at the conservatory all day."

"Like I said, you don't care."

Bronya let exasperation creep into her voice as she dabbed the green antiseptic on Avsey's cut. "All I do is care. I don't have a choice."

Avsey brushed her hand away from his leg. "That's not my fault. I don't want you to take care of me."

Bronya put the cap on the bottle. "Careful, you'll have green spots everywhere. Want an ice cream?"

Avsey eyed his sister. "I'm not a little boy anymore. Ice cream doesn't work."

"Ice cream *always* works. For everyone. I'm going. Come if you want."

Bronya was almost right. Ice cream cured everything. Except the pocketknife. But this was his lucky break. With his sister out of the apartment, he could continue his search for the pocketknife without her prying eyes following him everywhere.

When Bronya had gone, shaking her head and muttering under her breath, Avsey scrambled under the bed on his stomach to retrieve his birch box. He needed to check it again. Maybe he'd missed the green case, or maybe it was stuck against the side, held in place by the roll of stamps. He listened briefly at the front door for Bronya's footsteps but the hallway was silent. He went into Mama's room to open the box, just in case Bronya returned. He hoped she'd find her friends and stand outside talking like she usually did when the weather was warm. That would give him all the time he needed.

Sitting at the edge of his parent's bed, Avsey popped the lid off the birch box and reached inside, searching with his finger-tips for the smooth case. He pulled out the roll of stamps, lingering over them for a moment. Avsey had stolen some of these stamps from the boys at school who'd tortured him. Surprised that Dima's friends felt confident enough to leave such treasures in their desks, he hadn't felt guilty about stealing from them. These boys considered themselves untouchable, and that was the thing, in the end, that bothered him most. Stealing from Dima's friends felt like justice, a kind of exhilarating revenge visited upon those who'd laughed when Dima spit into his hands and rubbed saliva into his hair or when Dima called him Christ-killer and demanded to know if he had horns. Stealing from them was payback for their arrogance. They weren't superior to him—they were mean.

In the weeks after Mama was taken away, the taunts from the boys at school worsened. It took all Avsey's strength to keep his composure when Dima whispered, "I heard she eats children and spits out their teeth." Avsey, close to tears, had kept his eyes trained on the portrait of Lenin above the teacher's desk while Dima grinned and slapped his thigh. Avsey's only solace came from addding the stolen stamps to his collection, pasting them carefully into his albums while Bronya and Papa slept.

As always, he talked to Mama in the dark while he worked. He told her about stealing from the other boys, not quite sure she would approve but knowing she would understand. To reassure her, he told her he'd made a friend at school, in the last few days before summer break. He complained that Bronya was obsessed with the Moscow Conservatory. He didn't tell her about Papa's sadness, his moody silences. He didn't want to worry her. Before he went to sleep he always told her he was waiting for her to come home.

When the box had been emptied of most of its treasure, and the pocketknife was nowhere to be found, Avsey admitted defeat. He tried to console himself with the small toys and Lenin medals he'd stolen from the neighborhood kiosks. They were, after all, a testament to his skill and courage as a thief. The women in charge of kiosks were hawklike, and to cover a small toy with his palm and pull it out unnoticed was dangerous, exhilarating. Still, the loss of the pocketknife was a blow. It didn't just walk off on its own. Was he losing his golden touch?

The room smelled like Mama. Avsey stretched his legs out on the bed for a moment, then turned on his side and curled up in a forlorn bid to be near her again, to bury his head against her shoulder and pretend to sleep. He hadn't done this for a long time and didn't know why this particular memory made him ache under his collarbone, but it did. He missed her. He sat up after a time, smoothing the coverlet on the bed to obliterate the impressions his body had made.

He went to the armoire. Maybe she'd left a scarf, something soft he could keep next to him while he slept. He opened the doors into the dark interior and paused. A series of small drawers below the shelves and several boxes looked promising. Curious, Avsey took a small brown cardboard box from one of the shelves and lifted the lid. A pair of baby shoes, nestled in old newspaper. Had they been his? He didn't remember them.

In another box, he found a small pair of blue shorts and a matching shirt, also wrapped tidily in newspaper. Why had Mama kept these things? On a small piece of paper tucked into the shirt sleeve, someone had written *Kuzma — two years*. Avsey closed the boxes and returned them to their places on the shelf. Was Kuzma the child of a friend? A relative he didn't know?

Next, Avsey turned his attention to the three small drawers. Bronya would be home soon and his adventure in his parents' closet would end. He had to hurry. The drawer on the right contained Mama's jewelry: a chain with a pearl pendant Mama always wore, her wedding ring, and a small gold pinky ring. He'd never seen his mother without her jewelry. He pulled the drawer out and dumped its contents into his birch box, his heart beating faster. What would Bronya say if she knew? He liked feeling scared, and besides, he could always put Mama's jewelry back in the armoire if needed. In the meantime, he would have her gold. She would be closer to him, and maybe magically, his holding on to her in this way would bring her home.

He opened another drawer. This one held a folded piece of paper, a photograph, and a thick envelope. He could barely make out the writing on the envelope but held it up to the light under the door and saw his mother's name, *Asya*. In the corner, where the sender might have put an address— an *S*, written in ink and underlined.

Avsey took the folded paper and photograph and placed them in his box. He would look at them later. He returned the letter to the drawer so no one would notice the missing items. Anyway, grown-up letters were boring.

The last drawer appeared to contain things that belonged to Papa, but just as he began to look through them, he heard the front door. Afraid Bronya might hear him, he held his breath, listening to footsteps in the hall. "Avseyka?" Bronya was looking for him.

Avsey let the air escape through his open mouth and tipped the drawer into his box, hoping the slide of Papa's possessions wouldn't be loud enough to alert Bronya to his presence in their parent's bedroom. "Avseyka, I'm back!" He could hear her moving around the kitchen. His hands shook as he pushed the drawer into place, closed the armoire, and slipped out of the bedroom. A few steps and he was in his room, sliding the box under his bed. He turned around just in time. Bronya stood in the doorway, her hands on her hips. "Why didn't you answer me? I called you several times."

Avsey ignored her question, "I'm going to meet Ilya on the corner. I want to show him my stamp album." He grabbed the green stamp album from his pillow and headed to the door before Bronya could say a word. He couldn't look her in the eye until he'd had a walk and time to think about what he'd just done—stolen from both his parents.

He heard Bronya call after him, "Only to the corner, no further!"

CHAPTER 2
ROSTOV, EARLY MORNING, JUNE 22, 1941

Bronya couldn't sleep. A mosquito buzzed in the dark. She considered closing the window, but decided the room would be too hot. She distracted herself with thoughts of Avsey at Artek, the summer camp she'd gone to last year on the Black Sea. Her smarter-than-anyone little brother would leave home, alone, for the first time in less than eight hours. She was glad for him, especially after all that had happened in the spring. Artek would take Avsey's mind off Mama. He hadn't been home when their mother, half-naked, had threatened to jump from the balcony. Bronya had kept the image of Mama, straitjacketed and screaming as she was taken away, to herself. Artek would be good for Avsey, allow him be a little boy again. He would stop asking questions Bronya couldn't answer.

She listened to Avsey's breathing from the small bed in the corner of their bedroom. Bronya envied his ability to sleep soundly. She tried to relax her shoulders and clear her mind but couldn't help worrying. Papa remained resolute in his opposition to her attending the conservatory in Moscow, but she was sure this was because of Mama's situation. Maybe everything would be better before it was time to leave. Somewhere deep down, she knew Papa was proud of her.

Giving up on sleep, Bronya sat up and propped her head against the wall. Through the open window, the scent of river water filled the air, rich with the runoff from a thousand kilometers of steppe. The cicadas' song waxed and waned—crescendo, decrescendo. She imagined the swirling water emptying into the Black Sea and the world beyond. felt her body floating on a tiny raft, alone in the dark. Her eyes began to close.

From a faraway place, someone pounded on a door. When the rattling sounded again, louder, Bronya jerked up, confused. Who was there? Had she been dreaming? She held her breath and listened.

Again, pounding vibrated through the apartment. A scream formed and settled at the top of Bronya's larynx. Was someone here to take Papa? Bronya knew something about middle of the night visitors—they all did. Her heart beat loud in her ears. The long moment was ruptured by the creak of Papa's mattress. Maybe she could stop him and they could turn back before it was too late. They could slip down into their beds and pull the blankets up over their heads and pretend to be asleep.

But Papa's slippers flapped down the hall, quick against the soles of his feet. The dead bolt slid open. Bronya heard a voice in the vestibule. Words, indistinguishable but clearly urgent, drifted down the hallway and into her room. She put her ear to the door and listened harder.

A rustle and a thud sounded from the other side of the bedroom. Bronya jumped again. Avsey had turned in his sleep, sending his stamp album to the floor, but his breathing remained deep and even. He hadn't heard a thing.

The voice in the living room registered louder, more insistent. Would the stranger hurt Papa? Bronya groped the chair beside the bed to find her sweater, to pull it on over her nightgown. As she pushed her arms through the sleeves, a familiar scent lifted from the sweater's fibers. *Mama.* Bronya's last image of her mother floated in the midair of her mind's eye until she swung her feet over the side of the bed and placed them on the wood floor. She turned to face the door.

The stranger in the living room was Stepan Ilyich, chief engineer at Rostov-Glavny, the main train station where Papa was director of the North Caucasus Line. He and Stepan Ilyich had been friends forever, as far back as Bronya could remember.

The sight of his grisly face was a relief. Her whole body relaxed. She wanted to throw her arms around them both and tell them how frightened she'd been. But Papa's face was stern and colorless. He stared at Stepan Ilyich, his dark eyes prominent in his pale face, his hands at his sides. Stepan Ilyich's eyebrows were arched high on his forehead, and beads of perspiration glistened around his hairline. The two men eyed each other like contestants in a boxing match.

Stepan Ilyich was aggravated. "With respect, Lev Moisevich, we have reports the rail stations at Grodno, Brest, Rodno, Kaunas, and Kiev have been bombed. The fleet, warehouses, Sevastopol. All bombed. There are casualties."

A hollow feeling spread from Bronya's chest into her limbs.

Papa folded his large frame onto one of the kitchen chairs and stared at the patterned linoleum, his palms resting on his thighs. He stretched his fingers toward his knees. He looked up at Stepan Ilyich. "I don't believe it."

Stepan Ilyich pulled his shoulders back, "Germany has attacked the Soviet Union, Lev Moisevich. Whether you believe it or not." Stepan Ilyich kept his eye on Papa while he took a handkerchief from his pocket and swiped at the sweat that had begun rolling down his face. His words settled around them like paper confetti.

Papa stood and paced the room, cracking his knuckles, one by one. Stepan Ilyich flinched with each crack, and the distress on his face deepened further into its already furrowed lines.

Bronya glanced at the clock on the bookshelf. Quarter to six. Her eyes moved back and forth between the two men, waiting for them to speak. The clock ticked seconds and Bronya felt them reverberate through her body. Papa and Stepan Ilyich were no longer boxers; they were storks, their great wings stirring slowly for flight.

Stepan Ilyich broke the silence. "Lev Moiesevich?"

Papa turned. "It's madness," he said in a quietly, "absolute madness." Papa only used his quiet tone in serious situations. When Babushka died, he had greeted relatives and friends who came to pay their condolences in a low, growly whisper. As if the burden of speech weighed so heavily on his shoulders, it might press him into the newly dug earth alongside his dead mother. Bronya had always been a little afraid when Papa whispered.

She looked harder at the two men in the room. They were shrinking in front of her eyes. Everything was shrinking: the living room, the city, the world. She was shrinking, too.

"I'll come with you, Papa." Bronya pushed against feeling small. "Please?"

Papa looked at her and blinked. He hadn't noticed her in the room. "Bronislava. Good. Stepan Ilyich was saying, well, you heard. Stay with Avsey until I can make sense of what's going on."

Bronya, desperate, tried not to beg. "Papa, I'll wake Avsey. We'll come to the station with you. I can run messages for you."

Papa attempted a smile. "Everything will be fine." His voice lacked conviction. "You'll go back to sleep." He left the room without looking at her.

Bronya was incredulous. *Go back to sleep?*

Stepan Ilyich cleared his throat. He held his cap in his hands and looked down at his polished black shoes. Bronya thought he might cry. Uncomfortable, she pushed her curls from her face and tucked them behind her ears.

Stepan Ilyich raised his head. "Your father tells me you've had all fives at school, in every subject. He says he's sure you'll be an engineer."

Bronya smiled politely, but her heart dropped into the pit of her stomach. Papa hadn't told anyone about the conservatory? "Thank you, Stepan Ilyich."

He looked down at his shoes and shifted forward slightly before he said, "Your mother is proud of you too, Bronislava." He paused awkwardly, "You've grown up; you're more like her now. I mean, no, just the way you look. You have her looks." He took a step back and blinked.

Heat spread from Bronya's cheeks to her forehead. She had Mama's green eyes and unruly hair, and she'd already noticed the way people looked away, as if to resemble her mother meant she might lose her way.

Papa emerged wearing his uniform tunic and holding his cap. He was more familiar now, though his face was still pale and deep lines etched the contours of his mouth. He put his arm around Bronya. "Promise me you'll stay inside. If anything happens, go to the basement and wait for me there."

"Yes, Papa. Don't worry." What did he mean by *if anything happens*?

Papa reached out and pulled the hair from behind her ears. He winked without smiling, tender nonetheless. "Your ears will stick out."

Just before they both disappeared, Stepan Ilyich turned back to look at Bronya. His eyes shone brightly in his tattered old face, and there was the hint of a grave but tender smile. He looked sadder than anyone Bronya had ever seen. Now it was Bronya who thought she might cry.

Bronya sat numb in the living room for some time, at a loss for something to do. The gray suitcase in the vestibule caught her eye. After supper last night, she'd added the pioneer scarf to Avsey's suitcase and sent him off to bed with a kiss. How could she have forgotten? Avsey was leaving for Artek today. Would she have to tell him he couldn't go?

She closed her eyes and conjured explosions and smoldering fires in her mind. Where would she hide if the Germans came? Would they all wear gas masks like they had last summer at

Artek? The drill in the woods wearing gas masks had been nonsensical at the time. She'd been unable to breathe, but the most discomforting aspect of the whole afternoon had been the way her friends appeared alien, their faces obscured, their bodies marching in single file like giant ants.

Light crossed the threshold of the balcony window, spilling over the trees and into the apartment. Bronya walked into the kitchen, opened the cold-water faucet, and leaned over the sink. The world was as it had been before the news, the dishes remained neatly stacked, the samovar still nestled in the corner next to the stove. The cupboards were clean, the counters, still covered in old copies of *Pravda* and wallpaper, were peeling but tidy. A small bowl of onions, a box of salt, and a canister of black tea lined the wall.

Disaster hovered and, like a fairy-tale villain in the forest, it was not quite believable. What would the German planes sound like? How would things break apart? Would the dishes, books, and ceramic figurines fall through the cracks? She imagined Papa and Avsey clinging to the roofless, open walls. She splashed cool water on her face and tried to steady her nerves.

Avsey's sleepy voice rang out from the bedroom, "It's Artek day!"

Bronya's throat tightened. Avsey's optimism had always been infectious, unbearable at times. She would lie—at least until she knew what to say.

"Bronya?" Avsey appeared in his underwear and sleeveless undershirt, his skinny limbs muscular, newly brown. "Papa asleep?"

"He went to the station for a minute. You want to put some clothes on?" Bronya tried to regulate her voice.

Avsey yawned and swung his arms. "When will he be here to take me to the bus?"

Bronya turned her back to Avsey. She pulled the cupboard curtain open and extracted a white enamel box. "You need to get dressed."

"But when will Papa be back?"

"He didn't say." She took the lid off the box and sighed.

Avsey hopped up onto the counter beside her and pushed his face into hers. "Are all sisters evil or did I get lucky?"

Bronya avoided his eyes and stood on her toes to reach a pot on the highest shelf.

Avsey swung his legs, thumping his feet against the cupboard. "Did you and Papa argue this morning? Did you make him angry again? Just do what he says, become an engineer. Anyway, the conservatory is a dumb idea."

Bronya turned, irritated. "Papa isn't mad at me. And what has the conservatory got to do with you getting dressed? You are ten, not three."

"When are you going to tell me what's going on?"

"Avsey, why are you so stubborn?"

Avsey frowned. "You aren't my mother, Bronislava."

Bronya sighed. "But that doesn't mean you don't have to listen to me."

"I am perfectly capable of taking care of myself. As you know."

"Does that mean I don't have to do it anymore? I can go to Moscow? Stop talking like a crazy person."

"The only crazy person in this apartment is you." Avsey hopped down and stomped toward the bedroom.

Bronya fought back tears. She couldn't cry now. "Wait."

Avsey turned, an exaggerated look of impatience on his face.

"Germany attacked the Soviet Union early this morning. Stepan Ilyich came early to tell Papa. They went to the station. I don't think you'll be going to Artek."

Avsey's eyes widened. "War? Like in the movie we saw with Papa?"

"War is not like in the movies. This is serious. The Germans have bombed several cities. Stepan Ilyich said people have died." Bronya looked down at the linoleum. A column of ants made their way along the crack between the balcony door and the floor.

"Why didn't you wake me up?" The freckle under Avsey's left eye, shaped like a teardrop, twitched.

"Why does that matter? What would you have done?"

Avsey raised his voice. "I understand much more than you think I do."

Bronya reached her hand out to touch his arm, a plea for civility. He'd missed Mama in the last few months. "I'm sorry, Avseyka, I know how smart you are."

"A war starts and you don't think you should wake me up?"

"I said I was sorry. I've been waiting for German planes since Papa left."

Avsey waved his hand dismissively. "The USSR has the best pilots in the world. There is nothing to worry about."

Bronya didn't know what to say. Maybe he was right. Maybe he wasn't. But Avsey didn't need to know about the slithery feeling in her stomach, about how Papa had shrunk before her eyes. She didn't want to mute his confidence.

Avsey marched around the apartment singing at the top of his lungs, "If tomorrow brings war, if tomorrow we fight, we'll be ready today."

Bronya humored him but wished she wasn't in charge. Why did she have to face all this alone?

By the time Papa returned a few hours later, Avsey was convinced the Soviet Union had already won the war. Papa put off Avsey's questions with bland, vague answers. "We are taking care of the situation." Later he said, "Let's not worry yet, Avsey."

Bronya and Avsey walked with Papa to listen to Foreign Minister Molotov's speech broadcast from loudspeakers around Gorky Park. Bronya looked for her friends in the crowd but didn't see anyone she knew from school. The neighbors who lived on the third floor, an older couple Mama called the aristocrats, stood nearby. The woman, Madam Alexandra, was a fine pianist. As the crowd moved into place, Bronya caught her eye and lifted her hand in a discreet wave. Madam Alexandra nodded without smiling.

Bronya had taken piano lessons with Madame Alexandra for a year when she was six. Every Wednesday afternoon. She played the violin by then, but Babushka had wanted her to play the piano, too. She'd convinced Papa, explaining that the piano was necessary for all musicians. The lessons lasted until Bronya was almost seven, around the time Madame Alexandra had given her a porcelain doll in a faded silk dress. Mama hid the luxurious gift, making it clear she didn't approve of *la poupee bourgeoise*. Mama spoke French when she disapproved of something, as if the class war was embedded in language. The next day, Bronya's piano lessons ended. Mama told her Madame Alexandra had said she was devoid of talent. *Devoid of talent.*

Bronya remembered the argument between Mama and Babushka as if it had happened yesterday. She'd lain awake in bed while Babushka demanded to know why no one had asked her, the professional musician, about stopping the piano. Bronya felt intense shame for her lack of talent, but more than that, she'd been embarrassed for having liked the doll, for wanting it more than anything. She wanted to tell Madame Alexandra about the conservatory, but she glanced at Papa and decided to turn away.

Molotov began to speak, and the crowd fell silent. It was as if the foreign minister, grave and majestic, was standing among them. "Today at four o'clock, without any declaration of war and without any claims being made on the Soviet Union, German troops attacked our country, attacked our borders at many points, bombed from their airplanes our cities, Zhitomir, Kiev, Sevastopol..."

Avsey nudged Bronya. His eyes were huge. He stood on his tiptoes to whisper in her ear, "Sevastopol. Near Artek." Avsey leaned into Papa and took his large hand in his own, much smaller, hand. Bronya couldn't tell if he was seeking comfort or giving it. Shock curtained the air in broad swaths of open mouths, hands on hearts, upturned heads. No one moved. The park was pin-drop quiet.

Bronya reached for Papa's other hand as Molotov ended his speech. " Our cause is just. The enemy will be smashed. Victory will be ours."

Rostov's citizens stayed rooted in collective stillness until an angry voice broke the spell of Molotov's dignified narration. "Bastards, I'll kill every last one of them with my bare hands." The woman standing next to Papa began to cry. Another woman began to sing the International. The crowd took up the song, and the breeze lifted their voices, carrying them over the city. Bronya held her chin high and sang with all her might.

The powerful spell remained as the crowd dispersed like a large flock of birds lifting upward in unison. Papa was somber as he navigated around the park and down Budennovsky Prospekt, passing queues of young men reporting to the recruiting stations around the park. Young mothers with prams clustered together as their husbands became soldiers.

"Papa, are you going to leave, too?" Avsey stopped next to a group of old men sitting on a bench next to one of the recruiting stations. The men held short cigarette stubs between their yellowed fingers and smelled of vodka. They turned toward Papa when they heard Avsey's question, poised for the answer.

"Stalin needs me to work for victory here at home. The North Caucasus Railroad will be important to the war effort."

One old man stabbed the air with his cigarette. "Where is Stalin, comrade? Why doesn't he speak to the people? What does he think of his friend Hitler now?"

Papa threw the old man a withering look and said, "I'm sure Comrade Stalin is very busy just now. Our motherland has been attacked." The men shifted uncomfortably on the bench. Papa looked at Avsey and continued, "Sometimes people aren't themselves when they're afraid."

"Have you ever been afraid, Papa?" Avsey's voice was earnest.

"Yes, Avsey, I've been afraid many times. Fear is just part of being alive, like love."

"Is Mama afraid? Does she know about the war?" Bronya watched Papa stiffen. She looked away.

"Mama knows. Everyone knows."

"Does Mama still love us?"

Bronya turned in time to see Papa's face freeze; he looked as if he'd been slapped by the question. He bent down and put his arms around Avsey. "Yes, of course she does. Mothers don't stop loving their children. Ever. She needs to rest. That's all."

Bronya squeezed her brother's hand hard. He winced and hung his head. She put her arm around him. He pressed into her side and whispered, "I'm a tiny bit afraid."

Bronya squeezed his shoulders and whispered, "Me, too."

LATE IN THE EVENING, WHEN THE HUMID NIGHT AIR WAS SO THICK she could hardly breathe, Bronya sat cross-legged on the kitchen floor, something Mama would have forbidden. The cicadas had ceased their night rhythms as if they, too, were listening for the growl of airplanes and lead stepping soldiers. Avsey, unafflicted by the silence or the humidity, had dropped into a deep slumber, his arms wrapped around his stamp album, his shock of red hair bright against his freckled face.

Weary, Bronya let her shoulder blades sink further into the cabinet with each rise and fall of her chest. A glimmer between the linoleum and the wall caught her eye. Curious, she reached toward it, half-expecting to find a small coin. A few seconds of forcing her finger into the narrow opening yielded a surprising reward: a shiny pocketknife. Perplexed, she pulled the blade out of its light green case. The knife was new or, at the very least, unused. She ran her index finger along the blade.

It didn't make sense. She knew it didn't belong to Papa. He

had a large pocketknife with a locomotive embossed on one side. And Avsey wasn't allowed to own sharp knives. This was an object from nowhere. Utterly out of place.

An out-of-place thing, like the bird she'd found in the corner of the living room on the evening before Babushka died. She'd cradled the limp creature in her palm, its delicate head dangling between her thumb and index finger, its eyes like small shards of black glass. Babushka had been alarmed. *A bird in the house is a bad omen, an out-of-place thing.*

Papa, angry, argued with her. "Superstition is anti-Bolshevik nonsense."

Babushka responded calmly as always, "Bolshevik utopianism is fantasy," then raised her voice and added, "Godless nonsense." Babushka always spoke her mind. And she had often been right. And Papa, who was practical, sometimes lost the deeper thread of things, saw the world in stale terms void of meaning. Babushka's superstition was canny and beautiful.

Bronya carved a tiny notch into the soft wood of the kitchen cabinet. *Day One.* She pushed the blade back into the green case and held the pocketknife in the palm of her hand. She'd keep it. Maybe an out-of-place thing could also bring luck.

CHAPTER 3
ROSTOV, JULY–AUGUST 1941

AVSEY CROSSED THE STREET WITHOUT LOOKING. THE CITY WAS QUIET in the late afternoon. A few weeks into the war, soldiers were the most visible presence. The lines at the recruiting offices were still long, and the scenes of young men taking leave of their families had become commonplace. Avsey wished with all his heart he was old enough to wear a uniform, to shoot a gun. He'd thought about running away to the front lines to become a sharpshooter or a scout. He played scenes in his head of his own heroism, his decorations delivered while Papa and Bronya looked on with pride.

Ilya appeared on the street, waving to Avsey, shouting his name. "Where are you going? You look lost."

"Nowhere. I have to stay close to home. My sister is paranoid." Avsey focused on Ilya's face, happy to see him. But Ilya looked terrible. "What's wrong?"

"My brother is leaving."

Avsey brightened. "He's a soldier?"

Ilya nodded.

Avsey had only become friends with Ilya after he'd stolen the pocketknife in the last few weeks of school. On the day Dima announced to the class that Avsey's mother was crazy, Ilya had joined him on his walk home. They'd walked in silence at first, Ilya adjusting his pace when Avsey walked faster, thinking he had better get away while he still could. When they were almost to Avsey's apartment building, Ilya had asked, "Why do you put up with him?

"Put up with whom?" Avsey stopped, looking at Ilya closely for the first time.

"With that stupid bully."

Avsey wanted to say that he'd never wanted to put up with anything, but that he'd been alone. Instead, he said, "He can't hurt me. Like you said, he's stupid." Avsey knew this was true before he said it, but once he heard the words, spoken out loud to Ilya, he felt better, more powerful. He'd stolen the pocketknife after all, proof of his intellectual superiority.

Ilya and Avsey began spending time together, and as it turned out, Ilya liked stamps and icebergs and numbers, too. He laughed at Avsey's jokes and admired his chess skills. Of course, Avsey had no intention of divulging his secret passion for theft. He'd been betrayed more times than he could count, and he was cautious, waiting for Ilya to turn on him as the other boys had always done. But Ilya never turned.

Ilya said, "I have to go. My brother, tomorrow…"

Avsey smiled. "He's a hero."

Ilya frowned. "It isn't heroic to die." He peeled away in the opposite direction before Avsey could think of a response.

In the evening, Avsey wanted to talk to Bronya about being a soldier, about Ilya's brother and the other brothers they knew who were going off to fight. But Bronya said, "Let's not talk about this tonight. Please."

Avsey was restless. Why couldn't she talk to him about anything serious? The Neva radio had been requisitioned, so there were no more wireless orchestra concerts from Moscow and no more stories about icebreaker skippers and Arctic explorers. All they had now were card games and blackout orders. Avsey missed the radio adventures of Ivan Papanin, the Soviet scientist hero who'd been swept 2,000 kilometers on an ice floe. As he and Bronya played cards by candlelight, Avsey said, "I bet Papanin will earn another Order of Lenin."

Bronya nodded absentmindedly.

Avsey tried again, "Didn't Natalya go to Pyatigorsk to stay with her grandmother?"

Bronya sighed. "I know you want to talk Avsey. It's not easy right now. Natalya's brother was killed in Ukraine. That's why she left."

Avsey was quiet for a long moment before he asked, "Papa is a lieutenant colonel in the railway brigade. Is he going to die?"

Bronya looked upset. "No, of course not. Don't worry, Avseyka. Papa will be fine. I shouldn't have mentioned Natalya's brother."

"People die in war, I know that." Avsey finished the card game in silence.

Life in Rostov changed dramatically in the following weeks. Avsey didn't have time to see Ilya. He and Bronya spent their days assigned to a Young Pioneer group tasked with fortifying the city, trudging off early each morning to dig anti-tank ditches on the northern outskirts, carrying long-handled shovels and baskets over their shoulders. By the time the sun crested over the steppe each morning, they were already digging, their heads covered with white kerchiefs, their shoes covered in dirt. They worked until their arms ached, their legs failed, and the light faded, and when the summer sky was at its deepest blue before dark and streaked with rosy light, Avsey and Bronya walked home.

They walked with Bronya's friends, Elena and Olya, taking their time, walking through the tattered streets crowded with soldiers and refugees, with disowned things—shoes, rotted vegetables, a gutted accordion inside a disabled wheelbarrow, and more dead dogs than Avsey could count. The debris and disorder in the growing twilight added to the quiet horror they spoke less and less about now. Skeletal orphan boys ran past them, weaving through the narrow alleyways crowded with makeshift shelters. They resembled fledgling chicks, their downy heads shaved against lice, their brown limbs golden in the fading light. Like boys everywhere. Avsey felt sorry for them, lucky he had a home. They waved packages of cigarettes in the air and chased one another, their fingers pointed, their thumb triggers cocked and ready to shoot.

He trailed behind Bronya and her friends while they held hands and giggled. Until Olya said, "My oldest brother left this morning. He looked so brave, so cheerful, but I could only see half of him on the train, as if he'd left some other half behind." She swallowed hard and turned, "I wish I could send one of those German fellows a swift punch in the eye."

Avsey, who'd suddenly become interested in their conversation, said, "You're a girl, Olya." Then remembering he, too, was limited in his ability to become a soldier, added, "We are all too young to fight anyway."

Elena, who was small and slight with nervous hands, said, "I'm taking a medical course. At the hospital. The army needs girls to help wounded soldiers at the front."

"The front?" Avsey's voice was tinged with reverence.

Elena brightened. "Some of us will be assigned to tank battalions."

In a small voice, Olya said, "My brother is in a tank battalion."

Avsey kicked an old shoe, sent it skidding through the dirt. "We all want to fight Fascists."

Bronya turned to Avsey. "I'm glad you're ten. I don't want you go anywhere."

Avsey looked at Olya. "I wish I were in a tank battalion."

LATE IN JULY, AS BRONYA PREPARED TEA ONE EVENING, THE FRONT door opened, and there on the threshold, holding a satchel and a suitcase, was Aunt Sara. "Hello, hooligans!" Aunt Sara's voice was big and bright. "Tidings from Taganrog and state aviation factory number 31." Sara smiled, but her skin was sallow, her shoulders hunched. She and Mama were identical twins but constitutional opposites. Even before Mama's troubles, she and Sara had been different, devoted to one another, but as far apart as they could be in outlook and personality—Mama mysterious, Sara openhearted.

Avsey blurted out, "You look awful, Aunt Sara."

Sara took Avsey by the shoulders and in a teasing tone said, "Thank you, brave nephew. Honesty is your best asset."

Avsey brightened. He liked being called brave.

Sara put her suitcase on the floor and reached into her satchel. "We've been making airplanes in Taganrog, to beat back the Hitlerites." She placed a small piece of paper on the entryway table. "The LAGG-3." A simple drawing of an airplane fluttered in the breeze from the open balcony doors. "Soon we'll be making six of these beauties a day. Nothing short of miraculous. And top secret, of course." She winked at Avsey.

Avsey inspected the drawing. "Are we going to win the war, Aunt Sara?" Bronya heard the slight tremor in Avsey's voice.

Sara put her arm around him. "We will, brave nephew. But it won't be easy. When is your Papa coming home?"

Avsey shrugged his shoulders. "No idea."

Sara looked from Bronya to Avsey and laughed. "Brigands, the pair of you, living an unburdened life, stealing from the rich to give to the poor. Good thing I'm here. We need to make plans."

Avsey brightened. "What kind of plans, Aunt Sara?

"We'll talk with your father. Patience, hooligan."

"Aunt Sara, do you think the Germans will get as far as Rostov?"

"I honestly don't know. I don't want to believe Hitler's army will march into Rostov, but we have to be realistic. The Germans are moving toward Taganrog, which is, as you know, close to Rostov. We should be ready."

Bronya asked, "But how are we going to get ready?"

Before Sara could answer, they heard the front door open. Her face relaxed a little.

Papa took his shoes off in the entryway and joined them at the kitchen table. He sat dowr and nodded wearily to Sara. "Good to see you. Taganrog ready? Factory working at full steam?"

"The aviation factory is being evacuated, Lev, to Tbilisi."

Papa ran his fingers through his hair and frowned. "When?" He glanced at Bronya and Avsey.

Sara cleared her throat. "Lev, I asked to take the children with me. I wanted them on the evacuation list for Tbilisi. But the factory won't allow it. I explained the situation. They offered to let me stay, which doesn't help the children."

"I see," said Papa. Bronya, alert to Papa's dry tone, studied her father and her aunt. She could see an old hurt drift between them, like smoke.

Sara cleared her throat. "We must find some way to take the children out of the city before it's too late. I may be able to take Avsey. One of my comrades wants to stay with his crippled sister, and Avsey can take his spot on the list. But I can't take Bronya."

Avsey blurted, "I don't want to leave. There's no reason to leave."

Bronya added, "I'm not leaving Papa. Especially if the Germans are coming."

Papa's voice was tired. "Children, let's listen."

Sara leaned forward in her chair. "I have an idea. Hopefully, it isn't too preposterous. Please listen first, before you say no." She paused and fixed her gaze on Bronya. "Stalin wants to send girls to Ukraine, to drive tractors, to bring in the harvest. Bronya, you're good with machines. Your skills would be valuable on the kolkhoz. And if the Germans push in, you will be considered an essential government worker. The kolkhoz is near Kharkov. It's affiliated with Tractor Factory 183. You'd be added to the factory evacuation list."

"Work on a kolkhoz?" Bronya turned to her father, wide-eyed, the idea blooming in her mind. Papa's face was rigid, and Bronya felt sure he would reject the idea. She knew better than to say anything yet.

Sara nodded. "Lev, without her name on an enterprise list as essential to the war effort, Bronya won't be evacuated. She won't be able to escape the front lines. You'll have to stay here to defend the station and she'd be here alone. If the worst happens."

Papa looked at Bronya. She could tell he was weighing the options, calculating the emotional and physical risks. Finally, he took a deep breath and said, "I don't want to separate Avsey and Bronislava. The situation has been difficult enough." His face looked as if it would break apart, like a puzzle, along the lines around his mouth and eyes, across his forehead.

Avsey tugged on Bronya's arm. "We can't leave each other," he whispered.

Papa continued, "I already feel I can't protect my children. How am I going to send them away where anything could happen? I won't know if they're safe. Can you imagine those poor kids at Artek? How fortunate we are that Avsey wasn't there when the Germans attacked. We have been lucky once. I don't want to test fate again. We'll have to find another way."

Sara kept her voice calm, but Bronya heard the tremor, the urgency in what she said next. "Lev, you can't deny the possibilities for disaster. You're a party member and, I might add, Line Director of the North Caucasus Railroad. On top of that, we are *Jews*. Do you think if we are stuck in Rostov when the Germans arrive, they'll treat your children well? Sara glanced at Bronya and Avsey again, and Bronya could tell she was leaving something out. "When we secure our country, we'll be able to protect our children. Not before. Besides, you don't believe in fate any more than I do."

Avsey sat straight up and said firmly, "I'll never leave Papa."

Papa put his arm around Avsey's shoulder and pulled him close. He took a cigarette and matches from his tunic pocket. As he struck a match, the flame lit his face in the dark and Bronya caught a glimpse of the deep sorrow embedded there, as if a curtain had fallen away to reveal a ransacked interior. He released Avsey, inhaled slowly, and blew smoke into the air. Bronya knew Papa was summoning his courage. He took another deep drag on the cigarette, staring at the ceiling. He exhaled and said, "Maybe Sara's right. Maybe we should separate."

Bronya closed her eyes. She thought about the kids at Artek, trapped without their parents. But to be useful, that was appealing. She opened her eyes and saw Avsey's pale face. Would he be all right without her? Would he ever forgive her? A cold trickle of sweat rolled down her back. Was this how it felt to be terrified?

She thought of Stalin's call for courage and sacrifice. All at once she knew. She heard her own voice from the outside in, deep and alien and scarcely believable. "Papa, Avsey, please don't be upset. Sara's right. How can I say no, Papa? And Avsey will be safe with Sara."

Papa stared at Bronya, his eyes shiny in the dark, surprised, the well of sadness he'd buried for so long, exposed. She put her arms around his neck. "All right, Bronislava. How courageous you are." He caressed the top of her head. "I wish with all my heart things were different."

CHAPTER 4
ROSTOV, AUGUST 1941

MAMA WASN'T ALLOWED VISITORS AT PSYCHIATRIC HOSPITAL NUMBER 20, and now Bronya understood why. Her mother sat on a thin mattress, disheveled, wringing her hands. Bronya inhaled. She'd asked to come, to say goodbye to Mama, and Sara had somehow succeeded in getting her here. It was too late to back out now.

Asya held her arms out. "I never told a soul." Bronya wasn't sure if this was a gesture of surprise or her mother thought she was being arrested. She had been afraid of arrest in the months leading up to the hospital, pacing the floor all night while Papa slept, sure her neighbors had denounced her.

Sara spoke first. "Asya, I've brought you a surprise. Do you see Bronya's here?"

Mama didn't move. Bronya remembered Mama didn't like surprises.

"Hello, Mama, I'm happy to see you." Asya lifted her head and let her arms drop.

A pitiful patch of sunlight from the small, square window high above their heads illuminated Mama's face. She squinted and lifted one hand to shade her brow but immediately gave up, looking down to pluck at bits of skin on her legs. "What have you done with my child?"

"Mama, I'm here. Sara and I came to tell you something." Mama looked at the window again. She didn't blink.

Bronya pressed, "Mama, please. I've missed you. Do you know about the war?"

Mama waved her arms in the air. "Where is Kuzma?"

Bronya stepped back. *Kuzma?* Who were these people in Mama's head? She knew Mama's voices scolded, chastised, and spied on her. She'd heard Mama admit she was to blame but for what? What crime could her mother have committed? Mama's mind had collapsed under the weight of the invisible conflicts in her head, and that was all there was to know.

Sara sat on the bed and leaned into her sister. "Asya, we've missed you. Bronya wanted to visit." Her voice was brittle, like hay.

Mama kept her hands over her face and shook her head.

Bronya tried again. "Mama, I'm going away to work on a kolkhoz." She reached across the space between them and took her mother's hand.

Mama screamed, "Sergei isn't here, you can't leave me!"

Sara soothed her sister in a calm voice. "Asya, it's all right. Bronya's here with us."

The stern woman in a white cap, whom Sara had bribed with a few rubles into letting them in, opened the door. Despite the document giving them permission to visit Mama, the white-capped woman had made it clear she was in charge. She signaled the visit was over by motioning with her head toward the front of the building. Irritation had redrawn her already harsh features. "You'll have me lose my job," she spit.

"Everything will be all right, comrade. We are saying good-bye." Sara's tone was authoritative, and the woman let the door slam behind her.

Bronya turned toward Mama, confused. What could she say to reach her mother? As if in response, Mama turned her head and locked eyes on Bronya. Her tone was softly intimate. "Never give up the people you love. Not for anything."

Bronya froze. She felt the slow rise and fall of her breath, waiting. When Mama tried to stand, Bronya half-expected her to reach out, to extend her moment of lucidity and take her hand. Instead, she fell back on the thin mattress. "You'll all be punished."

Sara smiled sadly and put a hand on Bronya's shoulder, "Let's go."

As Sara pulled Bronya from the green-walled room into the long, tiled corridor, Mama yelled, "I am to blame! It's my fault!" The words bounced around the cold walls. Bronya fought the urge to run.

On the street, Bronya felt weak, and her legs shook. The smell of disinfectant coated the inside of her nostrils, her throat. She thought she could taste urine. "I shouldn't have come."

"She isn't herself, my love. You mustn't take it personally." Sara reached for Bronya's hand and squeezed it tight. "This isn't your fault."

Bronya remembered the moment she'd seen Mama on the balcony, trying to swing her leg over the wooden rail. She'd panicked and run, desperate to find the doctor. "Yes, it is my fault. I told the doctor about the voices. Maybe she would have gotten better at home. Maybe this place has made her worse."

"You did the right thing, Bronya. They took her to save her, not to punish her."

"Aunt Sara, are Kuzma and Sergei real people?"

Sara stared at the street ahead, her face immobile. "Yes, people she knew a long time ago."

"Why does Mama talk about them?"

"Because she's not in her right mind."

BEFORE SHE WAS READY, BRONYA STOOD UNDER THE OLD ONION domes of the neglected Cathedral of the Nativity of the Blessed Virgin, preparing herself to say goodbye. Papa stood nearby, holding her knapsack and violin case, looking for the Komsomol leader over the crowd. Avsey ignored them all and skipped ahead to mingle with the uniformed men. He turned and pointed to the army trucks and horses, the howitzer pulled behind a tractor, a look of glee on his freckled face.

A young man in uniform directed Papa toward several two-humped camels at the far end of the square. Three more camels appeared, strapped with green provision bags. Papa found the Komsomol leader, a serious young man who spoke in a clipped manner. He looked at Bronya and pointed to the string of camels a few meters away. "Trucks in short supply."

Avsey skipped toward her, wide-eyed. "You're riding a camel to Kharkov!"

Bronya eyed the animals warily. They were the color of sand but dirtier, their faces placidly indifferent.

Papa and Sara closed around her to give last-minute advice, but Bronya paid no attention. She watched her reflection in Papa's sad eyes until finally she put her arms around his neck and whispered, "Am I doing the right thing, Papa?"

Papa took her arms from around his neck and squared his face to hers. "We can't be sure about what is right until after we do it. When this is over, you'll go to Moscow, and do the right thing for your talent."

Bronya kissed Papa and whispered, "I always knew you understood."

A smooth-faced soldier with calm brown eyes led Bronya to a sitting camel with a shaggy neck and long eyelashes. The young soldier, Bronya realized, had come to look like his animals, his liquid eyes deep and undisturbed. He took the camel's lead in one hand and instructed her, "Don't make eye contact with him. Put your foot in the stirrup and swing the other leg over quickly."

Bronya followed his instructions, wondering if the animal might bite her. She settled between the camel's humps and realized she hadn't said goodbye to Avsey. Where was he? All at once, she didn't want to leave. She fumbled for the stirrup with her foot, frantic. How could she get down?

The soldier, impatient, said, "No stirrup. Grab onto the pommel and lean back." He made a clicking sound with his tongue and the camel rose on its back legs. "Now lean forward."

Bronya leaned forward, panicked. It was almost too late. Where was Avsey? The camel straightened its front legs, rising up. Bronya swung higher. Her stomach lurched. "I've changed my mind," she said weakly.

Papa handed her the knapsack. He hadn't heard her change of heart. The camel-eyed soldier attached the violin case to the saddle with a strap. Avsey appeared out of thin air, high up on Papa's shoulders, his face tilted toward hers. Was this what it meant to sacrifice? Bronya fought not to cry. "I don't want to leave you."

Avsey said, "I don't want you to leave." He handed her a paper package folded into a triangle. Bronya could see he was fighting tears. "It's from my collection. It will remind you of me, at least for a little while."

Her voice broke. "I'll be back in a few months."

"No, you won't. Just don't leave me forever."

Bronya swallowed. "I won't leave you forever. You'll wait for me and I'll be home soon."

The camel moved forward, and Bronya grabbed the saddle's pommel as she swayed from side to side, dizzy. Avsey extended his arms, stretching his fingers toward her, leaning over Papa's head, but the camel's wide, gaited rhythm took her further and further away.

She held the triangular package against her heart and mouthed, "Be brave, Avseyka." She craned her neck to keep sight of him until she rounded the corner of the cathedral and her family disappeared. She'd never imagined how it might feel to leave. The urge to turn back, to stay with her family, was almost too much to bear. Why had she thought she could ever leave them?

Hours later, when the last remnants of daylight had accumu-
lated at the horizon, Bronya opened Avsey's gift. There, against a
message written in colored pencils and decorated with scrolls
and hearts, was a brilliant blue butterfly, its dove-gray underside
and delicate wings fringed with yellow and orange eyes.

Avsey had written: *Everything changes. Nothing changes.*

CHAPTER 5
ROSTOV, SEPTEMBER–OCTOBER 1941

A MONTH AFTER BRONYA'S DEPARTURE, THE BOMBING BEGAN IN earnest. Avsey missed his sister in the worst way, especially at night. He admitted to feeling envious; she was the lucky one. Stalin had asked girls to help harvest the wheat in the fields because all the men were at the front, but Avsey struggled to understand why he couldn't go, too. He could work as hard as any girl. Harder. He finally decided it wasn't Bronya's fault he'd been left behind. And he was glad she didn't have to see the destruction that surrounded them all now.

When the bombing first began, the neighbors took to scurrying down the basement stairs to stay underground until dawn. Gradually, people discovered other, more fortified shelters, of which there were a few—the sewer pipes close to the park, and a large wine cellar on Sedova Street. The problem was getting to those places quickly.

Papa stayed in the train tunnels or the grain elevator close to the station but made Avsey promise he would run to the basement when he heard the sirens because "it's close and safe and I'll know where you are." Once, despite his promise to Papa, Avsey had stayed in the apartment after the sirens sounded, just to see. He'd spent the night spread-eagle on the bathroom floor with Bronya's blanket over his head. After it was over, he'd watched the sweep of searchlights looking for enemy aircraft and listened to the neighbors calling to one another from their apartment windows. He vowed he would never stay above ground again.

The heaviness in Avsey's sternum eased a bit underground, though it did not disappear completely. He didn't need to hold his breath between the sound of the bomb whistling toward earth and the explosion. Even so, the basement air was fetid with claustrophobic fear. He missed Mama and Bronya and the endless waiting, night after night, weighed heavily on him. Eventually, he found relief by playing chess with the neighbor from the fifth floor, a mathematician from the Institute and a reputed genius. More often than not, Avsey won. His opponent shook his head and accused Avsey of sorcery, the embarrassment evident on his red face.

When Ilya appeared underground on a ferociously loud night, Avsey couldn't believe his luck.

Avsey and Ilya took up where they'd left off in the final weeks of school. They laughed and traded stamps. Ilya said, "Poor Dima. He has no one to pick on."

Avsey thought of Dima's green pocketknife. He'd never found it and wondered if the loss he felt was what he deserved for taking it in the first place. "Don't worry. He'll find someone else to persecute."

Avsey and Ilya spent the interminable nights talking about everything: polar bears, arctic expeditions, Jules Verne. When he was with Ilya, Avsey forgot the queasy pleasure he'd derived from theft, delighting in a new feeling shimmering deep inside him—friendship.

One night, when the bombings went on longer than usual, Ilya proposed a distraction. "Let's share our deepest secrets, the things we've never told anyone."

Avsey agreed without thinking, and Ilya said, "You go first."

Avsey felt the vein in his neck pulse harder. Should he tell

Ilya about the revenge he'd extracted at school for every bruise, for every insult to Mama? About the birch box full of treasure stolen from the other boys stashed under his bed? Surely, Ilya would understand.

"Well," he hesitated, "I stole a toy truck from the kiosk near Gorky Park."

Avsey saw Ilya's face drop.

He added quickly, "A long time ago," thinking of the hawkeyed old woman at the kiosk who had almost caught him. "But I gave it back."

"I'm glad," Ilya said. "Stealing is terrible. We're lucky to live in the USSR where people don't steal from one another."

Ilya must have shared his deepest secret, but Avsey didn't hear what it was. He was deeply worried. Had Ilya seen his face turn red? What if Ilya found out he was a thief? What if he found out Avsey had stolen from his own parents, first from Mama's drawer and then Papa's? What if he confessed that it was hard to stop, that it felt good to steal? Would Ilya understand? In the end, he kept the details to himself, afraid Ilya wouldn't like him anymore.

A week later, Ilya stopped coming to the basement. Avsey waited for him, and when the planes were silent, walked the streets looking for him. He had never bothered to ask Ilya where he lived. Had Ilya left the city without saying goodbye? Had he been the victim of a German bomb? Or had he discovered Avsey's secret? The loss was devastating. Not knowing why Ilya had disappeared added to Avsey's heartache.

On top of everything else, Aunt Sara had disappeared. She'd gone back to Taganrog to prepare the factory for evacuation and had not returned to take Avsey to Tbilisi as they had planned.

Papa reassured him as best he could. "Sara wouldn't leave you."

Avsey was not comforted. Had something happened to her? The weather turned colder, and still there was no sign of Sara.

One night, the bombing began early, and Avsey, lonely,

trailed down to the basement to wait alone. At the bottom of the stairs, he stepped over a young woman, holding a sleeping baby swaddled against the chaos. The girl's skin was transparent, her eyebrows like eiderdown. She couldn't have been much older than Bronya. The building above their heads shook as another bomb found its mark. An old man wrapped his arms around his head, squeezed his eyes shut, and moaned. Avsey walked the perimeter of the basement looking for Ilya. He told himself this would be the last time he cared, the last time he would hold out hope to find his friend.

When he was certain Ilya wasn't there, Avsey decided to spend the night above ground. At least in the apartment, he wouldn't miss Ilya. He'd rather face the explosions than the loneliness in the basement. He had already placed a hand on the wall above the steps when he heard a woman's voice say, "Kiev is almost surrounded. They'll turn for Kharkov next."

Avsey froze. Bronya was near Kharkov, on a kolkhoz not far from the city. As casually as he could, his heart pounding, Avsey turned and looked for the voice.

An old woman leaned against the wall, a dirty red kerchief around her neck. She spoke knowingly to the young mother Avsey had passed on his way in. Avsey bent over and crouched on the bottom basement step, listening. The pounding in his head made it difficult to hear, so he inched closer. Both women were gaunt. Fatigue deflated their chests and lowered their voices. Avsey leaned closer still, trying not to appear obvious.

"Are you from there?" asked the young mother, her eyes closed.

"Lubny. A boy from our village came to tell us the Germans were on their way. I didn't wait to meet them. We have nothing but the clothes on our backs."

Humming softly to the sleeping baby resting on her outstretched knees, the young mother opened her eyes and scanned the cellar. "We walked for weeks," she said, "from

Belaya Tserkov. Baby came on the way, outside Dnipropetrovsk. We had no choice."

The young woman paused. Again, her eyes darted around the dimly lit room. She swaddled the baby tighter and tucked him against the wall. She slid closer to the old woman. Avsey shifted closer too, taut, straining for every word.

"The Germans shoot people, lots of people, into ditches. I saw with my own eyes, in the forest. Twice. My belly was too big to run. I hid behind a clump of trees and watched. I didn't want to, but I couldn't help it."

The old woman appeared not to be listening. She looked the other way.

The young mother pulled at the old woman's sleeve. "Once, before we left, in Belaya Tserkov. Then in Boguslav. We walked through the woods. Naked women, Jews, falling into ditches. Babies."

Avsey felt a wave of nausea seize his insides. He tried to stand, to run away, but his legs felt heavy, as if encased in cement. As he struggled, his body released and he shot up, charging up the steps two at a time, as fast as he could, knees trembling. He paused when he reached the top. He thought he heard the old woman laugh.

On the street, Avsey ran faster than he had ever run, faster than he ran when the boys from school chased him. He couldn't feel his feet touch the ground. The buildings whizzed by. Faceless people, huddled together in doorways and around basement steps, turned their heads to watch him. He ran faster.

Panic pressed into his chest. He felt like a small animal, ensnared. Sweat trickled down his temple and into his eyes. The sky flashed in the distance, but Avsey wasn't afraid of the bombs anymore. The thought of losing Bronya was worse than any bomb. What if he never saw her again?

His feet slapped through dirty puddles, splashing his shoes and pants with thick sludge. When he tripped on a flat crate and fell, he picked himself up, and without brushing the filth from his face and hands, continued to run. He felt the pain in his knees, in his head. He didn't care. His stomach churned, but he did not stop. He ran until his lungs could no longer take in enough oxygen to keep his body moving. He stopped and bent over, hands on his knees, and heaved.

When at last he straightened and wiped his mouth with his jacket sleeve, he noticed a large hole in the ground. Acrid smoke rose from the hole and the smoldering rubble all around. Avsey heard the tinkle of falling debris and watched as one corner of an apartment building collapsed in slow motion. People screamed, and men with shovels ran to rescue those inside.

Avsey turned in the direction he had come and limped toward home. At dawn, he heard a familiar sound, water lapping against the riverbank. He was on Sedova Street, alongside the psychiatric hospital. This was where Mama lived. Should he find her and tell her about Kharkov?

Bronya had tried to hide the hospital from him, pretending Mama was far away at a sanitorium outside the city, but Avsey knew better. He knew where Mama was because he'd followed Papa and hidden behind a tree until he emerged. The frozen expression on Papa's face told Avsey everything he needed to know. Mama was unreachable, just around the corner. Pretending only protected Papa and Bronya from having to talk about her, but it did not ease Avsey's heartache. Mama's absence followed him everywhere. He dreamed of her—her beautiful fingers with their half-moon cuticles, the way she used them to brush the hair from his face before she kissed him. He couldn't pretend the hurt was gone.

A face appeared at one of the windows as Avsey heard the whistle of another bomb and threw himself to the ground. He covered his head with his hands and closed his eyes. *Please. Please, don't let it hit the hospital.*

A loud explosion rocked the street, so loud he wasn't sure he was still alive until he noticed his ears were ringing and he could hear bits of debris detach and hit the ground. He lifted his head and wiped the dust from his face. He scrambled to his feet and searched for the face, but the window was empty. Screams and sirens filled the air again, but the hospital stood unharmed in the haze.

The sun was midway up the sky when Avsey opened the apartment door and found Papa at the kitchen table, head in his hands, sunlight streaming through the open balcony windows. The air was hazy, full of dust particles. They looked like gold.

"Where have you been?" Papa's voice was angry. "I went to the basement. Where were you?"

"I don't know."

Papa's jaw tightened. "What do you mean you don't know?"

Avsey stopped and stood very still. He could hear his heartbeat, hear the birdsong outside, and in the distance, an unidentifiable drumming noise. Someone climbed the stairs, quietly wheezing from exertion, then, a cough on the landing. The morning smelled of oil and mildew. He began to cry, his thin body rattled with hiccups. "I'm afraid, Papa, afraid we won't ever be the same."

Papa dropped to his knees and pulled Avsey into his chest, holding him tight in his arms. He brushed the dirt from Avsey's cheek. "You're as light as a feather, Avseyka. Your trousers are torn. Are you hurt?"

Avsey, still racked with hiccups, insisted, "Will we all die?"

Papa pushed his hair back from his forehead with both hands and Afseav thought he saw something close to despair in his eyes. Had something already happened to Bronya? "Papa, what is it?"

Papa squeezed Avsey tight against his chest. "The station was bombed last night. I couldn't find you. I thought you were gone, too."

CHAPTER 6
KHARKOV, SEPTEMBER–OCTOBER 1941

BRONYA FOUND SOME SOLACE ON THE KOLKHOZ DESPITE HER homesickness. She liked the tractor barn, where, if her timing was right, she could play her violin late into the night without anyone bothering her. She liked the mangy dog that accompanied her to breakfast every morning, waiting with moon eyes for the scraps she fed him. But it was friendship that sustained her most and helped ease her longing for home. Bronya and Vera, in particular, had been friends from the start, from the first week when they'd been alone in the crumbling kolkhoz dormitory, before the other girls arrived.

Bronya had been unnerved by the wind whistling eerily through the farm buildings at night and the creaky doors that wouldn't lock. She had trouble sleeping. On the worst nights, she crouched on the floor against the wall of the room she and Vera shared, singing solfège in the near total darkness. On the best nights, bone-tired from work in the fields, she slept fitfully until the rooster crowed at dawn, rousing her from the recurring dream she had of playing on an unfamiliar stage. The dream always ended as she raised her bow and looked out at the audience. All the seats were empty.

Vera teased her. "You're afraid of the wind?"

"It's more than that. Actually, I'm not sure what it is."

Vera softened. "I'll tell you stories. That's what my father did when we were afraid of the dark."

But it wasn't until Sveta arrived that Vera kept her promise. Sveta was from Kiev, a city like Rostov, and she, too, appeared nervous when the sun went down. She cried herself to sleep on the first night. "I didn't know it would be like this. I want to be brave, but I don't know how."

The next night, Vera sat on her bed, pulling her long blond hair into a bun. "We'll do this together, with stories." Vera's voice was soothing; she was a natural storyteller. "This is the story of Iron Wolf…" Bronya relaxed, her eyelids increasingly heavy. Sveta crawled into bed next to her and they fell asleep.

After that, Vera told stories every night. Sometimes they were funny, sometimes tragic, but they were always about clever peasants and forest animals and the wind, not unlike the fairy tales Bronya remembered from her own childhood, albeit more comforting, wiser. Vera told them, "We are sisters now, all country girls. We are brave together."

The bombings began shortly thereafter, and all the stories in the world couldn't quell the terror that rolled through the dormitories. The girls listened for the planes, worked in the fields, and tried to distract one another. Bronya was sure she'd never had friends like the girls who shared the turmoil of those first days of bombing. She wrote home about her friends, wanting Papa and Avsey to know she was working hard, doing her part but that she wasn't alone. She did not write about the German airplanes or the panic she sometimes felt in the middle of the night or about the Red Army soldiers traipsing backward through the fields, their eyes huge in their thin faces.

Instead, Bronya aimed to distract Papa and stop him from worrying. She wrote about the harvest, about the crates filled with wheat and loaded onto flatbeds, about the coal cars and locomotive tenders filled with grain and about the heroic work to move the harvest out of German reach. She wrote about the other commodities—lard, seed oil, and rosin, following the wheat into the Soviet hinterland. She described the beauty of the fields in the early morning, the tractors and combines in constant motion against the wide sky.

She told half-truths, too. She wrote that she'd played a concerto for the kolkhoz workers, which was partially true. She'd played for the director and a few others when she first arrived but had never been asked to play again. She didn't tell Papa that it was harder and harder to play her violin, that sometimes her fingers refused to move. She worried she might never play again, never attend the conservatory. But she didn't want Papa to know about all the ways in which life had extended beyond the borders of her agency.

Papa's letters were cheerful. It appeared to Bronya that he too told half-lies. His last letter arrived in early September. It had been posted in August, the day before Avsey was meant to leave for Tbilisi. Bronya read it sitting on the dormitory steps in the morning sun, Avsey's departure gift in her lap. She'd made it a habit to look at his butterfly whenever she missed home, to remind herself that the war would not last forever. The butterfly had gently come apart over the weeks, the delicate wings detached from the brittle thorax. Everything was brittle and tenuous now. But Avsey was by now far from the daily grind of war on the other side of the great mountains with Aunt Sara.

Bronya held the butterfly up in the light, reveling in its faded beauty, a way to remember the way things used to be. But as she cradled the butterfly in her palm, a gust of wind lifted the aggregate parts from their paper package, and Bronya watched them swirl and float away. Like Avsey—*free*.

Soon after, the Germans encircled Kiev. Sveta confided in Bronya, "I don't know where my family is."

"Maybe they were evacuated. Let's hope for the best. At any rate, it's all we can do."

But rumors about the large numbers of prisoners of war and speculation about what would happen next dominated their conversations and haunted their waking hours. With the harvest completed, Bronya, Vera, and Sveta worked at the tractor factory disassembling machinery that was then dispersed into boxcars or piled onto flatbeds and sent to safety in the Urals. The kolkhoz workers left incrementally, following the machinery to new lives. Whole columns of tractor drivers sputtered east atop their machines.

The German bombing increased in intensity over Kharkov, and all the factories prepared for the same dismembered fate, to be reborn somewhere beyond the fighting. The kolkhoz and the tractor factory gave orders to evacuate the workers, and the girls prepared to leave.

Despite their efforts to bolster one another, Sveta remained grim and Vera became more and more irritable. The veins in her fair skin were visible, as if she were turning inside out. She had stopped telling stories. In the dormitory, Vera told them all, "Sonya promised she'd come for me."

Sveta, always reading, looked up from her book. "She's a nurse at the front, right?"

Bronya knew Vera had waited all summer for a letter from her sister. "Can she leave, just like that?"

Vera, standing at the window, looked uncomfortable. "I don't know."

Bronya was surprised. "Did she write?"

Vera turned away without answering. Sveta looked at Bronya and put her index finger to her temple. She mouthed, "Crazy."

Bronya frowned at Sveta and put her arm around Vera. "Tell us a story tonight, Verunya. I miss your stories."

Vera shrugged Bronya's arm away and left the room. Sveta said, "Why isn't anything the way it was? What has happened to everyone?"

"We're all anxious. Better to be kind and not ask questions."

As the chaos around them intensified, Vera began to disappear. She missed mealtimes and was often sullen and uncommunicative. Bronya often walked the kolkhoz looking for her, wondering what had happened to her friend. Sveta was right. Vera had changed.

One evening at supper in the canteen, Sveta leaned over Bronya's shoulder and said, "Vera's stealing food. I've seen her, *twice* now. She hides potatoes in her blouse. Who knows what's going on with that girl? Something's wrong."

When Vera began sliding out of bed before dawn every morning and making her way to the road, Bronya became more alarmed. She studied Vera's morning ritual from under her duvet for a few days. It was always the same: Vera slipped her dress over her underwear and tied her hair back with a kerchief before she splashed water on her face from the bucket in the corner and stuffed her feet into her shoddy shoes. She opened the door, and without so much as a backward glance, slipped out. Finally, one morning, Bronya followed her. She walked to the road and stood next to her. "What is it, Verunya? What's happening?"

Without looking at her, Vera said, "Sonya will be here soon. You'll see."

"How do you know?"

Vera never took her eyes off the road. "The Germans are close. My father might be close, too."

Bronya, exasperated, said, "When did you decide to stop talking to me? None of this makes sense."

Vera looked down at her feet, and Bronya thought she saw the girl she knew for a moment, but Vera walked away, leaving Bronya more bewildered.

By the time Bronya could sneak away to the tractor barn with her violin, the wind had settled into a soft breeze and a spread of stars curled around the kolkhoz like a cocoon. The whole world, in all its beauty, appeared gentle, hopeful. Bronya knew this was an illusion, but she wanted to pretend, just for a while.

Inside the barn, she'd already opened the violin case and was lifting the instrument when Vera came up behind her, startling her. "Please don't tell anyone. He's with the Germans. My father. Please."

Bronya almost dropped her violin. "Your father is a prisoner?"

Vera was trembling. She folded her arms around across her chest. "No, he joined them. "He left us alone. Sonya went to find him."

Bronya blinked. "Why didn't you tell me that before?"

"Do you think I would be welcome here if anyone knew? My father, they might—well, I don't know. Besides, the other girls don't like me. They'd betray me in a heartbeat." Vera's body shook violently.

Bronya returned the violin to its case. "He left you alone? How could he do that?" She put her arm around Vera. "I won't say a word." But Bronya was unsettled. "Shouldn't you tell somebody?"

Vera shook her head so vehemently that Bronya promised again she wouldn't say anything about Vera's father.

The next day, Vera was caught by the kolkhoz director coming out of a small shed, a place where equipment was stored, off limits to the girls. Vera shrugged when the director challenged her. She said, "I was looking for the cat."

Bronya noticed the suspicion on the director's face and wanted to explain, to defend Vera, to tell the director Vera had been abandoned. She was sure the director would understand. But Vera would never forgive her. Her unease grew.

Later, Bronya found Vera sitting alone outside the dormitory in the dark, her head tilted to the sky. Vera whispered, "Do you believe in God?"

Bronya thought about the arguments at home between Babushka and Papa. "I'm not sure what I think about God."

Vera pulled a wooden cross on a long piece of twine from under her dress. She spit on her thumb and rubbed it. "Papa told me never to take it out."

"My Babushka was religious."

Vera kissed the cross and dropped it inside her dress. "Did she talk about God?"

"No, but she told me stories about my rabbi grandfather. He was murdered before I was born. She and my father argued about the Revolution. I think Babushka blamed it for my grandfather's death."

Vera sighed. "My father thinks the Revolution was a crime. He says the Bolsheviks killed my mother."

"Why would they kill your mother?"

"They took our grain. She died of starvation when I was six. She was everything."

Bronya was stunned. "That's awful, Verunya." She wondered how this could be true.

"Sonya hates the Bolsheviks because of it."

Bronya wanted to argue, but she felt sorry for Vera. Papa was a Bolshevik and he wouldn't take anything from anyone. Bronya thought about Mama, about how alone she was without her. No wonder Vera waited for Sonya.

"I'm going to stay here. I've hidden some potatoes. We won't starve."

"You hid potatoes in the shed?"

"I had to. I have to wait here for Sonya."

"But what if Sonya doesn't come and you end up here alone, or worse, with the Germans?

"I'm not afraid. The Germans won't hurt me."

"Are you sure?" Bronya was incredulous. Vera's plan was all wrong, dangerous. "You'll be considered a traitor."

"Is it treason to want my sister?"

Bronya remembered wanting more than anything to stay with Avsey. Was it treason to love your family? Maybe Vera had a point. Still, it was too dangerous to stay. She would make sure Vera boarded the evacuation train. She'd make sure she was safe.

CHAPTER 7
ROSTOV-ON-DON, OCTOBER–
NOVEMBER 1941

THE RAIN CAME EARLIER THAN USUAL AND ROSE TO FILL THE ANTI-
tank ditches, the furrows in the fields, and all the kitchen
gardens around Rostov. Swollen rivulets swept up small objects:
thin-soled shoes, rags and wooden spoons, clumps of garden
debris eddying around dead branches and leaves, and unknown
things bobbling in the muddy water—and once in a while, the
dark brown corpse of a rat could be seen floating. Avsey
worried. He stopped counting the days he'd waited for Aunt
Sara.

Papa spent his days and nights at the station, working to
send trains full of men and supplies into the areas where they
were needed. He constantly muttered to himself about daily car
loadings and freight categories. "Every military operation in the
war is dependent on the railroads," he told Avsey. The circles
deepened around his eyes, and once or twice, Avsey found him
in the living room in the middle of the night, his head in his
hands.

Rain rinsed the haggard city, but the frozen mist and dull
skies darkened the mood; a deep foreboding hung over everything, a fog of the unimaginable. Still, Avsey refused to give up

on Sara. On the occasions they sat side by side, Avsey leaned his head on Papa's shoulder. They did not speak.

Sometimes, Avsey descended into the basement shelter, glanced around for Ilya, and then climbed the stairs to the apartment, afraid to think about what might have happened to him. Maybe he'd left for the mountains like Bronya's friend, Natalya. Maybe he hadn't been able to say goodbye. He tried not to think about Ilya. Instead, he read *Around the World in Eighty Days* for the third time. He flipped through the pages of his stamp album with a loupe and dreamed of the adventures celebrated in their tiny pictures. But Ilya's absence made his heart ache.

When the Germans took Taganrog in mid-October, Papa paced the floor and talked to himself, stopping once in a while to pound his fist on the table. Avsey followed him while he paced. "Papa? Sara wouldn't leave me," he said, relieved to finally say it out loud.

"I know, son." Papa's face was haggard. He put his arm around Avsey.

"Do you think she's there, trapped?" Papa squeezed Avsey's shoulders without giving an answer. Avsey wanted to ask Papa if he thought Sara was dead but couldn't, afraid he would make it true by asking. The weather turned colder. They took to walking along the river and looking out toward Taganrog, though they couldn't see the town. Little white chunks of ice floated in the water. When Avsey stubbed his toe on a piece of cement in the dark, the cold made it hurt more.

Then, one desperately cold night in November, Sara knocked on the door. She smelled of cigarettes, woodsmoke, and motor oil. Her hair was tied back and tucked under a dark green cap, and she wore a thick belted jacket over loose trousers. At first, Avsey thought she was a man, but she smiled and he threw his arms around her.

Sara kissed Papa on both cheeks while he repeated over and over again, "I can't believe it." He looked Sara up and down. "You're frozen through. I'll make tea." Papa took Sara's jacket and hung it on a hook in the entryway. "My God, I'm relieved. Where in the hell have you been?"

Sara tugged her cap off and let her hair spill over her shoulders. "Actually, funny you should mention hell." She smiled, put her cap on Avsey's head, and hugged him again. Avsey wanted to hang on to her forever.

Papa handed Sara a cup of tea. "Let her drink, son. Can't you see she's shivering?"

Sara laughed and rubbed her hands together. "Hell is actually cold—it's not like they say." She sat down, lit a cigarette, and patted the chair next to her for Avsey to sit. Papa boiled potatoes and plied Sara with questions.

"Have you been in Taganrog all this time?"

Sara lifted her chin and blew smoke at the ceiling. "Yes. It's bad, Lev." She looked at Papa with gray eyes. Avsey knew Sara was sad when her eyes turned from green to gray. "The Germans are putting their policies into place, as they do."

"How did you get out?"

"You're ahead of yourself, Lev. That's at the end." Sara looked down at Avsey. "I can only tell you a little now. Maybe one day, I'll tell you the whole story."

Papa put plates, forks, and a bowl of boiled potatoes on the table. He poured Sara a glass of vodka and then one for himself. Sara pushed the cigarette into her saucer, sending a thin line of smoke curling around her face. Papa brought a dish of smetana and placed it ceremoniously in front of Avsey, whose eyes grew wide with pleasure. He hadn't seen sour cream for months. "A gift from Stepan Ilyich. Perfect timing. Just don't ask me where he got it," Papa said. He laughed.

Sara raised her glass. "To our health." She and Papa clinked their glasses together and drank. At last, Sara looked down at Avsey, her face serious. "Someone asked me to be on a kind of team, hooligan, to pester the Germans behind the front lines. I said yes, but it meant I couldn't contact you. I couldn't leave

Taganrog. Some of the team went to sabotage the German supply lines, to cut communications."

Avsey stopped eating. His mouth was open. "Are you a partisan?"

"No partisan ever answers that question, but yes, all-knowing-nephew."

Papa asked, "How many people?"

"Not enough. Eleven."

Avsey was impatient. "What happened?"

"We let the Germans build up an arms depot. They brought truckloads of weapons to a warehouse on the waterfront." Sara pushed her plate away and lit another cigarette. "Two nights ago, we blew it up." Sara's voice cracked. "Flames as high as the stars. I left while they were distracted, trying to put out the fire."

Papa was impressed. He stood up and made a funny bow toward Sara. They all laughed, but his tone changed toward her and his questions became more technical. They talked about explosives and the way the Germans had organized their occupation of Taganrog. Before he knew it, Avsey's head began to fall on his chest and he couldn't keep his eyes open.

Papa kissed him and pushed him off to bed. Avsey stretched out on the divan in his bedroom but left the door open a crack. He couldn't bear to miss any part of the conversation in the living room. He fell asleep for a while, but the low buzz of voices drifted into the bedroom, waking him.

Avsey listened lazily, but when the tone of the conversation changed, he wrapped the blanket around his shoulders and crept into the hallway. He might be missing something important. Sliding to the floor, he pulled the blanket up to his neck and rested his chin on his folded arms. Papa and Sara were sitting at the kitchen table smoking, their faces lit by a candle on the table between them. Avsey was close enough to hear every word.

"Have you visited her?" Sara exhaled smoke with a heavy sigh.

"Once. A bad idea. She thought I was someone else."

"I'm sorry, Lev."

"The doctor advised me to stay away. She's agitated after a visit."

Sara took a drag on her cigarette and exhaled slowly. "I thought when she married you, everything would be fine. She'd finished with Sergei because he was never there, always off on some geological expedition. But Lev, we have to admit we were wrong. She didn't want to leave her son or his father. We pushed her into it."

Papa crushed his cigarette into his plate. "I know she suffered. But I gave her two more children."

"Maybe she needed something else."

"Do you think she ever loved me?"

Sara turned and blew smoke in the air toward the ceiling. "I honestly don't know who she loved or didn't love. Maybe we all wanted too much from her."

There was a long silence between Papa and Sara. Papa poured more vodka. Avsey was confused. Who were they talking about? When had Mama left him with Papa? Who was Sergei?

Papa drained his glass and looked at Sara. "Lyosha was arrested right after Sergei was arrested. Have you ever thought there might be a connection?"

"Why would my husband's arrest be connected to Sergei? They were in different places, different professions. And Sergei was released."

Papa lit another cigarette and studied the ember. "Because Lyosha and I were involved in an incident a long time ago. We were at the wrong place at the wrong time. I believe Asya told Sergei about it."

"Incident?"

Papa shifted uneasily in his chair. "We found a boxcar full of bodies at the train station. Dead peasants, boxcar from Ukraine. Their bodies were emaciated."

Sara was silent for a moment. "Lyosha would have told me that."

Papa continued, "When I was arrested, I thought that it was because of what we'd seen."

"Lev, every line director in the Soviet Union was arrested. Remember the accusations? Saboteurs and wreckers? But you were released."

Papa leaned forward and flicked his cigarette ash into a glass. "Then why didn't Lyosha come home?"

Sara leaned across the table. She looked hard at Papa. "Do you know something I don't know?"

Papa leaned in close to Sara and said, "There had to be a reason, right?"

Sara frowned. "Makes no sense. Sergei didn't have a motive. Maybe Sergei ruined your life, but I don't think he ruined mine.
"

Papa sat back and crossed his arms over his chest. "It is easy to pull information from certain kinds of people. Even Asya didn't trust Sergei. "

Sara took a deep breath. "Asya didn't trust you either. Says more about Asya than about you or Sergei. She was paranoid."

"She trusted me." Papa's voice rose a notch.

"Remember after Bronya was born? She'd disappear. We'd look for her, your mother took care of Bronya. You sent Asya to Sochi, to rest. All that nonsense about air and sun. Uncluttered hygiene, the smelly waters of the Matsesta river."

"But she was better for a long time. She had Avsey and she was fine."

"And she was seeing Sergei."

Papa glared at the table, at nothing. He picked up a spoon and tapped it lightly against a glass, deep in thought. Then, to no one at all, he said, "By my account, he is responsible for all of the heartache—yours, mine, Asya's."

"But aren't we responsible, too? However well-intentioned

we were? Not easy to admit, but I've lost more than a few nights of sleep over it."

Avsey kicked the blanket away and rolled over onto his back. He was hot, his hands clammy. Did Mama lose her mind because of someone called Sergei? Did anyone's mind ever come back once it had been lost? He pushed himself forward with his feet, his back sliding on the floor until he was so close, they could have seen him had they looked. The smoke from their cigarettes floated into white tendrils in the candlelight. Avsey heard his name.

"Avsey needs to leave. I came to warn you. The Germans are massing as we speak."

Avsey lifted up on one elbow. They still meant to send him away. Why? He was strong. He'd do whatever Papa told him to do. The only thing he wanted was to stay here with them.

Papa's voice was grave. "I have nowhere to send him, Sara. You can't take him now. It's too dangerous."

Avsey shot up. Sara gasped and dropped her cigarette. He saw she was unsettled, her face frozen in surprise.

Papa reached his arm out and gestured for Avsey to approach. "What are you doing out here?"

Avsey picked up the blanket. He did not approach Papa. "I'm not leaving. No one is safe anywhere. Germans are shooting people into ditches."

Papa lifted his eyebrows. Then, as if admitting it to himself, he said, "You're right. No one is safe."

Sara regained her composure and asked, "Where did you hear about shooting people into ditches?"

"I overheard it downstairs, in the basement shelter. A woman said she saw it in the woods. Jews."

Papa opened his mouth like a fish, but Sara smiled sadly. "We forget that children are listening." In a hoarse whisper, she added, "Now you know."

Avsey lay awake for a long time in the dark. The only way to stay in Rostov was to find another basement and wait until it was too late to send him anywhere else. He'd be a hobo. He'd steal away at dawn. He was ten after all, not old enough to fight but old enough to make up his own mind. He wouldn't go far—somewhere he could hide until it was too late to send him out of the city.

An enormous boom followed by a longish burst of gunfire sounded too close for comfort. Avsey sat up.

Papa flung the bedroom door open. He threw the coverlet back and lifted Avsey from his bed. Papa was in uniform and held Avsey in his arms for a moment. He was shaking. "The Germans are here, Avsey. Get dressed." He handed Avsey his pants. "The neighbor, Novikov, has a car and an evacuation order. He'll take you to Bataysk, not far. I have to help defend the city, but as soon as I can, I'll come for you."

He crouched down. "This is important, Avseyka. If something changes, send me a letter. Remember, you can fold a piece of paper into a triangle, the way I taught you. You don't need stamps. He stuffed a pencil and a thin roll of paper inside Avsey's knapsack and tightened the strings.

Avsey pulled a sweater over his head and pleaded, "Don't send me away, Papa. Please."

Papa stopped and put his hands on Avsey's shoulders. "I promise. I'll find you."

At the front door, Aunt Sara handed him a small parcel tied in string. "Potatoes, tins of fish and bread. You're on your own for a bit, brave nephew. Keep your wits about you."

Avsey buried his face into Papa's shoulder and squeezed his eyes shut. The string around the parcel cut into his fingers. He felt the birch box, nestled at the bottom of his knapsack, against his back. At the bottom of the stairs, a blast of cold air pushed his head further into Papa's vatnik. Avsey felt a small reservoir of resolve tighten inside his chest.

They walked to the kiosk while the night sky lit up at short intervals, punctuated by the distant roar of guns. Avsey had never heard this kind of roar. He covered his ears with his hands.

A black sedan, moving slowly, pulled alongside them. It came to an idling stop, and Papa opened the door. As he bent to put Avsey in the back seat, the sky lit up, and for one instant, the people standing on their balconies became visible in the dark. The car was filled with bundles and blankets, boxes tied with string. A sewing machine was perched on the back seat. Papa found a place for Avsey on the floor and squeezed the knapsack beside the sewing machine.

Avsey was cramped but sat still, holding the food parcel in disbelief. Papa's eyes and the flashes in the distance were the only lights in the dark.

"It's safer if you stay down, out of sight," Papa said. He leaned forward and whispered something to Novikov and his wife, who both glanced worriedly at the street ahead of them.

Aunt Sara knelt on the street beside the car and reached in to kiss him. "I love you, Avseyka. You are the bravest boy in the world."

Papa, in his turn, kneeled in the street beside the car and held Avsey tight in his arms. As he stood and reached his head in to say one last thing, Avsey heard someone shout, "There's a car! Take it!"

Novikov gunned the engine and the door slammed shut, leaving Papa standing with his arms stretched out wide in the middle of the street. He ran after the car, slipping in the patches of snow. "I love you!" he shouted. From the back window, Avsey watched Papa grow smaller and smaller, until he disappeared completely.

The scent of home—laundry paste, cigarette smoke, and boiled vegetables—clung to his clothes as the car sped away. Avsey doubled over, wrapped his arms around his head, and cried.

CHAPTER 8
KHARKOV, OCTOBER 1941

THE GERMAN ARMY WAS CLOSE TO KHARKOV, AND THE DAMP AIR was heavy with speculation. Would the Red Army be able to push them off? Bronya wasn't sure. She'd seen the soldiers moving east and wondered if they were repositioning. Or leaving. The train station was heavily defended as the factories, in pieces and loaded onto flatbed cars, departed. And as the bombing intensified, the citizens of Kharkov crowded the platforms, clamoring to leave, anthills of human striving, of willpower and desperation, their misery compounded by the rain and mud.

Children, sick from the damp, barked like hoarse dogs, their small bodies racked by coughing fits. Bronya was fortunate. She was evacuating with the tractor factory like all the girls who worked on the kolkhoz. She had a ticket and housing in Chelyabinsk. A ration card. The women and children sleeping around the station had nothing of the kind.

On their last night on the kolkhoz, the girls could not sleep. The silence Bronya had become accustomed to, the dark nights, were broken by loud explosions and flashes of light in the distance. Bronya and Vera crept down the stairs together and watched the western skyline from the small window in the entryway, their backs against the opposite wall. The farm buildings were illuminated by the flashes of light, their rickety skeletons exposed. Occasionally a scream punctuated the otherwise voiceless landscape. The sky lit up again.

Bronya thought she heard the dormitory building crack. "Tomorrow at this time, we'll be far away."

Vera hugged her knees into her chest. "I'm not so sure."

"You are coming with me, Vera. Better to be on the train than alone here with the wolves."

Vera shook her head. "Wolves don't scare me. People do. Sonya says people are cowards, and that makes them untrustworthy. She's right."

Bronya whispered, "I'm trustworthy."

The morning revealed an eerie, crystalized world. A deep, nocturnal freeze had pushed the kolkhoz into acute panic. The girls gathered their belongings, yelling to one another to hurry. The ground was frozen, the mud no longer an impediment to the German armored vehicles. The earth had changed its mind and steadied itself to accept the enemy.

Bronya and Vera hurried to the station with the other girls, knapsacks on their backs, hands balled in their pockets. The sun made no appearance. Bronya had strapped her violin to her knapsack but worried the cold would crack the old wood, so she pulled the case onto her chest and wrapped her vatnik around it. Maybe in Chelyabinsk she'd be able to play more.

The girls passed soldiers hauling sandbags to fortify the anti-tank ditches across the city, pushing metal contraptions called hedgehogs into place. A sapper planted a mine beside a small bridge, soldiers protecting the spot, urging silence. Closer to the station, another sapper descended into the sewer, disappearing like an earthworm ahead of the sun.

The camps of women and children and old men around the perimeter of the station were squalid affairs. Bronya had never walked through them, but today, she, Sveta, and Vera hurried past the women, warming their hands and drying their clothes

over meager fires in metal barrels. An argument broke out—
whether over a lost possession or a territorial incursion, Bronya
couldn't tell. One of the men, his nose red, yelled, "I warned
you! You took without asking!"

A plaintive mother scolded her children for straying. Old
men stood together, unusually silent. One feeble voice intoned,
"Where were you in '38?" A world ripped apart at the seams.

Bronya smiled at a little girl with a runny nose but continued,
pushing through the crowd.

Losevo Station teemed with people elbowing their way
toward the platforms, large bundles on their backs tied around
with rope. When rumors of bridges collapsing from the sudden
cold reached the crowds, loud cheers erupted. An old woman
next to Bronya said, "Even the weather knows the Russian heart
is harder than German armor." The crowd pulsed together for a
few beats, passing along the hopeful news like a giant lung
contracting and expanding, fueled by the oxygen of last-minute
hope. The Germans had been stopped for one small moment,
though everyone knew the equation hadn't changed. The station
windows rattled. All eyes turned to the sky.

Bronya studied the station windows taped with large Xs to
protect the crowd from shattering glass. If only tape could hold
everything in place. The airplanes overhead looked like toys in
the distance, deceptively thin, glinting in the sunlight. Plumes of
dust lined the horizon in a neat line like pillars of salt formed
from the cherished particles of everyday life. Bronya's chest hurt
from the smoke in the air. The desire to run intensified and made
her skin itch.

The girls entered the station together, Bronya and Vera holding
hands, Sveta behind them, her hand on Vera's shoulder. On the
platform, the crowd tightened around them like a drawstring, until
no one moved. A few bodies over, two men came to blows and the
scuffle vibrated through the crowd, pushing an old woman to her
knees. Bronya let go of Vera's hand to help the woman, but she was
shoved further away as the instigators reignited their feud. The

crowd turned on the men, heaving them into compliance, but in the push and pull, Bronya lost sight of Sveta and Vera.

The woman stood and wiped the blood from her knees with a white handkerchief. She scolded in a loud voice, "Shame on you, all of you!"

Bronya stood on her tiptoes to look for her friends, but she was pinned, like a chloroformed butterfly, to a large, perfumed woman, blocking her view. The woman, coatless, her flowered dress clinging to the opulent curves of her body, cursed and began to cry. Close by, an invisible child called in a voice so heartbroken it sounded like glass, "Dedushka, Dedushka!"

Through an opening between the bodies, Bronya saw kolkhoz workers, just out of reach, board a teplushka outfitted with wooden beds stacked one on top of the other, a metal stove in the middle. Two adolescent boys squirmed through the riot of legs, reached the train, and boarded, refusing to be removed. Sveta and another girl from the kolkhoz mounted the steps and scrambled for a place inside. Afraid she'd be left behind, Bronya turned her body sideways, squeezed the violin into her chest, and with one last burst of strength, pushed through. She lifted herself up onto the metal step and turned to scan the crowd behind her. Vera wasn't there. She craned her neck to look down the teplushka's long corridor. No Vera.

The train whistle blew and the clouds of steam reduced the crowd to mere ghosts. Where was Vera? Bronya maintained her position at the door, certain Vera would appear at any second. She leaned out, holding tight to the metal rail, scanning the crowd. Two women saw their opportunity and pushed into the gap. Bronya's grip gave way and she lost her footing. She was unceremoniously shoved onto the platform while the crowd folded around her.

Standing on her tiptoes, Bronya pushed onto an anonymous shoulder and searched for Vera. Had she gone back to wait for Sonya? Bronya fought against the tide of people clamoring for the train and made her way outside. She circled the station twice. Vera wasn't there. She'd changed her mind. Bronya had to find her and convince her to leave before it was too late. She adjusted her knapsack, wrapped her arms around her violin, and set off running. She and Vera could be on the next train if she hurried.

She reached the tractor factory just as another bomb found its mark somewhere in the distance and the earth vomited its entrails into clouds of smoke. Sweat rolled down Bronya's face into her eyes. Soldiers on bicycles, their guns over their shoulders, pedaled toward the city. They were in a hurry and waved her back toward the station. One shouted, "Don't be afraid of death, devushka! Be afraid of shame!"

When Bronya reached the kolkhoz, she stopped and bent over to ease the pain in her side. The doors to the farm buildings swung in the breeze like laundry hung out to dry. She walked, the sound of her own footsteps loud in her ears. The whole place frightened her. When she reached the dormitory, eerie in the frozen mist, she hesitated. Rendered spare, the familiar building appeared alien. Her home of the last few months reeked of desperation and despair. She climbed the stairs, her heart pounding. Articles of clothing, books, and dead leaves littered the floors, the details of their former lives abandoned and forlorn. This was a waste of time. Vera was probably on the train heading away from the bombs.

At the front door, Bronya thought she heard a voice. A chill ran down the length of her spine. Spooked, she turned to leave, but from nowhere, as if conjured out of the frozen air, Vera appeared. She too was alien; she'd lost a shoe and her dress was muddy.

Bronya shuddered. This wasn't the Vera she knew. "Let's go back to the train station, Verunya. It isn't too late."

Vera did not respond. Her eyes were small and dark on her face, curiously uninhabited.

Bronya held her hand out to her. "I've looked everywhere. Why did you leave me?"

Vera whispered in a hoarse voice, "They've killed her. They've killed my Sonya."

"What are you talking about, Verunya? Everything is all right." Vera's hair was covered in dead leaves and twigs, as if she'd dug herself out of the ground. "Take my hand. We have to go now."

"She's dead." Vera turned to face the clump of trees at the edge of the field in front of the dormitory. Bronya followed her gaze. Smoke rose in solemn white columns from somewhere inside the kolkhoz.

Bronya, still confused, asked, "Who?"

Vera grabbed Bronya's hand, dug her nails into Bronya's palm, and pulled her toward the trees. Bronya struggled to free herself, but Vera circled her waist in an unrelenting embrace. They moved, oddly conjoined, toward the clump of trees. "You're hurting me. Where are we going?"

Vera did not answer and she did not let go.

Inside the trees, a woodpecker's roll reverberated through the haze. Thin rays of light pierced the heavy limbed pines from several angles, illuminating tendrils of debris, a tiny, floating world. Bronya had been afraid of these trees and had never ventured inside. When they reached a small clearing, Vera loosened her grip and pointed to a prone figure on the forest floor. Bronya edged closer, instinctively searching for a face. Vera backed away, her eyes on Bronya, her features tight, now distorted beyond recognition.

Sonya's blond hair was matted with black blood on one side of her head and dark shadows rimmed both eyes. She was beautiful, like the sorrowful icons of the golden haloed Madonna one saw in old picture books. Bronya fell to her knees, stunned. She brushed the frost from Sonya's hair and lifted her hand. Sonya's lifeless fingers were cold and white.

Bronya let her eyes travel down the length of the dead girl's torso. Her dress was torn and pushed up over her thighs to her waist, while her pale legs, spread at a horrifyingly unnatural angle, were bruised and bloody. Little buttons lay scattered like white pearls on the forest floor.

Overcome, Bronya cried. She cradled Sonya's hand, the fingernails black with dirt. It occurred to her that Sonya had fought to live. Bronya felt herself sinking, overcome by a wave of nausea. She looked at Vera, standing motionless next to her sister's body. Her friend needed her. Frailty wasn't an option. She pushed against the horror and pulled herself up. "Who did this?"

"You know perfectly well who did this." Vera stabbed her finger in Bronya's direction. "The Bolshevik Jews did it. *You* did it."

Bronya took a step back. Vera was in shock. Bronya reached toward her friend to comfort her, "It's me, Verunya."

Vera yelled, spit forming at the corners of her mouth. *"Don't you touch me, filthy vermin. I know you."*

Bronya's legs began to shake uncontrollably. "We'll find who did this. I'll help you."

Vera laughed. "My father was right. Scum of the earth. I should never have gone with you."

Bronya took another step back, confused.

Vera turned her gaze toward Sonya. She tore at her hair. "What will I do now without her?"

Bronya stretched her arms out. "Come with me, Verunya. I'll take care of you."

Vera stopped crying all at once. Her hands fell at her sides.

Bronya moved toward her. "Whatever you need, I'll do it."

A meager light of recognition appeared in Vera's eyes. Bronya, relieved, moved to put her arm around her friend. When Vera attacked her, Bronya was caught off guard. She staggered backward.

Vera was surprisingly strong. She pulled Bronya's hair, dug her nails into Bronya's scalp. The bile rising in her throat, Bronya pried Vera's hands loose and pushed her away. Strands of hair fell all around them, shimmering in the dim light.

Breathing hard, she choked, "Have you gone mad? I am not your enemy." Bronya glanced around the clearing, spooked.

Vera laughed. "I've always hated you." She jabbed her finger in the air to highlight her words. "I. Hate. You. All."

Bronya shoved Vera away with all her strength, searching for words of recrimination. Nothing came. Vera wouldn't listen anyway. Her mind was shattered.

Bronya looked at Sonya's battered body one last time, then at Vera. A small, hard knot formed in her chest, a stone between her ribs. Without another word, she turned and ran.

A ferocious howl had engulfed the kolkhoz by the time Bronya reached its center. Black smoke billowed into the air around her, bruising the stone sky purple. *Fire.* Bright flames curled from the farm buildings, the barns, licking the flat rooftops, devouring the old wood. She turned to look at the dormitory one last time. Flimsy curtains waved wildly from the upper windows, burst into flames and fell in charred pieces to the ground. Ash rained on her head and shoulders, her arms. The kolkhoz wept.

Bronya pressed her palms into her eyes. It wouldn't help to cry now. She saw two men in the distance, tiny as toy soldiers. They held torches above their heads at the far edge of the field and watched as they swept their arms in slow motion like dancers.

Smoke rose from the earth in tiny wisps, the field smoldering for a moment before the fire surged upward. A choreography of destruction to make sure the earth did not yield its bounty to the enemy.

As she ran, Sonya's image, her bruised body, burned into Bronya's mind. She prayed Vera was running, too. The Germans were close.

At the station, desperation had reached a fever pitch. Bronya pushed back inside, her determination to leave itself a kind of violence. A train pulled alongside the platform, belching steam. She filled her lungs with the stale air and made a path through the crowd. She'd missed her slot in the evacuation, but it didn't matter. She had to leave. How she made it through the chaos to the steps of the passenger car, Bronya had no idea. The green benches inside appeared as a mirage, a harbor. She fought hard for its shelter. At the door, the official in charge, a man in uniform with white piping around the collar, said, "Aviation factory?"

"No—I mean, I missed my train."

"Only aviation workers."

Bronya grabbed the door handle and held tight despite the tremors that shook her whole body. She scanned the length of the train. She'd clung to trains for thrills and bragging rights; she would cling to this one for her life.

The official began to close the doors. The crowd howled.

Bronya put a foot on the step and said in a firm voice, "Please, I'm with the tractor factory, but they've left."

The official studied her and asked, "Can you work, comrade, in Saratov?"

"Comrade, I'll work until victory and beyond."

"Then, devushka, we need you." He opened his arm to let her pass.

Inside, Bronya found an empty seat and sank into it. She let the knapsack slide from her back, wriggled out of her vatnik, and placed her violin case on her lap. She found a comb in the knapsack pocket and made an attempt to tidy her hair, her hands shaking so violently she was afraid the other passengers might ask her to leave. She wiped the ash and sweat from her face.

At last, she looked around. The car was packed with women sitting nervously, some with their eyes closed, their rough hands clasping handkerchiefs, tattered bags, the worn hems of their coats. Bronya couldn't make out the details of their faces because each woman had Sonya's features, her dirty hands and bloody legs, the bright buttons scattered around her body.

CHAPTER 9
RAILROAD LINES SOUTH OF ROSTOV, NOVEMBER–DECEMBER 1941

AVSEY KNEW THE NOVIKOVS WANTED HIM LOST BEFORE THEY GAVE him one last tin of fish and told him to wait at the Bataysk station. Fyodor Alekseevich and Maria Borisovna had never been particularly pleasant people, but the further they traveled from Rostov, the more nervous and unpleasant they became. Fyodor Alekseevich had a nasty habit of shouting at his wife. Sometimes he shouted about Papa. "I never promised that man I'd feed his brat!"

Of course, Fyodor Alekseevich never named names. Even far away from home, he was a coward. Avsey knew this because Fyodor Alekseevich had trouble looking him in the eye. His outbursts grew uglier. So, when the Novikovs whispered in the dark, Avsey listened.

One night, as they slept in the car in their coats, the doors open to the cold air, he woke to a whispered argument between Maria Borisovna and her husband. Avsey lay very still as Fyodor Alekseevich snarled and threatened his wife. "We can't take him back. We'll be arrested. You know as well as I do. So take him if you like. Then I won't have to feed you either."

Right away, Avsey understood the silence that followed. Maria Borisovna, in the face of her escalating domestic war, was recalculating her position. After a long pause, she said with no trace of disagreement or regret, "I'll tell him."

Still, Avsey couldn't imagine she'd do it—leave him. He drifted in and out of sleep until morning.

The next afternoon, Maria Borisovna reassured him with a smile so compelling, he almost believed her. She would be back for him soon. The tinned fish would hold him until they returned. She warned him not to wander off or they wouldn't find him again. Avsey nodded politely. What else was he supposed to do?

When the Novikovs had gone, Avsey searched for his ration card. The card was nowhere to be found. Had the Novikovs stolen it? How would he eat without the card? Avsey considered walking home on his own, but he remembered Fyodor Alekseevich's worry about arrest. Would Papa be arrested if he went back? Papa said he would come and Avsey decided to wait. Just as he had promised.

Bataysk was full of refugees, all of them looking to fill their bellies. The streets and canteens had become mean, hard places. Fights broke out, gangs of children ran through the marketplace stealing food. Women spat and brawled and pushed through the crowds while pale, disabled soldiers on leave waved for help. They paid with swigs of vodka and puffs on their cigarettes, but a few swallows of vodka did nothing to satisfy the hunger that chewed Avsey's bones and addled his brain.

He considered joining the orphans who slept under wagons and on city benches, but they were often in trouble with the militia. Even so, he took the time to carefully weigh the group's merits. He watched their deft maneuvering, the way they shared food, and most importantly, their defense of one another. In the end, he decided that if he was going to steal, he would do it on his own terms. He didn't want to join a gang of thieves. He'd never trusted other boys. Why start now? And besides, thieving was a complicated enterprise, and he had his own rules.

But Avsey's scavenging yielded little—bits of potato, ends of sausages, hard crackers abandoned on a bench, and once, a lump of sugar, right there in front of him on the street. Then he found the bulrushes.

Luckily, last spring, during a long walk along the river, Papa had taught Avsey that bulrushes were a source of nutrition. He'd pointed this out as a matter of interest, not because he thought Avsey needed this information or might need it in the future. He'd called them "Cossack candy." The name had made Avsey laugh, because bulrushes did not taste like candy. Not even close.

He found the bulrushes in a marshy area south of the Bataysk station. Some of the plants had retained their brown seed heads despite the cold weather, so Avsey tried to eat them first. They were dry and difficult to swallow. The bulrush roots, while tougher than those he'd tasted with Papa in the spring, weren't at all bad.

Admittedly, foraging in the water was cold work. He stopped frequently to blow on his fingers or warm them under his armpits. At one point, he slipped and almost fell, but the threat of cold water didn't stop his foraging; wet clothes on a cold night were better than an empty belly.

He rubbed the roots clean with his fingers, peeled them with his teeth, and dropped them into his knapsack. After a few hours of steady work, the knapsack was satisfyingly heavy and Avsey turned his attention to the other parts of the bulrushes. He made cords from the fronds and pushed these through the belt loops on his trousers to keep them up. He stuffed his valenki with seed heads to insulate his feet and keep them warm and dry.

Later the same night at the train station, his head resting on his lumpy harvest, Avsey felt his stomach rumble and growl. He spent the rest of the night behind the station with severe stomach cramps and diarrhea. Cossack candy took a heavy toll. In the morning, weak and dizzy, Avsey almost dumped his harvest into the dirt. It was only because he thought it might be possible to trade them that he kept the bulrush roots at all. Just in case.

Avsey had no other choice but to walk into town to find something else to eat. Sitting on a patch of dirt, too weak to walk further, he thought about giving up. It was then that a sweet-faced young woman from the bread factory across the street took pity on him and dropped a pile of rusks into his lap as she passed on her way home. Just in time. She did this the next day and then the next. Avsey began to think he'd found his luck, his own angel.

Word got out though, and the next day, a crowd of hungry orphans rushed the door at closing time, temporarily trapping the workers inside. After that, the practice ended. The young woman disappeared, and Avsey felt real despair for the first time. He'd lost the rusks and the only person who seemed to care anything about him.

In Bataysk, the refugees wanted to stay close to the places they'd left, hoping the battle lines would change in their favor. Everyone talked of going home; it was a matter of when, not if. But the waiting, the refusal to abandon hope meant Bataysk grew more and more crowded, meaner and meaner.

Avsey had already decided home was not a good option, that it would be best to move further away from the front lines and send Papa a letter letting him know. He extracted a piece of paper from his knapsack, smoothed it over his knee, and wrote, as he and Papa had agreed.

Leaving Bataysk. Going to Salsk or Tikhoretsk. I'll write again to tell you where I am. Please Papa, come find me.

He did not tell Papa he was hungry. He simply folded the paper into a neat triangle the way Papa had taught him, and gave it to the heart-faced woman behind the counter at the Bataysk post office.

IN THE YARDS, AVSEY CROUCHED, BALANCING ON THE BALLS OF HIS feet in a frozen rut next to the main track, his knapsack between his ankles. He would hop a train. His only hesitation had to do with the wheels. For as long as he could remember, Avsey had been terrified of the bone-crunching steel wheels of a train. They had rolled through his childhood and haunted his worst nightmares for years. But in all his time at the station with Papa, he'd never confessed his fear to anyone. He'd never overcome the sweaty palms and pounding headache he experienced when he was too close to the trains as they screeched into the Rostov-Glavny station.

Workers in the yard moved back and forth between cars, too busy to notice Avsey shivering, partially hidden behind a string of flatbeds. The late morning sun warmed his back while he rocked back and forth on his heels. His stomach hurt, and rocking sometimes helped. The railyard smelled of creosote, animal dung, and cabbage. A raft of steel track stretched out before him, as far as he could see, into the vast steppe and beyond the horizon.

Avsey knew two things: He was hungrier than he had ever been in his life, and he was going to leave Bataysk and all his rotten luck behind. He couldn't imagine the beyond, but it had to be better than his present predicament.

He listened to the workers shout to one another across the tracks as they coupled a string of tankers to an engine. The tankers looked particularly dangerous. The ladders made for temptingly easy access, but once on top, there was nowhere to sit. It would be too easy to slip down the slick surface. Sitting on the edge of the tanker wasn't an option either. He imagined his feet dangling over the side, swaying to the rhythm and click of the wheels and felt lightheaded. One false move and the wheels could easily grab his leg, sever a foot, drag him along the tracks.

He prayed for a long line of flatbeds, or better yet, a string of open freight cars—somewhere to sit on the moving train in relative safety. Anyway, the tankers would be filled with oil and going north, toward the fighting. He knew he wanted to go south or east. He figured if he hopped a southbound train, it would continue in the general direction it was already going and he'd end up in Salsk or Tikhoretsk. It was a matter of luck, like everything else. He'd have to take his chances.

He'd brave the terrifying wheels for something to eat, but first he had to remember what Bronya taught him about hopping trains. Avsey placed his palms on the ground in front of the track and hovered his ear over the cold rail. He didn't dare touch it, afraid his skin might stick to the metal in the freezing temperatures. He listened. The steel was eerily silent. He sat up and swallowed hard.

Avsey had been eight when he was allowed to help at the train station in the summer. By then, Bronya had already spent three summers roaming Rostov-Glavny and knew her way around. And she had big plans for her little brother's initiation into station life.

She began the summer by sharing her deepest secret—a way, she'd said, of testing his trustworthiness. Avsey had wanted more than anything to pass this test, but when Bronya told him it would involve grabbing hold of a moving train and clinging to its sides, he was terrified. She described for him how it felt to hold on as the train left the station, to hover in the space between two cars, the thrill of jumping off just in time, before the train picked up speed. She'd confided that train hopping was the most adventurous, courageous thing she'd ever done.

Avsey, slack-jawed with awe, swore he'd never tell Papa. He wanted his sister's approval at any cost. If he could master her lessons, he'd gain her trust. And respect.

The first thing Bronya taught him was to listen to the steel, to align his body with the track and put his ear to the rail so he could hear the vibrations of an approaching train long before he could see the steam or hear the whistle. She'd even taught him how to jog alongside a train, how to grab hold of the railing as it was accelerating and place his foot on the step, to make sure he had three contact points with the train at all times.

Everything went well for the first week of lessons. Avsey managed to follow Bronya's instructions without revealing his secret terror. But soon after they'd begun, Bronya cut her knee open on the jump-down. She'd clung too long to the train while it picked up speed, faster than she expected. She lied to Papa when he asked about the cut, saying she'd tripped, all the while keeping her eyes on Avsey.

After the fall and the lie to Papa, Avsey suspected Bronya had been terrified of being swept away, of being carried too far from home. He'd come to his hasty conclusion when he saw her limping on the platform, blood running down her leg. The injury hadn't bothered her, but she'd rambled on about how far she'd been taken outside the yards, further than she'd ever been before. Avsey felt better knowing his sister was afraid, too.

After her fall, she'd lectured him on the dangers of the yard. She'd held his arm behind his back and made him swear he'd never grab hold of a moving train. It hadn't been a difficult promise to make or to keep. But Avsey could hear Bronya's voice in his ear even now. *A train is an unforgiving beast, little brother.*

Avsey tucked his hands over his heart and pressed his chest into his knees. She'd taught him to do something dangerous for all the wrong reasons. And now he had to remember her every word in order to survive.

He took a deep breath. He put his ear close to the rail. At the end of his exhale, he heard it—the strain in the metal, a dull vibration, an oncoming train. He glanced down the main track for a concealed spot from which to hop aboard unnoticed. He found nothing but open space. He'd have to move quickly or he'd be seen. More importantly, he'd lose an opportunity.

The billowing steam appeared like a great phantom, and Avsey lifted up onto his toes. He flinched when the whistle blew and his heart thundered in his chest. The engine and the tender passed in a spray of ice as the train strained to slow down. He resisted the urge to cover his ears. He needed all of his senses if he was to succeed.

The train stayed on the main track just as Avsey had hoped it would, southbound. He watched the flatbeds roll by and then felt a surge of hope as a string of freight cars approached. The yard trembled, the sound of the engine, the wheels on the tracks, and the rail workers' shouts and whistles rattling Avsey's whole body. He wrapped his fingers loosely around the strap of his knapsack.

Avsey remembered something else. *If you can count the drive wheel bolts, you have time to hop the train.* Bronya told him this over and over, but he'd never been able to look at the wheels, let alone count the drive wheel bolts. He swallowed hard and forced himself to look at the wheels. A flash of nausea threatened to overwhelm him, but he fought it and focused. The tightness in his chest eased a bit. He counted the bolts. A new energy mobilized his limbs.

The door of one of the freight cars was open, a bit of luck. He glanced around the yard before he sprang up into a run. As he neared the car, he realized the bottom was too high. He couldn't place his hands on the floor and swing up. The rhythm of his breath and the thud of his footsteps, heavy in his ears, kept the panic at bay. He noticed a thin metal rail on one side of the freight car door and a step at the bottom.

Flooded with relief, he remembered something more. *Three contact points. One hand and two feet.* He threw his knapsack inside and jogged alongside the train, hand on the wood. The rail was cold when he grabbed it. He lifted his foot onto the step and pulled up.

Half his body hung in the air, agreeably, as if gravity no longer mattered and he could fly. Anchored by one hand and one foot, he felt liberated, foolishly joyful. The cold was exhilarating. This was what Bronya had loved, the giddiness of speed and air.

The train lurched forward, almost throwing Avsey to the ground. Two contact points, it was clear now, weren't enough. He turned his body to face the opening and made another mistake; he looked straight down. His free foot hovered close to the wheels. The old terror roared back. His confidence evaporated. Grasping wildly for the railing with his free hand, his body swung back and forth.

On the third try, he grabbed the doorframe and pulled himself close and tight, hugging the side of the freight car as he placed his other foot on the narrow step. Again, the train jerked violently forward. Sweat rolled into his eyes. His hand slipped down the metal rail. The train picked up speed. He glanced down and saw the track whizzing by. Bronya's voice whispered in his ear. *Keep your head.* He closed his eyes, bent his knees, and pushed hard with both feet to propel his body into the freight car.

Collapsing inside, he lay splayed out on the rough wood. He was sure his heart would burst through his chest and beat there, on the floor outside his body. He rolled over, lay on his back, and wrapped his arms around his rib cage. Bronya had been right to warn him against train hopping. But now he knew it was the second most thrilling thing he'd ever done in his life. Almost as exciting as stealing.

The freight car smelled of sweat and urine. *Reassuring.* Others had been here before him. He wasn't alone. Steadied, he pushed up to look around. In one corner, he found an abandoned foot-cloth; in another, a blue-and-white package of Belomorkanal cigarettes. Soldiers' things. He felt a rush of solidarity for the young men fighting on the front lines. He felt like a soldier, like the men before him in the freight car. He wanted to sit with them and dangle his feet over the side and slap them on the back. Comrades.

Avsey inspected the unopened package of tobacco. He had never wanted to smoke like the boys at school. Cigarettes made those boys cough and swear. But he could trade tobacco for something better, maybe even food. The footcloth was valuable, too, though Avsey felt sorry for its owner. It was a disaster to lose a footcloth at the beginning of winter. He stashed it next to the tobacco at the bottom of his knapsack. His luck had begun to turn.

From the half-open door, an icy steppe glided by in the after-noon sunshine. Avsey leaned over and draped his arms around his knees. He suspected Salsk would be the next stop but had no way to know. He passed cattle, small outbuildings, stumps of withered corn in half-frozen fields, idle tractors. Small boys ran alongside the tracks and waved at him. Wherever he was going would be different from where he'd been. That was all that mattered.

Avsey crossed his fingers and tucked them over his heart. He rested his chin on his knees. Now, the letter he'd sent had to make its way into Papa's hands. Avsey had more paper, just in case. But Papa would come. He knew it.

The sun disappeared, and with it, the view of the country-side. Avsey rolled further into the boxcar's interior and sat with his back against the wall. He'd suddenly found it impossible to keep his eyes open. Fatigue seeped through him like rainwater in sand. He thought briefly about the possibilities of dying in the cold, hungry and alone, but chased these thoughts away and foraged in his knapsack for some dried Bulrush root.

He'd discovered if he didn't eat too much of it, he could control his hunger without getting sick. He curled up on his side, adjusted the knapsack under his head, and chewed on the root. The train clicked through the night while the odor of the wood and the rocking freight car cradled him to sleep. Bronya's voice, lilting and lazy, sang a lullaby:

HE'LL SNATCH YOU UP BETWEEN HIS TEETH,
If on the bed's edge you sleep
And drag you to the forest deep.

HE WOKE WITH THE SCREAM OF BRAKES AND HIS BODY SLIDING across the floorboards. Momentarily confused, Avsey crawled to the door and stuck his head out into the cold morning. The sun had not yet crested the horizon, but he saw the sign for Salsk drift by and was pleased. He'd calculated well.

Rubbing the sleep from his eyes, he pushed the door open and grabbed his knapsack. One of the yard workers yelled obscenities when he jumped down, but no one bothered to give chase. Avsey shouldered his knapsack and set off at a run. He'd done it. He'd braved the wheels alone.

PART II DEFIANCE

NOVEMBER 1941-JUNE 1942

Wait even when from afar, no letters come to you,
Wait even when others are tired of waiting...
Wait even when my mother and son think I am no more,
And when friends sit around the fire, drinking to my memory.
Wait, and do not hurry to drink to my memory, too;
Wait, for I'll return, defying every death.

K. Simonov - translated by Alexander Werth - 1964

CHAPTER 10
OCCUPIED ROSTOV, LATE NOVEMBER
1941

THE GERMAN OFFICER TURNED THE HANDLES ON THE ASYLUM doors, pushed them open with two fingers, and peered quickly inside. He didn't expect to find anyone. The hallway had already been cleared, the patients herded into the courtyard. He'd seen them there, standing, shivering in new snow. The asylum, as asylums go, was satisfyingly sterile, though the beds were decrepit, the windows too small, and the slight urine-tinged odor about the place, pervasive.

A voice whispered in the stillness, from out of thin air. The German's neck hairs prickled. He shivered involuntarily, slowed his pace, and quieted his steps as much as his black boots allowed, heels first. He listened for another whisper and then shrugged it off as one of the familiar machinations inside his own head, those he ignored, albeit with some effort. Ghosts whispered often.

At the end of the hall, he turned and retraced his steps. *All clear.* He relaxed, took a cigarette from his jacket pocket, and paused to light it. With a deep inhale, he felt his shoulders release despite the shouting outside. The cigarettes had only recently become a necessity and one of the few pleasures since the work in Rostov began. He exhaled. Smoke lifted toward the ceiling, and through it, he noticed a figure midway down the hallway, nearer rather than further away, clad in white.

He closed his eyes. Another ghost. When he opened them, he saw that she was too close and her features too distinct to be a ghost. Lush brown curls, arched eyebrows, full lips. She certainly didn't belong to his memory. Too beautiful.

She reached out her hand and spoke, her tone imploring. "Sergei, is that you? I've waited so long."

He tried to make his voice harsh but failed. "Where have you come from, Fräulein? You belong outside." He pointed to the window. "Outside." He spoke a little Russian but didn't bother with it now. Language didn't matter for the mentally ill, and from her smile, he knew she wouldn't understand. She took another step toward him, an arm's length away.

When she reached for his hand, he felt a jolt, a current of electricity so strong, he was forced to loosen the collar of his shirt with his thumb. He did not drop her hand but held on to it firmly, its voltage pleasing. She moved closer, so close he felt her warm breath on his face. He noticed her green eyes were hazel-rimmed and ached to smell her neck and bury his face in the hair haloed around her face like fine gauze.

She brushed his lips with her finger and whispered, "Sergei. Don't make me wait."

He knew she was mad, like the others, and as such, unworthy of life. After all, his name wasn't Sergei, and he had never seen her before. The internal fight wasn't about what he should do—she was too beautiful to shoot. The tug of war was between his solid, loyal wife—the woman he'd married in a patriotic fervor and the mad woman in front of him. He justified his desire; the mad woman was clearly willing. He would die far from home, and so she would surely die here, sooner rather than later. There was also the cold fact of his trousers, taut with restraint. He'd need to take her out of here, in no small measure because the smell of urine had become stronger, but more importantly because he would want her more than once.

Three days into it, despite the heavy bombing and the daily aktions he commanded, his physical ecstasy was so great, he felt he was floating far above the earth.

The rooms they inhabited had large windows from which the officer could see the street below. Other officers inhabited the lower floors of the 19th century building that had once been a private home, since converted into a series of depressingly cold apartments. He imagined this had occurred because the Bolsheviks didn't like spacious, 19th century houses unless they were shared. At any rate, the squalid residents had been turned out and the Germans installed. The arrangement was perfect. He climbed to the top of the stairs at the end of the day and shut the door.

He didn't know her name, and he remained Sergei. Without reason, the madwoman defied physical limitations, washed his memory clean of the pimply girl behind the shed, the hungry secretary who had introduced him, after hours, to alternate orifices of pleasure and his aproned, unresponsive wife. This woman was a carnivorous plant, a Venus flytrap, and he, an insect, trapped inside the leaf of her limbs, the sticky mucilage of her brown curls—happy prey.

His zeal in skirmishes with the Soviets, in the search for Jews, increased despite his lack of sleep. Only his men could see he stood on the thinnest razor's edge between clarity and what they thought was the delirium of war. Still, they admired his good cheer, his strength and energy, his adaptation to the Soviet hell— the dreary, rubble-strewn streets.

Sometimes, he found her in the corner of the room talking about bodies in boxcars, about betrayal and a boy called Kuzma. She repeated over and over again, "I never wanted to leave him."

He wondered once what it all meant to her, but only for a minute. She had come from a psychiatric hospital after all. None of it was real, except what happened in the room and the deep inhalation afterward. Even so, he had difficulty trusting his senses. He questioned his own sanity more than once, but the pleasure restored his sense of well-being.

On the sixth day, the Soviets came from nowhere and pushed the Germans back to the city's northern outskirts. He ran without returning to the room, blocked by fierce fighting near the river, nauseated, his addiction curtailed with no possibility for a slow tapering off.

CHAPTER 11
SALSK, DECEMBER 1941

AVSEY DIDN'T REMEMBER WHY HE THOUGHT SALSK WOULD BE EASIER than Bataysk. The truth was Salsk wasn't easier; it was more complicated. The market—where old kolkhoz farmers sold pumpkins, dried herbs, and potatoes from their kitchen allotments, where refugee women hawked the remnants of their former lives: coffeepots and samovars, underwear, forks and knives, padded jackets, fabric remnants, and odd bits of costume jewelry—was so thick with people, the militia had trouble catching thieves as they vanished into the crowd.

Soldiers on leave watched stony-eyed as rail-thin mothers swaddled babies in dirty rags. Old women watched the soldiers, a mixture of pride and hope illuminating their lined faces. Powerful odors emanated from the crowded streets: shashlik; cubes of lamb meat grilled on an open fire; rotting trash, thick with flies despite the winter cold; and smoke from the dung and dried sage patties peasant women burned to purify the air.

Amid the confusion and chaos, Avsey made a plan to survive. He devised a set of rules he called the Salsk code of conduct: avoid trouble, remain wary, and search for opportunity. It wouldn't be long until Papa arrived.

He found his first opportunity at the municipal canteen. He

queued politely and was allowed into the milk room. Surprised, he filled his bowl and felt, for the first time in months, like a child, drinking milk reserved for children. He returned the next day, his stomach anticipating a warm belly full of milk, but the woman at the door with kind eyes who'd beckoned him in initially had disappeared, replaced by a younger, harder overseer who stopped him cold at the entrance.

Avsey tried again the next day. He stood next to a group of small children, and when no one was paying attention, slid past the young sentry as she talked with a friend. Avsey added perseverance to the Salsk code. He was satisfied with himself and laughed with the other children over things only children understood—burps, a dribble of milk, a stern look from an adult. His whole body delighted in the gurgle in his throat and the absence of hunger.

The next time Avsey made his way into the milk room and raised his bowl in anticipation, the attendant gave him a hard knock on the head with a ladle. Rubbing his head outside, he thought about where he'd gone wrong. Maybe it had been inevitable. He was a head taller than the other children. At any rate, the milk room opportunity was exhausted.

He felt a little sorry for himself before he heard Bronya's voice say, *Pity and scorn are two sides of the same coin. Noses up.* Bronya had told him this when Mama was taken and he'd had to go to school anyway. He'd seen the school principal whispering to his teacher, their faces etched in pity when he passed. He didn't know why, but he'd felt ashamed, even though he hadn't done anything.

Avsey thought about shame again when he saw the young amputees in Salsk. Their loss was raw and on display for all to see. He was embarrassed watching them. He didn't want them to see his pity, nor could he look away. One, in a wheelchair tended by a young nurse, never looked up. Another sat on a park bench every morning, arranging and rearranging the army blanket that covered his stump, shouting obscenities at passersby. Avsey wanted to shout back, tell the young soldier he was sorry for what had happened to him.

One of the amputees, Mikhail, appeared to inspire both fear and respect among the adolescent refugee boys, including Avsey. Mikhail had lost both legs. He pushed himself through the market each morning atop a crude board outfitted with four small wheels, his hair falling into his eyes, a metal cross stuck to his neck, drenched in sweat despite the cold.

Mikhail was hard to ignore—his bravado was legendary, as were his good looks. He wore short sleeves, even in nasty weather, and his muscled arms were covered in deep scratches. The older kolkhoz women at the market giggled like schoolgirls as he passed, flashing his wide smile, winking, his blue eyes dazzling. Perhaps it was because Mikhail had made the ultimate sacrifice for the motherland, or maybe his charm and good looks were irresistible, but the kolkhoz women vied for his attention with jars of honey, sausages, pickles, and moonshine. He was a rich man.

Mikhail's charisma and—in particular—his wealth had wide appeal. He ruled over a gang of orphans, all willing to do his bidding for cigarettes and potato vodka and a chance to own any one of the enticing objects so loved by adolescent boys everywhere: small knives, army caps, and tin boxes. Mikhail's command over the orphans was absolute. Once, Avsey saw him hold out a wristwatch to one of the older boys, while covetous onlookers trembled with desire.

Avsey lingered at the far edges of Mikhail's circle, wary but curious, aware that most of Mikhail's boys were older and bigger and governed by their own lust for treasure. Avsey steered clear for another reason; these boys would do anything for Mikhail's approval. Their thirst for his attention was perhaps more powerful than their longing for his riches. Avsey had ample experience with boys who, needing approval from other boys, lapsed into cruelty they'd never dreamed of alone. If you don't like wolves, stay out of the forest.

Avsey managed to keep his distance until one cold afternoon when Mikhail displayed, for everyone to see, several dozen chocolate pieces wrapped in gold foil and blue paper, temptingly arranged on his wheeled board.

Right off, one of the taller boys stepped forward to offer Mikhail a fistful of rubles. The rapid exchange completed, the boy unwrapped three of the chocolates and flat-palmed them into his mouth. Avsey could see the boy's ribs through his shirt as chocolate infused saliva ran down his chin. The other boys stood stock-still, their mouths open, their tongues sliding across their teeth. Avsey imagined the creamy texture and sweet taste of the foil wrapped chocolate. Another boy tried unsuccessfully to offer a pocketknife for one piece of the chocolate, the same knife he'd bought from Mikhail days earlier. Mikhail shook his head.

Avsey edged closer to the little circle, dizzy with desire, lured by the small blue-and-gold packages. He weighed one of his rules—opportunity—against another, avoiding trouble. A small interior voice warned him to stay clear, but opportunity won handily. He told himself this was simply candy. How could there be trouble in a few pieces of chocolate?

One eye on the other boys, Avsey fumbled with the strings of his knapsack and shifted his gaze downward. He saw the tobacco and the footcloth but rejected these items immediately. Mikhail always had plenty of tobacco. And to offer the footcloth to an amputee might be an insult. He reached in and pulled the top off his birch box. He'd never taken anything out of it, never traded any of its treasures for food, for anything. He rummaged inside the box and pulled out the rolled pages of stamps. Maybe, just maybe, Mikhail was a stamp collector.

Avsey stood alone, and for a moment, he hesitated. He'd collected most of the stamps over many years, pouring over them by lamplight, carefully sticking each one onto the right box and page in the album. The stamps he'd stolen from the boys at school were the most valuable. They were souvenirs of triumph.

Last but not least, the stamps were beautiful. He'd studied their images, dreamed of the places and the heroes etched into their surfaces. He'd loved them because until now, they had been his only adventure. He thought about returning the album pages to the box and walking away.

But life had changed. He no longer needed to feel superior to the boys at school. Revenge was the last thing on his mind. Standing in front of Mikhail and the other boys, so far away from home, Avsey realized he no longer felt the same way about the stamps. In fact, he hadn't had the heart to look at them since he left Rostov. While the heroes and their exploits remained enticing, he no longer dreamed of grand adventures in the Soviet hinterland. Adventure, he realized, wasn't as fun as he thought it would be. It was difficult and risky and no one ever knew how it might turn out. Adventure was lonely.

He approached Mikhail slowly. When he was close, a meter away, Mikhail looked up. His smile faded. He studied Avsey, nostrils flaring.

Avsey took another step toward the board.

Mikhail adjusted himself to sit up taller without taking his eyes off Avsey.

His hands shaking, Avsey unrolled the album pages and thrust them under Mikhail's nose. He kept his ears open and his eyes on Mikhail's face.

Mikhail brightened, almost imperceptibly. A boy standing close by whistled appreciatively and said, "Mischa, you lucky bastard."

Mikhail cast an angry glance at the boy before turning to Avsey and letting a slow, sly smile fill his face. At this, the boys moved closer to admire the offered goods, their eyes shiny and wide. An older boy cracked his knuckles.

Avsey nodded toward the chocolate and said, "All of it."

A hush fell over the boys; conversation, restless movement, whistles, all ceased. The silence rumbled like thunder through the group.

Mikhail, never breaking his eye contact with Avsey, slowly pushed the chocolate pieces to the end of the board, into a little pile. Avsey bent over and placed the stamps next to the chocolate. He felt Mikhail's heavy breath on his neck. The fumes of last night's vodka assaulted his nose, and he remembered that trouble lurked in these encounters. Speed was essential. He widened the opening of his knapsack and, with one swift sweep of his hand, pushed the chocolate into its interior. He stood up, bowed slightly to Mikhail, and backed away, pulling the knapsack strings tight.

That was when he saw Mikhail look to his left and flick his finger toward Avsey. A nearby voice yelled, "Get the bag!"

At least five boys were at his heels. One of them screamed, "Stop, weasel, or you'll be sorry!"

Avsey ran as fast as he could, certain his life depended on it. The birch box and all his treasures depended on it. His feet hit his bottom as he ran, clutching his knapsack to his chest. He jumped over people sitting on benches smoking, over crates of vegetables and a bicycle with a bent wheel. He ran straight down the middle of the road. A truck swerved to avoid the running boys, honking as it ran over a ditch, narrowly missing a woman pushing a pram.

Avsey ran. He heard one of the boys scream and turned to see him fly through the air and land on his side. Out of the corner of his eye, Avsey saw two other boys, gasping for air, give up. The two who remained gained on him, pulled at his shirt, and grabbed at his arms, but Avsey pulled away and ran faster.

Just when he thought he might be clear, he tripped. On nothing. He fell over his own feet and landed in the dirt, skidded to a stop on his back, and lay stretched out and vulnerable on the ground. He watched as if from above while the boys approached. They were breathing hard, and Avsey could see their teeth as they stood over him. They kicked him viciously in the ribs, grabbed his knapsack, and tried to pull it from his hands. "Give it up, you filthy dog," snarled a boy with dull eyes.

Avsey gripped the cloth and prayed the straps would not tear away, determined never to give up.

One of the older boys landed a vicious blow to Avsey's head with his foot and growled, "Your life's worth nothing now." Avsey felt his arms weakening and his breath slowing. From out of nowhere, a long stick swung over his head. He waited for the final blow. He closed his eyes.

But his knapsack remained in his arms, tight against his chest. He pinched the skin on the inside of his arm. Was he dead? He opened his eyes and sat up. The boys were running away.

In their place stood a girl leaning on a solid stick she held at her side like a staff. She bent over and said, "You alive?"

The stick was taller than she was. Her face was dirty and Avsey noticed two bald patches on her scalp. She stretched out her hand and pulled him up. "Cowards," she said. "Afraid of a girl with a stick." She held the stick up like a trophy, still staring at Avsey.

"It is a pretty big stick," Avsey said, eyeing it warily. The girl was thin and wore a man's jacket inside out, the wool against her skin. Her trousers were tied with a rope around her middle. She looked older than him, but he couldn't be sure. No one appeared the way they were supposed to these days. There was an air of experience about her though, a toughness Avsey had never seen in a girl.

"Why'd you help me?" He winced as he spoke. His sides ached and his head hurt. He reached to check his face for blood.

"Your eyes are turning black. No blood though."

"Why'd you chase them away?"

"Because they beat me once, too. Then I made this thing and they stopped. You need a weapon." The girl showed Avsey the bent nails protruding from one end of the stick.

Avsey's eyes grew to twice their size. No wonder the boys ran away. "Where'd you find the nails?"

"Just around. I hammered them in with a rock."

"Well, thanks for saving me." He began to limp toward the station, pulling his knapsack to his chest. He wanted nothing more than to lie under a bench and cry.

"I'm Lali." The girl stayed where she was.

Avsey continued walking. "Thanks again, Lali."

"Hey, where are you going?"

"Station." He raised his hand in a wave. The movement hurt. On top of everything, he felt lightheaded, a little nauseated. He tried to walk faster.

Lali caught up with him. "You're not right, are you?"

Avsey shook his head no.

Lali took his elbow.

Avsey hesitated. Did he want this girl to help him? For some reason, it felt wrong. He thought about the nails in the stick, the bald patches on her head. The nausea became worse. His ribs were tender, and it was hard to take a deep breath, to clear his head. He pulled his elbow away from her. "I can walk on my own, thanks."

"I'll walk with you to make sure you get to the station. You don't want to meet those boys in the state you're in."

She had a point. When they reached the train station, Avsey continued toward his sleeping place under the metal bench on a sparsely populated side of the waiting room, out of view of the platforms and away from the doors. He sat on the ground, stretched his legs out in front of him, and groaned. Lali leaned her stick against the wall and sat down next to him. Avsey studied the sores on her lips. Her red-rimmed eyes. He stared at the bald patches at the back of her head and realized he'd seen her before. But where?

"What's in your bag?"

Avsey realized he was still clutching his knapsack. He wrapped his arms tighter around it and said, "I traded all my stamps."

Lali rested her back against the wall. Avsey glanced at her sideways a couple of times before he remembered where he'd seen the bald patches. But that couldn't have been the same girl, the one he'd seen under a tree behind the market, two women slapping her. Avsey had felt a churning rise from his stomach to his throat. He'd hurried away and not looked back. He hadn't seen the girl's face because she'd been hunched over in a tight ball, dirt flying all around her frail body. He could still hear the dull thuds from the blows. That couldn't have been Lali, though.

Lali rose to leave. "Make yourself a weapon, kid."

Avsey felt a tiny stab of loss. "Sure, thanks."

He thought about Sara, about her favorite story, David and Goliath. *Your brain is all you need. David beat Goliath because he was smart.* Until now, he'd thought Sara meant he should outwit the mean boys at school. It occurred to him that David used his brain to make a slingshot.

Lali turned and walked down the platform. At the end of it, she looked back and waved.

Avsey waved back. He watched Lali disappear, then knelt and pushed his knapsack under the bench. He eased himself in after it and stretched out. His whole body was bruised, every point of contact with the ground painful. He gently shimmied his body further underneath the bench until he was completely hidden from view. His muscles relaxed. He unclenched his jaw.

It felt good to lie down. The low murmur of others coming and going, the shuffle of feet, the whistles, even the wheels, soothed him. No place on earth was as comforting as a train station. The noises, the odors, were a part of his childhood landscape, as familiar as his own fingers and toes. He took deep breaths of creosote, brake dust, and coal smoke. His muscles relaxed a little more.

He reached for the knapsack strings without moving his back, pulled it near, and then with one hand, dug inside for the chocolates. They were, after all, the source of all the trouble. And the reward. The bruises would feel better with chocolate. He held one piece above his head and carefully unfolded the corners of the blue paper. He peeled back the gold foil. The chocolate was dry, the rich brown color marred by a dull, white sheen. It didn't matter. He stuck the piece into his mouth and let it melt slowly. He ate three more in quick succession, feeling tears well in his eyes. The pleasure was almost too much to bear.

With difficulty he decided to leave the rest, to save them for later. He wasn't sure his stomach would allow more. He knew from experience never to push through, even if the hunger was terrible. He sucked his teeth clean, moving his tongue to dislodge any bits that remained while he considered what he might trade next. He'd have to give something up or he wouldn't last until Papa found him.

Avsey pushed himself onto his left side with some difficulty. When he'd found a relatively comfortable position, he pulled the birch box from the bottom of his knapsack and placed it on the ground. He popped the lid and cleared the space in front of him.

Papa had made the box from a birch log he'd carried home from a walk in the forest. He'd used the bark for the body and the wood for the top and bottom so that the box was light but strong. He'd given it to Avsey for his ninth birthday. The box was his prized possession, the container for his treasures—the things he'd stolen from the boys at school, Mama's gold, and the objects he'd found in Papa's drawer. The coins he'd initially kept in the box were long gone like the stolen pocketknife he'd prized above everything else. There was no point in going over the incident now.

He dumped the contents onto the concrete and felt a nauseating wave of regret. The images that used to delight him— comets, icebreakers, dragons, and dirigibles—were gone. He closed his eyes. The regret coursed through his whole body and pushed his heart into the bottom of his belly. He longed to take the stamps back. But Aunt Sara would be proud of him. She had been the one to console him when, in a fit of anger, he'd thrown his electric train over the balcony and broken it beyond repair. When he'd burst into tears, it had been Sara who said regret was a part of growing up, a test of one's maturity. He'd be better for it. Still, he didn't care for the hollow feeling; it was like castor oil.

He turned his attention to the objects in front of him. What else might he have to sacrifice in order to eat until Papa finally came?

He picked up the birth certificate he'd found in Mama's drawer. It belonged to a boy he didn't know. The family names and patronymics on the document had been cut out, replaced with ragged rectangular holes made with scissors. Avsey remained puzzled about the birth certificate. A boy's given name and his date and place of birth remained intact on the document: Kuzma, born 1924, three years before Bronya, in Rostov-on-Don. Avsey put the birth certificate back in the box. It wasn't worth anything.

The photograph of a tanned, muscular man, his sleeves rolled high above the elbow, wasn't worth anything either. The man stared directly into the camera, his gaze either shy or indifferent, impossible to tell. Avsey flipped the photo over. On the back, words had been inked out, leaving only a part of a sentence— *you alone*—and a signature—Sergei—in a neat, unfamiliar hand. Was this the same Sergei, the one Sara and Papa talked about on the night Sara came back? He had no idea who Sergei was or why his picture had been in Mama's drawer. The photo made him uncomfortable.

Next, he arrayed Mama's long chain, her wedding ring, and the other gold ring on the cement. The gold chain was thin with a pearl pendant. Avsey knew Papa had given this to Mama on their wedding day. He didn't remember who'd told him, but he'd always known it. He remembered playing with the pearl when he was little, white against Mama's soft skin. The skin that smelt of minerals and roses and milk. He'd been surprised to find the necklace in the armoire. He had no memory of her without it. It was the same with the rings. She wore them every day.

As Avsey considered whether he would trade Mama's

jewelry for food, the old brine of guilt rose gently under his ribs. While he never felt guilty about stealing from the bullies at school, he'd needed to think hard after he stole from Mama. He'd been surprised when for a time his act of disloyalty had freed him from the grief he felt in her absence. He had her secrets, and one day, he would ask her what it all meant. In time, the grief returned, accompanied by an acute sense of shame. He'd compounded his sadness when his only wish had been to banish it.

He didn't want the acid under his ribs to rise up again. He'd keep Mama's jewelry.

He decided Papa's tarnished silver cigarette case could be traded. *If* he were desperate. It was engraved with the initials *LMA* for Lev Moisevich Abramov. Stealing from Papa had been easier than taking Mama's things. That was until he'd opened the cigarette case one morning, outside, behind the apartment building. The odor had taken him by surprise—trees and tar, cigarettes and engine oil. Papa's odor.

He'd opened the case several times on that first day, to inhale, to ease his unease, until the odors bled into the fresh air and wafted away. Since then, he'd rubbed his finger over the engraved initials so often he was sure they'd rub off. He stuck the case in the front pocket of the knapsack. In the maybe category.

The blue stone was a mystery. Avsey had no idea if he could trade it or not. He wasn't even sure what it was or why Papa had it in his drawer. Avsey cradled the stone in his dirty palm and prodded it gently like he would a captured insect. It sparkled like Venus in the night sky. At first, he'd believed it was crystal. The crystal glasses Babushka had given Mama were almost the same color, and the facets caught the light in the same way.

He remembered seeing paintings of the tsars, their jeweled crowns, the blue and green jewels sparkling around their necks. But why would Papa have a jewel? It didn't make sense. Avsey dropped the stone back into the box. Better to figure out what it was before he traded it. He added the cigarettes and the foot-cloth to the front pocket. Everyone knew these items were valuable.

Avsey scooped the remaining treasures into the box and nestled it into his knapsack. He slid his body from underneath the bench, pulled the knapsack strings tight, pushed his arms through the straps, and sat up. As painful as it was, he had to pee. Stifling groans, he made his way to the field at the side of the station, away from the yards. His whole body ached.

On the way back inside, in the crowded waiting room, Avsey saw Lali from a distance and tried to raise his hand to signal her. Pain shot through his side. His heart beat a tiny bit faster. He was glad she'd returned. She probably wanted to check on him.

It was then that Avsey saw who she was with; two of the bigger boys from Mikhail's group walked beside her. Avsey blinked. He watched Lali, his breath shallow. A pit in the bottom of his stomach opened up. He felt his heart sink into the pit.

Lali and the two boys were headed to his bench. She had her stick. Was she on their side? Or had they threatened her? It didn't matter. He ducked under the stairs and pressed his body against the wall, every hair on his neck standing on end.

A few minutes later, Lali and the boys circled back and climbed the stairs. Avsey saw their feet over his head and shivered. Lali thumped the stick on the step. Avsey heard her say, "That's where I left him. I swear." She thumped the stick again to punctuate her words.

Avsey did not need to think. He had, without cause, believed Lali's good intentions. Why had she saved him in the first place? He felt doubly betrayed. Lali, like the Novikovs, had helped until some invisible tide had turned. He was angry at himself. The changes in the hearts of others were unknowable. Until they weren't.

He'd had no choice in the beginning; he'd been naive. Now he knew.

He was lucky. He'd carried his knapsack with him. He shuddered to think about what might have happened and added a new rule to the Salsk code of conduct: Never trust anyone until they had proven themselves at least three times.

He headed for the yards, limping, glancing over his shoulder for any sign of Mikhail's gang in pursuit. He knew what he needed to do. He would leave Salsk now, hop a train to Tikhoretsk, and send Papa another letter.

CHAPTER 12
THE STEPPE, NOVEMBER 1941

A SHADOW DARKENED THE WINDOW BEFORE THE BLACK WING TIP appeared on the right side of the train. Bronya jumped up between the seats, eager to catch sight of the whole bird as it soared over the steppe. The train, bound for Saratov, was slow and the appearance of a Steppe eagle was a gift. The monotonous beauty of fresh snowdrifts, ice castles, and frozen ponds was made majestic by a wide-shadowed wingspan or the mutinous glare of an antlered mammal.

Steppe eagles were Bronya's favorite. These birds were lushly feathered with pale bands braided through their tawny wings. Bronya was surprised they had stayed on the snow-covered steppe, but rats followed great armies, and more than once, Bronya had spied the vile creatures high in the air, writhing in the talons of an ascending eagle.

The train quit Lesovo station in a hurry, and Bronya had, despite everything, pressed her face against the window to look for Vera. But black smoke had poured over the train like oil, blocking the light and any chance of reconciliation. She'd overheard later that theirs was the last train out of Kharkov. Even now, weeks into their journey, the train moved east by day, only to retreat at night to allow the Red Army to move troops to the front on the single track. The mood on the train had nonetheless been lighthearted, perhaps even triumphant. And once the steppe was laid bare before them, a cheerful invincibility took hold of the women that persisted even after cold gripped the train and frosted the windows.

But Bronya had never cheered. The further the train took her into the interior, the more her dream of a short war withered and faded. It was one thing to work on the kolkhoz, quite another to watch the snowy steppe deepen its hold on her, solidifying the impossibility of home. She was thrilled to have escaped, but the violence in the clearing, Vera's outburst, all remained taut in her mind. She withdrew and said little to the women around her, sure if she spoke the horror would spill out.

They, in turn, called her, "our shy one, our dove." She sent Papa a letter from a post station along the way to tell him she would be at aviation factory 292, in Saratov.

The bombs exploded as she lingered between the seats. The middle cars buckled inward and slipped the tracks, throwing Bronya down the aisle, knocking the air from her lungs. She hadn't heard the whistle, the parting of the air as the bombs hurtled toward the train, only the sound of breaking glass, like the clinking of birthday toasts. Her last thought before the explosion was that not even a steppe eagle made such a shadow.

An eternity of silence followed. Nothing moved. Was this how it felt to die? Then, as suddenly as it had gone, her breath returned. She choked air into her lungs and coughed. Expecting the planes to return for a second pass, she curled herself tight into a ball, her head tucked toward her belly, wondering what it would feel like to be blown apart. She didn't want to be a moving target, her image inked against the snow, a dark bull's-eye seeking its scatter of bullets.

She pushed her fists into her eyes and thought of Avsey, his face and freckles, his laugh. She searched her mind for a happy childhood memory but found only static images: an articulated eight-shelled mollusk, a chiton, her pencil case from school, the number eight, closed things. She curled tighter and waited, the hush of shock loud in her ears. She pressed her fists harder into her eye sockets and stifled the urge to cry out.

When the planes did not return and the stillness became too much to bear, Bronya lifted her head and pushed herself up. She felt hollow, as if a ferocious wind had ripped the organs from her body. The emptiness hurt.

The other passengers were bloodied, trembling. One by one, they stood and moved cautiously toward the door. Bronya saw her own bloody knees, the shattered glass, the snow beyond the windows. Nothing made sense. She wished she knew these women, their names, their stories. They were all aviation factory workers, and before their panicked flight from the Kharkov station, she'd never seen them before. One of the women stopped, took Bronya's hand, and leaned in close to speak to her. Bronya watched her lips, puzzled. No sound issued from the woman's mouth.

Outside in the snow, several train cars were splayed on their sides like dying insects, the passengers and their possessions scattered in the frozen wilderness. Several women sat in the snow looking bewildered, others picked through debris, salvaging belongings. Bronya watched without understanding as one of the rail workers waved his arms dramatically, pointing passengers down the track. The world slowed and she walked in circles, disoriented. One eagle, then another, soared above her, square wing tips and white wing bars rippling in the wind. An eagle pair. Bronya felt a surge of sympathy for the small mammals on the ground. *Prey.*

A uniformed man stood close to her and gestured toward a group of passengers walking down the tracks. His mouth moved at a furious pace, and his forehead glistened with sweat. Bronya focused her attention on his lips and tried to clear the sludge from her mind. What had happened to his voice? Then, as if awakening from a dream, she understood; her hearing had been stolen by the explosion. She screamed, felt her chest vibrate, but didn't hear her own voice. Her frozen breath hung in the air.

From out of nowhere, her knapsack and violin appeared, and Bronya, grateful, took them. She followed the other passengers down the track, feeling the crunch of the snow under her boots, the insidious silence from the outside in, cruelly depleting. By the time a fresh train arrived at a lonely watershed, Bronya had stopped putting her hands on her throat, had stopped reciting poetry, straining to catch a familiar syllable. She blew on her fingertips and told herself she could learn to read lips. No one would know. Then she thought about never hearing music again, about Beethoven, and felt she might faint. One of the aviation factory women held her arm and pushed her forward.

The replacement train had more flatbeds and teplushki than passenger cars, and Bronya couldn't help but feel desperate. She'd heard stories from the other passengers about teplushki uncoupled from the rest of the train, abandoned at watersheds and small stations and left to wait for days, even weeks, before anyone noticed. All she wanted was to be out of range of the airplanes.

As luck would have it, a young rail worker, his unkempt black hair falling over his eyes, ushered her onto a passenger car ahead of the others. He spoke to her and pointed to a group of women still outside. Bronya nodded and tried not to scream. The young worker blushed bright red and hurried away.

The women boarded slowly, some pointing at her or patting her on the shoulder. Did they know she was deaf? Bronya avoided eye contact; the sound of the blood pounding in her ears was enough. The passenger car filled with women, and when the seats were taken, they sat in the aisles, some on top of suitcases. Bronya was happy to have a seat with easy access to the gangway. From there she could escape, inhale the scent of metal and winter pine, and avoid the press of warm, unwashed bodies and pitying glances. *Noses up.* She'd said it to Avsey a hundred times. Humiliation was more difficult than she'd imagined.

Bronya recognized passengers from the previous train, all disheveled and exhausted. They sat smoking or hung from the windows, haggling with kolkhoz families for metal combs and kasha. A few passed provisions they'd bought from the peasants through the windows and a meaty odor filled the train. *Dumplings.* The woman seated in front of her, turned to offer her a dumpling.

Bronya took a bite and let the dumpling melt in her mouth, closing her eyes to savor the rush of flavor. Their purchases complete, the women snapped the windows closed against the cold. The peasants backed away from the tracks, their pockets stuffed with rubles. Tobacco smoke filled the car, blurring the outline of the faces around her. By then Bronya was too tired to care.

The late afternoon sun slid down the horizon and still a large crowd of people remained shivering outside, waiting to be let in, or perhaps waiting for another train. She didn't know. The train's steam whistle sounded, high-pitched and shrill. Bronya jumped up, banged her knee on the seat in front of her, and toppled onto the woman across the aisle.

"Excuse me, I'm so sorry." Was this her own voice? A soft laugh floated through the car. The sounds bounced inside Bronya's head. Her ears worked.

She heard other voices. "Are we leaving then?"

"Cigarette?"

"I shouldn't have told you."

Bronya turned to look outside at the crowd. Tears of relief blurred her vision. The snow sparkled rose and violet, reflecting the wisps of sunset color. She wiped her eyes and noticed a tall boy in a thin coat, his arms wrapped around his torso, and a sheepskin hat pulled low over his brow. He was looking straight at her. He wore clean valenki while the rest of the crowd appeared disheveled and caked in mud. *Odd.*

The woman across the aisle tapped Bronya's arm. "Feeling better, daughter?"

Bronya turned and smiled politely. "It came back. Just now. I can hear. It was nothing after all."

The woman leaned closer, patted her on the shoulder, then turned to pass the news to the women in front of her. "She's fine. She can hear!"

The women clapped.

A pinprick of light from beyond the window distracted Bronya. The boy had backed away from the tracks and stood flashing a shiny piece of metal in his hand. It caught the last rays of sunlight at just the right angle, spreading sparkles of light over her face and beyond her seat. Blinded, she lifted her hand to shade her eyes, but all she could see were the little balls of light playing around her head.

The train began to move as the last sliver of sun made its final bid for attention. When the train slid past the watershed and trundled slowly out into the wilderness, Bronya made her way to the open gangway connection between the cars. Here was the view she'd wanted: a wide indigo sky, illuminated by remnants of the waning light curdled at the edges of the world. A crescent moon lay pasted above the thin arc of earth's crust. Bronya scanned the sky for black dots—German planes. Only the stars appeared, lit by the universe's blind lamplighter as he roamed the heavens.

Bronya couldn't remember how old she was when Papa began to tell them about the lamplighter's task, each star a rekindled soul. There hadn't been a time without Papa's stories, without his constellations. Now she remembered something else: Papa said that an early glimpse of the lamplighter, just after sunset when the sky hovered between dog and wolf, was lucky, a time to make a wish. Wishes, he'd told them, only worked if they were uttered out loud. They had to be thoughtful. Avsey always wished to be somewhere else, on the Amazon or at the North Pole. Papa told him, *Careful. You may not really want what you want.*

Bronya said out loud, "I wish for the war to be over, to be in

Tbilisi with Sara and Avsey and Papa." She reflected, then added, "And Mama to be better."

A voice in the dark said, "This war isn't over. That's for sure."

Bronya almost fell off the metal step. She hadn't noticed the boy on the other side of the gangway, the one who had made the train sparkle with his piece of metal. "Forgive me. I didn't know anyone else was here. Weren't you out there?" Bronya gestured toward the snowy banks on one side.

"Yes, but now I'm here, same as you."

Bronya looked at him. "You escape the bombs, too?"

"I escaped something worse. I ran away from vocational school." He moved to stand beside her and looked up between the cars into the star-filled space. "Do you remember how innocent the sky was? Before the war?" He turned his head to consider her. "I'm Piotr."

Bronya nodded. "Bronya. Why'd you run away?"

"It was awful, that's why. And a letter from my mother. The Germans got there first though. I had to cross the front lines to get home."

Piotr's eyes shone in the dark. They were almond-shaped. His eyebrows were dark, perfectly shaped against his pale forehead, and his nose was beautifully straight. His smile revealed crooked teeth with large gaps between them at the bottom. He was extraordinarily thin. He reminded Bronya of a circus acrobat she'd seen years ago with Papa. The acrobat stood on the shoulders of an enormous brown bear and back-flipped, landing on the straw floor, his hands in the air. *Bold.* Piotr had the same swagger about him. "Was your mother all right?"

"The Germans didn't hurt her, if that's what you mean."

"Where are you going now?

"Need work. I'll try Saratov. On my own."

They looked at the sky without speaking until all the color washed away and they couldn't see each other's faces. "I can share my seat, inside, if you want to be out of the cold."

Most of the women were asleep by the time Bronya and Piotr

opened the gangway door. Already exhausted by the bombing and the long walk to the watershed, the train's soporific movement was impossible to resist. One of them, a fat woman who claimed she would be the cook in the aviation factory canteen, snored loudly at the head of the car.

Bronya looked at Piotr. They both smiled. Bronya asked, "How old are you?"

Piotr pulled the hat from his head and sat on the edge of Bronya's seat, his feet spread wide on either side of two leather suitcases in the aisle. "Fifteen, you?"

"Fourteen. Almost fifteen."

Bronya paused and whispered, "Were you afraid to cross the front lines?"

Piotr looked around at the sleeping passengers before he responded in a low voice, "I speak a little German, but it was dark. No one stopped me."

"Where'd you learn German? School?"

"My father is German. He was taken, right at the beginning, enemy of the people and all that." Piotr looked at his feet. "That's when they sent me to that wretched school."

"Where'd they take him?" Bronya let the question escape and immediately regretted it. She knew things were not always as they seemed. She remembered Uncle Lyosha's arrest. He'd been called an enemy of the people, but Bronya knew that Lyosha had never been anyone's enemy.

"No idea. Gone, that's all." Piotr looked down at his clean valenki and took a deep breath, "On the way, I saw a cottage split open, right down the middle, by a shell. A dead peasant inside." Piotr made a cutting motion in the air.

"You were lucky."

Piotr shook his head. "The table was clean. The tea was hot. Boiled potatoes, sausage."

"I wouldn't have gone in."

Piotr chewed on his fingernails, lost in thought. He lifted his head and said, "I couldn't look; his face was gone. But I was hungry."

Bronya's eyes widened. "You *ate*?"

"I couldn't help it. I swear." He ran his finger over the embroidery on the valenki and looked at Bronya. "I pulled these off his feet."

Bronya had already noticed the detailed embroidery. "Didn't it feel bad?"

Piotr pushed the hair from his face. "When I opened our front door, she was lying on the stove. Her skin was transparent, like onion skin. Her hands were cold." Piotr looked out the window. "The war has made us all into thieves because it's robbed us of everything. Anyway, that's how you survive, you take what you can."

Bronya shivered a little.

Piotr turned. "What happened to your mother?"

Bronya stammered, trying to think of the right thing to say, "She's in hospital."

"Hospital." Piotr let out a low whistle. "Never knew anyone who went to hospital."

Bronya stiffened. "She's sick. It was my fault."

"You made your mother sick?"

"No, my fault she can't come home."

"Won't she get better?"

Bronya shifted in her seat. "I don't know."

Piotr sat looking ahead into the darkness. "Sounds like you have nothing left to lose, like me."

Bronya closed her eyes. She remembered Sonya's dirty fingernails. She thought about Avsey. She had plenty to lose.

"Wasn't my father's fault he was German. He was born that way. It's done now."

She watched Piotr stretch out on the floor between the suitcases, his feet near the door. He turned his face away, but Bronya heard him say, "All I've got is me."

The conversation dwindled, and eventually, she fell into a

strange sleep, her cheek against the cold window. She dreamed she was jumping over fires, flames shooting from the steppe, burning her calves, her dress.

When she opened her eyes, she didn't know how long she'd slept or where she was. Remembering the train, Bronya realized it had slowed its forward motion and was rocking disconcertingly in the darkness. They had stopped on a timber-and-iron frame—a trestle bridge. Water lapped against the bridge's pylons.

The night was quiet. From the window, small lights winked on a distant shoreline over a pitch-black expanse of river. Thinking they must be over the Volga, Bronya turned to look for Piotr on the floor, to point out the lights.

He was gone.

CHAPTER 13
THE DON RIVER BASIN, JANUARY 1942

IN THE BLUE COLD OF JANUARY, PAPA FOUND AVSEY AT THE Tikhoretsk train station huddled against a wall. Avsey saw Papa first and raised up on one elbow to follow Papa's head floating above the crowd. He couldn't believe his eyes. The scabs on his arms and around his mouth were painful, and in the mornings, his eyes were often crusted shut with puss. It was only when Papa circled back around that Avsey knew he was not hallucinating.

When Papa was standing close, almost on top of him, Avsey summoned all his strength and called out.

Papa looked down and dropped to his knees like a stone. He gathered Avsey's frail body to his chest. His shoulders shook uncontrollably. "It's a miracle. You're alive."

After a long moment in which Avsey worried he wouldn't be able to breath, Papa pushed him away to take a better look. He inspected Avsey's arms and legs as if every inch of his body had to be accounted for, a final tally of miracles. Avsey didn't have the heart to pull away. They had been severed from one another, and Papa was gluing them back together.

"I knew you'd come."

Papa wrapped his hands around Avsey's face, utterly speechless.

"It's me, Papa, I swear." Avsey buried his head against Papa's chest, pressed into him while Papa kissed Avsey's ears and the top of his head. Then, all at once, Avsey began to cry. He hid his face in Papa's wool coat, "Don't leave me again, please."

"I'll never leave you again. I promise." Papa lifted him up, cradling him in his strong arms. He slung Avsey's knapsack over his shoulder and carried him out of the train station. Papa carried him easily, and Avsey felt like he had as a small child on the way home in the night, safe and warm.

Avsey woke up and had no idea where he was. Shadowy forms surrounded the cot where he lay, and while the coal fire spread warmth in a small circle, everything else was wrapped in frozen mist. For a second, he imagined he'd been stolen by gypsies or black crows or worse—giant spiders. Only then did he register the damp cement walls and the pipes in the ceiling.

Papa sat down next to him.

Avsey rubbed his eyes. Maybe he was still half asleep and this was a dream. He had a vague memory of being carried through empty streets, the back of a truck. "Where are we, Papa?"

"Right bank. Donets River. Supply depot."

Avsey sat up. The red glow from the coal stove lit their faces.

Papa poured a cup of tea from a tin samovar and handed it to Avsey. The glass was warm. Papa looked at him. "You slept a long time."

Avsey watched the light flicker around Papa's face. The lines on his forehead and around his mouth were deeper, his lips were dry and chapped. He was thinner than Avsey remembered him. "Is this where we're going to live?"

Papa laughed. "No. We're moving supplies and rolling stock while we can. We'll live on the railroad, like vagabonds."

"While we can?"

"The Germans are pinned down north of here. We're pushing

them back. Slowly, slowly. We have time. Winter weighs every-thing down. I'll leave for a night, a few days, once in a while. Otherwise, we'll stay together."

Avsey gripped the glass tighter. He felt his breath, thin in his chest. "Why do you have to leave?"

"Don't worry. I'll come back." Papa reached out and brushed the hair away from Avsey's forehead like Mama used to do. "I work on the Committee for Freight Disposal, moving supplies to the front lines and rolling stock to the interior, so we can trans-port troops. Back and forth. And we're trying to supply the partisans when we can." Papa winked at Avsey. "You ready to enlist, Comrade Abramov?"

Avsey felt his face flush with pleasure, "Will I be a railway soldier then?"

"Yes, comrade. My right-hand man."

Papa ladled something from an old pot on the stove into a chipped porcelain cup. He took the glass from Avsey's hand and replaced it with a cup of warm shchi and a tin spoon. The odor of cabbage, savory and sweet at the same time, made Avsey homesick. He couldn't remember the last time he'd had hot food. He swallowed his first bite. Nothing, ever, had tasted this delicious.

Papa sat down on the cot, his own cup of shchi in his hand. Avsey closed his eyes. Hunger had dulled his senses, and the odor—the sensation of hot food in his stomach—revived his desire to eat. Papa ate silently, glancing at Avsey from time to time. When Avsey had finished, Papa refilled his cup. Avsey felt warm through and through, a sensation he hadn't felt since his last night at home. "What'll I do? I mean, as a soldier." Avsey wiped his mouth with his sleeve and looked up at Papa.

"Let's start with moving crates and running errands. I'll give you more to do when I see how things develop. We need to keep rolling stock out of German hands, keep our supply lines open. Lots of moving parts, going from one place to another."

"What about the partisans?"

"They need material to blow up ammunition warehouses, engine sheds, keep the Germans guessing. We're getting ready for whatever happens next, when the snow melts."

Avsey's face lit up. "Will I get to blow things up?"

"No, Avsey." Papa's tone quieted. "Yours is the most difficult job—small tasks, anything we need done. Ready for everything."

Avsey was quiet for a long time. "I'd rather blow things up. Like Aunt Sara."

Papa smiled. "I know but for now we are pushing the Germans toward Kharkov. We'll push them all the way out if we do this right. Are you ready for victory?" Papa's eyes shone in the dark.

Avsey smiled. "Yes, Papa, I'm ready. For victory."

"How about you take the oath of allegiance."

"The oath of allegiance?"

"The Red Army oath. Every soldier swears allegiance to the motherland."

"I'll be official, a real soldier?"

Papa nodded. He looked Avsey in the eye and asked in a serious voice, "Do you solemnly promise to be an honest, brave, disciplined, and vigilant fighter, to protect military and state secrets, and to unquestioningly obey all military regulations and orders of your superiors?"

Avsey's tone was grave. "Yes, Papa, I promise."

Papa stood and shook Avsey's hand. "Congratulations comrade soldier."

Avsey smiled when Papa ruffled his hair. "What about Bronya? Mama and Sara?"

Papa's smile evaporated. He cleared his throat and adjusted his tone. "Mama's at home, in the apartment, with Sara."

Avsey thought Papa's voice sounded false.

"I showed them your letters."

"Mama's home? Is Bronya home, too?" Avsey held his breath before Papa answered. If they were all home, could he go home, too?

Papa's face tightened. "A letter came the second week of December. She'd written because she was evacuating to Saratov. She sent her love. She's far from any fighting now."

"Don't you miss her, Papa? Like I miss her?"

"After we win the war, we'll all be together again. Not long now."

AVSEY WAS THRILLED TO BE A SOLDIER. HE LOVED THE VIEW FROM the freight cars, their doors open to the elements, the sound of the wheels rolling him to sleep, sunrise and sunset, the unknown. Papa was always close, checking tracks, speaking with the men on the platforms, in small station houses, writing in his logbook in the early mornings. Sometimes, when Papa rested his head against a hard surface—a window, a desk, the rough inside of a freight car—his eyes closed and his shoulders relaxed. He'd sleep for ten minutes.

When Papa was tired, Avsey worked harder. He loaded and unloaded crates and perched in station houses to listen to old radios in back rooms, hunched against the cold. Papa poured over grimy maps and Avsey marked the battle lines with metal pins. He memorized the rail map, so he knew where the rolling stock had congregated and where it was needed. Every so often, Avsey noticed Papa watching him.

Once, Papa smiled and said, "You are quite the soldier for such a skinny boy."

Papa's friends brought Avsey gifts: lumps of sugar, slices of dark bread wrapped in paper, chocolate, and once, a small polished stone, light brown with gold veins running through it, like so many sunlit rivers. Avsey added the stone to his birch box but always ate the chocolate. Once at the Golubovka station, an old Civil War soldier with a white beard, gave Avsey a black-and-white kitten. Avsey tried to convince Papa, "I can feed her, Papa, I know I can."

"We can't find enough milk for you, Avsey. I won't let you

feed an animal with food you need." Needless to say, Papa hadn't let the kitten come with them to the next station. He'd asked the old soldier to take care of it until the spring, when the war would be over.

Papa's best friend in the field, Nazim, was a young rail engineer from Pyatigorsk. He was taller than Papa and spoke in a throaty voice, which he used to great effect in the evenings when he sang mournful ballads and recited poetry. He loved backgammon and danced the Lezginka, a courtship dance from the mountains. He tried to teach Avsey to dance in front of a warm coal fire one evening but was quickly disappointed. Avsey, embarrassed, moved listlessly.

Nazim tried to encourage him. "You need passion in your movement. This is about courtship."

Avsey, annoyed, said, "All that arm waving, the girls I know would run away."

Nazim laughed. "Mountain Jews perfect the Lezginka as a matter of survival. No dance, no bride."

Avsey shrugged. "I don't want a bride." He thought for a minute. "You don't have a bride, Nazim. Maybe you aren't doing the dance right."

Nazim laughed until he had to hold his sides and stop to catch his breath.

Later, Papa said, "Nazim's father was my father's best friend. I've known him since he was a little boy, younger than you are now."

For as long as he could remember, Avsey had been fascinated by his grandfather's picture pinned into an old silver frame on the sideboard. He knew that he'd been murdered and that Papa never talked about him or about what happened. Ever. Avsey had learned about it from Bronya, who must have heard the story from Babushka. He didn't ask if Nazim's father had also been a rabbi, if they'd played backgammon together, their long beards floating above the board, tea on the table next to them. He wanted to be polite. Maybe Nazim's father had been murdered, too.

Nazim accompanied Papa and Avsey on the longer journeys to assess rolling stock and supplies on the rail lines between Rostov and Balaklaya. They checked the water and coal at the engine sheds and spent their days in the yards moving freight cars from one track to another, talking about load and capacity. For Avsey, it was one big chess game, only the stakes were higher. And it was always cold.

Nazim teased Avsey about the way his teeth chattered. "You'll give us away, starik. The devil may be blind, but he can hear." Avsey laughed at Nazim's jokes, but they didn't help the burning in his feet and hands. Then one day, Nazim appeared, hands behind his back, smiling broadly. "You are frozen purple. Hard to be a smart soldier without one of these." He handed Avsey a sheepskin hat.

Avsey couldn't believe his luck. A sheepskin. He liked that Nazim called him starik, old man. He was doing soldier's work and felt older. Everyone else, including Papa, thought of him as a little boy. He thanked Nazim and put the hat on his head. He never wanted to take it off. In fact, Papa had to pry the hat off when he wanted Avsey to wash, bribing him with biscuits from the ration box.

Despite the sheepskin, the cold was ever present. The pain settled into Avsey's hands and feet and made him cry, though he didn't let anyone see. His gloves and valenki helped, but the cold penetrated deep into his joints and bones, his soul. He thought of the soldiers on the front lines who were continuously frozen. Did they hide their tears, too?

The biggest challenge to Avsey's morale was not the cold though; it was the whistle of mortars and bombs on the front line at the Donets River, especially near Andreyevka, from where Avsey could see lights across the water. Though he couldn't see what was happening on the other side, he did see red blurs throw lines into the night like bloody, ruptured veins, just above the earth. He heard the explosions on his side of the river, at some distance, and heard the rumble of response from the Red Army.

Avsey knew this was the sound of men dying, the constant roar of death, blackened snow, and broken bodies. He saw the aftermath more than once, though Papa tried to shield him, his large hands over Avsey's eyes. Avsey finally stopped this charade when he told Papa, "If I'm old enough to be a soldier, I'm old enough to see what happens to soldiers."

Papa, grim-faced, nodded.

Avsey saw the frozen corpses of Red Army comrades: pieces of yellowed flesh in the snow, bits of cloth in the breeze, scattered like chicken feed. On one occasion, as dusk narrowed the landscape into shadow, he saw a fox dragging something heavy into the tree line by the river.

When the fox stopped to stare at him with yellow eyes, Avsey realized with growing horror the animal clutched a human arm between its teeth, the attached hand clearly recognizable in its last gesture, index finger pointing up. Despite the vomit rising in his throat, he watched the hand trail alongside the animal, leaving its trace next to the soft paw prints in the snow. The image haunted him for a long time.

Still, he decided, soldiering was the best job in the world.

CHAPTER 14
SARATOV, DECEMBER–MARCH 1941

THE FIRST NIGHT BRONYA APPEARED IN THE CANTEEN OF AVIATION factory number 292, one of the seamstresses, Galina Filippovna, sat down across from her and watched her eat. "Some motherly advice—slow down. You'll make yourself sick."

Another seamstress, Dorofeia Semyonovna, slid in next to Galina Filippovna and looked Bronya up and down. "She's too thin. And she needs a new dress."

Bronya sat up, mustered every ounce of restraint she had, and stopped shoveling food into her mouth. She did not want to be sick.

Later the same night, Bronya found herself standing barefoot on a stool in the sewing room wearing only her underwear. Galina Filippovna draped the fabric over Bronya's shoulders, around her waist. "Hold still. You'll ruin my reputation as a dressmaker. It's bad enough I'm making parachutes."

Bronya held her breath and watched Galina Filippovna push straight pins into the fabric at her waist. "I didn't mean you should hold your breath, silly girl."

Feodora Kirillovna, who had not been in the canteen, circled around Bronya, casting appraising looks. "Look at her ribs.

Leave a little room to fatten her up, otherwise you'll be making a new dress next week."

Galina Filippovna laughed. "I don't want her to look like a marionette in a floppy dress. She's too pretty for that."

Bronya knew immediately that she'd had a stroke of good luck. After the terror of Kharkov and the bombing, she felt coddled. *Safe.* In a matter of hours, she'd been fully adopted by the three seamstresses who worked in the sewing room.

Galina Filippovna fussed over what Bronya ate and gave her special treats. Dorofeia Semyonovna loved the violin and was thrilled Bronya could play for them. "A real artist in our midst," she repeated every time Bronya lifted the violin from its case.

Feodora Kirillovna braided Bronya's hair and shared her sugar ration, believing, as she said, "in the health-giving properties of sugar and vodka." Bronya didn't like the vodka but eagerly accepted the sugar.

In no time, life in Saratov settled into a strange reprieve. She wanted to stay in the sewing room forever, mothered by these women she barely knew, making parachutes. Or at least until the war was over.

The seamstresses talked all day long. They shared their letters, stories of husbands and sons, of married daughters in the villages they'd all inhabited before the war. Bronya, in turn, cautiously began to share her own stories, concentrating mostly on Papa and Avsey. When Bronya told them Sara had evacuated with the aviation factory from Taganrog to Tbilisi, the women's faces were shiny with admiration. She omitted Mama's voices, and when they asked if Sara's husband was serving, she did not tell them that Uncle Lyosha had been arrested and never seen again. She lied.

Dorofeia Semyonovna said she'd been to Tbilisi "with Alexei, when he was small." Alexei was Dorofeia Semyonovna's youngest child, and Bronya could tell from the way she brightened when she said his name that he was her favorite. "Walnuts the size of my fist and wool as thick and soft as butter. Long sticks of dried apricot, sweet as candy. Paradise, I'm telling you, a real paradise."

"Your Avsey will be fat the next time you see him," said Feodora Kirillovna.

The sewing room was beautiful, filled with piles of clean, white nylon. Bronya liked cutting the trapezoid shapes for the parachutes. She liked the straight lines and the measuring sticks, the high-pitched whir of the sewing machines and the two gleaming metal tables against the walls. When the parachutes had been sewn together, she inspected the seams for strength, to make sure there were no small tears in the fabric or loose threads at the edges. "Because," said Galina Filippovna, "your young eyes are sharper than mine."

The seamstresses told Bronya stories about the Locust Warriors and the secret parachute operations underway even as they spoke. "These men's lives, all our lives, depend on clouds of white nylon, sturdy sewing machines, and your sharp eyes. Imagine that," said Feodora Kirillovna.

Dorofeia Semyonovna looked at her fingers and wriggled them in the air, "And my old fingers."

"Why are they called Locust Warriors?" Bronya hung on every word.

Dorofeia Semyonovna whispered, "They land behind enemy lines to sow havoc. Like locusts. They're unstoppable."

Bronya thought about the Locust Warriors behind enemy lines. Had any of them been killed or captured? She didn't ask, not wanting to spoil the mood.

The sewing room was best in the evenings, after supper. The samovar was nestled in the corner between the cutting machines. Bronya played her violin for the seamstresses and they, in turn, praised her playing.

The evenings ended with card games. Feodora Kirillovna was astonished at how quick and ruthless Bronya was at Durak.

"My brother is the genius in the family," Bronya told them. "He's the smartest person I know. Sometimes I had to cheat a little to win." She cleared her throat and looked away. "I should have let him win."

Feodora Kirillovna said, "Oh, nonsense. You made him a better player." Feodora Kirillovna always won at Durak.

"Play one more piece, please." Dorofeia Semyonovna closed her eyes and Bronya picked up her violin.

AT THE END OF BRONYA'S FIRST WEEK AT THE AVIATION FACTORY, Dorofeia Semyonovna paused from her work at the sewing machine. "I have good news!" She pulled Alexei's latest letter from her apron pocket, holding it high in the air. "He is south of Moscow."

No one was ever sure where their soldier sons and husbands were located; the censors were ruthless and everyone was careful not to say too much. Soldiers had to be vague, for obvious reasons, but somehow Alexei's letter had slipped through with specifics.

His mother was elated. "We are pushing them back," she said in a hushed tone, "He's in the thick of it now." She waved the letter above her head like a flag. "He's sure the war will end in the spring."

Galina Filippovna and Feodora Kirillovna lowered their heads and glanced at each other. After a short silence, Galina Filippovna said, "We'll need to make you another dress, Bronislava. I have just the fabric for it, to match your eyes." She smiled. "Won't your mother be pleased?"

Bronya coughed. She'd woken up with a throbbing headache and hadn't felt well since. "Yes, thank you, Galina Filippovna. She'll be pleased you were so kind to me." Bronya disliked lying more than she disliked losing at cards. She wondered about the look that had passed between Galina Filippovna and Feodora Kirillovna. Were they worried about Dorofeia Semyonovna? Wasn't the war going well?

In the evening, after tea, the seamstresses settled into a round of cards, but Bronya couldn't keep her eyes open. She politely refused Feodora Kirillovna's offer of sugar and took herself off to bed early.

The dormitory was empty. Bronya was glad for the silence. Her head pounded, and anyway, it was too cold to talk. Her breath hung ghostly in the cavernous room. The local women who worked in the factory were sure God had sent the cold to stop the Germans. Bronya changed into her nightdress under her blanket and reached down to search for her ribbon at the bottom of her knapsack, the one Feodora Kirillovna had given her to tie her hair back.

The ribbon was nowhere to be found, but her fingers closed around the pocketknife from the kitchen linoleum she'd found on the first day of the war. A sudden, terrible longing for home reached down into her gut and pulled her entrails into her windpipe, blocking her breath. Closing the pocketknife inside her fist, she slid deep under the blanket in the dark. She thought of Alexei, Dorofeia Semyonovna's favorite son, how lucky they were to have his letters, to know how the war was going. Bronya thought it might be nice to be Dorofeia Semyonovna's favorite child but quickly changed her mind. She didn't want to be anyone else's child. When the war was over, she would show Mama her new dresses. Mama had always liked pretty dresses.

Bronya woke in the middle of the night, her headache worse, clutching the pocketknife in her sweaty hand. The whir of the aviation factory's machinery was deafening. The factory buildings were always brightly lit in the dark, but tonight the machines throbbed and pulsed through the dormitory walls louder than she'd noticed before. She had, once or twice, worked eighteen-hour shifts in the sewing room and then dragged herself to bed in the deepest part of night, reassured by the factory's continuous hum. But now her head pulsed along with the unbearable rhythm of the heavy machinery. She kicked the blanket from her legs and pushed the wet hair from her face and neck. Her whole body was hot, her nightdress soaked, heavy against her skin.

She pushed up with some effort, dizzy, telling herself she'd eaten something at supper, something in the soup. She'd go to the infirmary and ask for medicine. The blanket around her shoulders, Bronya tiptoed past the rows of beds. Several of the women turned in their sleep, their breathing heavy, but no one woke.

Bronya walked over the patches of ice and snow between the buildings in her bare feet, slipping several times, throwing her arms out to balance her body, shivering. Her muscles ached as if she'd been bent in half over the cutting table for days. She stopped to press her fist into the small of her back and pull the blanket tighter around her shoulders.

Inside, the factory lights pulsed brightly. Why had she never noticed the brightness, the throb of the factory at night? She passed the machine room, the canteen, then turned left at the end of a long narrow hallway. The light under the infirmary door appeared as a mirage.

The young nurse looked surprised to see Bronya but said nothing and went back to her book, waiting for Bronya to write her name on the infirmary list. Bronya picked up the pencil, but her fingers refused to hold it. She pulled frantically at her frozen nightgown to keep it from touching her skin. She pressed her head between her hands to stop the pulsing. She begged the young nurse, "Make it stop, please," and sank to the ground with a thud.

TIME STRETCHED UNTIL IT STOOD STILL. THE DIFFERENCE BETWEEN day and night was elusive, filled with feverish dreams, whispered conversations, and ghosts with dark holes for faces.

When Bronya opened her eyes, she didn't remember the infirmary, the young nurse, the lights. She had no idea where she was. She searched for the piles of white nylon and the samovar.

Her body ached, as if there were bruises deep inside her bones. The ceiling lamp above her head, askew, struck her as odd. She'd never seen it on any of her visits to the infirmary.

She lifted her head and shoulders and realized with no small degree of horror that she was in a room with long rows of white beds and shiny floors. No one spoke in full voice. All sound, in fact, was muffled. Whispers, the rustle of fabric, and the quiet din of metal against metal.

A door opened on the other side of the room, and a figure dressed in a long white gown and wearing a white mask and gloves walked to her bedside. The voice under the mask reassured her. "There, there, lie down."

Bronya asked, "Is this a hospital?"

"You're in the sick ward, in isolation. Try to stay still." The masked figure took Bronya's pulse and gently pushed her back onto the pillow. The door opened again and two porters, a stretcher between them, walked to the far corner of the room. They tipped the stretcher to roll a seminude woman onto one of the beds. More white-robed figures entered and pulled a nightdress over the inert body. The woman's head had been shaved.

Bronya reached for her own head. At first, her fingers felt only cloth. Queasy, she tugged at the fabric and searched for her curls. Only stubble and skin remained.

"Stay still, Abramova. You need rest."

"What's happened to my hair? I don't belong here. I've done nothing wrong."

"Calm down. No typhus patient leaves the infirmary without my permission. Lice. Couldn't be helped. You don't remember? You pitched a fit."

Bronya lay back, despondent. She'd never been so tired. "Typhus?"

"Lice like crowded trains. Other than the factory women, did you see anyone on the train?"

Bronya remembered Piotr with a sharp intake of breath. "Yes."

The mask looked up. "Who?"

Bronya nodded. "The boy, next to me. I don't know where he came from, and he was gone when I woke up."

"Gone? You didn't see where he got off?"

"No, I was asleep."

"Did he leave anything? A suitcase, anything?"

Bronya thought about the valenki Piotr had taken from the dead peasant. She thought about his dead mother. "No." She closed her eyes.

The doctor's tone softened. "You'll need a few weeks. You're young. Some of the women in your dormitory haven't been so lucky."

"What do you mean?" Bronya felt her head pulse harder.

"We've burned all the linen and the clothing, but typhus does what typhus does."

Bronya tried to sit up. Who was here with her? She remembered Babushka's tales of typhus, how the disease had almost stopped the Bolsheviks during the Civil War. More than anything, she wanted to ask if the women in the sewing room were ill but couldn't summon the courage. She'd invited Piotr to sit next to her on the train. Had the typhus come from him? It was all her fault.

The doctor lifted the blanket and examined Bronya's torso, arms, and legs. Bronya saw the tops of her own hands were covered in a red rash. She wasn't able to lift her leg, but she knew that it, too, was covered in red blotches. She tried again to sit up.

The doctor's soft tone disappeared. "Enough, Abramova. It isn't worth the effort."

AFTER A MONTH IN THE INFIRMARY, BRONYA RETURNED TO THE dormitory. Outside, the temperature had plummeted and the women wore overcoats over their nightdresses. Half the beds were empty, and yet, the women who remained were happy to see her. They couldn't imagine she'd played a part in the tragedy.

Feodora Kirillovna reassured her, "Your hair will come back, it's already started to grow."

Galina Filippovna wrapped another blanket around Bronya and lamented her weight loss. "You're like a stalk of wheat. I'll have to take your dresses in or feed you more."

Bronya didn't care about her hair, or how thin she had become. She looked around the room. "Has Dorofeia Semyonovna had more letters from Alexei? She must be in the sewing room." The women looked at their shoes.

Galina Filippovna put her arms around Bronya. "Alexei's gone, too. The notice came two days after she left us. She never knew."

Bronya was inconsolable. She howled in the night like a wounded animal. The women held her, caressed her head when she cried. They brought her apricot gazirovka, full of bubbles, ticklish in her mouth. They fed her spoons of jam and honey. They held her up as she walked to regain her strength. She tried to tell them she didn't deserve their attention, and didn't deserve to be loved ever again. She brought bad luck. They held her head against the tide anyway, all their mothering poured into the only child at hand.

By the end of March, the doctor decided Bronya wasn't gaining enough weight. She signed the necessary papers to send her to Zheleznovodsk, a sanitorium in the Caucasus. "The earth is full of iron there, Abramova. You'll eat and regain your strength and leave all this behind." The doctor touched her arm, smiled kindly, and whispered, "Typhus is a harsh master. It doesn't take sides or make friends. Try not to take it so hard. The last years of childhood are important. You'll finish the war out safely."

Bronya wondered how the doctor knew she'd blamed herself. She was guilty nonetheless, and the regret, incised in her gut, did not ease. She kissed Galina Fillpovna and Feodora Kirillovna goodbye at the train station and thanked them for loving her. They promised they would read her letters aloud in the sewing room and tucked a needle and some thread alongside a deck of cards in her knapsack.

She boarded the train and remembered it was her birthday. Fifteen felt old. She had the feeling she'd kept her eyes open too long and wasn't able to distill the images that paved the insides of her mind.

As a final goodbye, Bronya played her violin as the train pulled from the station while the seamstresses waved and blew kisses. She would play her violin in the mountains. Maybe music would help her understand.

CHAPTER 15
THE DON RIVER BASIN, FEBRUARY–
APRIL 1942

ON THOSE SINGULAR NIGHTS WHEN THE STARS WERE OBSCURED BY clouds, Avsey belly-crawled on the ground with Papa and his friends to load crates into small sleds on the frozen river west of Krasny Lyman, then huddled alone in tunnels or underpasses and waited. Papa wouldn't let him cross the river.

Avsey never knew where Papa went exactly, but he knew there were certain things no one spoke of—names, destinations, the horrors behind the front lines. Silence was part of the partisans' code. Following the code meant Avsey never told Papa the tunnels were full of rats. He did wonder how he was supposed to remain disciplined when rats scurried across his legs, or alongside his torso, so near to the exposed skin on his face that he could almost feel their whiskers and tiny clawed feet, their small eyes shiny in the dark.

On the nights the rats propelled him out of the tunnels and down into the gullies and roads, Avsey buried his hands inside his armpits and pulled the sheepskin hat over his ears. He stomped his feet to keep the circulation going and regretted his promises to Papa. He cursed the code of silence.

One night, Nazim stayed behind in an overpass with Avsey and experienced the vermin firsthand. He shook his head and whistled through a narrow gap in his front teeth, the whites of his eyes bright in the dark. "This is what I call bravery. I had no idea the real threat was on this side of the river." He did not laugh.

The next time Nazim stayed behind, he brought his home-made slingshot and a pocket full of stones. "Just aim at the red in their eyes."

Avsey wasn't sure if he actually hit any rats, though he could hear the scurry of tiny feet as the stones landed near their positions. He thought he heard yelps, and even if these resided solely in his imagination, they were satisfying. Nazim and Avsey took turns with the slingshot, called each other Rat Slayers of the Dark Night, and invented astronomical tallies of dead rats—an effort to earn the bragging rights associated with such prowess.

"How many do you think we killed tonight, Comrade Abramov? Ten thousand?"

"Oh, easily ten thousand, if not more. We have them on the run."

"You've earned the slingshot, Abramov. Congratulations. The order of the wooden artillery slinger, the highest honor for a Rat Slayer."

Avsey found new energy in the rat wars and eventually felt he'd conquered the menace of the tunnels and could endure anything if Nazim was around. He kept the slingshot in his pocket, periodically patting it for reassurance. He thought of the Young Voroshilov sharpshooter badge he'd win someday when he was old enough.

Avsey and Nazim began to spend more time together after Papa decided to leave Nazim on shore when he crossed the river, to sound the alarm if the party didn't return by morning. Avsey was relieved. He liked Nazim's uncanny ability to light up the darkest places, effortlessly, as if the sun rose in his presence. Better still, Nazim explained things. He told Avsey the Germans were on the run; they were sick. They'd wanted Moscow, but the Red Army had pushed the Nazi criminals back.

In the warehouses and station rooms, Avsey never left Nazim's side. He drank Nazim's elixir of life—pine needle tea—and learned to play backgammon on a small leather board. Nazim taught him to make an anthracite coal fire with kindling, showed him to how choose the smallest, shiniest pieces of coal. "Anthracite is dense," he said, holding out a small piece. "Lighting a fire is an art. Even coal needs a butterfly touch, starik."

Avsey liked the sheen of the coal and the warmth it provided. "Am I a butterfly, Nazim? Have I done it right?"

"You're getting better. Remember, precision plus delicacy equals strength. Brute force only offers short-term gain."

Avsey wasn't sure he understood but nodded anyway. He thought maybe brute force referred to the Germans.

One evening, in one of their warehouse camps, Nazim sat next to Avsey, explaining strategy and weaponry in front of the coal fire. He drew maps, adding arrows to illustrate the direction Soviet troops would need to push to consolidate their gains. Papa's forehead folded into an accordion of worry. His eyes on Avsey, he said, "Little boys should not know this much about war, Nazim."

Nazim countered, "I did try to teach him how to dance, Lev. You saw how that went." He winked at Avsey. "He needs to know what's going on. He's here."

Papa shook his head. "No, he needs to go to sleep without all this nonsense in his head."

Later, when Avsey was supposed to be asleep, he heard Papa tell Nazim, "We've taken his childhood. I have a bad feeling about it."

"What else can we do, Lev? You made him a soldier."

What was wrong with Papa? Why had he changed his mind? Nazim had passed Avsey's Salsk rule about trust. He'd come through three times, at least. And besides, only Nazim treated Avsey like a real fighter.

By early March, the ice had begun to melt and steppe scrub

poked through patches of dirty snow. Avsey had spent so much time with Nazim that he'd adopted Nazim's mannerisms, his swagger, the way he spread his fingers out in front of him when he asked a question. Avsey mimicked Nazim's way of talking, referring to the Germans as *Nazi criminals* and *scurrilous jackals* instead of Hitlerites. Nazim refused to utter the German leader's name, and Avsey did likewise, which made Papa smile.

The snow melted and the mud insinuated itself into every corner of their lives. Even the morning tea tasted of mud and mold. The Freight Distribution Committee settled at the train station in Krasny Lyman. Avsey thought of Krasny Lyman as the center of the earth, the molten middle from which it belched coal, sending it north on coal cars, toward Moscow. The place tasted of metal and smelled of unwashed soldiers, and, as the snow continued to melt, rotten potatoes. The train station was alive night and day, a bright beacon of activity—repair shops, soup kitchens, and a warren of small rooms where men played endless card games, their faces shrouded in great clouds of cigarette smoke.

The trees budded, delicate, barely-there shoots, slowly stretching into the sunlight, hinting at change. The river flowed again, at first moving large chunks of ice downstream and then gradually, swelling with the spring rains, washing the basin area clean. The swollen river spilled into lagoons where Avsey saw cranes, skylarks, and an occasional eagle.

At dawn, the mist rose from the water and Avsey felt his heart swell at the sight of it. Papa now crossed the Donets in a dugout canoe, hidden by the fog. The cloud cover protected them from the Luftwaffe, and for a brief period, nature reigned majestic and made them forget.

But by late April and the encroaching warmth of late spring, the war din crashed up against their positions, louder and more strident than before. Papa left to bring rolling stock from the Barvenkovo salient and to check the bridges across the river. "Nazim is your commander, Avsey. I know you'll follow his orders." Papa held Avsey tight in his arms and whispered so no one else could hear, "Maybe soor you can be a normal boy, go to school."

Avsey squeezed Papa's neck in return but didn't know what he meant. He would never be a normal boy again.

For a short while, Avsey did not miss Papa. During daylight hours, Nazim filled Papa's place easily. The nights, however, were a completely different matter, and gradually, when Papa had been away for longer than expected and days turned to more than a week, Avsey took to lying awake at night on his cot, listening for the sound of footsteps. His heart felt leaden and bruised in his chest. He slowly stopped sleeping because he wanted to be awake when Papa came through the door. He felt the tight vice of dread gripping him tighter each day, squeezing the blood from his body. He told himself not to worry.

When April turned to May, even Nazim became grim. Heat descended on the steppe, and with it came flies, great black clouds of tiny flies with bluish wings and green eyes.

Late one afternoon in the station house, Nazim sat down next to Avsey to give him news, "Listen, starik, your Papa has more work to do with the brigade. You'll have to wait for him a little longer."

Avsey swatted flies and watched Nazim. Something was wrong. He let the flies settle around his eyes and nose while he waited for Nazim to tell him more. He knew by now that fear could swallow him whole in one neat gulp, and he wasn't sure if he wanted reassurance, truth, or both. "How long? Is he all right?"

Nazim's eyes met Avsey's. "I'm sure he's fine. The waiting is the hardest part of all this."

Later in the evening, when sorrow had fed his fear and inflated the worst of his imagination, when thoughts of Papa, lost or sick, had reached a fevered crescendo, Avsey sat in front of the unlit stove and pulled his birch box from the bottom of his knapsack. He wanted to rub the initials on the silver case and hold the stone in his palm. Maybe holding Papa's possessions would bring him sooner. Maybe he could keep Papa safe if he was sorry for stealing his possessions.

Nazim sat dozing on a wobbly chair close by, his feet on a pile of bricks, his large hands folded over his chest. Avsey thought about keeping the box hidden from Nazim but decided it might be better to show his treasures to one person. If he was truly sorry, he would need to confess. And he trusted Nazim.

Nazim opened his eyes. "Beautiful box. Where'd it come from? Is it birch?"

"Papa made it for me. When I was a kid. I keep my things in it, my treasures."

Nazim lowered his feet to the cement and bent closer to Avsey. "First of all, you're still a kid. An old soul, but still a kid." Nazim smiled and ruffled Avsey's hair. "I'll give you a haircut before your father comes back. Treasures?"

Avsey took a long breath, then exhaled slowly until all the air had emptied from his lungs and they felt flat inside his chest. He looked Nazim in the eye. "Things I stole. Things I stole from *Papa*. And from Mama, things I took from the boys at school."

Nazim arched one eyebrow high on his forehead. His smile melted as he let out a long, low whistle. Avsey held out the silver cigarette case. Nazim took it in both hands. He examined the engraved initials, the intricate letters, and the decorative scrolls around the edges of the case. Avsey expected a scolding, but Nazim whistled again. Emboldened, Avsey reached into his knapsack and scooped the blue stone into a tight fist. He took his time, withdrawing his hand slowly, hesitating. Should he show Nazim the stone?

With a burst of courage, Avsey thrust his hand toward Nazim and opened his palm. The stone felt heavier than he remembered. His bravado quickly evaporated. Was he proud of stealing from Papa? He waited, head bowed.

Nazim was incredulous. "You stole this from your Papa?"

The look of confusion on Nazim's face bolstered Avsey's

regret. He shouldn't have shared the stone. He snapped his palm shut. "It was lying there, in his drawer."

Nazim shook his head in disbelief. "Show it to me again."

"Why? What is it?" Avsey opened his hand.

"It's a sapphire, malchik, a big sapphire."

"Like in the tsar's crown?"

Nazim let out a curt laugh. "Yes, like in the tsar's crown. Any idea where your Papa got it?"

Avsey shook his head.

"What else have you got in there?" Nazim looked down into the birch box.

Avsey pulled the box close to his chest. "Some of Mama's jewelry. I did have a pocketknife, but I lost it and traded the stamps in Salsk for chocolates.

Nazim reached over and pulled the package of Belomorkanal cigarettes from the box. "Where did you steal these?"

"I found those on the train. I didn't technically steal them."

"You don't strike me as a thief. So why?" Nazim's voice was serious.

Avsey shrugged, his eyes filled with tears. He swallowed hard and allowed the words to pour out. "Well, the boys at school were mean to me. Mama left, and I wanted to keep her gold because I missed her. Papa's things were right there, in the drawer in the armoire, so I took those, too. I also took things from the kiosk in the park and, well, I don't know. It's something I do. It makes me feel better."

Avsey swallowed and wiped his nose on his shirt sleeve.

Nazim placed his hands on Avsey's shoulders. "Look at me." He brought his face close. "You feel better when you steal?"

Avsey let his head hang. "I'm sorry. I shouldn't have taken the Red Army oath. I'm a thief."

"You aren't a thief. I know you aren't, deep down, dishonest. Some boys steal from their friends, maybe all boys, But from your parents? Whole different order of magnitude."

Avsey looked up. "If I give you everything in the box, will that make it all better?"

"No, of course not. You'll have to return these things to their owners." Nazim paused. "Except for the stamps, which you've already traded, and the pocketknife you lost."

Avsey nodded toward the tobacco in Nazim's hand. "You can have it if you want. I swear I didn't steal those." He dug again at the bottom of the box and extracted the footcloth. "And this, you can have the footcloth." He held out his hand. "Nazim? Are you going to tell Papa?"

Nazim was silent, then earnest, when he said, "It's your responsibility to make things right. I won't have to tell your Papa, because you'll tell him when he comes back." He pointed to the stone. "Keep everything in the box until then. And don't tell anyone about your treasure. Understand? Until you tell your Papa."

May was glorious on the river. The trees filled out, vast greens and silvers draped luxuriously over the Donets, and in between the roar of guns came full-throated birdsong, insects, frogs and toads, men's laughter. The heat rose, the soldiers stripped down to their underwear. They cleaned their weapons. But Papa did not return.

On the morning of May 12th, Avsey's eleventh birthday, Nazim was agitated. He told Avsey in a somber voice that Marshal Timoshenko had ordered the army to attack the German lines on the outskirts of Kharkov. "It's beginning," he said, pacing up and down, around the crates and machinery, outside and around the building, once, twice, until he turned and disappeared.

By late afternoon, Nazim's mood had shifted. He was elated, bloated with good news. He found Avsey in front of the station, on the steps and hauled him inside. "We've truly caught them by surprise. Our radio silence has worked." He grabbed Avsey under the arms and swung him in the air. "Your Papa's been moving tanks into the salient. He's sent you birthday wishes by courier." Nazim opened his mouth, threw his head back, and laughed. He hugged Avsey.

Later, Nazim and the Krasny Lyman stationmaster, Vasil' Pavlovich, toasted Avsey's birthday with army samogon. They ate pickled vegetables and bread and shared a small cake from the women in the welding workshop. Vasil' Pavlovich was proud of his homemade alcohol. He lifted his glass. "To our brave little soldier." Nazim winked.

By the night of the 13th, Nazim's mood had changed again. He paced the train station, stalking the repair shops lit by welders and ironworkers while Avsey followed him, watching from the sidelines, worried Nazim knew something he couldn't share.

Late in the night, when much of the rumble of the station had quieted, Nazim came looking for Avsey, who had fallen asleep in a corner of the stationmaster's office, his cheek stuck to a newspaper on the desk. Nazim shook Avsey's shoulder, and when Avsey opened his eyes, handed him a cup of dark tea. "Drink, starik. We're out of time."

Avsey sat up and wiped the saliva from his cheek. He rubbed his eyes and yawned. "Is Papa here?"

Nazim shook his head. "No." He looked down at his hands. "I need you to do something, Avsey. You can say no, but I hope you won't."

Avsey was suddenly wide awake. "Do something?"

Nazim closed his eyes and whispered something to himself. When he opened his eyes, Avsey noticed they were dull—the sparkle had gone. "I want you to cross the river, then the front lines, and report on what the fascists are doing. We don't have much time."

Avsey wanted to scream *Yes, I'll do anything you want me to do.* Instead, he heard himself ask, "Why me?"

"Because the jackals are on the move, in a hurry. They won't pay attention to a red-headed kid."

Avsey looked at Nazim thoughtfully. "What would I be looking for?"

Nazim pushed his hands through his dark hair and wiped his mouth with his hand. He looked unkempt, the stubble on his face thick for the first time Avsey could remember. Nazim glanced around the station house before he whispered, "Timoshenko is hesitating. If the criminals hit us on our left flank before we've pushed more tanks in to secure our gains, we're in trouble."

"What do we do?" Avsey whispered, too.

"I want to know if the Germans are massing troops and equipment. I want you to go and see."

"How?"

Nazim looked at the map on the wall and traced his finger along the blue line that represented the twisted Donets. "We'll take you across the river on our side and then you'll cross the front lines. Here. I'll give you instructions on where to go and how to come back."

"Will it help Papa, Nazim?"

Nazim smiled sadly. "I honestly don't know."

"I'll go no matter what, but I want to help Papa."

Nazim was very serious. "I can't promise you anything. But it's possible."

"We'll leave in the morning?"

"No. Now. We have twenty-four hours. Probably less. One last thing—if for some reason you can't get back before midnight tomorrow, I won't come for you. Understand?"

Avsey nodded solemnly. "Yes."

"Every hour counts, Avsey. Every minute."

Nazim didn't talk while he stuffed Avsey's pockets with hard biscuits and watched him drink one more cup of tea and eat a tin of stewed meat. He studied Avsey's every move. "Why are you looking at me all the time? It's creepy."

Nazim shrugged and looked embarrassed, "Sorry, starik." Then he pushed an old cap onto Avsey's head. "Ready?"

It was then that Avsey saw something had changed. Nazim's face was flat and joyless, almost hard.

Avsey thought he understood. "This isn't pretend anymore is it, Nazim?"

"Nope. The real thing."

When Avsey grabbed his knapsack, Nazim shook his head. "Leave it. I'll give it to your Papa if you, if I need to."

Avsey looked at Nazim, then stashed the knapsack under a small table by the coal stove. "I'll come back. Don't worry."

Vasil' Pavlovich drove them south in an old truck littered with cigarette butts. The night was humid but clear and moonless. They turned to the west and crossed the river over a narrow wooden bridge hidden by trees. When they emerged into the open, Avsey hung his head out the window to gawk at the explosion of stars in the expanse of inky universe above their heads.

The night sky was infinite, and Avsey liked thinking about infinity. The universe was reassuringly immense, bigger than tanks and Germans, bigger than Papa or Nazim or himself. Infinity whittled the worst of life into trinkets, mere tokens.

Light is forever. Everything else is dust. This thought consoled him, but he had no idea why it should. Infinity was also terrifying.

As they made their way west, the road narrowed into a rutted dirt path and the trees grew taller, gradually obscuring the sky. Avsey pulled his head into the truck.

Vasil' Pavlovich kept the headlights off and cursed under his breath every time the truck hit a hole. He said, "Lucky there's no moon. Except I can't see the holes." They hit another crater in the road with a loud scrape of metal. Avsey looked up at Vasil' Pavlovich, searching his face for signs of anxiety. The old man's face remained placid. Avsey was sure that Vasil' Pavlovich had seen terrible sadness, or his face might have been less inscrutable, more elastic. The steering wheel jerked sharply to the left, and Vasil′ Pavlovich cursed softly. His cigarette remained tight between his teeth.

When the truck reached a clearing, Vasil′ Pavlovich stopped, cut the engine, and leaned forward, listening. Nazim listened, too, and then, hearing nothing, exhaled and pushed the door open. He motioned to Avsey to get out. "Time to go, soldier."

The truck stood in the road next to a pile of branches. Nazim bent over and began to clear the pile, throwing branches in all directions, underneath the trees on either side. Every few seconds, he stopped and listened, his ear cocked to one side, before he continued his work. What was going on? Avsey wondered if Nazim was getting ready to light a fire and felt the alarm rising in his throat. When Nazim swept more leaves and twigs off to the side and Avsey could make out a black frame, he laughed with relief.

Nazim asked, "You do know how to ride a bicycle, right?"

"Of course. Mama taught me." Avsey thought of the green bike stored in the basement against the stairs at home. It had been too big for him in the beginning. Maybe now he could pedal while sitting on the seat. Nazim shook the debris from the bicycle, dusted off the saddle, and handed it to Avsey.

"Hop up, see if your legs are long enough." Vasil′ Pavlovich took a wrench from the truck, but they didn't need it. Avsey's feet reached the pedals at just the right angle.

"Now, then." Nazim stuffed his hands in his pockets, and keeping his voice low, explained, "You'll stay on this path. It bypasses a village called Khristishche. Do not go into the village. We had enough trouble there in January. From there, it's twenty minutes to Slavyansk. Ride through Slavyansk, but pay attention to what's happening there. Tanks, soldiers. Remember what you see. If you can, keep going toward Kramatorsk. Not far, maybe an hour. Check the airport on the southwestern side of town. My guess is they are using the airport for something. Don't get too close. Understand, starik?"

Avsey nodded.

"Questions?"

"Where's the airport again?"

"At the edge of Kramatorsk, on the west side. Look for two things. The first, a small rock quarry. The second, a bit further along, a small rail station. You'll turn left after the station. The airport is at the end of the road."

Avsey, concentrating, repeated the instructions under his breath, one by one. "Kristishche. Slavyansk. Tanks. Soldiers. Kramatorsk. Quarry. Turn left at the station. Airport."

"Return the same way. If all goes well, you'll be back before sunset. Don't talk to anyone, don't answer questions. Do not under any circumstances ask any questions yourself."

Avsey repeated, "No questions."

"Do not linger. Keep moving. You have until midnight. Plenty of time to get in and out. Do not appear to be in a hurry. Stay nonchalant but focused." Nazim stood and straightened his shoulders. He shook Avsey's hand. "Good luck, scout."

Vasil' Pavlovich, a newly lit cigarette hanging from his lips, took both of Avsey's hands in his own and muttered, "Good luck, young man."

Avsey rested his hands on the handlebars. He did not want Nazim to see he was shaking.

Nazim put one foot inside the truck and then turned back. He looked hard at Avsey. "The sun will be up soon. Remember, enemy territory, best to get out as quickly as you can."

Avsey didn't feel afraid until the truck disappeared into the night. A forlorn feeling, terror mixed with loneliness, the likes of which he'd never experienced before, seized him. He felt a wave of nausea, but the lingering scent of Vasil' Pavlovich's cigarette helped calm his nerves. He could see the cigarette's tiny red ember through the back window of the truck as it receded into the trees. He swore he could see Nazim's palm flattened against the window, too. The darkness eventually swallowed the tiny red dot, taking the pale skin with it.

Avsey was on his own. He repeated the Salsk code of conduct. Avoid trouble, remain wary. Look for opportunities. Persevere. He already knew there was no one he could trust on this side of the river. He turned the bicycle toward the first village, swung one leg over the bar, and sat tall on the seat. He pedaled steadily into the darkness, buoyed by the light spilling over the treetops.

CHAPTER 16
DON RIVER BASIN, MAY 1942

BY THE TIME AVSEY HAD PEDALED PAST KRISTISHCHE AND COULD SEE the vague outline of low buildings on the outskirts of Slavyansk, the sun had cleared the tree line and was firmly ensconced in a pale blue sky. The dirt road turned to pavement, cobblestones, then pavement again. Remembering Nazim's advice to appear nonchalant, Avsey pedaled lazily, made figure eights on the road, and stopped for a small army of geese as they crossed in front of him.

In the center of town, cicadas pushed the humid morning air into a hum that rose and fell in waves through the tree-lined streets. Stray cats prowled for breakfast, their tails swishing hard back and forth as they closed in on mice and small beetles scuttling in the cracks. Avsey pedaled around a gold-domed church and over the river. An old woman, bent over with a brush broom, cleaned a walkway with rough strokes back and forth. She stopped and watched under hooded eyes as Avsey passed. He felt uneasy and avoided staring back. The locals would know he wasn't one of them.

He rode through a park and around a small lake. He crossed over thin rivulets on foot bridges, the bicycle shaking against the wooden structures, rattling his ribs. He opened his mouth to hear the sound of his voice articulated in the bumps as he pedaled over the bridges, the only human voice in the town at this hour. When he was through Slavyansk, he stopped to look back, perplexed. What had he expected? He glanced up at the sky. He'd been gone a couple of hours already.

On the road toward Kramatorsk, the pavement gave way to dirt again, then narrowed considerably until Avsey was surrounded by fields. He stopped to dig in his pocket for the hard biscuits, leaned the bike against a low stone fence, and ate while he scanned the countryside.

There, right in the middle of the field, was a long line of mounded dirt, as if an anti-tank ditch had been filled. Avsey thought maybe this was important; this filling in, too tidy. Covering an anti-tank ditch with dirt required effort. *What for?*

He hopped over the fence to take a closer look. Green groped riotously everywhere, invading every crevice and cranny of fertile soil except for the long line of dirt that ran perpendicular to the road. Nothing yet grew on it.

He climbed to the top of the mound and looked down its length. Were the Germans so confident the Reds would never be back this way that they could afford to fill in the anti-tank defenses? Something wasn't right.

As he turned to descend the mound, the soil gave way under his feet. He slid down a little, left foot in front of his right, shoes sinking into the soft earth. He struggled as he tried to pull his right foot free, waving his arms to maintain his balance. The earth released his foot, and with the sudden upward movement, Avsey lost his balance and toppled over. He pushed up, but his hands sank, and a hint of soft color appeared below his chin, a light blue morsel of fabric. He reached for it and stood, pinching the fabric between two fingers. It was a small coat encrusted with mud and dead leaves.

The coat had once been a beautiful blue, and even now, all its buttons remained attached. The little piped collar featured a deli-cately embroidered bouquet of yellow flowers. A little girl's coat.

Had the little girl run away to play in a ditch wearing her best coat? He noticed rips in the fabric, at the back. Avsey shuddered involuntarily and let the coat fall back into the soil, glad to be rid of it. He wiped his hands on his trousers and wished he hadn't climbed the mound.

Nazim's voice echoed around him in the empty field. *Get out as quickly as you can.* Avsey made his way down the mound gingerly, in case there were other mysteries in the dirt. At the bottom, he emptied his shoes and slapped them together to free the clots that clung to the soles. He sat down to slip them on. He could not waste more time.

A little further on, when the road had dipped into the tree line and the branches reached for one another in an archway across the sky, he saw the tanks. The earth was covered with them, a plague of metal boils covering the peaceful countryside. Turreted, they pointed north, their tracks visible through the green fields awash with yellow flowers. In the middle of it all stood a hunting shelter, a small white-washed hut and several grass covered dugouts in the distance.

A sentry leaned against the wall smoking a cigarette and biting his cuticles, immobile in a beehive of activity. The scene swarmed with dark uniforms. They reminded Avsey of village chimney sweeps, black-clad and perched in precarious places, peering into hatches, on the backs of trucks, throwing off the branches that had camouflaged their lethal weapons.

Avsey shivered despite the heat. From somewhere inside his own head, a high-pitched whistle sounded. He stuck his fingers in his ears and jiggled them to be rid of the unwanted noise. Did fear make a sound? He left the field, looking back as he pedaled away.

Back along the river, the road widened again. Trucks honked past him, forcing him to stop and watch them pass. The truck beds were full of clean-shaven young soldiers, their rifles slung casually across their torsos. They paid him no attention. The convoy passed without slowing, sending a quiet wave of relief through Avsey's whole body. He focused on the road ahead and pushed his feet faster.

He hadn't ridden a bicycle in many months and just for a moment he imagined himself at home, carefree, his biggest worry— pedaling fast enough to escape the bullies from school. But the trouble at school paled in comparison. Escaping the bullies was nothing like riding around the German Army. Once or twice, the road threatened to unseat him; rocks and ridges caught at the tires when he wasn't looking, while little gullies and streams ran down one side of the road, leaving the road slick with mud that splashed his shoes and pant legs. He gripped the handlebars and pedaled standing.

He reached Kramatorsk before the sun was at its zenith. The town reminded Avsey of Rostov, only smaller. Pretty stone buildings adorned with small balconies, the sound of fountains in the central square, like home. Nothing bad could happen in a place like this. Avsey rode past women in small market stalls rummaging through piles of fragrant herbs, past neat kitchen gardens and children sitting on concrete steps in the sun.

More German trucks rumbled by, then a long line of open-air Kübelwagens, just missing Avsey, waking him from the dream of normalcy. Again, he stopped to let them pass. Trucks loaded with horses and soldiers called to one another, laughing. And still, no one paid him any attention. They were well cared for, these men. Their teeth were white, and their skin glistened in the sunlight. They were like postcard images of Crimea, their open shirts exposing suntanned skin. The picture Nazim had painted of a German Army, sick and weakened, wasn't true. Why had he lied?

Avsey put his head down, his chest tight, his hands balled into fists. He couldn't let them see his anger, his disgust. He'd thought maybe the German soldiers were frightened, too, that they hadn't wanted to come to where he lived. But that's not how it looked now. He hated these carefree invaders who rested their hands on the backs of their fellows, their weapons hanging like schoolbags from their shoulders.

When they had passed, Avsey pedaled deliberately, acutely aware he was now surrounded by the enemy. He slowed at the sight of rubble, huge mounds of concrete and debris on the right side of the road. He straightened his legs on the pedals to stand up. A vast field of bent metal and scorched timbers spread out before him, as if a whole town had been destroyed, its remnants sorted into piles.

He hopped off the bicycle and stood for a long while trying to make sense of what it had all been, and why it had been destroyed. Again, a queasy feeling urged him back to the road. He reached the quarry pedaling much faster, his legs and lungs burning, only slowing at the train station to make sure he turned left toward the airport.

When at last the airfield came into view, he stopped, stupefied, and laid his bike down in the dirt. The sun had climbed higher, and with it, the heat. Avsey wiped the sweat from his forehead and walked behind a tree to pee, never taking his eyes off the activity on the airfield. Dust hung in a fine haze over swarms of soldiers moving heavy equipment. He lay down beside the bike on his belly, head in his hands, to watch.

Dotted around the runway, between the farm buildings and the small outhouses, Avsey counted six heavy antiaircraft guns. Soldiers were busy moving two smaller guns and several searchlights into position. Nazim had been right. The Germans were ready for something big. The low whistle in his ears returned. Annoyed, he pressed his hands into the sides of his head, desperate to be rid of it.

The soldiers yelled to one another across the small airfield, and at one point, two soldiers walked a few meters from where he was lying, unzipped their trousers, and peed. They were engrossed in conversation and did not see him. Avsey listened but understood nothing in German. All he could do was watch, the pit in his stomach widening, the bile collecting at the top of his throat.

When he'd memorized the situation—the placement of the guns and searchlights, the numbers of soldiers—he slapped the dust from his trousers, jerked the bike around, and pressed his feet into the pedals to stand. He took one last look at the equipment arrayed around the stubbled runway, then launched the bicycle back the way he'd come, legs trembling, a fire in his belly. He leaned forward into the handlebars, longing for speed, wanting to race back across the river as fast as he could, to shout a warning at the top of his lungs. He restrained himself. The whistle between his ears was gone.

The light had shifted by the time he arrived in the center of Kramatorsk. A group of soldiers talked with pretty girls at a cheerful green kiosk. Avsey held his breath as he rode around them and counted to twenty. He prayed they wouldn't see his wobbly legs, the sweat on his upper lip. He stopped to sit on a bench just past their position, in case they'd noticed his urgency, before he finally pushed out toward the field road where he had first seen the tanks. Maybe there he could pedal faster. He was in a hurry to tell Nazim what he'd seen.

Well into the trees and pedaling hard, Avsey heard a yell. He slowed and scanned the leaves for movement. He didn't see the three German soldiers until they were right in front of him. He pushed the pedals backward to avoid hitting them, and skidded to a stop. One of the soldiers took hold of his handlebars. Had they jumped from the trees?

Avsey looked up. Maybe there were more of them. They were so close, he thought he might faint. More sweat collected around his upper lip. The soldiers were pointing up into the trees and laughing. The tallest soldier ruffled Avsey's hair, held up a strand to show the others. Avsey had no idea what they were saying, but they seemed to be having fun at his expense. Their jackets were unbuttoned, and their weapons lay across bare skin.

They pressed their faces into his and spoke louder. Avsey shrugged and shook his head.

The tallest soldier, the one who had touched his hair, held out a small piece of paper and pointed to the hut in the middle of the field. Avsey realized, with a lurch in his stomach, the hut was the one he'd seen earlier in the morning, a sentry still leaning against its side. The tall soldier pushed the paper into Avsey's hand and pointed to the hut again. Avsey swallowed hard and looked at the paper, then at the hut. The tanks sparkled in the sun. Did they want him to deliver a message?

The soldier holding his handlebars let go and dug into his pocket. He held a coin in front of Avsey's nose and nodded toward the hut. Avsey didn't move. The sun was at the three-quarters point in the sky, and he wanted to be far away, on the other side of the river, on the other side of the *world*. He sucked his lip into his teeth and bit down on the insides of his mouth.

The soldier pressed the coin into his hand and gave him a little push toward the field, pointing in the direction of the hut. Avsey stared at the foreign coin in his hand. Any other time, he might have been fascinated, might have wanted it. But now all he wanted was to leave the road and the soldiers behind. He inched forward with the bicycle, but the tall soldier stepped in front of him, blocking his way.

A third soldier, thin, with a barely-there mustache, dug into his pocket and pulled out a brightly wrapped candy. He smiled and pushed it into Avsey's hand next to the coin.

Avsey thought maybe he was kind. He smiled back, thinking surely this fellow would understand. He pushed his bike forward. "Please? I have to go."

The soldier took the handlebars and shook the bicycle, snatching the candy from Avsey's hand. He was not smiling anymore.

Avsey was trapped. He rested the bike against a tree and climbed over the fence. The soldiers cheered.

He ran toward the white hut, following the vehicle tracks, the green crops trampled and broken all around him. The sun, still piercingly hot, would start its descent soon, and Avsey longed to be on his way back to Nazim. He wiped his face with his shirt as he ran wishing for water.

In front of the hut, he held the paper out to the sentry and pointed to be let inside. The sentry slowly lit a cigarette and blew smoke in Avsey's face. He spoke Russian with a heavy accent, "What do you want?"

"The soldiers over there wanted me to bring this note here." Avsey pointed toward the road. The sentry eyed him suspiciously and craned his neck to look for the soldiers through the trees. Avsey shifted from foot to foot.

"Wait. No move."

"Would you have some water?" Avsey made his voice as polite as he could.

The sentry stared at him. Angry voices floated into the air. The sentry disappeared. Avsey waited, scarcely believing he was standing in front of a field command post inside enemy territory. He waited for a very long time, watching the sun and wishing for water. The minute he decided to give up and run, the sentry stuck his head out and waved Avsey inside.

The hut was occupied by two officers who stood beside a wooden table. They turned to him, irritated, their faces set in stone. Avsey realized they had been arguing. He handed the note to the officer in front of him and couldn't help but stare at the man's smooth, delicate hands and the gold ring he wore on his right pinky finger. He smelled like grass and wild boar. Both soldiers wore gleaming German crosses on the left, under the brass button pockets of their jackets.

Avsey had never been this close to a German officer. His stomach felt as if he'd swallowed thousands of tiny live minnows.

Before the officer could unfold the note, a loud bang echoed around the field. Avsey jumped. The officer with the gold ring ducked slightly. Outside, engines revved and men shouted at one another. The officers rushed from the hut without looking at him. Avsey stretched his head out into the sunshine and watched them run, along with the sentry, toward the shouting behind the tanks. He was alone, improbably alone. He could go.

He turned to make sure, one more time, that no one else was in the hut. A pile of papers on the table caught his eye. Maps, telegrams, papers embossed with eagle insignia, scribbles, lines, and arrows of all sorts. Avsey remembered Nazim's battlefield illustrations. It dawned on him—some of these might be valuable. He lifted several of the papers to see what was underneath. More drawings.

He noticed a carafe of water on the table and, forgetting the papers, seized it with both hands and drank, water spilling around the sides of his mouth. He reached to return the carafe to the table, but it slipped from his hands, hit the ground, and shattered. The sentry walked into the hut, breathing hard. He said something in a harsh tone. Avsey stood very still, his hands at his sides, waiting for the sentry to arrest him and call for more soldiers. His head spun. He was sure he would pass out. But outside, the noise of a new commotion reached his ears. The sentry, a look of panic on his face, bolted out the door.

Dizzy, Avsey turned toward the desk. This was his last chance. Ever so gently, his fingers tingling, he slid a pack of papers out from the middle of the pile, making sure to leave the top documents arrayed as he had found them. Hurriedly, he folded the stack in half, sucked his stomach in, and slid them into his trousers.

Avsey bolted from the tent in time to see the sentry headed in his direction. He slowed his pace and let his arms hang. Perhaps nonchalance would earn him time. His heart beat so wildly, he was certain he would stop breathing. When he thought he might be far enough away from the hut, he gave into the panic and ran, pumping his arms, slashing at the knee-high vegetation that now felt like tentacles grasping at his legs.

He glanced back toward the tanks once, surprised no one had

followed. His next worry was the soldiers on the road. What would he say to them? Would they see the papers stuffed into his pants? But when he reached the bicycle, they were gone. He didn't stop to catch his breath.

Shaking, he grabbed the handlebars and hopped on the bike, gulping air. Sweat poured down his face, into his ears. He paid no attention to the bumps and crevices on the road. He slid once and fell into a muddy puddle, and for a split second believed he was finished. But the road behind him remained as it had been—peaceful, green, empty. He leaned forward, steadied himself, and didn't look back again.

There were plenty of German trucks and motorcycles in Slavyansk. Avsey heard shouting as he passed through town but didn't turn his head. He expected a truck to screech to a halt in front of him, a soldier to jump down and grab his arm. He wheeled around the park and back out onto the road toward Kristishche as the sunlight succumbed to dusk.

Avsey couldn't shake the image of German officers, their chiseled faces, the crosses on their breast pockets. The whistling in his ears had completely vanished, but now he was so hungry, his whole body trembled. He reached down to make sure the papers were still in his pants and groped his pockets. The hard biscuits had been lost in his escape. His stomach rumbled. But hunger was the least of his worries. The Germans had been busy. They didn't pay attention to a red-haired kid on a bicycle because they'd been planning an attack.

Around Kristishche, Avsey heard laughter drifting through the trees. He was grateful the sun had disappeared but worried anyway—enough light lingered to expose him on the road. The smell of them—alcohol, sweat, and roasted meat—was pungent. The soldiers were close. He pedaled faster. His knees and shoulders hurt, but his stomach stopped rumbling, a small consolation.

By the time he'd left Kristishche well behind, his anxiety was almost unbearable. Would Nazim be there, waiting?

He reached the road where he'd watched Nazim slide away hours before. It was dark and empty. He stood up on the pedals, hoping to be seen, searching for Nazim. The forest was quiet.

He crossed the road and laid the bicycle on the forest floor. The stolen papers cut into his belly, the back of his neck burned. A familiar tingle electrified his spine all the way to his fingertips. Nazim hadn't believed him, said he wasn't really a thief, but the truth was there, in the way his chest felt it might burst open, in the satisfaction settling over his whole being. He didn't feel guilty this time. His gift was useful.

The scent of the pine forest cocooned him. Something moved through the underbrush, but Avsey was too tired to care. One by one, every muscle in his body released. He let his head hang over his knees and felt oddly relaxed. He wasn't afraid of anything now. His left shin hurt. He listened to the crickets.

He didn't see the truck until it was so close, he thought it might veer off and hit him. It glided past him on the road, as if from the depths of a distant ocean. Watching from the underbrush, he stood and peered out to make sure it was Nazim at the wheel. When he recognized Nazim's sharp profile, he stood and limped out of the forest.

Nazim stopped when he caught sight of him and reached over to push the door open, a finger on his lips. Avsey crawled into the truck and pulled the door shut with a gentle click.

They didn't speak until the truck was in the middle of the wooden bridge, but once Avsey began his story, he couldn't stop. He started with the camouflaged tanks in the field, then described the handsome soldiers, the huge pile of rubble, the antiaircraft guns, and the white hut. He ended with the laughter he'd heard in Kristishche just as they reached the station at Krasny Lyman.

"Nazim, they have searchlights, so they can see our planes and shoot them down."

Grim, Nazim said, "I had a bad feeling."

Avsey pulled the stack of papers from his pants. "I took these."

Nazim raised his eyebrows and whistled. He rifled through the papers, shaking his head, a look of admiration on his face. "You are a real spy, starik."

Avsey looked down at his hands, their cuticles rimmed in red earth. He hadn't mentioned the anti-tank ditch and the little blue coat. It didn't matter. The papers and the airfield mattered. Helping Papa mattered.

Nazim leaned over the steering wheel and turned to face Avsey. "I was afraid. If you hadn't returned, I couldn't have…" His voice broke, and he looked out of the window. In a whisper, he said, "I shouldn't have asked you to go."

"Why? I did it, Nazim. I'm a real soldier now, a spy, like you said."

Nazim stepped out of the truck, but not before Avsey saw a flash of despair in his eyes.

Inside the station, Nazim disappeared with the stolen documents.

Vasil' Pavlovich looked after Avsey for a few minutes, gave him bread, and let him sit in the wide chair behind his desk. He said, "You're a hero now." He smiled in his stoic way and left to join Nazim.

Alone, Avsey curled his feet underneath him and tried hard to keep his eyes open. He wanted to talk to Nazim, to ask about Papa, but despite his best efforts, he drifted into sleep, calling to Papa in his dreams.

Avsey felt something gently push his shoulder. He opened his eyes. "Papa?" He sat up, expecting Papa's smile, his tight embrace.

Instead, Nazim's face came into focus. Vasil' Pavlovich's face was there, too, hovering at Nazim's shoulder. They looked like puppets, their disembodied heads moving in unison. Nazim's mouth opened and closed several times.

Avsey rubbed his eyes, uncomprehending. He heard Nazim say, "Wounded. We have to go now."

Avsey, still orienting himself, watched them. Their faces moved closer. Nazim and Vasil' Pavlovich spoke at the same time, "Your father."

"What?"

Nazim expelled his breath forcefully. "Avsey, your Papa has been wounded. He's in a field hospital near Balakleya."

Avsey felt himself sinking. "How can that be?"

"We'll go to him, starik. Don't worry."

"Is he going to die, Nazim? Is my Papa going to die?"

CHAPTER 17
ROSTOV-ON-DON, JUNE 1942

Asya had plumped up since Sara found her wandering the riverbank in December, the Don frozen solid, asking anyone who passed where her suitcase was, as if she'd been dropped off at the wrong station in the middle of a journey. She was wearing a flimsy nightdress and carrying a tapestry pillow. Sara did not ask where she'd been. She did not ask where the bruises on her arms and legs had originated either. She didn't want to know, not really.

Nonetheless, a queasy worry took root about what had happened to Asya during the short German occupation in November. Sara, thinking she should return Asya to the hospital, found it deserted. Lev was called to the Freight Committee the day after Sara brought Asya home, bathed and fed her, cut her hair and nails, tweezed her eyebrows. Asya did not speak, did not acknowledge her husband or look for her children.

Lev held out Avsey's letters. "Don't worry, I'll find him and keep him with me."

Asya stared blankly out the window, and Sara knew it would be easier to care for her without Lev.

Asya did not speak for weeks. She followed directions and generally complied with the routine of everyday life Sara established until, on the outside, she began to resemble her old self. Sara, sitting by the window, mending the holes in their socks, felt compelled for her own sanity, to converse. "When they took Lyosha, I thought I wouldn't survive. I miss him every day, the way he made me laugh."

Asya showed no sign she'd heard.

Sara smiled sadly. "I know, Asya, I know you've deserted me." Her sister's disengagement wasn't a moral failure, despite what the doctors said about reformism, insinuating Asya had betrayed her socialist core. Sara experienced Asya's delusions as a desertion, an abdication of their bond, but she knew they were beyond Asya's control. "You haven't chosen this, sister. Like Lyosha, he didn't choose either."

One warm spring morning, Asya spoke. She stood in front of Sara as the sun filtered into the living room and asked for the boy. "You want to reclaim him? It's been such a long time. Would he know you?"

Asya never answered Sara's questions but made the same request every day: "I want Kuzma."

Sara logged Asya's need into the ledger of her transgressions against her sister. She and Lev were responsible for the abandonment of Kuzma to his grandmother. Asya had been tired of Sergei's long geological expeditions in which he was away for months, mapping the Caucasus. Lev had appeared in her life, ready to, as Asya said, love her blind. And while it was Sergei who'd demanded Asya leave their son with his mother, Sara had supported the idea, worried Kuzma might hinder her new life with Lev.

Kuzma was a strange, mute little boy with imploring dark eyes. Lev had always been jealous of anyone near Asya and never offered to take Kuzma, to love him, too. Asya, her choice impossible, had finally agreed. Sara didn't know if Asya saw her son. She never spoke of him, but Sara suspected the boy had been protected from further incursions into his stability by his grandmother. Agrippina, if she remembered correctly, was a force to be reckoned with.

Why did Asya want to see Kuzma now? Was it remorse? Where was the boy anyway? But Sara knew: He was somewhere in Proletarsky, among the Armenians, his grandmother's people. Agrippina was considered by some to be a medicinal healer, an alchemist of sorts. Her power had not extended to the boy, who, as far as anyone knew, remained mute and remote, just as they had left him at the age of two.

On the hottest day of June, Sara woke to a silent apartment and noticed flies had congregated on the white tablecloth she'd spread the night before to brighten breakfast for her sister, whose sanity often clung to objects rather than people. Asya wasn't there.

Sara set off for Proletarsky on foot through the neat piles of rubble and glass, swept up by the citizens of the city to restore, at least, the facade of order. She walked quickly, keeping her eyes peeled for her sister's head of undulating curls, her graceful limbs. Sara remembered she'd been born first, was the oldest by twenty minutes, a fact she'd taken as proof of her greater responsibility in the relationship. She straightened her spine and stepped over a wooden beam resting in the garden of a collapsed whitewashed house, its contents spilled like entrails onto the street.

The Proletarsky neighborhood had changed, not least due to the weeklong German residency in November. Sara came upon a street of modest houses, their windows boarded or broken, their outside walls black with traces of smoke, evidence of the murderous German proclivity toward arson. On the street, someone had assembled small piles of stones to remember the dead. She did not stop to look. She already knew what this was, having already heard of the Proletarsky Jews the Germans shot one afternoon as their neighbors tucked into their suppers.

She'd not ventured out during that long November week of German occupation, but sequestration had not stopped the stories from reaching her. She'd been relieved that Avsey had escaped the city before the Germans settled into their routine. Lev had disappeared, too, to fight the intruders from the outskirts while she'd stayed alone listening to the whispered warnings through cracked doors and open balcony windows.

Stay inside. Prepare a hiding place.

The panic of that week returned at the sight of this destruction and bore its holes into her chest.

Sara walked past the bazaar and turned left at the blue Armenian church, trying to remember her way to Agrippina's cottage. The landscape had changed in the intervening years, reshaping the neighborhood's contours, blurring the edges between garden and street. More recently, the beautiful old buildings had been covered in the scattered debris of conflict, their facades discolored and chipped, the formal landscapes and wrought iron flourishes speckled with dirt. Bullet holes and rubble, sagging cement siding, threatened the older buildings with collapse. Balconies hung useless, shuddering in the breeze, while shattered glass windows sparkled in the sun like attractive older women—diminished but pleasing.

The streets were empty except for small children and stray dogs who stood still to watch Sara pass. The children ran to tell their mothers, whose faces appeared behind lace curtains moments later.

Sara had seen the wood fence at Agrippina's house exactly twice. The first time was seventeen years ago, the day she'd first met Kuzma. Then, once again two years later, when she'd walked away with a stone-faced Asya, leaving Kuzma on the porch, invisible in the richly patterned skirts of his grandmother. Asya married Lev three days later.

Sara walked, alert, ready to argue with Asya, but she was nowhere to be found. Dejected and footsore, she turned into a small side street and stopped to take a stone from her shoe. As she stood on one foot and turned her shoe upside down, Sara reached to steady herself against a tree.

There, across the road, was Agrippina's fence. To be sure, it no longer marked the perimeter of her garden which had outgrown its boundary, but it was hers nonetheless. Now the fence provided wavering support for woody branches of sage, lavender, and rosemary. In places, it was almost flat against the ground, huge pink peonies pushing between the unpainted slats alongside purple lavender spikes, all bent under the weight of buzzing bees and the delicate touch of butterflies.

A broad-shouldered adolescent boy wearing dirty overalls stood in the doorway looking out, his face lifted, as if the scent of invaders had infiltrated his territory. His hair was matted and stuck to his forehead in the heat. He moved cautiously onto the little porch, turning his head from side to side, nose up, eyes narrowed.

In time, he walked down the steps and into the side yard, shifted his gaze downward and set about his daily tasks. Kuzma had become his grandmother's gardener. He moved confidently around the small piece of earth around Agrippina Artyomova's decrepit cottage, and it was obvious that he had coaxed the soil into luxuriant life, a jungle of herbs and medicinal plants surrounded by peonies, the whole of which was guarded by a platoon of feral cats.

Sara moved closer. Hidden by the overgrowth, she followed Kuzma around the house toward the southern wall of the cottage, covered in pink damask roses and beds of sorrel, oregano, and thyme. A border of wild sage had crept in between the roses, covering the thorny branches in gray and green.

Kuzma did not look anything like Sara expected him to look. Not like Sergei, who was small and muscular, and not at all like Asya, whose dark hair contrasted with her fair skin and light eyes. This boy was an Armenian like his grandmother—strong nose, thick eyebrows, dark eyes. He was beautiful.

With small clippers in hand, Kuzma picked up a basket and began to fill it with flowers. The scent was intoxicating even from where Sara stood, and the boy stopped periodically to bury his nose into a bloom as if to check its potency. He smiled, which struck Sara as inward, awkward. He tilted his head back and scanned the wall for more blooms.

Sara surveyed the perimeter of the garden and the small street. Asya wasn't there. Satisfied her sister had not found her boy and not wanting to be seen, she turned to leave. She would have liked to watch him for a few more minutes but prudence called her to turn away.

Sara was already moving down the road when a loud banging made her jump. She turned to see Kuzma hitting a watering can with his clippers, his dark eyebrows furrowed, his mouth open.

He was shooing her away.

He kept at it as Sara hurried down the shabby street, twice looking back. Kuzma stayed behind the fence, banging the watering can, apparently practiced at warding off strangers. Sara had, of course, always been a stranger to the boy, but it was not lost on her that he might have thought she was Asya. She also realized that the rumors were true; Kuzma remained without speech, though not inexpressive. This, Sara knew, was wholly due to Agrippina's willpower, her ironclad spirit.

Walking home through the dusky gloom of rubble filled streets, Sara quit Proletarsky and continued toward the apartment along the river. The sky spread out beyond the water and the trees, purple and orange, vast and satisfyingly calm. Weariness settled into her muscles, deep into her joints and bones, her mind. She gave up on finding her sister. It was too much, walking the city, constantly alert. She let the urgency slip away and eased into the memory of Kuzma's appearance and disappearance from their lives, the heartache they had endured, his innocence in all that had transpired.

As always happened when Sara gave up on Asya, she mysteriously reappeared. Sara recognized her from behind, sitting on a broken bench, her hair hanging over the back, gently lifted in the breeze. She faced the sky. Perhaps she'd been there all along.

Sara approached quietly, resigned to the limits of her knowing. She sat down next to Asya on the bench without a word. The sky collected color, splashing deeper hues further along the horizon, a sinking crescendo. The sun was almost gone.

Without looking at Sara, Asya said, "You'll suffer most when we die."

Sara turned to stare at her sister.

Asya often spoke in terms of prophecy, had done so since she was a girl. One of her quirks. And yet Sara understood now that Asya's prophecies always focused on loss. "Who is *we*, sister? You and me? No one is going to die. Besides, suffering is an inescapable matter for all of us."

"You'll be fine, in the end. You have an important task."

Sara took Asya's hand and admitted failure. There was no task, no mission to complete. Asya was the unruly consequence of whatever unknown force had seized her mind, and there was nothing more to say.

PART III LUCK

JULY-DECEMBER 1942

And let those who did not wait say that I was lucky;
They will never understand that in the midst of death,
You, with your waiting, saved me.
Only you and I will know how I survived:
It's because you waited, as no one else did.

K. Simonov - translated by Alexander Werth - 1964

CHAPTER 18
ZHELEZNOVODSK, JULY 1942

MANY PEOPLE HAD FLED TO THE SANATORIA TOWNS AND VILLAGES IN the Caucasian foothills, thinking themselves safe, shrunk into the sides of the mighty mountains whose peaks were themselves, more often than not, shrouded in clouds. Zheleznovodsk was beautiful, the little town charming and there was theater in the evenings. Residents and refugees alike were lulled into an uneasy truce with fear. Uncertainty hung in the air, but no one spoke of the worst that could happen—of further incursions by the enemy or bombing raids. It seemed to Bronya that only she imagined catastrophe under the snowcapped peak of distant Mount Elbrus. Other people smiled and walked and took their time. They ate vegetables and unadulterated bread. They smoked and talked about books.

Bronya hedged her bets. Should she stay or go? Who could she trust? One thing was certain: There were no safe harbors, no anchors. After Kharkov and Saratov, the horizon appeared false, a mirage wavering in the heat. She lived between the fictions of others, watchful, as the people around her made their own deals with reality, aware that what she couldn't know was more important than anything she could.

The tall matron whose age, in Bronya's mind, was indeterminable, pulled the chaise out onto the terrace while she gave orders. "Lie still, devushka, and close your eyes."

"What is a moon bath?" Bronya allowed herself to be covered with a thick wool blanket, too hot for the evening temperature.

"The moon aids blood circulation. Take deep breaths." The matron closed her eyes and inhaled, an exaggerated breath to demonstrate for her patient. Bronya kept her eyes open.

The mountains, backlit by a crisp full moon, loomed larger than they did during the day, their crags and rifts illuminated in reflected light. A spread of stars blistered the purple sky. Bronya always missed Papa most when the sun went down—Papa, who'd made her memorize the constellations and their brightest stars, quizzing her on clear nights all year round.

Avsey hadn't taken an interest in their astronomy evenings, often falling asleep at the start of Papa's lectures. He'd always been more interested in solid ground—the earth's mountain peaks and frozen tundra. She hoped Avsey remembered something of Papa's sky lectures, that tonight from Tbilisi, he recognized Ursa Major and Leo, whose brightest star, Regulus, was the lion's heart, directly opposite Denebola, the lion's tail. In case they were ever lost, Papa always said, they'd navigate their way home like ancient mariners. Would they all be able to navigate their way home when the war was over?

Bronya spent the spring in treatment to regain her strength, escorted over mosaic floors, in and out of small pools of rust-colored water, and harangued into lying still under the sterilization lamps, the matrons constantly urging her to eat her porridge, take her time, sit in the sun. "Typhus can reoccur, even years later," one of the feldshers told her, "You need to rest and eat."

Mandatory nap time, an hour and a half every day, was more than Bronya could bear. She soon became restless and took to creeping out of her room to roam the sanitorium's halls, avoiding matrons, feldshers, and nurses—anyone who wanted to tell her what to do. She especially avoided the director of the sanitorium, Zalima Ashamazovna, a rose-perfumed Circassian woman who often finished her sentences with, "I speak truth." Bronya decided that anyone who staked a claim to truth was especially untrustworthy. Besides, Zalima Ashamazovna was cold and imperious. Bronya hid behind the linden trees in the garden whenever she heard her high-pitched voice.

By the time the cold winds subsided and Beshtau's trees budded tender green, Bronya had regained her strength. Galina Filippovna's dresses no longer hung loose, and her arms and legs were brown. She was allowed to spend the day walking up, through ash and oak, to Beshtau's treeless summit. By the time summer arrived, she had chosen a stand of birch trees three-quarters of the way up the mountain as a respite from the matrons and the heat. She took to playing her violin there, alone, for hours.

One warm afternoon, not long into summer, Zalima Ashamazovna called Bronya to her office. Despite Bronya's dislike for the director, Zalima Ashamazovna's demeanor demanded a straight back, and Bronya complied. She stood at attention in front of the director's door, her hands at her sides, wondering what she'd done to deserve an audience.

Zalima Ashamazovna went straight to the point. "If you had not had typhus, you'd be in miserable lodging with the other refugees. Fate is on your side, Abramova, but you can't play your violin all day if you want a ration card."

Bronya had never met any Circassians, though she knew from school of the long Caucasian wars waged by the tsars and the celebration of the peoples of the Soviet Union in her textbooks. She'd read Lermontov's poem "The Dagger" and wondered if Zalima Ashamazovna kept a dagger, *a friend of iron*, in her ample bosom. "Yes, comrade director, I am grateful."

Zalima Ashamazovna nodded toward the door. "You'll work in the kitchen garden. I have written to your family to tell them you are ready to leave."

Bronya had already moved from the deserted typhus ward to

a dingy room situated along the same corridor as the sanitorium kitchen. The green walls were peeling and water-stained, but she was free to take books from the library, and she read, often until the sun came up. She waited eagerly for a response to Zalima Ashamazovna's letter home.

The ancient gardener, Radomir, stooped from years of bending forward, took Bronya as his helper to do the things he could no longer do easily. She dragged heavy sheets piled with tree cuttings, pulled the wagon through the trees, and most vitally, remembered which tools Radomir needed and where they were kept.

Bronya was happy working with Radomir, but there was one alarming inconvenience—the kitchen garden was fiercely defended by the cook's helper, Old Maria, who chased Bronya away with a machete in her hand. Bronya never bothered to mention this fact to Zalima Ashamazovna because Radomir protected her from Old Maria with a steady look and a machete of his own. An uneasy truce took hold; the machetes were withdrawn and Bronya settled into her work.

She learned to pull weeds from the flower beds, firmly coaxing the invader root systems out of the dark, rich soil. She gathered linden flowers and strung them out to dry for tea and spread rose hips and rosebuds on mesh frames to whither and shrink in the sun. On her solitary walks, she foraged wild sorrel and sage, and Radomir, pleased with her efforts, sold them in the peasant market.

Periodically, he dropped several kopeks into her hand. "Your share," he said, winking, his other hand on his stooped back. Once, he brought her a broken piece of rosin for her bow.

Bronya kissed him on the cheek, wondering how he'd known she needed it.

Radomir blushed. "It's the least I can do for you and your beautiful music."

Bronya wanted to go home. She was glad the director had written to her family. But she hadn't heard from Papa in nine months and had almost given up. Through early spring and the heat of summer, she waited, determined not to succumb to the evil thoughts that formed somewhere between midnight and dawn, the deep worry that told her in her own small voice that the worst had happened. She calculated the train routes their letters would traverse between Rostov and Zheleznovodsk, the barriers they might encounter—weather, fighting, loss. The calculations helped her wait, but they did not stop her worry. Where was Papa?

Sara's letter of May 20th arrived two months after it had been posted, well into July. Bronya leaned against a linden tree and stared at the familiar handwriting on the mailgram—Sara's perfectly formed letters. Why was she in Rostov and not in Tbilisi? Did something terrible happen?

She held her breath and peeled back the edges of the thin envelope.

MAY 20, 1942

DEAREST BRONISLAVA,

JOY AT FINDING YOUR LETTERS. TODAY WE RECEIVED THREE AT ONCE, like three golden apples. Real happiness to know where you are and where you've been, that you are safe and in good health. I am caring for Mama in the Turgenevskaya Street apartment. The hospital was destroyed by the Germans months ago. Avsey is with Papa for now, far from Rostov.

Nothing has turned out as we planned but then nothing ever does. One day we'll tell each other everything. If I could fly to you, I would. My only wish, to be together again.

. . .

A million kisses, from Mama too.

SARA

BRONYA READ THE LETTER THREE MORE TIMES BEFORE SHE FOLDED IT and stuffed it into her pocket. *Nothing has turned out as we planned.*

All this time, she'd pictured them in the wrong places. They were further away and closer than she'd imagined. She cursed the censors. Sara couldn't tell her, even if she knew, where Avsey and Papa were or why their plans had changed. Still, they were alive. Bronya closed her eyes and covered her face with her hands. In the deepest part of her mind, she'd imagined they weren't.

The first thing to do was to tell Zalima Ashamazovna. She patted the sweat from her face with the hem of her skirt and reminded herself to be polite and matter-of-fact. Home was within reach.

As if fate had arranged it, Bronya rounded the corner of the main building and found Zalima Ashamazovna walking toward her, dark shoes crunching in the gravel, arms swinging.

"Why are you so hard to find? Go for bread, Bronislava, and stop lazing about."

"Yes, comrade director. Right away. But I have news."

Zalima Ashamazovna examined Bronya with a raised eyebrow.

"I've had a letter from my aunt." Bronya pulled the letter from her pocket and held it out, smiling politely. "I can go home." She was sure this news would please the director.

Zalima Ashamazovna pulled her bosom into an authoritative stance, head thrown back like a bird.

Bronya secretly called her the Pigeon—not out loud, of course, only under her breath.

"You haven't heard, Abramova? The Germans took Rostov two days ago." She made a small noise at the back of her throat, not unlike the rooftop pigeons she resembled. "I suppose that's that, then." She clapped her hands together as if to shake the dust away. "The wagon is at the kitchen door."

Before Bronya was able to say another word, Zalima Ashamazovna turned and walked down the gravel path.

Though it was still early, the day was already particularly hot. Cicada crescendos broke in waves through the trees. Bronya pulled the wagon toward the bread factory, her thoughts focused on Mama and Sara.

Were they safe? Alive? Where were Papa and Avsey?

She crossed the street. A boy on a bicycle narrowly missed hitting her, and in the heat-induced shimmers of light, she saw Avsey on his bike, laughing. The boy yelled and raised a fist as he wheeled by.

Bronya turned toward the park, where clusters of people stood talking or smoking under the trees, everyone discussing the German advance. "I've heard they're moving east, coming here."

"Where can we go now?"

"Maybe it's better to stay."

"Tbilisi? Baku?"

At the bread factory, Bronya waited patiently while a woman in a white apron filled the wagon with dark loaves of heavily scented bread. Her stomach growled. She nodded her thanks and turned to pull the wagon back through town and up the road toward the sanitorium.

The sun, merciless, burned the back of her neck. She could go home on her own, couldn't she? If she had to walk all the way to Rostov, she would.

The kitchen door banged open. Old Maria eyed her crankily. She pulled the wagon handle from Bronya's hand, almost toppling herself over in the process. Bronya thought of Old

Maria's machete but snatched a loaf of bread anyway. For a second, she felt powerful.

"Thank you, Old Maria." One loaf would last a couple of days on the road. She didn't need to think more; she would take her knapsack, her violin, and leave.

Before Bronya reached her room in the corridor, she heard the metal springs of her bed groan from behind the door. She pushed the door open cautiously, and stuck her head inside.

When her eyes adjusted to the shift in light, she was startled to find Zalima Ashamazovna perched on the edge of her bed, hands folded on her lap. Bronya hung, half inside, half outside the room.

Zalima Ashamazovna unfolded her hands and placed them on her knees. Why was her bearing always so sanctimonious?

Zalima Ashamazovna leaned forward. "Greeting proceeds conversation, Bronislava."

"Hello, comrade director."

"I don't condone thievery, but you'll need more bread if you're leaving."

Bronya tightened her grip on the loaf.

Zalima Ashamazovna waved a fly away in the dim light and motioned Bronya to stand in front of her. "The Germans are on their way, and by all accounts, they move quite fast. Soon, we'll all be neighbors. Better to stay here until we find someplace safer."

"There is no safe place. It's all the same, here or there—I want to go home."

"Always a good idea to have a plan, Bronislava. You are Jews, yes?"

Bronya stiffened. Sara had always worried about what the Germans would do to them if they rolled into Rostov. But Bronya persisted. "I have a plan. I'll take my chances."

Zalima Ashamazovna straightened her skirt over her knees and leaned further forward, until Bronya thought she might tip over. "Good sense and patience go together, Bronislava. It's safer here than out there. This is a sanitorium, a place of typhus. No one likes a place touched by disease. The German Army is particularly sensitive in this regard."

Here, Zalima Ashamazovna paused. Her eyelids were puffy, heavy over her eyes. "A solution will appear." She smiled sadly and added, "I will help. On my Circassian honor."

Bronya softened a little, the muscles in her neck relaxed. "Thank you, comrade director. I plan to walk home with or without bread." She held the loaf out, "Please accept my apologies. I wasn't thinking clearly."

Zalima Ashamazovna waved the bread away. "I admire your determination, Bronislava. But one truth is better than a hundred lies. You don't know what an army can do to a pretty young girl."

Bronya flinched. She *did* know.

The director's face lost its haughtiness, and her shoulders slumped. "Don't antagonize Maria. She is by nature unfriendly. And no violin playing. Understand?"

"Why?"

"You will not want to call attention to yourself, under the circumstances. I want you to survive, Bronislava."

CHAPTER 19
PYATIGORSK, AUGUST 1942

In Pyatigorsk, on the first day of August, Papa sat on a long, metal table while Mila, the nurse, applied layers of gauze and mud to the surgical wounds on both his legs.

"Last round of mud treatments, lieutenant. No more surgeries." She winked at Avsey.

The Yermolov baths had been Avsey's introduction to Pyatigorsk, the first place they'd come from the ambulance train and the only place Avsey had felt safe after Papa's rescue. Avsey imagined Pyatigorsk as a haven where the heavy odor of the earth's elements and the echoes of underground lakes sheltered them from war.

Black mud permeated everything at Yermolov. From breakfast to late afternoon, after Papa's treatments were finished and he was lying on his cot in the ward, Avsey tasted the mud at the back of his throat. He liked it, even craved it. Outside, alone, he scooped up fistfuls of dry dirt from the roads and flower beds, breathed its odor, and put it on his tongue.

He'd confessed his craving to Mila, who shook her head sadly. "Lots of children are eating their minerals this way."

When he'd first arrived, exhausted and frightened from the field hospital where Papa had been unconscious for days, it was

Mila who'd found Avsey a bed in one of the nurses' rooms in the dormitory. She'd had a difficult time prying Avsey away from Papa. It was only by promising him that Papa wouldn't leave again that she loosened his grip on Papa's arm.

It didn't take long for Avsey to become the nurses' pet. They played games with him, washed his clothes, and mandated he eat soup every night. Mila sang to him in the dark when his nightmares returned him to the evacuation train crawling at a snail's pace, chased by enemy shells. In her company, Avsey gradually came to believe he hadn't seen all those dying men, that the mud and body parts hadn't been real, but rather a part of the nightmare world he inhabited at night.

At least that was what he let Mila believe, to make her happy. She reminded him of Bronya, the way she moved through a room or folded clothes or tried to comb his hair by wetting it first to make it lie flat on his head. He found the ache for his sister intensified when Mila was nearby, as if he'd placed it under a magnifying glass. That which was almost invisible became more intense, jagged in its detail. He decided he would marry Mila one day, despite their age difference.

Nazim had stayed in Pyatigorsk, too, though at first, Avsey did not see him.

Papa explained, "Nazim has work to do. He was chief engineer here in Pyatigorsk before he joined the Freight Dispersal Committee."

Since Pyatigorsk was home for Nazim, Avsey imagined he stayed with his elderly mother. He knew of her because once or twice she sent Papa fruit and flowers. When Nazim brought these gifts, Papa's eyes changed, half happy and half sad. Avsey didn't ask him why, in part because Papa had been closed off since his close call with death, and Avsey thought of himself as Papa's protector, the guardian of his peace of mind. It was his task to keep sadness away.

Besides, Papa hadn't slept well since his injury and was irritable most of the time. And things only grew worse. Nazim rushed in one afternoon to tell them the Germans had captured Rostov. The nightmare was repeating itself, and now Mama and Sara were unreachable behind enemy lines.

In the days that followed, Papa's anger festered, curtailing his speech. Papa had always kept his feelings inside, had always been quiet when troubled, but now his eyes sank into his face, as if the pressure were collapsing him. Sometimes, after Avsey asked a question three or four times, he had to tug on Papa's sleeve to get his attention, to wake him from the taciturn state he appeared reluctant to abandon.

It was lucky Mila was there when Papa received Sara's letter from Rostov, posted a few days before the Germans arrived. Papa pounded the table with his fists, but Mila remained calm. She'd seen wounded men read their letters from home a hundred times. Her eyes filled with pity for Papa without knowing the circumstances of his loss, and Avsey felt grateful to her for this.

Papa held Sara's letter and raged out loud to no one in particular, finally letting his anger find its course. "They were ready to leave. I knew they'd put it off too many times." Papa caught sight of Avsey and snapped, "Tuck your pockets into your trousers!"

Avsey bristled—it wasn't fair to blame him. He was worried about Sara and Mama, too. He pushed his pockets into place. Obedience was, for the moment, better than rebellion. No need to push Papa into an argument.

Avsey pulled a small pebble from one of his pockets; he'd emptied them of dirt earlier that morning, worried someone would discover his secret craving and punish him. Mila watched him, her hands on her hips. Was she scolding him, too? He hung his head and pushed his embarrassment deep down in the pit of his stomach.

Papa lay back and shouted, "Damn, rotten, bastards!"

Avsey jumped. Papa never cursed. Avsey had been with him in the field hospital while flies buzzed around his bloody bandages in the sweltering heat, been with him when the doctor said he'd never walk again. Papa hadn't cursed or lost his temper, he'd simply ignored the doctor. Avsey knew Papa's distress meant that the situation in Rostov was a great deal worse than the first time the Germans had vacationed there.

He touched Papa's arm, "It's all right. Aunt Sara said we'd win the war. Remember? Sara's always right, isn't she, Papa?"

Mila smiled and put her arm around Avsey. She squeezed him tight and then dabbed a bit of mud on his nose. "Sweet boy. Of course, she's right."

Avsey felt his cheeks burn.

Papa paid no attention to them. He turned to the letter, muttering to himself until he reached the last page. Then his head jerked up, eyebrows high on his thin face. "Bronya is in Zheleznovodsk. That's what Sara says here." He held the page out as evidence.

"Where's Zheleznovodsk?" Avsey had never heard of it.

Papa, incredulous, almost shouted, "On the other side of Beshtau, the north side of the mountain, closer to Mineralnye Vody. We can walk there."

Mila raised a finger to Papa, her young face serious. "You aren't supposed to be walking up mountains, Lieutenant Abramov." She turned back to the mud, spreading another layer over the gauze on his right leg.

"I know, I know, Mila. Don't worry. I'll find someone else to go."

Avsey couldn't believe his ears. "How'd Bronya get to Zheleznovodsk?"

Papa glanced at the letter. "Sara says she had typhus. In Saratov. She was sent to a sanitorium in Zheleznovodsk to recover."

Typhus. Saratov. It had been over a year since Bronya waved goodbye from the back of a camel on her way to Kharkov. At the time, he'd thought she was the lucky one. Now, of course, he understood how silly he'd been. They were all lucky until they weren't. "Can we go to Zheleznovodsk, Papa? Now?"

"We'll find her, Avsey. Let me talk to Nazim."

But Nazim did not appear at the hospital for a week, and only then to tell them German artillery was approaching Pyatigorsk. "They've overrun the NKVD on the Kuma and are approaching Mineralnye Vody. All we have are the tractor school cadets."

Papa stared blankly at nothing. Mila ran sobbing from the room.

Panic spread in the city, initiating evacuation efforts. All thoughts of walking over the mountain to find Bronya vanished.

They began to hear sporadic small-arms fire around town but could see nothing. The dust and high temperatures had created a hellish haze, an otherworldly atmosphere. As night fell, the silence was punctuated by screams and outbursts, their sources unseeable. Avsey stayed in Papa's hospital room. No one slept.

In the morning, before Avsey could digest any of it, he walked the hospital corridors as the staff, under evacuation orders, hurried to load trucks with medical equipment and patients. Avsey heard angry shouts, women crying. No one came to Papa's room to check on him, and no one brought breakfast.

By the early afternoon, nurses piled into trucks and roared off to the train station. Mila found Avsey before she left, hugged him, and said, "I'll see you at the station, Avsey. We'll ride together. Don't be afraid, sweet boy."

He noticed how big Mila's eyes were in her wide, heart-shaped face, how viciously her hands shook. He hugged her but felt dishonest for not telling her he wouldn't be on the train. He stood as tall as he could and kissed her on the lips.

Mila smiled. Avsey knew she knew he had a crush on her, and he was grateful she hadn't reacted with disgust. Instead, she chastised him.

"Cheeky, boy. That will be quite enough." She kissed the top of his head.

Avsey watched Mila walk away. She couldn't know he had

no intention of evacuating. He would never leave Papa, and Avsey knew Papa wouldn't leave.

Nazim was in Papa's room when Avsey returned. They were arguing. "The cadets failed, Lev, and have retreated to the forest on Mount Mashuk. They haven't stopped anybody. You have to evacuate."

"I'll do no such thing." Papa's jaw was tight. He was restraining himself.

"Lev, you are of no use here. The cadets have one machine gun between them, a few anti-tank guns. Manpower won't help."

"After all these months of radon baths and mud, I should be strong enough to take them out on my own." Papa's tone was sarcastic. "Besides, I'm not going anywhere without my daughter, Nazim. Do you hear me? I won't leave her behind."

"Lev, I'll go for her, I promise, but listen to me now. You've *won* this one. You can walk. No one beats the odds forever, not even you."

Papa glared at Nazim, and Avsey sensed Nazim's desperation.

Nazim, usually so full of bravado, fired his last shot, "What about Avsey? We should have sent him out last week when the cattle were evacuated. Take him out, Lev, while you still can. Please."

Papa chewed on one side of his mouth while Avsey braced himself. Papa turned to him. "Nazim is right. You need to evacuate, stay with the nurses. I know, I promised, but things have changed. One of us needs to be reasonable." He waved his hand in the air, as if separation was nothing.

Avsey was indignant, surprised at the force of his own voice. "I am *not* going to be reasonable if you aren't!" he shouted. He'd done enough shrinking recently, and this was deeply unfair. "You said we'd stay together." He looked at his hands, the dirt under his fingernails.

He lowered his voice. "Besides, you need me to find Bronya.

Nazim doesn't know her, wouldn't know her if she walked in here and tapped him on the shoulder."

Nazim looked at his feet, but Papa stared at Avsey.

Avsey saw he'd opened a crack in Papa's resolve. He continued, "How's Nazim going to recognize her if she's there? Please, Papa."

Nazim and Papa were quiet. Papa sat silent on his bed, shoulders hunched over his knees while Nazim watched them both. In the end, it was Nazim who said, "I'll take him to my mother's house."

Avsey's anger dissolved. He walked to the bed and wrapped his arms around Papa. "We'll find her." He pressed his cheek against the rough bristles stretched over Papa's cheekbones.

Papa patted him on the back without looking at him.

Avsey whispered, "We always beat the odds, Papa. Don't worry."

Papa forced a smile, looking out of the window, eyes opaque. He squeezed Avsey's shoulders. "I'd rather worry. It's the only thing I can do."

A few days later, the Germans moved into Pyatigorsk along Kalinin Avenue while the cadets retreated across the river. The rumble of tanks was terrifying, but the battles continued as the cadets tried to dislodge the enemy from Mashuk, the highest point in town. Avsey wanted to join them, but he kept his promise to Papa to stay inside.

In the end, the cadets made their last stand on Svobody Avenue. Avsey heard the explosions, the screams. Later, he heard the fragmented stories, whispered among the terrified citizens about the cadets' fiery end. All anybody could do now was watch as the Germans made themselves at home.

AVSEY SLEPT BY THE STOVE IN YANINA DANIILOVNA'S COTTAGE, ON the cot Nazim had slept on as a boy, feeling unmoored and lonely. Nazim's mother reminded Avsey of a rodent. She preferred the corners to the middle of the room, keeping to the edges of her life, head down. But the old woman was the least of it.

Papa and Nazim had imposed a total ban on information. He would know nothing of where they spent their time or what they were doing. Avsey guessed they were organizing partisans just as they had last winter on the Donets, but why they didn't include him or need his help as they had before was a mystery.

He'd listened to their reasons. *You're too young. Occupation is different from the battlefield.* Hadn't he been too young before Papa was wounded? Hadn't they been in danger last spring?

He reminded Nazim in a low voice, so Papa wouldn't hear, "I stole papers from the Germans in enemy territory!"

Nazim pleaded with Avsey. "Please, there is nothing I can do. Your father..." His voice trailed off.

Avsey fumed. "It isn't fair. And you know it."

In the first few days, Avsey's unease with the old woman heightened his feeling of betrayal. Yanina Daniilovna was as blind as she was stubborn. She navigated life with an extended arm, tapping a cane in front of her to gauge the depth of a step or the consistency of the ground, to feel for obstacles, from cracks in the cement to holes in the garden soil.

She never spoke to him. She simply moved around the cottage as if he wasn't there, the only sounds the drag of her worn slippers and a kind of clucking she made with her throat. Avsey thought she did it for company, a substitute for human conversation.

To ease his boredom and help him feel a part of whatever action Papa and Nazim were fomenting, Avsey took to roaming through town in the early morning and late afternoon, when the heat was at its least oppressive. He watched the Germans from a distance, though on occasion, a soldier called him over, ruffled his hair, and offered him candy.

The Germans loved Avsey's red hair.

But he disliked these encounters. He found he wanted to

avoid their touch, their smiles, to stop the red-hot anger that rose in his throat when they were close to him. The rest of the time, he lounged in the yard at the back of the cottage, kicking rocks and playing solitaire at a small metal table under the date plums and figs. The depleted deck of cards he'd stolen from the hospital contained one king, two queens, and no aces.

When Nazim made his first visit to check on Avsey, Yanina Daniilovna cut figs and cucumbers and arranged them on a plate. She sat near her son at the metal table in the sun, attentive to the sound of his every movement.

Avsey whispered to Nazim, "Have I done something? She never says a word to me."

"She doesn't speak Russian very well. Never has. She prefers Tat. Be patient. She birthed me when she was older, past her time to bear children. She's an old woman."

Avsey was relieved but wondered why Nazim's mother spoke a strange language he'd never heard. He hesitated. "What's Tat?"

"The language spoken by Mountain Jews. She didn't learn Russian in school, the way you and I did. She learned enough to get by. When we came to Pyatigorsk, my father insisted on Russian. He didn't want the neighbors to know we were Jews. When he died, she stopped speaking it, stopped talking to anyone, except me."

Avsey understood but remained uneasy, resolved to stay out of the old woman's way. He was surprised then, when after Nazim's visit, she acknowledged him for the first time. She reached down and patted him on the head as she walked by. When he brought her a pillow for her feet the same evening, she patted him on the shoulder and the strange stalemate was broken.

They fell into a rhythm. She sliced and fried eggplant from her garden, leaving it for him on a small plate along with figs and date plums from the trees he sat under every day. Occasionally, she offered him a piece of honeycomb from a jar she kept in the corner or left him gifts on the kitchen table before she went out—small things like almonds, a coin or two, rarities.

For his part, Avsey ate whatever she prepared, and that pleased her. She held the empty plates in one hand while she ran her fingers over the top with the other, a satisfied smile creasing the lines around her empty eyes.

More touching for Avsey was her listening for him. Even before he opened the door at the end of an evening foray, she rose and shuffled over to light the samovar, feeling for the matches and the teapot with her spider fingers. As if she'd been waiting all day to do this one simple thing. He admired the way she made her way across the room, her cane in one hand, the glass of tea shaking against its tiny glass saucer in the other. Avsey loved the gentle tinkle of the glass. She never spilled a drop.

Nazim took to visiting in the dead of night when Yanina Daniilovna was already curled on her mat in the corner with the cotton coverlet over her head and shoulders, snoring loudly. Avsey was often asleep, too, but Nazim shook him gently, then sat at the edge of his old cot to talk. "Your Papa sends his love. Still too dangerous for him to come."

Why did Nazim need excuses for Papa's absence? "Why can you come and he can't?"

Nazim said the same thing he always said. "Just the way it is right now. Nothing to do with you."

Yanina Daniilovna turned in her sleep and sputtered. Avsey tilted his head in her direction and said, "She misses you."

"You remind her of me when I was little. And despite what you think, your father misses you, too."

They gossiped, Nazim always interested in the things Avsey heard or saw. About the man next door, for example, to whom Avsey had lied, claiming he was Yanina Daniilovna's grandson from Rostov, or about the woman in a white headcloth holding a basket of purple plums, who'd said, "Tell blind Yanina that

Zhelznovodsk and Mineralanye Vody have been cleansed of the Bolshevik vermin."

The woman had handed him a plum and smiled. Avsey told Nazim, "She only had one tooth, one tooth in her whole mouth."

"You're my eyes and ears, starik. To listen well is a valuable skill."

"The Germans are in Zheleznovodsk?"

Nazim nodded. "Yes."

"When are we going to find her?"

Nazim repeated the usual excuse, "The conditions need to be right. You know that. I'll let you know."

"I'm sick and tired of waiting. We have to hurry. I have a bad feeling."

CHAPTER 20
ZHELEZNOVODSK, AUGUST 1942

THE GERMANS ARRIVED AS LONG RIBBONS OF REFUGEES FORMED ON the roads east of Zheleznovodsk. Days later, the town appeared deserted. Bronya didn't know whether anyone had been able to escape or where they might have gone. She was no longer asked to go to the bread factory, and she didn't dare climb into the mountains, choosing instead to remain on the sanitorium grounds. Radomir gave her more to do in the garden, but even he was watchful.

In the first week of the German occupation, before they had settled into a routine, Zalima Ashamazovna beckoned Bronya to join her on the garden bench one morning before breakfast.

"Sit with me. It is better to speak here where only the birds can listen."

Bronya lowered onto the bench. "Are you sending me home?"

Zalima Ashamazovna's tone was gentle. "I have a plan—not the plan you want, but a plan to survive. You will trust me, no?"

Bronya studied Zalima Ashamazovna's formidable face, her high cheekbones, the prominent bump on her nose. Her eyebrows, overplucked, had been etched onto her broad fore- head with a chemical pencil. Bronya imagined her in front of a small mirror, carefully drawing the arch of each brow. Proud. Like Babushka.

She shrugged. "Maybe."

"Good girl. We will trust each other." Zalima Ashamazovna smiled. "It just so happens that my brother, a printer by trade, also has a passion for calligraphy. He's a real artist."

Bronya smiled politely. "I don't understand."

"Some days ago, several trucks arrived in my home village, several hours west of here. In it were half-starved children, evacuated from Leningrad, months ago, when the ice was still thick on Lake Lagoda. The drivers, on their way to Teberda, saw the Germans on the roads and stopped in the village to ask for shelter. Our women took the children into their homes and began to care for them. These children are Jews. Of course, there was a small panic. It is dangerous to care for Jews. The Germans shoot those who show compassion for your people."

"Will they make the children leave?" Bronya tried to disguise the tremor in her voice.

"Of course not." Zalima Ashamazovna took Bronya's hand. "My brother, the calligrapher, spent the night forging birth records for these children. Last night, he came to me for supplies and I told him about you."

"About me? Why?"

"You can go there, stay as a daughter of the village."

"Why can't I stay here? No one knows anything about me."

"Child, I'm afraid many would not want you here. Already the Germans are taking Jews off the streets, helped by those who support them, and know who is who. Already there are enough staff here who know your name. In my village, no one will betray you. You will be one of us."

"What happens to those they take from the street?"

Zalima Ashamazovna closed her eyes and shook her head. "My brother will come for you tonight. You are to stay in your room until you hear three quiet knocks on the door." She wiped the sweat from her broad brow with a handkerchief and put a hand on Bronya's shoulder. "Do we have an agreement?"

Bronya looked at her feet. She could refuse, could leave on her own, but something inside her wanted to trust this woman who had after all delivered on her promise to help. Bronya nodded. "We have an agreement."

Zalima Ashamazovna rose, patted Bronya on the shoulder again, and said, "Do not leave your room for any reason."

By nightfall, Bronya was already restless. She didn't try to sleep. She sat on the floor in the corner next to her bed, running her fingers over her violin, the urge to place her fingers on the strings—to take her bow—steadily persistent, like her desire to stay alive. The fact that the violin had belonged to Babushka had always made it special.

But now, Bronya took comfort in it, as if Babushka were there, whispering to her that everything would be all right. She traced the F-holes, the decorated scroll, the tiny mother-of-pearl Star of David on the neck of the instrument, at the back. Babushka had often rubbed her finger over it before she played, knowing where it was and that no one else could see it. Bronya often rubbed it as well, and Babushka was right. Knowing it was there calmed her nerves.

Zalima Ashamazovna took Bronya's knapsack with her dresses but left the violin, securing a promise from Bronya to slide it under the bed before she left. Bronya toyed with the idea of putting it under her skirt, but it occurred to her that Babushka wouldn't have wanted her to risk discovery because of her beloved instrument.

Zalima Ashamazovna was right. The violin was not only a hindrance, it put her in danger. She'd put the green pocketknife in her pocket instead, having decided long ago it was an omen for good. It would serve as a reminder of everything that was missing: the people she loved, music, possibility.

She placed the violin in its case and whispered, "Don't be mad at me. I don't have a choice. We will meet again."

All at once, Bronya heard a rush of boots and slamming doors, loud voices from the sanitorium kitchen. Was this Zalima Ashamazovna's brother? Had he brought friends? The heavy footsteps made their way toward her little room. She heard German, then Russian, then German again.

Hitlerites were walking on the tiled sanitorium floors. Had she been betrayed? Could they hear her breathing? The little room pulsed with the hammering inside her chest.

Zalima Ashamazovna's authoritative voice rang out above the fray. "We were a sanitorium, but we function now as a hospital for typhus patients. We keep the bodies in this room until they can be taken away under cover of darkness. The wagon will be here to collect yesterday's dead."

Bronya listened while she eased herself under the bed and curled around the violin case, her knees touching its handle, her nose against the smooth wood at the top. Zalima Ashamazovna did not claim to have spoken the truth.

For what seemed an eternity, she listened to the back and forth: German in demanding tones, German-accented Russian, and then Zalima Ashamazovna's explanations.

"Of course. You may enter, but I wouldn't advise it. We've had typhus here since January." When she finally heard the footsteps recede, Bronya crawled out long enough to peek under the door, to search for signs of movement, for light. Finding neither, she returned to her spot under the bed.

Another eternity passed. Dawn leaked into the little room, and as it did, Bronya gave up. No one was coming for her. She was on her own. Her back ached from lying on the floor in one position for so many hours. The quiet was deadening. Had the Germans taken everyone away? When she heard the three soft knocks on the door and heard the hinges creak open, she didn't believe her ears. It wasn't until she saw the men's muddy shoes from her place under the bed that she believed they had finally come for her.

One of the men whispered her name. Bronya opened the violin case, lifted the violin, and quickly rubbed the star one last time. "Wish me luck, Babushka." She closed the case and slid out from under the bed, headfirst.

Two men stood in front of her holding a stretcher between them. They nodded to Bronya but did not speak.

Zalima Ashamazovna's brother had her dark eyes and commanding posture but nothing of her haughtiness. He was tall, almost regal, his hair flecked with gray. A string of amber beads attached to his belt moved as he walked. Most striking of all were his hands—long slender fingers, parchment paper skin, manicured nails, the nail on the index finger longer than the others. He wore a fez and a dark jacket despite the heat. As he winked, Bronya thought him the loveliest man she'd seen in a long time. She trusted him immediately.

The other man was small and stocky, much older than his friend. Dark sweat stains under his arms had spread down his sides, all the way into his belt. He had a pronounced limp, but his shoulders and arms were broad and muscular. His head was bare. He put an index finger to his lips, beckoning Bronya to lie on the stretcher with a nod of his head, then covered her with a coarse linen sheet that smelled of hay and mold.

Bronya caught her breath as she was jerked up and spirited down the hall and past the kitchen, her feet higher than her head. Outside, sunlight filtered through the linen fibers of the sheet, warming her body.

One of the men groaned as they slid the stretcher into the wagon. "Stay still," they whispered in unison.

The horse moved slowly past the sanitorium gates, then faster when they reached the paved road out of Zheleznovodsk, toward the truck waiting to take Bronya to Zalima Ashamazovna's village.

Bronya sat between the two men, dozing, listening to their strange language, their soft assents, one to the other, back and forth. Once, they saw a truck on the road ahead and Bronya curled into a ball on the floor before it reached them, but they crossed the Kuban and arrived in the village before dusk without incident.

She was settled into a whitewashed cottage within minutes, sitting on the floor in front of a small, three-legged table, eating warm bread and apricots.

Someone in the room said, "Hunger is the best spice." The room, full of women, erupted in quiet laughter.

She was the oldest of the adopted children. "Old enough to be a bride," said Gulya, her new sister, who was still a few months shy of sixteen, the marriageable age. Since Bronya had arrived with nothing of her own, Gulya gave her a white dress and a cotton scarf to tie around her hair.

It was Gulya who chose Bronya's new name. "I'll call you Zhana. It means princess." Gulya was small, dark-eyed, and round. She held Bronya's hand right away. "Best friends," she said.

Bronya repeated her new name over and over to make the foreign syllables sound natural in her mouth. "*Zhana Datova Dzharimova.*"

Those orphans who were old enough to talk repeated their new names and played quiet games, calling to one another. The babies listened from the laps of their new mothers, listless. All the children were thin. One little boy, who must have been around four, did not speak at all and sat alone in a corner, uninterested in the activity around him. After a few days, the children were separated and not allowed to play together again. A precautionary measure.

It did not take the Germans long to make their presence known. They arrived late in the night, their vehicle headlamps flooding the village with light. Bronya listened to the commotion caused by rousing families from their beds, the women screaming, children crying. She pulled the coverlet over her head and considered climbing out of the window. But Gulya pulled her into the living room, where they stood watching from the open door as headlights illuminated the soldiers walking through the village.

The village held its breath.

The Germans stayed all night, overturning furniture, and inspecting the identity of mothers holding tightly to their children. Door to door, house to house. One soldier took Bronya's chin in his hands and turned her head to examine her profile. He smiled while his hand tilted her face toward his. Gulya hid behind her mother's back, holding one of the babies. Gulya's mother, a naturally quiet woman, shot daggers at the soldiers with her eyes.

In the late morning, the villagers, bleary-eyed with exhaustion and fear, watched the Germans stroll through the village again, overturning flower pots, searching sheep pens and chicken coops. They appeared jumpy and smelled of stale drink.

As they entered her house for the third time, Bronya blinked in disbelief. The soldier who had held her face in his hands now held a violin, its scroll exactly like hers. Was it possible? Was this her violin?

If it was, it would mean the Germans had returned to the sanitorium. Had they hurt Zalima Ashamazovna? Did they know something?

The soldier passed close to her. He spun the violin over and over in his hands, like a top. Bronya saw a flash of ivory inlay on the violin's neck. *Babushka's star.*

Her eyes widened before she composed herself and prayed the German hadn't noticed. He sauntered around the room, returning to stand next to her after each circle of the cottage perimeter.

When he'd circled three or four times, he stopped beside Bronya and smiled unsteadily. She wanted to turn her face away, but an unexpected surge of anger electrified her, made her face and fingers itch. Beads of sweat broke out on her forehead. If she moved, he'd know.

The soldier looked down at the violin, then thrust it toward her, looking away awkwardly, a shy adolescent rather than a soldier. Bronya shook her head. She noticed the steel blue of his eyes, the blackheads on his nose. His smile disappeared. Was it because she had refused the violin? She thought he might grab her hair and drag her out onto the street.

She continued to meet his gaze and remembered something Zalima Ashamazovna said at their last meeting: *Where there is no decency, there is no fortune.* If only this were true.

A thick scream penetrated the house from outside. Everyone flinched. No one dared move. Only the soldier remained as he had been. He lingered, staring at Bronya while Gulya and her family trembled on the other side of the room. He plucked the violin's strings and turned the instrument over to examine its back panel, holding it expertly between both his hands. He ran his thumb over the grain in the wood and held the violin up to the light, taking his time. A half-smile lingered on his lips as he plucked the strings again, holding the instrument close to his ear.

Bronya understood. This German knew the violin's worth. He'd found a treasure. He peered inside the F-holes, tilting the violin to see what might be written inside. *He's a musician.* The thought enraged her.

Just when she thought she couldn't hold back any more, the soldier tucked the instrument under his arm and swung from the room.

Gulya rushed to the window, and Bronya followed her in time to see soldiers converging across the road at the corner, two houses away. They congregated in the yard of one of the white-washed houses, upsetting the hens, turning over a pail and a long-handled rake.

Soon after, gunshots reverberated from behind the little house, rolling over the village like an avalanche. The women looked around the room, eyes wide, but no one dared move, except Gulya, who, still holding one of the babies, trembled so violently that Bronya had to lean into her to keep her upright. When the Germans climbed into their trucks and roared off in clouds of dust, Gulya, Bronya alongside her, ran to the yard. The baby she was holding had started to scream. No one consoled him.

The villagers gathered at the far end of the street behind a ramshackle henhouse. The hens, skittish, circled nervously around the body of an excruciatingly small boy in the dirt, black blood pooled under his head, his little hand wrapped gently around an unbroken egg. The village wept.

Bronya, in the midst of people she didn't know, let the sorrow settle around her, felt she could hear it course through the veins of the villagers, a sympathetic resonance vibrating on a single note.

In those hours before the little boy was buried, Bronya watched grief blanket every particle of the village, like a fog embedding itself in the soft tissue of the women, in the exhale of their babies, in the metameric folds of centipedes and earthworms, seeping into the soil that would cradle his little body.

After the burial, grief became the forward motion of life. The villagers went about their chores, shoulders hunched, gaits labored. Bronya was mired in anguish. Sometimes she had difficulty breathing for no reason and was forced to sit to collect herself, the sweat collecting around her hairline. How was it that this small child deserved death?

CHAPTER 21
ROSTOV-ON-DON, TUESDAY, AUGUST
11, 1942

FROM THE BALCONY WINDOW, SARA WATCHED AS THE PARADE OF old men, women, and children, fat with layers of clothing, moved down Turgenevskaya Street in the habitual heat of a summer morning. They were on their way to one of six registration points in the city, the closest on Stanislavskogo Street, on their way to resettlement. The women carried suitcases in one hand, small children in the other, bedding on their backs, food parcels wound with string, and baskets of produce harvested from their shared garden plots.

An old man pushed a wheelbarrow full of books. They'd all been reassured by Dr. Lourie, head of the Council of Elders, that they would be resettled for their own protection, exactly as the Germans had outlined in the posters they had affixed at various points around the city. His appeal to the community to register, printed five days earlier in the Voice of Rostov, had caused controversy. Yet here they all were, doing as they were told and walking to the registration point.

Sara didn't believe anything Dr. Lourie said. She'd told Asya, "We'll stay until dark and then leave." She had no inkling of what resettlement meant, but she suspected it was a German ruse, a euphemism for something worse. Still, she had no idea where they might go, where they might hide. She needed more time.

But when, from the balcony window, Sara spied Kuzma in the crowd—his lip bloody, his grandmother, Agrippina, nowhere in sight—she knew immediately everything had changed. She knew the plan she hadn't formulated would never come, though in the moment, she pushed the crushing despair away and resolved to find a way out.

She watched Kuzma follow the crowd, as if in a daze, staring into the distance. In an uptick of unease, she wondered how he'd come so far into town. Was he lost? Was it a coincidence that on the day they were meant to leave the city, Kuzma appeared alone? He carried nothing in his hands except a small stick he tapped nervously against his leg or ran along the wall as he walked.

"Asya!" Sara lowered her voice. The neighbors needn't hear her panic. Her next exhortation was a whisper, her voice hoarse. "Come to the window."

In the silence that followed, Sara caught a whiff of Asya's scent and felt the air move over her shoulders. She turned toward the door. Particles of dust swirled up the stairwell, catching the sunlight like fairy dust. Asya was gone.

Alarmed, Sara pocketed the apartment keys she'd prepared, on a wire, labeled with Asya's name and address as the occupant of Turgenevskaya Street No. 27. She'd followed the instructions for leaving the apartment, written the address out on a thick piece of paper, pierced it with the wire, and looped the wire to attach the key. She'd locked the dishes away, swept the floors, and folded the blankets, stacking them neatly on the beds. Methodical, measured, all the while searching for an escape from resettlement, some way to trick the would-be captors and thieves. Far more important for now was the need to find Asya, who, searching for Kuzma in her housedress, would attract male attention—easy prey on a street teeming with soldiers.

Singularly focused, Sara pocketed their documents, locked

the door, and walked down the stairs, the bile of pure terror rising in her throat. Outside, she tried to push her way through the slow-moving parade. Kuzma had disappeared, and the street was more chaotic than it had appeared from the balcony. There were piles of rubble, remnants of shattered buildings, abandoned bicycles, upended families, and children chasing one another, changing directions while parents doubled back. Old men, stymied by the beauty of the early morning and the unknown, fingered small coins in their pockets.

Sara stopped to help an elderly man navigate the side of a shattered apartment building, a minefield of crumbled cement and broken fences.

Memory harnessed her to these people and these places. She heard one young mother whisper to another, "This is where I had my first kiss, under that tree there, on the way home from school. Remember Natan?"

Sara thought she saw the top of Kuzma's head and pushed past a woman admonishing a small girl to keep her shoes clean. "The last pair I'll buy you."

Kuzma floated, as if lifted by the crowd. Sara followed, anxious not to lose sight of him. Where Kuzma went, Asya would go, though there was no sign of her yet. Kuzma submerged into the crowd, and Sara followed, turning left on Gazetny Lane. He appeared a block later, standing next to a group of younger boys, their eyes directed upward, toward the open windows of Doctor Goldshteyn's third-floor apartment.

Someone in the crowd said, "What's that boy doing up there?" Sara edged closer to Kuzma until she was standing so close, she could touch him. She had no idea what to say, wasn't sure he'd remember her from Proletarsky all those months ago or if he would mistake her for Asya. He was transfixed by the scene above him.

"That's Timofei, from school," said one of the boys on the ground, pointing up.

The boy in the apartment was at the forefront of an effort to haul a large desk up and out of the window. At last, it teetered over the windowsill. The crowd watched it fall and splinter, sending shards and loud cracks through the air. The boys below flinched visibly and looked away. They slipped the wire key chains from their wrists into their pockets.

One of the boys said, "I'm not sure I locked our door. I should go back."

"It doesn't matter," said another, "the locks won't hold."

Sara wasn't shocked by Timofei. The Germans had simply sanctioned the hatred that had simmered beneath the surface for ages. The neighborly bloodlust had always been at hand, quietly shocking, no matter how many times they'd been reminded of it.

In the upheaval, it must have appeared to some as if the Germans were protecting the Jews, doing them a favor.

Kuzma followed the boys, who had quickened their pace and were moving resolutely down the street. The parade slowed again at 28 Gazetny Lane on the corner of Stanislovskogo. Some in the crowd averted their eyes, but some, mostly older men, stopped and stood still. Nothing remained of the Artisan's synagogue except curling wisps of smoke and dust the color of eggshells and lapis.

Through the haze, Sara saw Asya in her flowered housedress and felt a twinge of tenderness she hadn't felt for a long time. Asya was further down the street, her eyes fixed on Kuzma, her hair gathered at the nape of her neck. Sara had always known that once Asya found him, she would never leave her son again. It didn't matter if the years of her absence had been filled by his grandmother. He was hers forever now.

Sara joined Asya without reproach, and together they walked to the registration point at 188 Stanislavskogo in silence, Kuzma in front of them. At one point, Sara tried to turn back, to pull her sister away, but Asya resisted with surprising agility.

She glared at Sara. "You can't take him from me again."

Sara understood. Asya, bewitched by the sudden fullness where for years there had been only sorrow, blamed her, and she was right. Sara had stood on Agrippina Artyomova's porch all those years ago and waited while Asya wept. She had been cruel. And cruelty always had a reckoning. Sara followed Asya, who trailed Kuzma, all the while looking for a way out, until all thoughts of a quick escape quietly drifted away.

The crowd, funneled from the registration points, thinned, and in orderly fashion stepped up into waiting trucks. A soldier tried to push Asya into the back of a windowless van, its motor idling, while others led Kuzma away toward a large truck. Sara stood in the queue, a soldier blocking her path.

When Asya broke free to join Kuzma, Sara, eyeing the gray uniform, cursed under her breath, sure she'd be shot if she followed. As luck would have it, the soldier was distracted by an argument further down the line, and Sara soon found herself unharmed in the back of the open truck next to Asya, across from Kuzma, as they wound their way out of the center of town. The convoy of trucks ahead resembled a metal snake slithering in the dirt, the sun hot on its steely back.

One old man in the truck wept openly, saying, "Masha, Masha," over and over again. The other men inched away from him, but Kuzma reached out to touch the man, his eyes full of sorrow. Sara saw innocence in Kuzma's kindness, an oblivion to his own peril. The blood on his lip had dried, but the skin around it was swollen purple. The man swatted Kuzma's hand away.

Asya, watching this, leaned forward to caress Kuzma's shoulder. He looked at her without smiling, yet moved closer to her, receiving her caresses as if they'd always been there. Sara, confused by the intimacy the gestures implied, wondered if Kuzma might remember his mother after all. But then, nothing was as it should have been.

When the trucks stopped at the ravine, Sara was surprised. *Resettled here?* Near the ravine where they'd been afraid to play as children because of the vipers known to lurk in the crags and grasses? Nothing about this ravine made sense. She remembered her mistrust of Doctor Lourie, cursed herself for forgetting it and cursed him for his betrayal. Still, she only half-believed the situation she was actually in until she became aware of loud voices shouting orders in German and Russian.

She lifted Asya over the side of the truck and jumped down after her. Asya walked at some distance behind Kuzma, calling his name. She tripped in her eagerness to catch up with him, and Sara took her arm and pulled her up. By then, the old men, Kuzma among them, were herded away from the truck and randomly struck with rifle butts, sending some to the ground before they were made to stand again.

Sara saw the rifle butt raised for Kuzma and shoved Asya behind her, shielding her from the vision of violence against her child. Asya protested loudly. Sara pleaded, "Please, Asya, you'll see him soon." She dragged her sister up the rise of a little hill, out of sight.

The first thing she noticed in the landscape was the large pile of clothing—gaily patterned dresses sprinkled with the same light-colored sandals all women wore in the summer. And stockings, a large pile of stockings.

Sara blinked several times to bring the scene into focus, to take in what was happening. The nude women appeared as if in a painting, posed for pleasure, or as Eve, misrepresented in the garden.

A volley of gunfire brought her back to her senses. Several men in police uniforms were staggering, grinning. They held pistols and bottles. Oddly, there were no screams as the women walked, naked, down the other side of the rise. Another volley of gunfire.

Asya was beginning to panic and struggled to break free. "Where is he?"

Sara, holding her sister by the arm, was surprised by her own strength, the grip she had on Asya's skin. They would stay together at all costs.

Her voice was steady. "Let's not be afraid. Remember when

we used to say that to one another?" She took the wire key chain from her pocket and flung it as hard as she could away from the ravine. Could they run away into the woods?

Sara undressed quickly, maintaining a strong hold on Asya, switching hands as needed to pull first one sleeve off, then the other, finally throwing the dress into the pile. Asya calmed at the sight of Sara's nakedness. "That's good, Asya, stay with me and let's not be afraid."

Asya nodded, but as Sara helped her lift the housedress over her head, a thick handful of her hair caught on a button and she began to scream. Sara soothed her sister, aware of the way the other women linked their naked torsos to walk further up the rise.

"You're fine, my dove, you're just perfect." She held the dress up, gently pulled the hair away from the button. and straightened to stand face-to-face with her mirror image.

Sara touched the large brown birthmark on Asya's right thigh, near her hip bone, and ran her finger over her own birthmark on the left thigh. She did the same for the birthmarks on their foreheads, both now faded. As children, they'd played games, one the mirror to the other, anticipating movement to keep the game alive. They'd marveled at the reflective nature of their features, the teeth that appeared and disappeared on opposite sides of each of their mouths at exactly the same time, one slightly bigger eye staring into its opposite likeness.

The only physical distinction between them, inflicted at the age of four, was a raised scar on Sara's forearm where she'd fallen from a tree and broken the bone cleanly in two. It had been Asya who'd held her sister's arm up for their mother to inspect, the injury somehow hers, bawling with the pain.

Sara hadn't been aware of her limb at the time. She'd thought Asya's arm was broken and watched as if from a great distance as the doctor took her into the exam room, separating them. She remembered the bewilderment that such a thing could happen to one of them and not the other. Until Asya's voices congregated and spoke only to her, the scar was the only difference in their beings, the remainder of their division.

They moved into the line of women on the hill and walked together down the other side of the rise, closer to the ravine. Some of the women cried softly. Sara focused. She leaned in close to her twin's ear. "I'm sorry I made you give him up. I know you loved him."

Asya looked up, mouth open, her gaze distracted briefly by the noise from both sides of the little hill. "Where is he?"

Sara turned to stand in front of Asya, face-to-face, insisting on her attention. She wasn't sure, but somehow time was short. "Sergei divided us, pillaged me. But forgive me. It was your right to choose, not mine."

Asya flinched again and smiled sadly. Taking Sara's hand, she kissed its fingertips. "I thought you'd never come."

Sara reached to smooth Asya's hair. Who did her sister think she was? They walked a few more steps. Sara stared at the edge of the ravine and wondered how she ever thought they could run. She whispered as she squeezed Asya's hand, "Let's not be afraid."

They walked to the edge and took the last steps in unison. When they fell, they fell together, at the same instant, on the same intake of breath, intertwined over the ravine of snakes they'd feared as children.

CHAPTER 22
PYATIGORSK, AUGUST 1942

THE GERMANS MADE THEIR PRESENCE KNOWN IN EVERY FACET OF life in Pyatigorsk, occupying the nicest apartments and plastering imposing announcements on all the public buildings. These were instructive, the rules of a new regime. Only Germans could go to the Yermolov mud baths or take the mineral water cures, for example. Every poster featured the phrases: *No Jews allowed. No Bread for Jews.*

Avsey remembered the young woman he'd overheard in the basement in Rostov and worried. But maybe these Germans were like the boys in school who made him ashamed when they spat on him. He'd always ignored them, and that was what he would do now. These Germans didn't know him. And anyway, the mean boys at school were not as good as Avsey in arithmetic or poetry or chess. Maybe the Germans were not as strong as they believed.

They were, however, hard to ignore. They were *everywhere*. On the roads around Pyatigorsk, the German infantry made themselves comfortable. They slept in open Kübelwagens and rose in the early mornings to shave in front of small mirrors they hung from slim branches in the trees. They feasted on fruit and cigarettes, the side cars of their motorcycles heaped to the top with striped watermelons, plums, and cucumbers. In the evenings, officers strolled through Tsvetnik Park, gleaming from head to toe, chatting with female companions.

Avsey recounted all this to Nazim, who said, "Bloodsuckers. That's all they are, bloodsuckers."

Avsey knew the bits of information he left out of his conversations with Nazim were equally important, but he couldn't bring himself to talk about them. He was sure Nazim already knew the occupation's gruesome details, but Avsey didn't want Nazim and Papa to know he knew them, too. Nazim would tell Papa, and they would send him away. So Avsey didn't mention he'd seen bodies near the hospital twice in the first week. At dawn.

The first time, he hadn't exactly turned away, but he hadn't let his eyes focus too long on the details: a hand, a shock of fair hair, flies. Vultures, the tips of their wings like feathered fingers, soared overhead. By evening, he thought he should look again and mark the spot in some way. The bodies were gone. He'd known they would be. The Germans were too fastidious to leave them, but he was unprepared for the lack of evidence, the pristine nature of the anonymous deaths.

He searched the dust for signs of struggle, for the imprint of the bodies he'd seen, for stray buttons, coins, blood. He doubted his memory, his sanity. Maybe he'd been mistaken. Maybe, unbidden, his nightmares had returned.

When it happened a second time, he didn't question his sanity. He let the images of pale skin, an elbow at an unnatural angle, settle and fester, struggling to hold reality at arm's length. His anxiety about Bronya worsened until it felt like a blister under his skin, pushing up, threatening to burst over him.

Though Avsey wasn't privy to the details of the work Papa and Nazim were doing, he knew that to sabotage the Germans, they had to move around Pyatigorsk in the daylight hours. He looked for them, on the streets, at the park, in narrow alleyways, always aware of his surroundings. Occasionally, he thought he glimpsed Papa.

His eye caught a stranger who either walked with a limp or tilted his head to the left, causing his heart to lurch. He was alert to the sound of a familiar laugh, a cough. Much to his disappointment though, no one was ever Papa.

Sometimes, when he'd spent the day searching, Avsey conjured the piles of the early morning dead in front of the hospital and imagined Papa among them. He didn't want these thoughts, but they appeared anyway, drawing support from his imagination without his approval.

Nazim appeared earlier than usual one evening as the moon rose before Avsey had settled into his evening routine of tea and solitaire. Nazim kissed his mother and said, "You ready, starik? We're going to Zheleznovodsk tonight, to look for your sister. The hike over Beshtau isn't difficult, but it will require a certain amount of stealth."

Avsey jumped up and hugged Nazim. All the loneliness emptied out of him at the possibility of finding Bronya. Stealth was his specialty.

Outside, Nazim took a piece of charcoal from his pocket and rubbed it on Avsey's face. "Camouflage, just in case we meet the enemy in the dark." Nazim winked, but Avsey knew he was serious. The Germans were nothing to joke about. Ever.

Nazim applied the charcoal to his own face while he explained how they would get to Zheleznovodsk, "We'll need three and a half hours if we keep a steady pace. But then we have to come back. Long night ahead."

Avsey wasn't worried about climbing Beshtau, especially because Nazim knew the terrain. He'd grown up in the mountains. The only thing he worried about was finding his sister. What would he do if she wasn't in Zheleznovodsk? Why did it feel as if his heart lived in his stomach?

To distract himself, he asked Nazim questions. "Have you climbed Elbrus, Nazim?"

"Of course. Only up the south side."

"Do you think the Germans are on Elbrus yet?

"They're there. They can't resist mountains." Nazim shook his head. "Hubris always brings bad luck. The mountains don't like it."

The climb up Beshtau wasn't easy. At the start, Avsey walked behind Nazim on a wide trail and wasn't even out of breath. But the terrain soon changed. The trail meandered and became steep and finally disappeared altogether. Their feet slipped on the loose rocks. Occasionally, Avsey was forced to use his hands to climb. Despite the moonlight, he couldn't distinguish roots from rocks or which parts of the terrain he could use to climb and which would fall away at his touch.

Nazim instructed him, "Don't pull yourself up. Use your legs, try to lift your feet a little higher. It isn't difficult if you sense the mountain, fall into its rhythm."

Avsey had realized months ago that "difficult" was a relative term and the only thing to do was to keep going, no matter what. He tried. He lifted his feet, but he had no idea what it meant to feel the mountain. He lost his balance and slid with a frustrated yelp. Before Nazim could help him up, they heard voices from below. German voices.

Avsey lay on his back in the spot where he'd fallen. Nazim crouched close by, the whites of his eyes barely visible, his hand over his mouth. Pinpoints of light swept the hillside. How had they passed these soldiers without being seen? Or had the Germans known they were there?

Loud laughter drifted over the rocks. Could the soldiers hear the rocks sliding down the hillside? He fought the urge to cough, sliding his tongue across his lips and swallowing hard. The voices receded and the pinpointed lights grew dim and finally extinguished, relinquishing the moonlight.

When the silence was complete, Nazim stood and offered a hand to Avsey in the dirt. "Keep up. We haven't got all night." Avsey did not fall again.

They found the sanitorium easily. It was situated close to the base of the mountain, the building recognizable by its size and grandeur. Even in the dark, Avsey marveled at the ornamented onion domes topped with slender spires. They walked cautiously up the front steps and into the courtyard, vigilant, looking for light, listening. The grounds were quiet except for cicadas and the occasional howl in the distance. Avsey wondered if there were wolves on Beshtau. He decided not to ask Nazim. He didn't want to know.

They walked through a series of small courtyards, all dark. The sanitorium buildings appeared deserted. At the window of a large, important wing, Nazim made a sling with his hands and gave Avsey a boost to take a look. Nothing but stillness. They crept past therapy rooms and a dormitory, around a corner, alongside the kitchen gardens where trellises supported over-grown vines. They looked in all the windows but found nothing. Nazim shook his head and shrugged his shoulders, puzzled.

Avsey decided the place was deserted, and fighting the ache he felt for his sister, strayed, walking in circles.

Nazim pulled him away from the gravel pathway more than once. "Too noisy," he scolded in a whisper.

Avsey pointed to the dark windows, frustrated. Wasn't it clear there was no one here?

Then all at once, as if on cue, they stumbled upon a section of building past the gardens where there were lights and voices emanating from a row of low windows open to the night air.

Nazim and Avsey surveyed the scene: An old man, a woman wearing an apron over her flowered dress, and a German officer, his dark tunic unbuttoned at the neck, sat at one end of a long oak table just under the window. The little company was close to the open windows, and as they approached, Avsey thought he could hear their breathing, the woman's phlegmy throat, the German's slight lisp in broken Russian.

They crouched beneath the window to listen, but Avsey

couldn't help himself. He straightened to look inside, keeping his eyes in line with the windowsill.

The woman was animated. "The Bolsheviks are finished. Thank God." She walked to the stove facing the far wall, and her voice became muffled, her words unintelligible. When she turned back toward the table, Avsey heard her say, "At your service, commander."

The old man spoke, but he, too, turned away from the window. Still, his last few words were clear. "You're the director now, Maria?"

The woman ignored him and addressed the German. "More tea?"

Nazim touched Avsey's knee and nodded toward the mountain. He wanted to leave.

Avsey heard the old man say in a loud, shaky voice, "And what's happened to the director?"

Nazim tapped Avsey's knee again, trying to get his attention, but the old man's voice had a plaintive quality to it. Avsey couldn't look away.

The old woman moved closer to the window, her voice a little louder. "She got what she deserved, Radomir. She helped them. That violin girl, she was a Jew, and suddenly she just disappeared? Where'd she scamper off to then? I knew I didn't want her in my garden. I would have used my machete, given half a chance."

Avsey pinched himself. Did he hear right? A violin girl who disappeared? Bronya? He pushed his head up a little further, a wave of stale terror passing through him.

The old man called Radomir was staring at his lap. Even from a distance, he looked unsettled. The man wiped his face with his big hand, hard, as if trying to erase himself.

In the next instant, Avsey felt Nazim pull on his arm, a signal for him to crouch down. Avsey knew he was taking a risk but couldn't tear himself from the old man's face, convinced he knew something more about Bronya.

Nazim tugged again, more insistent. Avsey wrestled his arm away, lost his balance, and landed with a thud in the dirt. The little group inside stopped talking. Avsey didn't move. He pressed his body into the earth and held his breath. He listened to the sound of footsteps approach the window.

Nazim stood and pressed his body flush against the wall. From the other side of the glass, the old woman said, "I better check the hens. Something's out there."

Nazim pointed toward a passageway to the right of the windows, at the back of the building, and signaled Avsey to follow him. Avsey crawled on all fours until he was past the window, and then they both ran, through the passageway and into the trees behind the sanitorium.

When they stopped to catch their breath, leaning against the trunk of a wide oak, Avsey said, "They were talking about my sister, Nazim."

Before Nazim could say anything, the hum of engines sounded in the courtyard. Headlights flooded the sanitorium.

Avsey scampered after Nazim, further into the trees at the foot of the mountain. They waited in silence until the lights flickered off and then waited more just to be sure no one was headed their way.

Some time passed without further commotion, and Avsey whispered, "I'm going back."

"No, you are not, Avsey. It's over. We mined that conversation for all it was worth."

Avsey stood up, determined, and started back toward the sanitorium, toward the kitchens. Maybe they were talking about Bronya even now.

Nazim grabbed his arm, but Avsey broke free. "Don't do it."

Nazim's voice was a warning, but Avsey ignored him and continued walking.

It was then that Nazim tackled him and pinned him to the ground. "You have your father's stubborn streak, his arrogance."

Avsey winced as Nazim pulled his arm behind his back.

"This is bigger than you or your sister. If they catch you, it'll all be over. Besides, she isn't there." Nazim pulled Avsey's arm up so that the pain radiated through his shoulder and down the middle of his back.

Avsey felt Nazim's breath on his neck and turned to look at him from the corner of his eye. Nazim's face was contorted, his teeth clenched. Who was this man?

The confrontation didn't last more than a minute. Nazim dropped Avsey's arm and stood up. Avsey pushed himself up to his knees and brushed the dirt from his trousers. "You didn't need to hurt me, Nazim."

"Yes, I did. I'll do it again if you can't follow orders." Avsey's arm ached. He couldn't look at Nazim.

They took the path further up the mountain, climbing for some time in silence.

Avsey hung his head and watched his feet. He couldn't rid himself of the image of the old man's discomfort, his gesture of distress. This man had seen his sister recently. He was sure.

Nazim tried to approach Avsey several times, but Avsey walked away, climbing faster than he had on the way there. "Look, I understand. You want to find your sister. Me too. But we've got to calculate our risks. I'm sorry if I hurt you, starik."

Avsey muttered under his breath, "I'd risk everything for my sister."

If he heard, Nazim didn't let on.

Halfway up the trail, Nazim changed direction and took a smaller path toward the summit. "Sky's clear. Let's check if the Germans are on Elbrus."

Avsey stopped. "We could actually see them from here?"

"'Course not. I just wanted your attention."

"You got my attention, Nazim." Avsey's tone was resentful.

Nazim softened, then stopped. "We'll find her. She got away. That's a good thing."

"How do you know? You didn't want to stay to listen."

The muscles in Nazim's neck and jaw tightened visibly, but he said nothing.

They climbed without speaking, stopping periodically to listen, wary of any movement in the forest. At the summit, Avsey heaved a sigh of relief and tilted his head. Elbrus rose up from the earth in front of them, its twin peaks opaque against the night, spewing stars—an open mouth speaking firmaments into the universe. The sight was dazzling.

Avsey could make out the base of the mountain by the veins of snow and ice etched halfway down its sides, the heft of its presence otherwise indiscernible, a giant asleep on its side. He stood, mesmerized as light gathered at the rim of the earth, then spread like butter over the mountains until he could see the giant's broad muscularity rippling in the dawn. He watched the peaks absorb the light, take on dimension, and ever so gradually articulate into cold, craggy masses of rock, majestic against an increasingly pale blue sky.

Avsey whispered, "What's it like, up there, Nazim?"

"Cold, breathtakingly beautiful. It's not a mountain; it's a volcanic tribute to the gods." Nazim sat on a smooth rock and leaned his chest into his knees. "You see the two peaks? They're like the five peaks of Beshtau, remnants of ancient lava craters. When I was your age, the local climbers used to say they could hear Prometheus moan at a certain point, midway up the mountain." He picked up a twig and put one end in his mouth. "You know about Prometheus?"

Avsey knew all about Prometheus. "He stole fire from Zeus and gave it to mankind. Zeus punished him by chaining him to Mount Elbrus. He sent an eagle to peck at his liver every night. Until Heracles set him free."

Nazim shifted slightly closer to Avsey, holding the twig between his fingers like a cigarette. He placed his arm around Avsey's shoulder. He sighed. "Where is Heracles when we need him, eh?"

Avsey shrugged Nazim's arm away. "We *are* Heracles. We have to free ourselves."

Nazim looked down at Avsey but didn't say anything. The silence and the stars settled into one another for a few minutes until Nazim stood and started toward the descent. He said, "We have to get back."

Avsey thought he heard a catch in Nazim's voice.

Before they reached the tree line on the way down, before he lost sight of Elbrus, Avsey turned for one last glimpse. He whispered, "Where could she be, Nazim? Is she alive? What if everyone dies except me and I'm here all alone?"

Nazim stopped. He bent over and took Avsey's face in his hands. "You aren't going to be here all alone. Someone helped her, someone who paid a price. Prometheus is out there, giving light. We'll keep looking. I promise."

Avsey wrapped an arm around Nazim's waist and leaned into him. His other arm still hurt.

CHAPTER 23
PROLETARSKY, AUGUST 1942

Sara woke and remembered the fall, the horizon's thin orange line, the air full of blast and smoke, the tilted pause. The alarming absence of light. She remembered snakes, a swollen lip, a blue-green flowered dress, Asya's hip, her scar, their sisters' pact. Lyosha dancing on the beach, years ago, when they first met. The green iron gates of a house on Engles Street, shards of wood, empty walkways littered with plums and sweaters and confetti identity papers.

She remembered the parade through the streets of Rostov, the children holding keys tagged with their addresses, wearing coats in the summer heat, one red shoe jettisoned as the crowd of onlookers cheered, a wheelbarrow.

Slowly, Sara noted the absence of air on her skin and began to move her limbs—a shoulder, a slow reach of her forearm through the gaps, the opposite foot struggling to push through a tangled mass. A liquid weight pressing down, surrounding her on every side. She clasped a lifeless hand and recoiled.

A cascade of memories washed over her: screams, sobbing, a man begging to die. More and more terrified, gasping for air, she moved the dead away, the panic turning and tossing her upward. Her muscles burned. She pushed, kicked harder. One hand broke free, then her face, her mouth wide, gulping oxygen and moonlight. She cleared the dirt from her eyes with the tips of her fingers and opened them. The sky tasted of iron and burnt leaves. Her heart pounded on the doors of her rib cage, lying to her, telling her she wanted to live.

Struggling to stand, Sara noticed the soil beneath her feet glowed white in the dark. *Quicklime.* She'd seen it before, knew to avoid it, but it was everywhere. Her arms wavered, balancing the bulk of her body while she listened for other voices, begging not to be alone. Teetering precariously on the mound of human flesh, Sara walked as lightly as she could, toward the ravine's edge. The darkest place on earth. Up against the wall of soil higher than her head, she hesitated. Why not stay here? What was left?

Even as she executed her escape, clawed her way up the earth, she didn't know why. Out of the pit, at the edge, she retched and dry heaved but did not turn away. She waited for other tremors, for movement in the dark beneath her. Adam and Eve appeared in her thoughts, along with the tree of knowledge. She thought of the couple covering their nakedness, remembered Cain's murderous nature, the earth soaked with Abel's blood.

The movement she longed for, when it came, did not come from the pit. On the field, a figure, fully limbed and upright, walked toward her in the dark. Sara flattened into a spread-eagle prayer, the earth clasped against her chest, cursing Cain under her breath while she waited for the click of the pistol. When, after a few seconds, the click did not come, she opened her eyes and turned her head ever so slightly to the right.

A man, bent at the waist, studied the pit. He wasn't far or near but did not appear to notice her. Even in the dark, she could see he was tall, thick through the middle. His dark shirt and trousers reeked of alcohol, but he was steady, his hands on his knees, balancing at the edge. And as abruptly as he had appeared, he straightened and slowly turned away, walking into what remained of the night without a sound.

Sara put her index finger in her mouth and bit down. She wanted it to be a mistake, to fight the need to breathe, the desire to hide. Staggering, her limbs weak, she found a dress in an adjacent field and pulled it over her head, covering her nakedness in another woman's loss. The dress smelt of Red Moscow and sweat.

WHEN AGRIPPINA OPENED THE DOOR AND SAW SARA STANDING IN the faint light, her face tightened into a howl that straightened her old back and snapped her head out of her hunched shoulders. A turtle forced from its shell. The skin on her neck quivered, and she clutched at her heart.

"I came to tell you. Kuzma is gone. Everyone died. Except me."

"Where?"

"At the ravine of snakes."

Agrippina's shock pushed her back on her heels as if by a sudden gust of wind. She came to rest against a wall, covered her eyes with her hands, and shook her head, sobbing.

Sara had never forgotten the day she and Asya left Kuzma in Agrippina's care. Agrippina knew her task was to shelter and protect her grandson, to compensate for his father's long absences and his mother's weakness.

She was a good grandmother by all accounts, pushing the shame and gossip away even when it had emerged that Kuzma was indeed different. She cocooned him in her healing world, believing the greatest gift she had to offer was an unbending stance against the unclean forces and her uncompromising love. She couldn't cure him, but then, Sara knew instinctively, Agrippina had never seen Kuzma as needing curing.

From behind her hands, Agrippina said, "He saw his mother, here in the garden. I don't know how he knew her, but he did. For a month, he's been tugging on my sleeve and pointing to the city."

Sara slumped into a chair. She remembered the way Asya caressed Kuzma. "Asya saw him in the crowd below our apartment from the window and followed him. I followed her."

The two women remained together in silence until long after the sun rose and settled into its place in the middle of the sky. Agrippina spoke after a time, to say, "The unclean force saw that he was pure. And vulnerable. He had a fever a few days ago. I suspected he'd been bewitched."

Sara looked up and blinked into the light. She'd forgotten where she was.

"Did you see my Kuzma die?

"No, we were separated at the end, but he knew he wasn't alone."

"And Asya?"

"We were together."

Agrippina paced, her back rounded, her gait wide. She put her hands on her hips, shuffled to the stove, and placed a kettle of water on the old stove to boil. Rosemary-scented steam filled the air. "We need to rid you of the spoiler's influence, get rid of the dust they've pushed into your soul with their evil."

Agrippina's words made their first impact on Sara. "Evil is what it is, Aggrippina. Not easily vanquished."

"Maybe not, but we have to try." Agrippina wiped her face with a thin apron and began to gather the herbs and potions she kept in jars in her kitchen. She talked to Kuzma as she worked,

"My beautiful boy. They stole your footsteps." She brought Sara a tray burdened with succulents, deep red leaves sprinkled with white powder, and wild grass tea. Sara complied with Agrippina's instructions to drink, inhale, swallow. She wanted nothing more than to close her eyes forever.

When Sara had ingested Agrippina's potions, the old woman washed Sara's face with warm water. She lifted the perfumed dress over Sara's head and left it in a heap outside her door.

"I'll bury it tonight." She pried the dirt from Sara's fingernails and combed the leaves and dirt from her hair before she wiped the quicklime and sand from her body. "We have to hurry, before the soul's life recedes."

"How did you know I wasn't my sister?"

"There was never sameness in your inner lives. Only in your limbs, the color of your eyes, the way your hair fell about your shoulders."

Sara looked at her bare legs, her hands, her feet. *Asya's.* "Why was I the one to survive?"

Agrippina shook her head sadly. "Reflexes saved you. They can save your soul, too." She handed Sara a pair of trousers and a shirt, then stood over her with a spoon and watched her swallow a foul-smelling tincture. "You need to sleep."

"I can't."

"No, but you will."

Sara's breathing relaxed. She closed her eyes cautiously, aware of the room, of Agrippina's conversation with her lost grandson. "Your breath is in my ear, sweet Kuzma."

Sergei opened the door of his mother's cottage in the late afternoon. Agrippina, who was urging Sara to take another dose of tincture, stood to face her son without a word. Sara rose, too.

Sergei was disheveled and frail, diminished, though his features remained sharply etched, his blue eyes bright. He swallowed and said, "Is it true? He's gone?

"Along with his mother." Agrippina remained standing next to Sara as Sergei sank into a crouch, his face close to the floor. He rocked quietly back and forth on his heels, his face in his left elbow, his right arm dangling uselessly at his side.

Sara wondered how it was they were all here, without the others, in Agrippina's cottage.

Sergei crawled to a chair. His mother sat beside him. He took her hand and held it to his cheek. Agrippina pressed her head into his shoulder. "My young men. One maimed, the other gone."

Sara wanted to say she'd tried, but it wasn't true. She hadn't devised an escape. "I'm sorry it wasn't me instead of them."

In the evening, a sliver of moonlight piercing the open window from the garden, Agrippina handed Sara a glass of tea. Sergei hadn't moved from the chair. Agrippina brought another glass and Sergei sat up to take the tea in his left hand.

Sara eyed his limp arm and quickly looked away.

Sergei forced a smile. "Courtesy of the NKVD."

"You were arrested the same year as Lyosha."

Sergei turned and gently raised an eyebrow. "Yes. They beat me, and when I came to, my arm was useless. They also left me this." He ran a finger over a small dent on his close-cropped skull.

Sara sighed. "Lev wanted to blame you for Lyosha. As if blaming you for every terrible thing would ease his loss."

"Lev always believed his own lies, especially about his wife. But somewhere, deep inside, he knew better."

Sara stopped. There was too much grief already.

Sergei handed her a cigarette, put one between his teeth, and struck a match. "He couldn't admit the depths of her betrayal. Or her despair."

Sara leaned into the flame. That was true. She took a long drag on the cigarette and exhaled. "Lev said you knew a story about them, Lyosha and Lev. About emaciated bodies stacked inside a couple of freight cars in the yard? He thought maybe you told someone what they'd seen and presumably never reported."

Sergei looked up at his mother, who brought him a cup for the ashes. "By the time Lyosha and I were arrested, that story had been over for years. No one ever knew anything about it."

Sara said, "I think he felt guilty that Lyosha didn't come home and he did."

Agrippina sighed heavily. She was pacing, her old face more haggard.

Sergei stood, took his mother's arm, and led her to the divan. "Sit down, Mama." He lifted her feet onto a small wooden stool and bent to kiss her on the forehead.

When he straightened, he looked at Sara and said, "You remember when Asya married Lev? After you brought Kuzma to my mother?"

Sara nodded slowly. "I've always regretted…"

Do you know when she came back to me?"

Sara shook her head.

"In 1933. Avsey was little. We'd go out to the far side of the rail yards, where we made love in empty boxcars or in the woods behind the station. Early one morning, Lev saw four freight cars in the yards. A few NKVD men hovered nearby, a warning sign he ignored. He'd been hearing rumors about his wife and demanded to see what was inside. These cars had been coming in and out of Rostov for months, and if Lev had not been in a blind rage, he might have been more thoughtful. But he was irrational, and the NKVD thugs obliged. I'm not sure what he thought he would find, but piles of dead peasants were not on the list. I never heard that Lyosha was with him. He said that?"

Sara let her body fall back against the chair. Agrippina stifled a moan.

"Yes. But I never heard any of this from Lyosha."

"Even if he was there, he wouldn't have told you. Boxcars full of starved Ukrainians—dangerous knowledge then and now. Lyosha was arrested at the same time Lev was, five years after the boxcar incident. I didn't spend time with the NKVD until after Lev had been released. Nothing to do with dead peasants."

Agrippina stood again.

Sergei spoke to her gently, "Mama, take some of your tincture." He put a shawl around her shoulders and led her back to the divan and handed her a glass of water.

When Agrippina dozed off, Sergei continued his story. "The sapphire came from the freight car. Lyosha never knew about it."

"Sapphire?" Sara looked up. "What sapphire?"

"You see, Lev didn't tell you the whole story. A former person was in one of the freight cars, still alive. She had been in hiding with her former servant in a small village since the Revolution. They lived together for sixteen years, but when the servant's family all died of starvation, their grain requisitioned by the Bolshevik agitators, the noblewoman ended up near death alongside her friend. Lev noticed the woman was alive and came back to check when the guards took a break. He smuggled her to his neighbors, the piano teacher and her husband, also former people. He was a kind of hero, risking himself for the sake of decency, a Bolshevik helping an aristocrat."

"How do you know all this?"

"As it turned out, a week later, the rescued woman spoke to Bronya during a piano lesson. The piano teacher was terrified they would be discovered. She gave Bronya a doll, perhaps to win her silence. Of course, Asya saw the doll and confronted the teacher. The whole story tumbled out. Lev hadn't told her."

"I still don't understand the sapphire."

"The former person kept a sapphire hidden in the hem of a dress all those years. She gave it to the piano teacher to give to Lev, to thank him. Sergei smiled softly. "I can see why Lev would keep such a thing despite the risks. It had a strange allure."

"How do you know? Did you see it?"

"Asya showed me the sapphire. Lev had no idea she knew about it."

"You're right. He only told me a small part of the story."

"Lev didn't tell himself the whole story about anything. He denied anything was wrong with Asya, even when she said crazy things. He denied Asya's longing for Kuzma. He had an unfair deal, and it isn't surprising he blamed me for as much of it as he could. It eased his pain."

"Maybe he wanted me to blame you, too. Makes sense. He couldn't accept his part in Asya's unhappiness or mine. He always wanted to be her hero, the answer to all her problems."

Agrippina grunted awake and rose from the divan, agitated. Sergei put his hand on her shoulder, but she waved him away, saying, "Enough of the past. Enough."

Sergei studied his mother's face. "Mama, the past what we have now."

Sara crushed the cigarette into the porcelain cup and reached for another. "May I?

Sergei struck a match and leaned forward. "Lyosha wasn't guilty of anything. Suspicion is always tangential. They shoot people because the line describes the curve."

"Why were you arrested?"

"My arrest was academic; my position on geography fell out of favor. The bigger question is why they didn't shoot me."

Agrippina scolded her son gently, "Enough. No more talk of the dead. Please. Let them be."

Sergei smiled again, his weathered face tender, full of sadness. "There's no one else to talk about, Mama. The dead can't let *us* be."

Agrippina hung her head, grief circling her like a hawk.

Sergei looked at Sara. "The Germans will be looking for Jews in the city, house to house. Eventually, they'll find their way here. We have to find a hiding place."

Sara hadn't thought about what might happen next. Could she go back to the apartment? She remembered throwing the keys near the ravine.

She approached Agrippina and took her hands. The old woman's eyes were swollen. "I'll go. Maybe the neighbors will let me into the apartment." She kissed Agrippina's cheek.

"No, child. No one will help you there. You'll hide here."

"You are better to me than I deserve, but it's too risky."

Sergei paced and lit another cigarette.

Sara stuck her hand out. "Sergei, I'm sorry."

Sergei waved her hand away. "I have a better idea. I'll take you out of here. I've been smuggling goods through the mountains for years. On roads no one knows, been selling tobacco and samogon to the Germans. I know their habits."

Sara shook her head. "I can't let you risk your life, Sergei."

"I've risked my life for lesser things. I can't undo what's

done, but I can take you through the mountains, away from the Germans."

Agrippina was animated. "He's right, child. Sergei's right, you're almost away. You've already escaped the ravine of snakes. Go. For Kuzma and Asya. For Lyosha."

Sara took a long breath. Would it be a betrayal? To live?

She turned to Sergei, "My sister loved you. I'll go with you."

CHAPTER 24
PYATIGORSK, SEPTEMBER 1942

AVSEY'S NIGHTMARES INTENSIFIED. AFTER THE NIGHT CLIMB TO Zheleznovodsk, he had a dream in which Mama and Sara appeared as chrysalises, transparent in the dirt. He stood at a distance, studying them, held by an invisible barrier. Their ribs and femurs were visible under a pink membrane, folded butterflies. He wanted a sign they might yet emerge.

A few nights later, he dreamed of a deep ditch, a thin plank of wood straddling its sides, a bridge, he thought—an escape. But when he tried to cross the bridge, it disappeared and he was left on the wrong side of the ditch, though why it was the wrong side, he couldn't say. The nightmarish terror and the dream's opacity haunted him for days, leaving him depleted and weak as if he'd forgotten to eat. Indeed, he often forgot to eat until in a frenzy, he devoured anything he could find in Yanina Daniilovna's cupboards.

The thought of his sister close by, somewhere obvious but unknown to him, left him hopeless. He was tired of cards, the garden, and cicadas. He shadowed Yanina Daniilovna, but she was set in her ways and waved him away. Avsey thought she must be lonely, too—self-reliant to a fault, even the neighbors avoided her.

The only crack in the old woman's veneer of independence was her longing for her son. Nazim's visits were rare, and he appeared only at night when she was asleep to avoid being seen. Avsey wanted to tell Nazim how his mother settled on a dilapidated chair in front of her house, slumped forward, tensing at the sound of footsteps. He wanted Nazim to see the way Yanina Daniilovna's chin fell on her chest when the footsteps fell away.

Avsey understood her. He, too, was a prisoner of longing. And he became more and more anxious for news, for the next foray into the dark to look for his sister. Where might they go next? Would Nazim keep his promise and come up with a plan? He remembered the way Nazim had hurt him and felt queasy. Should he go back to Zheleznovodsk on his own? The old man's words reverberated in his head, over and over. Would he be able to find Radomir?

Avsey's unease was magnified with the arrival of more soldiers in Pyatigorsk. These were hollow-eyed men who were prone to drink in the evenings. They never strolled in the park, didn't eat melons, or tousle his hair. They did not throw their heads back to laugh or show all their teeth or slap their comrades on the back. It was clear these men were peculiar, different from the other soldiers, though he was not able to tell why. They were somber. Arguments erupted between them and lingered over their evenings like smoke from a distant fire.

More posters appeared around Tsvetnik Park. Jews, the posters said, were required to register and present themselves on the morning of September 5th at the cavalry barracks for resettlement to less populated areas. They were ordered to bring their apartment keys, name and address tags attached to wire key chains, and a limited amount of luggage.

Avsey didn't have apartment keys, and he didn't want to live in a less populated area. He worried about the order and waited for Nazim or better yet, Papa, to tell him what to do. But no one came. Distraught, Avsey wandered the streets at night looking for Papa and Nazim. He thought about the woman in the basement, the things she'd seen in the woods. How was he supposed to decide?

Avsey hadn't realized his worry had turned into anger until Nazim appeared on the evening of September 4th. "Is Papa going to the cavalry barracks? Have you found Bronya?" His tone was demanding, disrespectful. He noticed the lines etched into Nazim's forehead, lines he had not seen before. He hesitated.

Nazim stood, forlorn, in the middle of the room, head sunk into his hunched shoulders, as if he were dodging enemy fire. "Slow down. Take it easy." He crossed the room to greet his mother, who was already preparing the samovar, and placed his hands on her shoulders. She turned, took his hand, and kissed it three times before she continued making tea. Avsey felt the familiar ache in the middle of his throat and turned away.

Nazim took the chair next to Avsey. "I have something to tell you."

Avsey couldn't help his sarcasm. "Maybe you should keep your secrets, Nazim. Keep me in the dark. I mean, I'm just a kid, right?"

Nazim glanced at his mother and kept his voice low. "Avsey, please listen." He took a deep breath and ran his hands over his face like Avsey had seen Papa do a hundred times. It was always a sign that things weren't going well. Nazim leaned close to Avsey. "I want to explain a few things, so you won't misunderstand."

"Misunderstand?"

"Listen. Please. That's all." Nazim wiped his face again. He began slowly, "The Germans created a unit of Soviet POWs, Caucasians, captured from the Red Army. These men are traitors. The Germans are using them for special operations in the Caucasus because they know the region."

Avsey was tired of listening. "So what?"

"I speak Azeri so I joined, as a spy."

Avsey sat back so abruptly he almost tipped over on the chair. "You're in a German unit?"

"We want to sabotage their operations, but we need to know what they're doing first. Makes sense to me."

Avsey felt as if his hair was on fire. "So where's Papa? Is he in this unit?"

Nazim had dark circles around his eyes. He looked haunted, disoriented. He cracked his knuckles one by one. "Your father doesn't speak Azeri. But it was his idea."

Yanina Daniilovna brought Nazim his tea, returned to the samovar, poured a glass for Avsey, and shuffled over to him. They watched her in silence. For the first time, Avsey was glad she didn't speak. When his mother went to her corner, Nazim asked, "Have you seen your father?"

"I'm not going to lie. I've looked for him, but no."

"I don't know where he is. I've lost him. I thought maybe he came here." Nazim covered his face with his hands.

Avsey felt the chasm of nightmares and heartache widen. *Papa?* The room spun around. "What do you mean you've lost him?"

Nazim faced Avsey. His breath was shallow. "We were supposed to meet. He didn't show up. That's never happened before."

"When was your meeting?"

"Yesterday. Morning. Maybe he was delayed or we missed each other."

"There's a chance he's fine, right?" Avsey imagined a tiny beam of light in the chasm, trained his eye on the beam, and held it in his mind.

Nazim's mouth was dry, his tongue slow, "It's possible that the streets weren't safe. Maybe he saw me in uniform and didn't know me. Maybe I frightened him."

"In uniform?" Avsey spit, "He was afraid of you."

"Maybe. But I told you, he knew what I was doing. The

whole thing was his idea. He heard men in German uniforms speaking Azeri and thought it was the perfect way to infiltrate." Nazim's voice cracked.

Avsey felt tiny needles prickling his skin. He jumped up and paced back and forth, looking at Nazim from the corner of his eye. He was ready to leave, to do anything, to search street by street for Papa.

"Avsey, I've looked everywhere. That's why I want you to stay inside, in case he comes here. He knows where you are. I'll continue looking, but he may come for you."

"But what about the posters, Nazim, the resettlement? Is your mother going to resettle?"

"Of course not. She'll stay here. No one knows she's a Jew. She learned that lesson a long time ago."

"What if they come here?"

"No one will come for you, Avsey. Promise me you'll stay here. If anyone does come, hide in the garden."

"Why?"

"Because it's the most important thing I've ever asked you to do. You have to trust me. Wait for your father."

"What if he doesn't appear?"

Nazim tensed. "This is an order. Stay away from the cavalry barracks, the resettlement nonsense. Stay inside."

When Nazim had gone, Avsey let all his doubts coalesce into one big lump that stuck in the middle of his throat above his Adam's apple. It sounded crazy, but what if Nazim had turned? It was almost beyond anything he could imagine. Nazim, a traitor?

But the thought wouldn't leave him alone. It rippled across his mind like wind on water. Was that why he hadn't wanted Avsey to go back to Zheleznovodsk? Hadn't wanted to really search for Bronya? Why Nazim stopped confiding in him? The man who wouldn't say Hitler's name wearing a Nazi uniform? Nothing made any sense.

As night fell, Avsey knew he couldn't let himself sleep. The nightmares would return if he slept, and he couldn't bear more. He listened to Yanina Daniilovna's loud snores, hoping she would keep him awake.

On his cot, his head propped up on one hand, he spread the contents of his treasure box out on the coverlet, holding each object in turn, his companions in the dark. He held the silver cigarette case over his head and rubbed Papa's initials. He swung Mama's pearl from its gold chain over his forehead like a pendulum. He followed it with his eyes until he felt dizzy and had to stop. He held the picture of Sergei above his head as well and put his pinky finger in the cutout holes in the birth certificate.

Then, for a very long time, he held the stone in his closed hand and shook it rhythmically, a tiny drum inside his fist. The objects didn't seem to matter as much as they had, their mystery dulled with sadness. The only thing he wanted was for everyone to stay alive—Kuzma of the birth certificate, and the muscle man in the photo, and Mama, so she could wear the pearl. And Papa and Bronya because they all needed one another, because they *loved* one another.

Nazim's story about Papa missing their meeting, his story about Soviet POWs in German uniforms, plagued Avsey all night. Just before first light, he stashed his treasure box and his slingshot in his knapsack and pushed it under the cot, then crept quietly out into the breaking dawn. He didn't believe anything the Germans said but headed to the cavalry barracks anyway. He was just a red-headed kid. He would observe, figure out what was going on, and decide what to do. In the meantime, he found it difficult to believe Nazim had lost Papa. It was easier to think Papa had decided to lose Nazim.

By the time the sun was up, hundreds of people stood in the yard of the cavalry barracks and more waited outside the open gates. They queued between two lines of uniformed men—some police, some soldiers—waiting to climb into open trucks. The process was extremely orderly, and in the early morning, the crowd was sleepy. Children slept in their mothers' arms. No one asked questions.

Avsey stood apart from the crowd as they moved onto the trucks and roared off, the early morning sunshine playing over their faces. More trucks appeared and people clambered onto them, wiping the dust from their necks with handkerchiefs. They reassured the children, who were thirsty and cried for water.

The dust caught in Avsey's throat and made him cough. The crowd became noisier. Avsey heard a woman scolding her children. "You will do as you are told," she said. He saw an old man decide he wouldn't go, and watched the soldiers drag him onto a waiting truck, kicking him mercilessly on the way.

It was then, just when Avsey thought it might be better to leave, that he caught sight of Papa, stepping up onto one of the trucks. He was thin and bent over, barely recognizable. A German officer, one hand on Papa's neck, helped to push him up. Avsey didn't want to believe his eyes, but when Papa lifted his right leg over the side of the truck with both hands, he knew. This was Papa's weak leg—the last surgery hadn't been that long ago.

Something told Avsey not to yell, but he ran to catch up, to join Papa. Why hadn't Papa come for him? Was he leaving him behind? Didn't he know they could go to the resettlement place together? He pushed through the crowd, ducking under arms and suitcases and small children resting on their mothers' hips, their legs dangling.

An old man caught him by the collar. "Slow down, young man. You'll get your place in paradise soon enough."

Avsey broke free, but Papa's truck pulled away.

The crowd settled into the waiting, part of an ebb and flow of bodies, surging forward and backward in waves. Avsey took his place in the queue. When the next series of trucks appeared, he climbed in and settled between two young women and the old man who'd held his collar. He pressed his back against the sides of the truck and covered his mouth with his arm.

One of the women held out a handkerchief. "Go on, you'll need it," she said.

Avsey smiled at her. He was even more grateful for the gift when the truck pulled away from the cavalry barracks and the cloud of dust overwhelmed him. He placed the handkerchief over his face and closed his eyes.

He felt a sudden wave of regret. His knapsack was tucked under the bed at Yanina Daniilovna's cottage. Everything he owned was in it. Wherever they were going, Avsey wouldn't be able to give Papa his silver box. His blue stone. He didn't have Mama's things either. Would she forgive him?

When the trucks stopped, Avsey saw more rows of soldiers on either side of a long line of people. There were blankets on the ground. Avsey noticed that people, urged on by the soldiers, were dropping objects onto the blankets as they passed. When he was closer, he saw the blankets were covered with donated possessions. Keys and eyeglasses and coins. Gold jewelry glinted in the sunlight. Silver candlesticks, watches, glass figurines, gloves, hairpins, bracelets, a small birdcage without a bird. Papa was nowhere in sight.

He stifled a scream when a hand grabbed him by the collar and dragged him backward, out of the line.

Nazim stood over him, wearing a uniform without insignia. No swastika, no eagle, nothing except the color and cut of the uniform to indicate what he was doing. He whispered harshly, "I told you to stay home."

"I saw Papa, on a truck." Avsey could see by the startled look in Nazim's eyes that he hadn't known Papa was here. He looked up, his gaze darting back and forth over the crowd, panicked.

"Go back, Avsey. I'll find him, but you have to leave now."

"I don't believe you, Nazim."

Another soldier wearing the same unmarked uniform

approached. He spoke in Russian, "Need some help? This one giving you trouble?"

"No, sir, he isn't a Jew, just a farm boy, so I've told him to leave."

"Don't waste your time. The kids like to watch. They're always hanging about at these affairs."

Nazim pushed Avsey hard. "Go home, kid. You have no business here." His mouth was contorted into an angry grimace. The other soldier laughed, and Avsey backed away, then turned to run into the woods. From there, he would creep forward and look for Papa without being seen.

Aware Nazim would be looking for him, Avsey scanned the crowd from between the trees. He stayed close to the lines of people, looking for Papa's distinct gait. Further along, Avsey noticed people separated into groups of men and women. They were climbing into two furniture vans. These vans had windows painted on the outside, and Avsey paused to wonder why anyone would go to the trouble to paint windows on the side of a furniture van.

When he came closer, he heard one of the soldiers say in Russian, his tone sarcastic, "That's why they're called soul destroyers."

Avsey backed further into the tree line, found a spot a little higher up, and sat down to wait. No one paid him any attention.

The loaded vans drove away. Avsey kept his eyes on the crowd. If he stayed in the same spot by the trees, Papa would appear eventually. That was what Papa had taught him on their walks in the forest.

If we lose one another, stay put. I'll retrace my steps to find you.

They had lost one another, and Avsey would stay put until Papa found his way. Then they would be resettled together. He thought about Bronya. He didn't know where they would be resettled or how they might find her, but maybe she would be resettled, too. They'd be together after all.

A short time later, two vans painted like the others backed up to an anti-tank ditch below his position, right to the edge. Avsey thought one of the vans might roll into the ditch, but it stopped just in time, its back tires triggering little cascades of dirt into the void. What were they doing now?

The driver cut the engine and hopped out, leaving his door open. He and a soldier in the same uniform as Nazim unlocked and opened the back doors of the van. At first, Avsey did not understand—all he saw were bright colors. Pink. Red.

When the driver began to pull the colored objects from the van, Avsey stood to get a better look. He refused to believe his eyes. The driver and the soldier were pulling contorted bodies from the back of the windowless van and throwing them into the ditch.

Avsey turned and retched, his arms wrapped around his torso. There was no doubt about what he was seeing. In fact, he'd been wrong all along. His nightmares had been the escape. The reality was much, much worse.

He caught sight of Nazim running through the trees toward him just as the first van drove away and the second van's driver opened the doors to unload his grotesque cargo. Avsey moved behind a tree where Nazim couldn't see him and watched the driver throw bodies into the ditch. It was clear the task was disagreeable. The driver, in a hurry, dropped several of the bodies and shoved them over the edge with a push of his boot.

The van emptied, the driver scooped up a handful of dirt and rubbed his hands together. The breeze lifted the fine powder falling from his fingers while the light caught flecks of gold in the suspended dust swirling over the ditch. The driver wiped his hands on the sides of his trousers before he shut the back doors.

Nazim caught up with Avsey just as the driver pulled away from the ditch to circle back around to the waiting crowd.

Avsey, quick on his feet, stayed just beyond Nazim's grip while Nazim pleaded, "Avsey, I'm begging you. Run. It isn't far."

Avsey surveyed the scene again. The van had returned to the

waiting crowd, and Avsey realized no one in the crowd could see the anti-tank ditch. They wouldn't know until it was too late. Nazim inched closer until he stood a few meters away, out of breath, his arms limp by his sides. "Avsey, please listen."

Avsey positioned himself to keep an eye on the vans and Nazim. More people climbed up, only this time they resisted a little. The soldiers pushed. Avsey turned to Nazim, "Look, *look* what they are doing. Is this what you wanted?"

"No, I didn't know, please believe me. I'll make it right."

"How will you do that? All your big ideas! You're helpless. Because you put on that uniform." Avsey jabbed his finger in Nazim's direction, his anger a tight ball in his throat. He choked back his desire to scream, and with great effort kept his voice to a growl. "You have all the information you need. Truth is, you can't save anyone now. Lucky you didn't find my sister. She might have a chance."

"Avsey, please, *please*, run as fast as you can. I'll get you away from here." Nazim choked. "Please."

Avsey caught sight of a familiar movement from the corner of his eye. He and Nazim turned their heads at the same instant and saw Papa lifting his leg into the van. A soldier helped push him up, gently.

Papa, lifted into the air, disappeared into the van.

Avsey took two steps toward the crowd. He was almost out of the tree line, sliding down a slight incline, his shoes covered with the dirt he'd craved for so many weeks. He realized the craving had gone and wondered when it had happened. When did he stop needing minerals?

Nazim pleaded, "Please, Avsey." He held out his hands.

Avsey shook his head. "You were my hero. But you're like Zeus. You don't care about us." He watched Nazim's mouth open. No sound came out.

Avsey turned and ran. The van wasn't far. He didn't look back. The crowd parted to let him through. When he jumped, he saw the look of surprise on the soldiers' faces and heard the crowd gasp.

Inside, he crawled on all fours, aware of nothing other than the need to be with Papa. In the dim light, the stench, Avsey took Papa's hand.

"I'm here, Papa. Don't worry. I won't leave you." The doors slammed shut.

CHAPTER 25
THE CAUCASUS, SEPTEMBER 1942

AFTER THE LITTLE BOY WAS BURIED, SEVERAL GERMANS CAME TO live in Gulya's village. A high-ranking officer occupied the doctor's office at the hospital along with his aide-de-camp and a female interpreter. Though only three Germans lived in the village, they were everywhere, a constant presence. Traffic on the single thoroughfare was so heavy, the Germans built another bridge over the river to accommodate their trucks and tanks. It mattered little that the vehicles did not stop in the village; the German Army owned everything it touched.

The Germans appointed Murzabek, the old man with a limp who'd rescued Bronya from the sanitorium, as mayor.

Bronya wondered if Murzabek might be a collaborator, and when one day she recognized the aide-de-camp as the soldier who'd held her violin, she was beside herself with fear. She whispered to Gulya, "How do you know Murzabek isn't on their side?"

Gulya was indignant. "Murzabek was responsible for the decision at the meeting of the Council of Elders to take the orphans in the first place. Despite the danger."

But Bronya worried. "I don't understand why he would

work with them if he wasn't on their side. Maybe he'll betray us."

Gulya drew her shoulders back and looked Bronya in the eye. "It's the obligation we have as Circassians to adopt orphans, to give hospitality. Murzabek came up with the idea to forge the household record book, too. He added the adopted children's new Circassian names and dates of birth, as if they'd been born to Circassian families. He wouldn't have gone to all that trouble just to betray you.

"But how do you know all of this?"

Gulya smiled. "I eavesdropped at the council meeting. I always do."

Bronya thought about how many times she'd listened to conversations that were not meant for her ears.

Gulya continued, "Murzabek is the oldest man in the village —he is a natural choice. We are lucky because he's smarter than they are. Do you know the Germans investigated but didn't find the truth about the children, about you? Because Murzabek is good at hiding things, at playing his role."

Maybe Gulya was right, but Bronya decided not to say anything about her violin. Especially not to Gulya. Bronya had trusted Vera and regretted it. She couldn't imagine making herself vulnerable to anyone else ever again. Besides, the pit at the bottom of her stomach widened when she thought of her violin's new owner.

Life in the village was tenuous enough, constantly fraught with the possibility of exposure. She found it difficult to sleep, aware she put the villagers in danger, always conscious of the favor they were granting her and the other children. What if someone decided to expose the whole scheme?

One afternoon, Bronya returned to the house to find Murzabek sitting by the stove with her adoptive parents, all with downcast faces. Before Bronya could ask what had happened, Gulya blurted out, "A man only visits a woman he wants to marry. I didn't know what else to do. You can't marry such a man. They aren't like us. They have no respect." Gulya wrung her hands.

"What happened? Someone wants to marry me?"

"That lizard, the German who was here on the first night, he asked for you, asked for the girl with green eyes. I told him you'd gone away, that you were sick."

The one with the violin?" Bronya felt the bile rise in her throat. "What did he want?"

"Sit down, child." Murzabek motioned her to a stool close to the stove.

Bronya did not move. "Did he have the violin?"

Everyone in the room turned to stare at her.

Murzabek asked, "What has a violin got to do with anything, child?"

Bronya fixed her eyes on Murzabek. She remembered his voice on the day he'd rescued her from the sanitorium, how kind he'd been. "It's my violin. I left it at the sanitorium. He must have taken it from there."

Gulya gasped. "Maybe he's looking for you because he knows. Not for marriage."

Murzabek fingered his amber beads, his eyes focused on the door. They waited in silence until Murzabek looked up and said, "When the wicked one arrives with a smile, we know he wants something. We have to take Zhana away and announce her death."

Gulya's mother rose up from her chair, her mouth slightly open but reconsidered and sat down again.

Gulya burst into tears. "It's all my fault."

Murzabek's voice was firm. "You did the right thing, Gulya. Zhana must leave before the German returns. For her sake and for ours. It makes no difference what he wanted. He came and that reason alone is sufficient." He nodded to Gulya's mother. "Lay out your mourning clothes."

Gulya sobbed louder, and Bronya, flooded with tenderness, put her arms around her.

Murzabek left Gulya's house before sunset and returned with a cart and horse like the one he'd driven to rescue Bronya from the sanitorium. He handed her a large drawstring bag full of provisions: dried sheep's side, maize rolls, hard cheese, and cucumbers. He pointed to the sickle moon that hung low against the horizon. "The time is ripe for leaving."

Gulya, who hadn't stopped crying, gave Bronya an embroidered shawl. "From my dowry. So you'll come back here to find a husband. We'll raise our children together."

Bronya hugged Gulya. It wasn't Gulya's fault she didn't understand what it felt like to be hunted, just like it wasn't Bronya's fault she hadn't been able to trust anyone in the village.

Murzabek loosened Guyla's fingers from Bronya's arm and said sternly, "It is what's best."

Bronya kissed Gulya's family and climbed up next to Murzabek.

He took the reins and whispered to the horse. "Let's go, Krasavitsa." Gulya pressed her face against the window.

Bronya watched her until the night closed in and the village vanished.

Murzabek avoided the German outposts, crossing the kolkhoz fields until they were far from the village and surrounded by forest. The moon rose higher in the sky, and at Cherkessk, they crossed the Kuban River over a long, low bridge. Halfway across, Krasavitsa stopped and refused to budge.

Murzabek sighed. "She doesn't like the black waters."

Bronya understood.

Murzabek jumped down to lead the horse across, all the while singing her name in low tones, coaxing her with his tender voice while reassuring his anxious passenger.

The Kuban behind them, Murzabek continued on the backroads, skirting the populated areas of Cherkessk, once again avoiding potential German encounters. Waving his hands around him, he gestured toward the forest. "There was a time when trees spoke. They know everything, see everything."

Bronya looked up through the branches. The sky was full of stars.

Murzabek smiled. "The trees helped to create the Milky Way —they are the wealth of the earth."

The forest gave way to cultivated fields where Bronya felt less protected, but Murzabek continued at a steady pace. He noticed Bronya's increased vigilance and said, "Relax, child, there is no danger here."

He began to sing in a language Bronya didn't understand, his voice cracking, full of emotion.

She settled into the sound of the cart wheels, the horse's breath, and Murzabek's odd song. Eventually, she was able to hum along.

He smiled and nodded and patted her hand. "That's right," he said, "you understand."

And she did. He was singing of courage and loss, of terrible journeys, preparing her for what was to come next.

Bronya leaned against the back of the seat, drifting in and out of light sleep, a kind of trance fostered by Murzabek's solid presence and the warm night. Only when the birdsong became insistent and full-throated did she sit up, fully awake. They passed a crooked sign for Svoboda, but Bronya did not see a town. The road remained deserted, and the fields gave way to forest once again.

Gradually, the soft morning light radiated through the greenery, illuminating the forest floor and the yellow eyes of animals surprised by the sound of the cart before they dashed into the underbrush. The forest lulled Bronya into a sense of well-being she hadn't experienced in many months.

Then Murzabek pulled off the path, stopped the cart, and turned to her. "This is the dangerous part."

"Because it's daylight?"

"We're near the spa towns now, more German patrols. I think

you know about the sacred mountain, yes?"

Bronya couldn't think which mountain might be sacred. Didn't all mountains fall into this category for Murzabek?

He prodded, "Beshtau?"

"Yes. I played my violin under the birch trees there."

"It is a familiar place, then, a place of memories. I'll leave you there, and you'll make your way. At the foot of Beshtau, there is an old monastery close to Pyatigorsk. It was a pioneer camp for a time. The Germans are there now, but their presence is small."

Bronya shuddered.

Murzabek, his tone grave, said, "Remember, the enemy has weaknesses. They make mistakes. Do not let them use your fear against you. Do not expose it to them. Ever."

Bronya nodded.

"I'm sorry I can't take you further, child, but the mountain will provide shelter until you find your bearings. Go south to Ordzhonikidze, and from there walk on the Military Road to Tbilisi. It is a long road, but the only way out now. Do you know how to follow the stars?"

"My father taught us." Bronya looked at Murzabek, overcome with sorrow and gratitude for this man who'd risked his own life for hers, searching for something more to say. "I don't know what I would have done without you."

Murzabek patted her hand. "I know. You belong to us now, and we to you. Remember, mistrust is a gift, a will to live. Trust only yourself."

Bronya climbed into the back of the wagon. She lay against the front end, under the seat, while Murzabek stashed her provision bag in the corner and adjusted a dirty tarp over her, blocking the light. "No matter what happens, make no sound. And when I tap three times, take your belongings, and walk away. Do not speak. I will watch until you're away."

The cart eased out onto the road, and after a short time, Bronya heard sounds of life around her. Trucks honked past, Krasavitsa's gait quickened. Bronya was reassured by the sound of the horse's steady hooves, but Murzabek called her to slow down. "Steady, old girl."

The cart stopped, and Krasavitsa snort several times. Heavy boots approached, and a vehicle stopped close by, its motor idling. Bronya tried to stop her shoulders from shaking, steeling herself for what might happen next. What would she say if they discovered her? Why hadn't she planned with Murzabek for this possibility? Her muscles tightened involuntarily as she tried to make herself smaller without moving.

Murzabek said something in a halting German that caused uproarious laughter. As quickly as he had slowed down, he pulled away with a click of his tongue. The clicks were directed at the horse, but Bronya knew they were meant for her, too.

The next time Murzabek pulled over, not long after the first, there was no laughter. The voices were harsh and again Bronya held her breath. The horse whinnied, and the cart rolled backward while Murzabek soothed the animal.

"Good, Krasavitsa, all is well."

She felt the cart tilt to the right and heard Murzabek's feet hit the ground. He spoke in halting German again, his tone serious. She could still hear boots around the cart while Murzabek's voice grew incrementally distant. A terrible weight pressed into her, as if her own breath might smother her and her heartbeat crush her insides.

Someone next to the cart lit a cigarette and spoke in a voice like gravel. Bronya didn't know if there were others present, but she heard no reply. When at last Murzabek returned, he remained beside the cart, waiting for something.

Eventually, Bronya felt the cart shift with a heavy presence, heard the jingle of metal and the thump of what she imagined was a rifle butt against the wood. Cigarette smoke, hair pomade, and sweat.

Murzabek climbed up and clicked his tongue again. The horse started, her passengers perched directly over Bronya's head.

Bronya wished they would speak so she could listen to the tones of their voices and prepare herself for what might come next, but they remained silent.

Soon, they were on a road with trucks and motorcycles, populated with the sounds of men calling out to one another. Bronya opened her eyes to look through the cracks in the wood but saw nothing more than passing flashes of light. Where were they now? Murzabek had not planned to come into any town. What had happened to make him change course? Where were they going? She closed her eyes but listened harder.

When the horse came to a halt, she felt the cart shift again. The heavy presence rose, the cart listed to the right, then sprung up as if pulled by a string from above.

Murzabek called out in Russian, "God save us!"

She heard the reins slap hard against Krasavitsa's neck and felt the cart lurch forward, the horse breaking into a trot. Murzabek began to sing again, the same song as before, and Bronya knew he was telling her the danger had passed for now but to beware.

The sounds from the world outside the cart fell away for a time, then rose again, a cacophony of everyday life—trucks, horns and human voices, Krasavitsa's hooves on cobblestones, her steady breath, Murzabek muttering to himself, a woman close to the cart yelling after a child: "Wait before you cross, little imp, you'll be crushed!"

The cart's wood slates, jolted by the road, knitted together, yawned, and moaned. Bronya's back felt bruised, but she did not dare shift her position. The road was longer than she'd imagined. More time for mistakes. The next time the Germans would find her, they'd know about the violin, the sanitorium. She would be taken away and something awful would happen to Murzabek.

The street noise fell away and the road drifted, bit by bit, back into silence. But as the noise receded, Bronya fretted more. Was this calm before the next disaster? How long would she have to lie here under the tarp? Sweat trickled into her hairline. She longed for Murzabek's song.

When the cart began to climb and Bronya had to press her feet into the wood to stay in place, she knew they had left the town behind for good. Still, she wasn't paying attention when the knocking came. It took a second to remember to throw off the tarp, climb over the sides, and jump down onto the road. The daylight startled her, but she saw the stone walls of a monastery ahead.

The day was bleak. She walked and did not look back at Murzabek and Krasavitsa until she realized she'd forgotten the bag of provisions in the back of the wagon, along with the pocketknife and her shawl. She turned around, half-afraid the horse and her master had already gone.

Murzabek appeared small next to the cart. He waved her back, holding the bag, looking nervously from side to side. Krasavitsa threw her head up and down. Bronya ran, glad for one last moment with her rescuers.

She wrapped her arms around Murzabek's waist. "I'll never forget you," she whispered. "Never."

She reached out to caress Krasavitsa's muzzle. Her whiskers were sharp against Bronya's palm. She leaned into the horse's head and put her mouth to her ear. "Thank you, old girl."

Murzabek cleared his throat and looked away. Bronya stood rooted, not wanting to leave him. He retrieved the shawl Gulya had given her and wrapped it carefully around her head, all the while humming his song.

Why couldn't she ride back with him? Remain with her adoptive family, with Gulya? It all seemed unreal, unnecessary. She hadn't appreciated the comfort of it until now.

Murzabek adjusted the shawl around her head and handed her the pocketknife. "You might need this. From here, it's two days of walking to the higher mountains. The front lines are around the Terek river. For now. Keep your wits about you. One always has fewer friends than one thinks."

He put his hand over his heart and bowed his head.

Bronya put her hand over her heart. The tension in her shoulders eased, but the empty place under her sternum filled with heartache.

Murzabek smiled. His eyes were tender. "Let's not tempt fate."

Bronya hesitated, then turned and walked toward the monastery.

She heard Murzabek say, "Look up, daughter."

CHAPTER 26
THE CAUCASUS, SEPTEMBER 1942

Bronya tried to sleep on the mountain, her arms wrapped tight around her torso for warmth, but the subtle noises in the dark unnerved her, and she climbed to Beshtau's summit before dawn. The sunrise in the east and the view of the higher mountains from the summit would help orient her. The night had been cloudy, and she'd worried about where to go next.

Hoping to see the peaks of Elbrus pushing above the clouds from the south, she reached the highest point as the sun pushed over the horizon, throwing decadent gold and pink strands of light like jewels over the earth. The higher mountain elevations remained shrouded. She would have to wait, watch the sun, and hope for a clear night of stars to guide her.

When the sun's orb was fully exposed, caught between the rim of the earth and the blanket of cloud above it, Bronya thought she heard a voice, the sound of sobbing. She froze. Who could possibly be on the summit at this hour? Feeling exposed, she sat hunched over, her back against an outcrop of rocks, a feeble attempt to hide. She thought about making a dash for the tree line but wasn't sure which direction offered the quickest escape. The sobbing, she thought, originated off to the left, a little higher up. Uncertain, she remained sitting and questioned her powers of perception. The sound did trail off for a time, as if moving down the mountain, but by then she had begun to mistrust her senses.

Besides, the forest wasn't safe either. Yesterday, she'd come upon a young German who looked to be about her age, smoking beside her favorite stand of birch, the place she'd spent her days defying the sanitorium rules in the early summer, playing her violin. He had been absorbed in thought, or he might have seen her. Her pulse raced at the sight of him, and she'd leaned into a leafy hornbeam further into the forest to calm her nerves.

Closer to the road, she'd seen several soldiers, their uniforms unbuttoned, holding bottles and peeing on the dusty trail in the late afternoon. They staggered around one another and laughed. Then at dusk, she happened upon an intertwined couple disrobing as darkness swallowed them, slowly shielding their nakedness. They did not notice her either, and she moved further up, keeping off the trail.

She wondered if it might be best to move off the mountain altogether, but she needed to orient herself, and as Murzabek had reminded her, *she needed the stars.* He was right in another regard: The mountain was familiar, the last safe place she'd known. She would start her long journey from a familiar place.

As the sky accrued light and the landscape came into focus, the mysterious sobbing sound ceased and Bronya pushed her head beyond the rock shelter. The summit remained deserted. Raptors stirred from their shadowed perches and began to hunt. Had her senses been playing tricks on her? Perhaps she'd mistaken the caws and calls of a bird for a human voice. Maybe it was loneliness? Yet something in the back of her mind wouldn't let her move on. The sound was human, distinct in the way humans cried, uncontrolled, burdened. Silence between periodic expulsions of air and grief.

The high peaks of Elbrus broke through the morning cloak of clouds. Elated, Bronya looked around her to familiarize herself with the rock formations, to check on which side the moss grew.

This would point her south when the clouds obscured the stars or the high peaks. The sobbing returned, and now, Bronya was sure the cries were human. And much closer than before. She knew the sound of a broken heart.

She peered over the rocks into the bald spaces, straining her ears. The sobs, which had become shorter and louder, emanated from a crop of three medium-sized boulders, not far from her position. Was this a soldier? She walked toward the grief despite the danger, as if pulled by a magnet.

The grieving man, his back to her, was crouched between two boulders. His shoulders shook as he muttered to himself.

Bronya told herself to run. He hadn't seen her, and she could escape easily down the hillside and into the trees. He was not wearing a uniform. Was he mad? Unstable? But Bronya sensed something more, something poignant—vulnerable.

She took another step toward him just as he jerked his head around and saw her. He scrambled to his feet, a look of surprise stretching his mouth open. He staggered slightly backward.

Bronya looked from the man's swollen face to the hole he'd been digging in the dirt between the rocks, to the object he was pressing against his chest.

His black tunic was covered in fine dust, and his face appeared bruised and haggard. He was unshaven. His hair was glossy and dark, the same color as the stubble on his chin.

Bronya thought he might be in his mid-twenties. He looked like he should frighten her, but somehow, he didn't.

Bronya spoke first. "Can I help?"

The man tightened his grip on the thing he was holding and took another step back.

Bronya worried she'd misjudged the situation. He didn't look like a German, but how did she know?

She lied, "My friends have gone ahead. They'll be back soon." She clutched her bag of provisions against her chest, facing him in a strange, mirrored standoff.

The man nodded, absent, his eyes cloudy with sorrow.

Bronya felt foolish. She didn't need to make up a story. This man was harmless, caught in something he couldn't escape, an insect spinning inside a web.

He nodded and turned back to his task, occasionally glancing warily in her direction. He took the object he'd been protecting and unwrapped it, placed it in the hole between the rocks, and then, with great care, brushed the dirt away and draped the dirty cloth around it. His efforts were tender, focused.

Bronya felt a small tightening in her chest. The object looked familiar. Her mind was playing tricks on her again. She walked closer until she was right over the man's head, staring down into the hole, but the cloth obscured her view. Bronya chided herself. Her imagination had run wild.

She backed away a little when the man stood. He ignored her and began rocking, almost imperceptibly, back and forth on his heels over the hole. His chant was rhythmic, a song, his melodious voice almost a whisper.

It took a few seconds before Bronya realized he was reciting kaddish, the prayer for the dead. In Hebrew. Papa had recited kaddish when Babushka died. She'd stood next to him, surprised her party member father, secular in every aspect of his life, knew the prayer. But Papa's father had been a rabbi, dead before Bronya was born. Of course, he knew kaddish.

Bronya watched the man in front of her. At the end of a phrase, she whispered a voiceless amen as she had learned to do in the sad week after Babushka's death.

The man turned his face toward her, eyes wide, but did not stop until he had finished and Bronya had whispered amen several more times. He turned toward her but said nothing.

Bronya had forgotten her initial interest in the buried object and stared back at him. She said, "There were Germans on the mountain last night."

His face relented a little, the lines softened. "How do you know it?"

"My father taught me when my Babushka died. He learned it

from his father. She left me her violin." Bronya felt awkward. No need to tell a stranger about the violin, but the loss was fresh, and particular to the place they were standing on Beshtau. He wouldn't understand or care.

The man, who had a second earlier looked almost friendly, backed away from her now. He ran his hands through his hair.

She didn't move, too puzzled to run, though a thin ribbon of fear threaded itself from her bowels into her rib cage. Had she revealed too much to a stranger?

He looked at her. "What's your name then?" He squeezed his eyes shut and waited for her answer, shoulders hunched as if expecting a blow.

Having decided not to answer the minute he asked, she blurted it out anyway, "Bronislava." She knew immediately it was a mistake.

The man turned away from her. He bent his knees and leaned over, breathing hard, as if winded from a steady uphill climb. His shoulders shook, but no sound came from him.

Bronya was afraid if she ran, she might upset him more, afraid he might run after her. She took several careful steps toward the trees, hoping not to disturb the pebbles underneath her feet, to avoid drawing attention to her misgivings.

She reevaluated the situation. She could steal away now unnoticed and forget the grieving man who'd been on the summit at dawn. If she took her leave quietly, he would forget her, too—they would forget each other.

The man stood and turned to face her, now steady in his torso, head back. "Do they call you Bronya?"

Struck by his altered demeanor, she decided he was a lunatic. "Yes, of course." She backed away further.

The man advanced.

She pivoted toward the tree line, ready to sprint, her calves tight, poised for escape.

The man trembled a little, not like before, but an aftershock in his body's earthquake. He took a deep breath and released a flood of words. "They're dead. I have to tell you all at once or I may never say it. Your father and Avsey." The man looked down at his hands and exhaled. "They're gone."

Bronya felt strange. All sensation left her. Though her limbs remained attached, she could not feel them, as if she were floating away from her body in slow motion.

"Excuse me? You couldn't possibly—you—I don't even know you." Bronya noticed the pitch of her voice was higher. She felt it unifying her body, pulling in its wayward parts, arms and legs rallying them to her cause. How dare this strange man think he knew her brother, her father. "Who do you think you are?"

The man put his fingers to his lips and shushed her while he looked around. A soft disturbance, a bird's wings, rippled the air.

Bronya flinched. An enormous speckled hawk rose above them, a bald dove fledgling, suspended in its talons. A dove fluttered in vain above the hawk's head, demanding its offspring. The hawk circled higher.

The man took a few steps in Bronya's direction. Her muscles tensed. She was ready to run, but he stopped short of her position and said, "My name is Nazim. I knew them. We spent the last year together."

Bronya, shaking her head, couldn't find the words to tell him she knew he was mistaken, to say out loud he couldn't know them because they were far away, somewhere else, she didn't know where.

The man, without taking his eyes off her, backed up the hole and crouched down. He reached inside, feeling his way, his eyes never leaving her while he took the object in his hands.

The cloth fell away, and Bronya saw he was holding a birch box, like the one Papa made for Avsey. The man extended the box toward her, offering his evidence.

Bronya knew she was sinking and tried to stop herself, thinking it a matter of willpower to remain upright. But willpower couldn't stop her knees from buckling, from hitting the ground. She felt herself fall, her arms flying, her eyes in the clouds. The next time she was fully aware of her surroundings, he was sitting beside her, a look of concern on his face. She tried to get up but felt lightheaded. Avsey's box was on the ground beside her. How did this man have possession of her brother's most prized possession?

"I'm sorry I told you the way I did."

She sat up to stare at him. "There has been a mistake."

"We were in Pyatigorsk because your father was wounded. In May. He was sent for surgery at the military hospital. His legs were shot through. We'd been together all winter, on the Donets."

"It isn't possible. No one knew where they were." Bronya knew this made no sense, but it was the only thing she could think of to say, a way of fighting the vacancy waiting at the edges of her mind.

How could they be dead? It wasn't true. There had already been too much tragedy. She heard Babushka's voice: *There is never more grief than we can survive.*

Bronya had taken this to mean tragedy was self-limiting, that it operated with respect to a certain equilibrium. Now, all at once, she understood. Babushka had been trying to teach her something else, something more akin to capacity, to the extension of what was bearable.

"I knew your father all my life. Your grandfather and my father were best friends."

The vacancy spilled a little further into Bronya, the edges of her defenses frayed.

"Your aunt sent a letter. It said you were in Zheleznovodsk. We went there to find you."

Bronya couldn't breathe. Then, all at once, her breath came too fast, out of control. She covered her face with her hands. "It isn't true."

Nazim hung his head. "With every fiber of my being, it weren't."

CHAPTER 27
KABARDINO-BALKARIA, OCTOBER 1942

By the time Bronya and Nazim arrived at the bottom of Beshtau in the late afternoon, Nazim had recounted Avsey's trek to Zheleznovodsk. How desperate he'd been to find her. She'd learned her brother and father had worked with partisans the winter before in the Donbas. She couldn't help feeling he was telling her too much. Her mind couldn't hold on to details. Nazim's claims were like mercury. They scattered when she attempted to pin them down into a coherent story, evading her grasp. She wanted this odd man to disappear.

Yet, when Nazim offered to help her move past the front lines and onto the Military Road, Bronya said yes. She remembered Murzabek's warning about trusting anyone. She decided she didn't have to trust Nazim in order to take his help. More than any help he might offer, she wanted his memories. If he'd been with Papa and Avsey, she wanted to know what had happened. Trust or no trust.

They were met by two white-haired men at the helm of a battered truck filled with sacks of sunflower seeds and dried tobacco. The men, unshaven, their eyes bloodshot, greeted Bronya with suspicion. One of them fashioned a bundle out of rags and pushed it roughly into her arms. "Hold it as you would a baby."

She nodded and climbed into the back of the truck, cradling the light bundle, her shawl around her head. She leaned against a sack of sunflower seeds for the ride to a kolkhoz outside Malka and wondered what she'd gotten herself into, especially when the German Army rolled by without stopping to check the occupants of the old truck. She watched, with a certain incredulity, as Nazim and his friends cheered and threw sunflower seeds at the soldiers in open vehicles.

They passed on the road beside them, so close they could touch. The Germans laughed but never stopped, never looked twice at the truck or its occupants.

She heard the man next to her mutter, "What they don't know will kill them."

While she took note of everything, Bronya felt outside of it all, a distant observer. By the time they reached the kolkhoz, she was no longer interested in her surroundings. She collapsed inside herself, pushing through the motions of living while time slowed and then disappeared altogether, sloughing away meaning like sunburned skin. She was strangely aware of the deadening and gazed out from its depths, curious about the cleft in her being—one part raw, the other, indifferent.

In the days that followed, grief tugged Bronya down an angry, windowless alley of despair, hemmed in on all sides by an invisible force she didn't understand. She was only nominally aware of where she was or what was happening around her. She was not aware of eating and slept little. If she closed her eyes, she was invaded by images and worse—voices. Avsey's face or Papa's, floating in a thin gruel of memory and despair. Avsey chided her or asked her questions.

After too many hours of troubled wakefulness, when fatigue dampened her ability to resist, she fell wherever she happened to be. In the trees, on the floor of a crumbling kolkhoz building. Once she woke up in a zemlyanka, a sour-smelling dugout where the lack of light emboldened rats and insects to investigate new occupants. She stifled a scream and crawled out. Was this what madness felt like?

Everything passed in a blur of cold air, cigarette smoke, and hard edges—crates, agricultural machinery, faces, the earth itself. She was aware of men and women cleaning weapons or loading carts, lighting fires. No one spoke to her. She assumed from their conversations they were partisans, though they never explained anything, never questioned her. She knew the sun rose and set but paid no attention to the emerging light or the total darkness. Nazim promised to take her to Ordzhonikidze so that she could cross the mountains, but she didn't know when or how they would leave.

When sleep did win, the dream world was clear. She knew where she was and where she was going within the confines of the past, itself a kind of prison. She was always in Rostov on the first day of the war, suitcases by the door, Stepan Ilyich's sad eyes deep in his lined face and Papa telling her to be brave.

Had they not been brave enough? Eventually, she asked Nazim.

He delivered his answer in an angry tone. "They were too brave. If they had been cowards, they'd still be here."

She avoided Avsey's box, made a vow not to open it, not for a long time. She'd found the green pocketknife in her supply bag, though she had no memory of putting it there. Her companion from home, it was enough. She couldn't bear more.

Nazim watched her. "The things we don't see hurt us more," he said.

"I know what's in there. I knew my brother."

Nazim shook his head. "It isn't possible to know everything about the people we love."

At least Nazim never offered pity.

Bronya took stock of him. What had Avsey thought of him? Nazim chain-smoked and bit his fingernails. He cracked his knuckles. He did not appear to sleep. And, in the short time she'd known him, his hair had gone completely white.

On one of the blurry nights, at the beginning, Bronya had made her way outside to pee. As she squatted, she noticed Nazim nearby, leaning against a tree. The red ember of his cigarette in the dark caught her attention.

In profile, his face was angular, lit by a full moon, a knife's edge. He didn't appear to have noticed her presence. When he held the ember of his cigarette to the inner part of his forearm, at the most tender, pink-skinned junction, and then, without flinching, brought it closer, she was sure he did not know she was there. He turned his head away from her so she could not see his face when he pressed the cigarette into his skin. Disturbed, she crept back inside and curled against the wall.

In the following days, three more partisans arrived at the Malka kolkhoz, another girl and two younger men. No introductions, no names. Nazim stood with them, looking in Bronya's direction. She overheard him say, "She isn't one of us. Leave her out of it."

Later, when she thought about his comment, Bronya felt insulted. Nazim didn't trust her?

But by the time Nazim was on his way out a few hours later, she was once again indifferent to everything around her, a willing captive in a distorted limbo. He whispered instructions, "Wait for us. Don't try to go south on your own. Wait a week, and if we do not return, then go alone." He left the building without giving her time to ask questions. She heard the rattle of the shaky kolkhoz truck moving down the road.

Bronya spent three days kicking around the abandoned fields, skipping rocks on the dirty pond, wondering if she should strike out on her own. She waited, not because Nazim had asked her to, but because she had no idea where she was and didn't care.

When Nazim and the other partisans returned, muddy and spent, they had more weapons with them than Bronya had seen before. They were also in a hurry. Nazim told her, "We have to leave. Now." When he reached the door, he turned back, adding, "No questions, leave nothing behind."

Bronya followed orders. She checked her bag for the green knife and Avsey's box. She wrapped her shawl around her head and climbed up into the truck along with one of the partisan girls. The girl couldn't take her eyes off Bronya's shawl. The scenario was the same as before—the fake baby, head coverings —only now Nazim warned them to remain silent, not to speak with one another for any reason.

"We are moving close to the front lines. If we are stopped, you are not to speak. Talking without thinking is like shooting without aiming. And no chatter among yourselves."

The girl immediately fell asleep in the back of the truck. They arrived in a village called Zayukovo without incident.

Here, more men appeared, stooping low to stick their heads into the shepherd's hut where Bronya, with the first group, had taken shelter. They signaled their presence to the others, then turned and went to sleep elsewhere, perhaps further up into the hills, in the woods, in their own camp.

By now, Bronya understood. The partisans spread out, kept their own council until they needed to cooperate. They only spoke in whispers and were wary of her presence among them.

In the morning, Bronya walked outside into the blinding beauty of the mountains and was touched by something outside her grief for the first time in many days. Zayukovo was nestled into the Baksan river valley, surrounded by emerald green foothills and the white peaks of the high mountains.

Fields of sunflowers extended to the edges of her vision, a raft of yellow floating on a lush green velvet sea. Workers harvested flowers in the distance, moving back and forth, felling the stalks with steady sweeps of their sickles. A dog barked somewhere. The fog of grief lifted and retreated a little into the hollows of her gut, still sharp, but the underside of a wave instead of the crest.

Nazim sat down next to her in the sunshine. His face was pale, his lips cracked. He smelled of tobacco. She noticed none of the nervousness she'd seen before. He was steadier, lighter.

Nazim leaned toward her. "You all right?"

Bronya shrugged. "I don't know."

He lit a crude, hand-rolled cigarette, inhaled, and then with his long exhale asked casually, "You ever heard the partisan's oath?

"No." Her voice sounded alien, far away, a stone down a well.

"The last bit of it goes like this: 'For the burned towns and villages, for the death of our women and children, for the torture, violence, and mockery of our people, I swear to take revenge on the enemy cruelly, mercilessly, and relentlessly. Blood for blood and death for death.'" He paused and looked at her. "Yesterday at Kamennomostskoye, the Malka river was clogged with German bodies. The Lermontov Brigade, all of us Jews, obliterated a German tank unit. For Avsey and Lev. I wanted you to know."

Bronya felt an inkling of satisfaction wedge into some remote part of her. This was the solution, she thought, *death*. "Can I join the brigade?"

Nazim's response was immediate. "No. I mean, you can't."

"Why? There are other girls. I heard one say she's a sharp-shooter. I can learn."

"Doesn't matter. I can't let you join."

Bronya was indignant. "I have more of a right than you to avenge my father and brother. You can't stop me."

"Out of the question."

She jumped to her feet, all the anger she'd harbored flooding in, spilling over her edges. "Why the hell not?"

Nazim motioned for her to sit with a calm downward gesture of his hand. He took a long drag on his cigarette. "Here, this will help." He held out the cigarette.

Bronya shook her head, refusing.

Nazim stamped out the ember in the dirt. "I have something to tell you."

Bronya sat down and crossed her arms over her chest. "What is it *you* have to tell *me*?"

Nazim's voice was gentle. "Did you know your grandmother and my father played music together? My father wasn't classically trained like your grandmother, but they played old tunes and gypsy music. He'd come to Rostov from Azerbaijan with his clarinet, after the Revolution. He had a fierce natural talent. He was fierce in every way."

"And this is why I can't join the partisans?"

Nazim lit another cigarette and watched the smoke curl up. "My father regretted that he wasn't with your grandfather on the night he was murdered. That regret never left him. I already have too much regret. My father's and my own."

Bronya blinked. "My grandmother never talked about that night."

"My father talked about it. My parents left Rostov for Pyatigorsk because my father said he didn't trust the city anymore, because he didn't want to remember. He never forgot. More than that, he hid his identity. He named me Nazim, so I would fit in with the neighbors. He lived a life of quiet fear. But revenge was not a word he ever used."

"Babushka wasn't afraid."

"I saw your father a few times when I was a boy. He was close to my mother. She'd taken care of him right after, when your grandmother lost her mind. I'm glad her loss turned to defiance."

Bronya had never imagined Babushka losing her mind or anything else. But when she thought about it, Babushka never spoke about how she felt. She'd told Bronya the facts in a dry, unemotional tone: Her grandfather and others had been murdered by their neighbors because they were Jews.

Bronya watched the sunflowers undulate in the breeze, their

heavy flower heads bowed, swaying like supplicants. "How did Avsey end up with you?"

"When the Germans took Rostov the first time, in November, your father sent Avsey out of the city with neighbors. Eventually, he wrote, saying he'd been abandoned by these people. He'd been hopping trains, trying to survive. When I met him, he was so thin, we thought he might disappear."

Nazim smiled softly and looked toward the mountains. He flicked the long ash of his cigarette into the dirt. "He wasn't scared of much. Rats. Losing you." Nazim lowered his head and took another drag on his cigarette, "When the Germans closed in, your father and Avsey decided not to evacuate. They didn't want to give up on you."

Bronya felt the breath leave her chest, felt it hover beyond her reach. They had stayed because of her?

Nazim swallowed hard, still looking at his feet. "It's my fault. Not yours."

Bronya said, "It's nice of you to absolve me, but…"

Nazim sighed. "Avsey lost his trust in me. I tried to keep him safe, but he wouldn't listen to me. He wanted to go back to Zheleznovodsk. I wouldn't let him. I was rough with him."

Bronya rested her forehead on her knees and closed her eyes. "I don't want him to be dead. I want them both alive." She put her face in the crook of her elbow while another wave of sorrow held her underwater. She sank, her arms and legs heavy, helpless. Images of death—gelatinous fish eyes, pale, unyielding flesh, black blood—crowded her mind's eye. She fought against the images of Papa and Avsey, threatening to form beyond her will.

Nazim cleared his throat. "The next time I saw Avsey, he was at the resettlement operation in a field outside Pyatigorsk and I was in a German uniform."

Bronya sat up. "What are you talking about?"

"I had infiltrated a German unit of Azeri POWs who'd turned to save their skins. I didn't know, but they were being used at the resettlement operations to murder Jews." Nazim bent and picked up several small stones. He chucked one hard into the field. "I begged Avsey to run away." His cheeks hollowed out, and deep lines cut across his forehead as he spoke. He launched another stone into the field. "He saw your father being loaded into a van and ran to him. They died together." Nazim tucked his hands in his pockets and faced Bronya.

"Are you saying Avsey knew he was going to die?"

Nazim took a deep breath, "He knew."

"Why didn't you stop him? He was a little boy."

"I tried. But he didn't believe in me anymore.

"Why?"

"I've asked myself that question a million times. I was a flamethrower, confident I could do anything. I leaned too far back and lit my own hair on fire. Avsey was standing too close." Nazim paused. "I know they're dead because of me. I should have sent Avsey away. Cowardice so easily disguises itself as love."

Bronya's gaze was unflinching. "So if I don't die, you're redeemed?"

Nazim was shaking. "I'll never redeem myself. Regardless, you can't stay."

"What if I want to?"

"Because for me, there is no escape. For you, there is."

Bronya felt her anger flare, burning the pit of her stomach, her nostrils. Her ears itched. She tightened her hands into fists. Her voice was low, barely audible. "I don't want to escape. I want to kill Germans."

Nazim spread his fingers and stared at his hands. "Believe me, it feels good for about a day and then it doesn't anymore. But fair enough—revenge is easier."

"Revenge is relief. You know that. I want relief, too. I don't care if I die."

Nazim stood, the lines around his mouth hard. "I understand. And of course, it's entirely up to you where you go and what you do. But you will not join the partisans. I'll make sure of it."

Bronya stopped. The anger drained from her chest all at once, as if a large hole had been slashed into her, an escape hatch. Another wave of sorrow immediately filled the space. She hung her head.

Nazim continued, "At any rate, it's time to go, if you still want to get through the mountains."

"Now?"

"Last opportunity. The Germans make one mistake, and when it happens, it's best to take advantage. On a long front line, they leave gaps. If you're coming, it has to be now. Soon you won't have a choice."

Nazim turned and walked away. He looked back once and said, "Never squander an opportunity."

Alone, Bronya thought about Avsey walking over Beshtau to rescue her. She yelled at him, "Why didn't you wait? You promised!" Her voice surprised her, but talking to him felt sane. "What should I do?"

When she thought she heard his voice in response, she panicked. "I am like Mama. Hearing voices."

His absence swelled.

"I shouldn't have left you."

In the wink of an eye, Bronya was at the crest again, sputtering into the depths of grief. She cried and begged the air, the mountains, "Please let him come back."

When she heard his voice, clear and strong, she was stunned. *Stay alive.*

And again, *Stay alive.*

CHAPTER 28
KABARDINO-BALKARIA, OCTOBER 1942

IN THE RIVERBED BELOW ZAYUKOVO, NAZIM NARROWED HIS EYES and scanned the Baksan's pebbled banks over the heads of the horses, from left to right. He grabbed the reins of Bronya's horse and held his index finger over his lips. Bronya held her breath until Nazim motioned her forward and the horses waded through water up to their knees.

Bronya scanned the riverbanks, too. "Where are we going?"

"Can't tell you until we're there. Caution is a matter of habit. We'll pass through the gaps in the German lines."

Bronya didn't ask any more questions. She listened, desperate to hear Avsey's voice again. They walked through gorges, through terraced fields surrounded by deep, wild undulations of the earth's surface, more rich green velvet. Bronya felt her anger, her sadness ebb into the landscape. The mountains, the sound of the water tumbling down the rocks far above them, brought her closer to Avsey, as if he shared the beauty of the earth from a great distance.

Nazim and Bronya did not speak. Farmers on small terraced plots raised their heads briefly as they passed. In the late afternoon, they approached Nalchik and checkpoints manned by young Red Army conscripts. Trucks and carts, artillery guns, armored tractors and bicycles, people pulling wagons, pushing prams, all streamed past the checkpoints, the bustle at odds with the deep serenity of the mountains. They rode through an alley of linden trees and saw the Red Army, the Lermontov Brigade tanks, men rushing about, women dragging heavy bags, pulling children, everything moving.

Bronya worried. They had crossed the front lines without notice, but Nalchik was on a war footing, its residents moving out of the way. The further they rode, the more people rushed in the other direction, their belongings loaded onto anything with wheels. Children whistled to their dogs and were scolded by their mothers, and when the clouds parted and gray-white Elbrus rose above them, Bronya was overcome by the magnitude of what needed to be done.

Nazim read her mind. "The mountain isn't unconquerable. Neither are the Germans."

Later, when they had left Nalchik well behind, Nazim told her, "We are going to Urukh. Not far now. I'll leave you with my cousin. I've heard she is evacuating with her children, through the Military Road."

It was almost dark when Nazim pushed open a rickety gate and led the horses through a yard full of apple trees and neatly stacked bricks. The night was cool and cloudless. Bronya shivered in the thin dress she'd been wearing since she left Gulya's village. She wrapped the shawl tight around her shoulders. Did she look as unruly as she felt? She'd long since stopped caring how she smelled. She smoothed her hair with the palms of her hands and turned to face the small brick house.

Nazim opened the door and shouted, "Anyone home?"

In the rush of arms and legs and a chorus squeals, a girl with a long black ponytail ran to wrap her arms around Nazim, followed by a small wiry boy who jumped up and down on his toes, clapping his hands.

A woman who had been tending the fire in the stove stood and wiped her hands on her apron before she, too, clasped

Nazim in a warm embrace. "What's happened to your hair?" She put her hands on his cheeks and looked into his eyes.

"Hello, Miriam."

"Nazim, you're an old man!" Miriam touched his head.

Nazim smiled. "So, I've been told." He turned toward Bronya. "Miriam, this is Bronya."

Miriam glanced down the length of Bronya's torso. "Welcome, child. You must be frozen." She motioned her children forward. "This is my daughter, Liya, and my son, Misha. Come sit by the fire."

Liya eyed Bronya without smiling, but Misha jumped up and down with excitement. "We are going on an adventure, all the way to Tbilisi!"

Liya looked at her little brother. "How do you know it will be an adventure?"

Leaning into Nazim, Misha ignored his sister. He stared at Bronya. "Is she coming on our adventure?"

Nazim laughed and bent over Misha. "Would you take her with you?"

Misha reminded Bronya of a cricket, all elbows and knees and forward movement. His black hair had a mind of its own and stuck out in all directions. He stood up tall and said, "I'm five."

He continued to watch her for a few minutes, as if debating her worth before he reached his hand out to take hers. When she smiled, he led her around the room, pointing out important objects. "This is the stove and this is my bed," he said with pride.

Bronya held Misha's small hand and nodded. She wouldn't let herself cry. Misha was sweet, like Avsey, and Bronya wondered why she hadn't appreciated Avsey's enthusiasm.

The floors and walls were covered with carpets, and in one corner, four mattresses covered with wool blankets lined the wall. On the opposite side of the room, three polished wood trunks stood next to one another. One of them was open and appeared to be full of fabric, whereas the other two were closed and piled with trays, cups, a samovar, books, and ornaments.

As her eyes adjusted to the light in the room, Bronya realized an old man sat in a chair close to the fire, eyes closed, hands folded on top of a sheepskin that covered his legs.

"Uncle Boris. He sleeps all the time." Misha dismissed him with a wave and continued.

"Misha, our guest has had a long journey. Maybe she's tired? Liya, heat water for a bath and find Bronya some clean clothes from my trunk."

Liya rolled her eyes.

Miriam invited Bronya to sit next to Nazim and placed an earthenware platter of herb pie on the round table between them. She shepherded Uncle Boris and Misha to bed while they ate, then returned to make tea for Nazim who looked exhausted, staring into the fire in silence.

Miriam strung a curtain around the stove and motioned for Bronya to join her inside. "Take off your clothes."

Bronya, embarrassed, looked around the curtained room before lifting the dress over her head.

Miriam laughed, pointed to a large tub, and said, "Stand here." She poured warm water from the kettle on the stove into the tub. "No need to be shy, devushka. We are friends."

Miriam scrubbed Bronya from head to toe with a huge slab of rough soap that smelled of rosemary. Bronya winced. The cloth was rough, the water a little too hot. Miriam ignored her, unfolding Bronya's arms talking nonstop. "Misha likes you already. He doesn't like everyone. You should be flattered. He has a heart of stone, that one."

Miriam helped Bronya dry herself with a warm towel and handed her a nightdress and a shawl. "There," she said, "you're beautiful again." She took the curtain down and moved away to pour tea for Nazim.

He stared at Bronya.

Miriam smiled. "She looks different clean. Must have been quite a journey."

Nazim looked away while Miriam continued, "Any trouble crossing the front lines? The Germans are everywhere."

Nazim shrugged, "Evasion is my specialty. I'm more worried about you on the highway. The snow will reach the lower elevations soon. I wouldn't linger anywhere for any reason.

Misha stirred on his mattress, whimpering in his sleep like a puppy.

Nazim nodded in his direction. "How's he doing?"

"He misses his father, but he doesn't know yet. I'll tell him when we're settled."

Nazim looked down at the floor between his feet. "I miss him, too."

Misha's blanket lifted, and he tumbled out from under it to stagger toward his mother. Miriam stood and held her arms out to him, her face drawn. Bronya wondered if Misha had overheard the conversation. He walked past his mother's arms, instead shuffling toward Bronya. He climbed into her lap, laid his head against her shoulder, and asked, "Will you be my sister, too?"

Bronya felt grief rise up and settle just under the surface of her skin, a deep purple bruise. Nazim shifted in his chair, watching her, uneasy.

Miriam looked surprised, but Bronya put her hand on Misha's head and whispered, "Of course I'll be your other sister. I've been needing a little brother."

She looked up, glad Misha couldn't see her face, and took a deep breath. He was already fast asleep.

When Miriam took Misha and lay next to him on his mattress, Nazim addressed Bronya in a quiet voice. "Do you think you'll ever return? I mean, when everything is over?"

"I don't know. I suppose... "

"I want to give you something, before I leave." Nazim pulled a piece of wood from his pocket. A slingshot.

Before she reached for it, Bronya knew it had belonged to Avsey.

"I made it for him, to help him stay courageous when he was alone. Now you need it."

Bronya stared at the rough bifurcated branch, perfect for a slingshot; the elastic slotted through slits on both sides, knotted to keep it in place, the leather pad at the elastic's other end, from which to launch stone pellets. The sorrow welled again, and she tried to swallow it, to breathe it away. She pressed the slingshot against her chest and hung her head. "Thank you," she whispered.

"He'd wanted a pocketknife, told me he'd stolen one from a boy at school but that he'd lost it. I taught him to carve with mine."

Bronya looked up at Nazim. "It isn't possible." She walked to her bag in the corner and pulled out the green knife. "I found this the day the war started, in the kitchen at home, stuck between the wall and the linoleum. It must have been his."

Nazim smiled and shook his head. "He was something special, your brother." He rose slowly and stuck his hand out. "I'm going to get some rest."

Bronya put her hand in his, and he held it for a long moment while he looked at her. "You're a warrior, but warriors swallow their grief. Grief held hostage turns to anger." He let her hand go gently, then turned and carefully shut the door behind him.

Regret drenched Bronya's insides. She wanted to run after Nazim, ride the horses back through the valleys together. Why, if she was a warrior, hadn't he let her stay? She had so many questions about Papa and Avsey. She'd miscalculated her time with Nazim, and now it was over.

Before the light touched the apple trees in the garden, Nazim was gone.

CHAPTER 29
THE GEORGIAN MILITARY HIGHWAY,
OCTOBER–NOVEMBER 1942

By the time the cart pulled away from the yard in the morning, the apple trees were barely visible. Fog had crawled into the earth's crevices and indentations to flatten and obscure the hills, the dwellings, and the people who lived in them. Only the rock promontories on either side of the road were visible, a kind of otherworldly maze from which there was no escape. The horse found the road and pulled the cart south, toward the high mountains.

Uncle Boris sat at the front of the cart with Miriam, taciturn but good-natured. He pretended to hide a coin behind Misha's ear, pulling it out with an exaggerated look of surprise. In the fog, his narrow head appeared disembodied, his ears overly large. He moved his fingers deliberately, so that every trick was obvious. Rather than diminish Misha's delight, the old man's practiced movements, his clownish appearance, enhanced the fun. Misha laughed harder with each reveal.

Liya rolled her eyes, but she, too, was kind to the old man. Bronya had watched her settle him into the cart and place the sheepskin over his legs, kissing him tenderly on the cheek. Misha moved to sit next to Uncle Boris, leaving Liya and Bronya the pile of carpets and sheepskins in the back.

At Ordzhonikidze, the sun burned the fog away, and the temperature rose. Bronya peeled off the vatnik Miriam had given her and rolled her sleeves up above her elbows. She and Liya both pulled their valenki off and let the sun warm their toes.

Liya said, "You aren't from the mountains."

"No, Rostov."

"How do you know Nazim, then?"

"He is a friend of my father."

Liya glanced at her mother and leaned closer to Bronya. "I want to marry Nazim, but my mother says he is too complicated. She says he wouldn't make a good husband."

Bronya thought about the cigarette marks on Nazim's arms, about the way he'd looked at her the night before. "Maybe she's right. He is older than you."

"That's not it. My father was fifteen years older than my mother. She says Nazim takes too many risks. My father took risks, and she doesn't want me to be widowed."

"Mothers. I guess they know. "

Liya leaned against Bronya. "I like you better now."

In Ordzhonikidze, the road along the Terek River teemed with Red Army tanks, soldiers, and militia. Old men strolled together or sat on the riverbank watching the commotion, gesturing with their hands in heated discussions. Sheep, and an occasional cow wandered freely, beholden to no one, stopping military traffic.

Miriam drove on, past a half-empty market in disarray after the early morning rush. Abandoned vegetables littered the ground, a small girl in a knitted dress—two, maybe three years old—stood in the middle of it all, crying. No one paid any attention.

An air of anxious anticipation permeated the air while women in colorful dresses hawked nuts, yellow apples, and pomegranates. People in carts and on foot, laden with bundles of various sizes, streamed out of the town and into the mountains. Some stopped to look back before they continued forward, heads down. One woman picked up a stone, kissed it, and put it in her pocket.

The staccato sound of airplanes, and the frightening maneuvers of tanks in the streets, turning, backing up, out of place in size and scale, heightened the tension. The bustle and drive thrilled Misha, who stood and waved at the tanks.

Only yesterday, Bronya had been in occupied territory. She thought about the people in Nalchik. In war, the status quo could change in an instant.

At the start of the Military Road, before they began the ascent, a military policeman stopped the cart. The traffic slowed behind them. "Where are you going, citizen?" The policeman was stern.

"I'm taking the children and the old man to my sister's home in Tbilisi."

"Where does the horse come from?" He bit down on the twig in his mouth and waited for the answer as impatience grew behind them.

"We are brickmakers. The horse transports bricks to the factories."

The policeman's eyes went from the front of the cart to the back, resting on Bronya and Liya. "The carpets?"

"I make them, comrade, at home."

The noise grew louder—horns, shouting, banging. The policeman, distracted, waved Miriam through, though he appeared reluctant and looked longingly at the carpets. When Bronya turned to look back, she saw him yelling at a shepherd whose animals had swarmed onto the road, urged on by the chaos around them. An old man on a dilapidated bicycle had been hit by a truck and sat, dazed on the ground, his battered bike beside him.

The little cart followed the Terek, climbing onto the Military Road surrounded by lush mountain pastures, a rich carpet of green and purple. Bronya was accustomed to the high mountains in the distance, but she'd never actually clung to their sides. The earth, she could see, healed itself, covered its ancient eruptions in vegetation. Could humans heal their chasms?

They entered the Darial Gorge. Bronya pulled her head into her shoulders and gazed up. Minerals in the speckled granite glistened, moss and ferns grew in decorative patterns in the shady crevices, and water trickled quietly down well-worn grooves into the river. At one point, the high granite walls engulfed the road in shadow, and though it was late morning, Bronya shivered. She and Liya pushed their arms into their vatniks backward and pulled sheepskins around their shoulders. Military vehicles towed antiaircraft guns, soldiers marched in both directions, and children nudged one another and pointed, stupefied by the height of the rocks surrounding them.

Liya cast a sideways glance at Misha, who had rejoined them and was lying on his back, looking up, his head cushioned by a pile of carpets. Eventually, he dozed off.

Liya turned to Bronya and whispered, "Is your father dead, too?" She looked up at the small sliver of sky above them as if indicating the place where dead fathers lived. Her face was serious, and for the first time, Bronya noticed tiny curls along her hairline that framed her pale face and dark eyes.

Bronya nodded slowly.

"I thought so," said Liya. "Misha doesn't know. We'll tell him in Tbilisi. Do you have brothers and sisters?"

Bronya shook her head and looked up at the granite. She'd admitted Papa's loss. There was no reason to share any part of Avsey with anyone.

Gradually, they climbed out of the gorge, high above the river, following the road carved into the mountainside. The mountain peaks were covered in snow while the lower elevations, remained startlingly verdant. They skirted the ruins of an ancient fort.

Below, the riverbed narrowed and the water gleamed, a thin ribbon of liquid silver. Misha opened his eyes and was frightened. "Take me out of the teeth, I don't like them." Indeed, the mountains above his head resembled giant teeth.

Liya calmed her brother by pointing out the river below.

After a long while, during which the conversation lagged and Uncle Boris napped sitting up, solitary headstones appeared on the hillside above them, sunken, lopsided into the earth. Further up lay a small graveyard, a neat iron fence around its perimeter. Miriam stopped, and they climbed to look at the graves. Tsarist soldiers who'd fought and died in the Caucasus and who'd never seen their homes again.

Misha was curious. He brushed the leaves from each one and asked Bronya to read the names and dates. Some were difficult to read, erased by time, covered in lichen. Forgotten soldiers, forgotten wars.

They left quickly, and to appease Misha, who'd grown irritable, Liya found a long stick. He waved the stick all the way down the hillside, lifting his legs into a march, a serious expression on his face.

At the cart, Bronya used the green pocketknife to strip the bark from the stick to make a smooth handle for Misha's little hand. Misha marched around the cart, kicking rocks, his arms swinging. Liya applauded. Uncle Boris stepped up and settled into place, ready to leave. Miriam occupied herself with the horse and scolded Misha for his exuberance, warning that the weather looked threatening.

They still had a long way to go. Bronya motioned Misha to climb up next to her when something caught her eye, a glimmer of silvery movement. She watched in horror as a snake coiled and raised its scaly head, poised to strike. Misha had seen the snake, too, and held himself still, his face pale.

The green knife was in Bronya's hand, the blade out. She heard Miriam laugh, as if at some distance, a tiny half-laugh. Uncle Boris coughed. Their heads were raised, and they were looking at something on the road ahead, in the direction they were about to travel.

A split second later, in one long, continuous motion, Bronya lunged. She scooped the snake up with the blade and flung it hard off to the side. The snake landed in front of the horse, writhed in the dirt, then untwisted itself and slithered away. Misha fixed his eyes on Bronya but did not move.

Miriam screamed. The horse, affronted by both the snake and the human panic, tossed its head and moved the cart backward toward the edge of the road. Bronya dropped the knife and grabbed Misha while Miriam struggled to hold on to Uncle Boris. The cart's wheels loosened the soil, throwing small pebbles and dirt clods skittering down the steep sides of the cliff. Miriam, ashen-faced, closed her eyes. It was Liya who grabbed the reins and pulled the horse away from the precipice.

For several minutes, the only sound on the road was Miriam sobbing. She held the old man, her whole body shaking. When she stepped down, holding firmly to the sides of the cart, she took Misha from Bronya and gathered all three children close. Her body shuddered every few seconds, and Bronya had the impression she couldn't speak.

When at last they were all loaded back on the cart, Misha sat between Uncle Boris and Miriam. He had wanted to sit next to Bronya, but Miriam, her hands still shaking, held on tight to her son.

She pointed. "Look up. It's Kazbek. Isn't it beautiful?"

A cold fog swirled around the high mountain, the white peak towering above the others, mighty and mysterious. Misha began to cry, and Miriam pulled him tighter to her side and urged the horse forward.

A cold rain began, and Miriam covered Misha and Uncle Boris with carpets while she drove the horse from under her own carpet. Liya and Bronya crawled under a layer of sheepskins covered by a thick carpet and lay there in the diminishing light. The horse climbed, slow but steady. Bronya thought of the coiled snake, its scaly back and triangular head. Chills ran down the length of her spine.

Liya pulled something from under her dress, from around her neck. "This is for you. It's an amulet. It will protect you from evil."

Bronya took the necklace and held it over her head. Composed of almond-shaped silver beads, small red stones, and coins, the necklace was unusually attractive. A round, silver pendant hung from the middle, engraved with crude Hebrew letters. "It's too pretty for me, Liya. I can't take it." Bronya held out her hand to return the gift.

"Put it on and never take it off. I have one, too." Liya pulled another long strand of beads from under her dress. "I wanted to give it to you before we left home, but I was embarrassed. One only gives an amulet with love, otherwise it doesn't protect. Anyway, I didn't love you until now."

Bronya slipped the necklace around her neck and wrapped her hand around the pendant.

"You dropped this." Liya pressed the pocketknife into Bronya's hand. "Good you didn't kill the snake though. That's very bad luck."

Bronya laughed. She liked Liya's superstitions. As she'd liked Babushka's. She'd been right to keep the pocketknife. It had brought good luck.

The rain did not let up, and the horse continued its slow progress as the mountains swallowed the light. Bronya lay in the back of the cart listening to voices on the road. She didn't know where they came from or to whom they belonged. Unable to see her hand in front of her face, she reached for Liya's, but she was fast asleep. Bronya kept her eyes open and listened.

When the sounds outside became muted, Bronya lifted the carpet shelter and sat up. They were in a long tunnel. The cart passed dark figures bent over small fires, oblivious to the wheels passing dangerously close to their feet.

Miriam turned to look at her. "You're awake. Let Uncle Boris stretch out and sleep in the back. Come up front with me."

Bronya shook Liya awake, and together they helped Uncle

Boris lay down in the back of the cart and readjusted the sheepskin and carpets to cover him. He was drowsy and lay down with a groan. Liya straightened his legs and kissed him on the forehead.

"Misha, do you want to lay in the back with uncle?"

Misha shook his head and lay down in Bronya's lap. He took her hand and placed it on his cheek. "Stay here."

Wisps of fog and mist curled eerily through the tunnel. Misha fell asleep.

Bronya had to fight to stay awake, miserable she hadn't taken the opportunity to sleep when she was in the back. Liya fell asleep, her head on her mother's shoulder. Despite herself, Bronya felt at home on the little cart.

By the time the cart exited the tunnel, the rain had stopped. Miriam pointed to the turrets of a fortress not far above their heads. "It's Ananuri." The stone structures were connected by thick fortress walls, the kind of walls one imagined in fairy tales, with small cutouts for archers to defend from invaders below. "I was inside once, when I was a little girl. Six hundred years old."

At dawn, the clouds stretched into thin strands of orange and scarlet over the valley while the stars sparkled, a scattering of tiny gems, polished by the light already spilling over the mountains. Liya and Misha opened their eyes and stretched. When a falling star streaked across the sky, Liya noted in a matter-of-fact tone, "Someone has died. It's a soul falling from the heavens."

Bronya watched another falling star, its trajectory shorter than the first. Wouldn't all the stars in the sky have to fall if each one represented a death?

The road now ran alongside a wide stretch of river close to the water; thin waterfalls sent trails of water down the rocky slopes to the river, and the sound of water and birdsong made the earth feel fresh, cleansed of its sins.

Ahead, a large flock of sheep, an army of marauders, shook the world awake with their vibratos. Low houses appeared, all with terra-cotta roofs and stone walls.

Miriam pointed to a great stone monastery on the side of the mountain. "Jvari. Christians believe this is a place of miracles. We are close to Tbilisi."

Misha climbed into the back to lie down with Uncle Boris. He'd only been gone a few seconds when a sheepskin flew off the side of the cart and landed on the road.

Miriam and the girls turned their heads in unison to see Misha, wobbly, standing in the back of the cart. Miriam, alarmed, yelled, "Misha, sit down! You'll fall out!"

Misha grasped the back of the seat to steady himself and said, "I think Uncle Boris is dead."

CHAPTER 30
TBILISI, NOVEMBER–DECEMBER 1942

BY THE TIME SARA WAS READY TO LEAVE SERGEI AND STRIKE OUT ON her own, she had learned that alcohol; a few bottles of Georgian wine and a bottle of cognac, bought safe passage across the front lines.

Sergei's cognac also bought several small pills the German Army issued its soldiers to keep them awake. The pills kept Sergei awake enough to drive through the mountain pass in the middle of the night. Sara understood the tenacity of the German army in a different light. The first snow fell two days later.

They arrived in a small village in the Georgian foothills and stayed the night with a family of winemakers, suppliers of Sergei's bribes.

In the evening, sitting in the cold garden in the dark, Sergei lifted a bottle. "To crossing boundaries, to mountains, to freedom."

Sara laughed. "What freedom? You are a dreamer."

"Maybe. But I never lose sight of it—too much time alone, I suppose." He lifted a bottle of samogon and added, "To the future." He took a swig and held the bottle out.

Sara's voice was quiet. "We'll never be free. But I am grateful."

She reached for the bottle and tilted her head back. The homemade stuff always burned the throat. "What didn't you tell me that night in Agrippina's cottage? There was something she didn't want you to say."

"It isn't important now. Honest."

"Something about Asya."

Sergei paused a long moment before he said, "Sara, listen. I don't want you to hate her. Just the opposite. I want you to stop blaming yourself. Her mind had gone. She was not in touch with reality."

Sara took another long drink. The samogon's burn crawled down her throat and into her chest. She handed the bottle to Sergei and waited.

Sergei's smile disappeared. He stared at his feet, and his voice cracked. "After I was arrested, Asya denounced Lyosha. She told the authorities he'd tried to change her mind. They interpreted her words as meaning he was ideologically suspect."

Sara's head spun, but the samogon, oddly, buoyed her. The sister whose left hand was her right, had taken her husband away? Sara couldn't believe it. "Why would she do that?"

"She thought Lyosha was putting ideas into my head, telling me to leave her. Her interrogators, institutionally delusional, failed to see her insanity. She didn't mean to harm him. In her mind, justice involved warnings about the devil. She told me when I was released. It brought me to my senses and I never saw her again."

"Why are you telling me now?"

"Because, we won't see one another again. And I don't want you, in your mind and memory, to doubt him. He was a gem of a man."

Sara took the bottle. "No wonder great armies trade in fire-water. Burns through all the bad news." She took a long swig. The burn, worse this time, made her cough.

Sergei smiled, "Samogon burns through more than bad news. Believe me, I know." He held his hand out for the bottle.

Sara put her hand on his shoulder. "Regret isn't as useful as it should be, but neither is denial. You're a brave man, Sergei."

SARA TOOK HER LEAVE OF SERGEI IN GORI, STALIN'S HOMETOWN, not far from Tbilisi. "Stalin should have stayed here," he whispered, looking around, "in the church."

Sara laughed. "He might have become a smuggler, like you."

Sergei smiled and raised his eyebrows. "Certain you don't want to stay on? A smuggler's life isn't so bad, and when the war's over, you'll be set."

"I don't trust the mountains in the same way you do, Sergei. And they don't trust me."

"All right, but I have someone for you in Tbilisi. Her brother shared a cell with me in 1938. He was a Georgian, a Jew, a writer. Just before he was shot, he told me about his sister. Fanny Baazova. Find her and tell her what's happened—your story, not mine."

Sara did not relish telling anyone anything of the kind, but she took the name and address Sergei wrote for her on a small slip of paper. There was a story to tell, an urgent warning about what the Germans were doing, what they'd done in Rostov. What they must be doing everywhere.

Sergei asked one of his comrades to drive her to Tbilisi in his battered truck. Leaning into the window, he said, "Backward is a step into the abyss, a promise broken before its made. My motto."

He kissed her on the cheek.

SARA FOUND NUMBER 3 ANTON CATHOLICOS STREET IN THE OLD Town of Tbilisi. She was surprised to see it was a synagogue, a square brick building with a low dome and a cupola rimmed with round windows, topped by a slender spire. The leaded windows around the cupola were decorated with Stars of David.

The door was unlocked, the building deserted. Cautious, Sara circled the room, staring up into the dome, marveling at the graceful simplicity of the leaded glass. A woman's voice behind her made her jump. "Are you interested in the building, or have you come for something else?"

A small woman, younger than Sara but square-shouldered and self-assured, stood by the door, her hand resting on the iron handle.

Sara addressed her as comrade. "I am looking for Fanny. I know someone who knew her brother."

The young woman smiled sadly. "I'm Fanny. Which brother are you referring to? I had two."

Fanny's eyes were deep brown, almost black. She wore a dark scarf over her long hair, tied at the back, and had an old-fashioned air of grace about her, as if she'd stepped from a 19th century painting. "What happened to them?"

"They were both shot."

Sara, who for years hadn't wanted to admit Lyosha's death to herself, let alone to a stranger, said, "I'm sorry."

"Where is this friend who knew my brother? Why did he send you?"

"He brought me through the mountains and thought you might help me. I have information about the Germans, about what they are doing. I want someone to know."

Fanny remained impassive. "Someone? My help will depend on what you have to share and who you want to tell."

"I have no idea if you can help. Maybe no one can." It was clear Fanny was a rebel. But reachable, kind.

Sara heard herself say, "My husband was shot."

"Is that the information you have to share?" Fanny's tone did not change, but Sara thought she saw a softening in Fanny's eyes.

"It's the first time I've said it."

"It isn't hard when you get used to it. Better than the lie."

"The lie?"

"Believing they're alive somewhere. My father is in Siberia. Every time I say it, I hope he's alive, that he'll walk through the door in an hour and ask for something to eat. Hope is another kind of lie. The finality of a bullet to the head is not much different from the finality of hard labor."

Sara lowered herself onto a long bench and repeated Sergei's declaration to Agrippina. "The dead are all we have."

Fanny eased in next to Sara and gently took her hand. "That's not true. We have life."

"The Germans are killing Jews by the hundreds, maybe thousands, shooting them into ditches. I have seen it."

Fanny sighed. "I know. But honestly, there is no one to tell, unless you leave here, unless you travel a long way, and for that, you need money. Do you have money?"

Sara shook her head.

"Better to stay then, isn't it?" Fanny touched Sara's shoulder, pressed into it with a firm hand.

Sara stayed, settling into a small corner in Fanny's apartment where she slept.

It was Fanny who urged Sara to become a guardian for the dead. Sara, who had known little of ritual and nothing of cadavers, began to ritually wash the stiffening corpses of the recently deceased.

After she'd washed a woman who'd died in childbirth, Sara felt the work as a calling and thought of nothing else. She learned that the face muscles, eyes, and mouth stiffened first, then the small muscles in the hands and arms. Every corpse gave up the suppleness of life in the same ordered way, but age determined the rate at which the changes occurred—babies and old people stiffened faster than youth and middle age.

Her devotion strengthened when she noticed that the dead frightened the living. The dead needed her to ease the wounded hearts of the grieving and the living needed her to help them let go lovingly, without lingering.

She washed and listened, all the while asking forgiveness

from each corpse for the imposition, the loss of dignity, the lapses of judgment she may have made or might make in the future, for complacency, for the trembling of her hands, her *heart*.

In point of fact, she asked forgiveness from all the dead as she worked, from Lyosha and Asya, from those she loved and those she never knew. From Kuzma. The act of asking for forgiveness, never mind the acquisition of it, was alone sufficient to keep her among the living.

Fanny, seeing her devotion, pushed her to the bathhouse, too. "The other half of the burden is to soothe and purify. The burial society and the bathhouse. Balance."

CHAPTER 31
TBILISI, NOVEMBER–DECEMBER 1942

THE FADED BEAUTY OF TBILISI DREW BRONYA IN AT FIRST SIGHT. THE narrow streets were festooned with iron balconies and winding staircases, laundry stretched between buildings like multicolored flags. There were white trams and blue doors and bearded giants, their stone muscles embalmed in thick porticos. Marbled meat hung on metal hooks in the markets and feral cats patrolled small courtyards where bright rugs hid secret doorways.

Miriam drove the cart carrying dead Uncle Boris through Tibilis's Old Town until she reached a stone house with a round wood balcony. Most of its glass windows were shattered, covered in brown paper, itself peppered with holes and tattered edges.

Their arrival had not been expected. Bronya hung back as the flurry of greetings and bad news traveled through the courtyard. Neighbors appeared, wondering who had died. The horse was taken away. Someone handed her a bowl of soup while Liya and Misha disappeared into the rhythm of the familiar household.

A group of men carried Uncle Boris's body into square room at the side of the house and lay him there. Bronya and Liya unloaded the rugs and sheepskins and piled them in the courtyard under the balcony to shield them from the threat of snow. When they returned from their task, the last remnants of dappled light from the small window danced over the mound of Uncle Boris's lifeless flesh, his head covered with a linen cloth. Two black-clad women appeared, dragging chairs behind them, then took up their posts as sentries. Liya whispered, "They watch over him until the burial." Others congregated to shout and wail over the body.

More men arrived, tasked with washing Uncle Boris's body, and the wailing women emptied out into the courtyard to quiet their children. Misha was in turn, called into the dimly lit room to pour a small vial of water over the body, the last step in the ritual before burial. Misha was small in front of the corpse, and Bronya, at the sight of him so close to the dead, felt lightheaded. She fought the urge to grab him, to hold him close.

As night fell, the women lit candles to accompany their vigil, and several men came to recite prayers. Bronya thought about all the unguarded bodies whose dignity had not been preserved. She thought about Papa and Avsey and about Babushka whose death had been marked with whispered condolences and quiet talk.

And the prayer for the dead.

Bronya thought about Papa reciting Kaddish. Because of it, she'd met Nazim, learned the truth about Papa and Avsey, she was *alive* because of the prayer for the dead. Papa's quiet fidelity to his mother, to his ancestors, had saved her.

WHEN THE MOURNING PERIOD WAS OVER, MIRIAM ARRANGED FOR them all to wash. "New beginnings," she said. Bronya had seen the brick molehill domes, richly tiled, steam seeping from their arched windows. She dreaded sharing a steam bath with others, as she had in the sanitorium. But Liya had looked aghast when she asked to stay behind.

In the anteroom of the bathhouse, a woman appeared at the door to tell them where to undress. Bronya lifted her head as the woman exited and thought she saw a resemblance, striking even from behind, to her mother. Her mind was playing tricks on her. She'd been dreaming of Mama.

Liya leaned over. "Bronya? Stand up. You'll be fine."

Bronya pushed herself out of the chair. The bathhouse couldn't wash away her loneliness, her guilt.

Liya nudged her. "Don't worry. No one will steal your clothes."

Bronya smiled at Liya. She was glad to have a friend when so much else was uncertain. Still, she wanted more—a tether, a way to stop floating. She undressed, sank into the sulfuric waters and closed her eyes.

Bronya let her shoulders relax. She remembered Mama tickling Avsey in his bed, his raucous laughter. She saw Mama in the kitchen, her head turned toward the table where they all sat attentive, expectant—of what, she did not remember. She remembered Avsey's note, pressed into her hand at their leave-taking. More than anything, she regretted abandoning him. Avsey, grown old at eleven, had wanted to die. Had she been there to arraign the wicked, to pierce the darkness, would he have chosen her? Could she have saved him?

The bath attendant washed Bronya's hair and scrubbed behind her ears with a rough cloth. It hurt, but Bronya gave way, as if the battle had finally collapsed the ramparts, taking the defenses with them in a slurry of mud and muscle. In the plunge, Bronya felt the longing for Mama more acutely, felt she might cry, but the attendant softened her touch, rinsed her gently, and wrapped her hair in a cloth to absorb the water. The unexpected tenderness soothed her.

Miriam had brought them all clean dresses, and when they were dry, Liya and Bronya slipped the dresses on and made their way to a small anteroom. They sat in flimsy chairs, their wet hair hanging down their backs, waiting for tea. It was in this defenseless, somewhat soporific state that Bronya raised her head at the sound of slippers, in expectation of a warm drink. She shivered and focused on the woman who approached with two glasses of tea, one in each hand. But as the woman's face came into focus, Bronya was confused, then stunned.

The woman who stood in front of her looked exactly like her mother. She was thinner, almost frail, her spine rounded forward, her beauty nostalgic where once it had been breathtaking. The resemblance was uncanny. Bronya closed her eyes. Surely, she was hallucinating. It was because she wanted to see Mama that this woman appeared before her, a ghost.

She opened her eyes. The likeness remained.

The woman had stopped, her mouth frozen open.

Bronya couldn't help herself. She whispered, "Mama?"

The two glasses of tea slipped from the woman's fingers simultaneously and shattered on the floor. Liya jumped up, alarmed.

The woman fell against the wall, edged to a chair, and collapsed. She lifted her head and said, "Your mother is dead. It's me, Sara."

IN THE EVENING, WHEN SARA RETURNED TO HER TINY CORNER AT Fanny's, she paused in the doorway, her arm around Bronya.

Fanny, at the table slicing potatoes, a cup of tea beside a pile of peels, raised her eyebrows. "Who do we have here?"

Sara, who was still in shock, said, "My sister's child."

Fanny's eyes widened, but she composed herself and motioned them to sit. She smiled, "Welcome, beautiful girl. How have you come to Tbilisi?"

Sara interrupted, "She gave me news of her brother and father and hasn't spoken since."

Fanny nodded. "Of course. Understandable. You've told her everything."

"Yes, We are..." Sara's voice trailed off, "all we have."

Fanny took Bronya's hand. "You are a gift." She turned to Sara and whispered gently, "She won't disappear if you take your eyes away. I promise."

"I should never have taken my eyes off her in the first place."

MONTHS PASSED. THE GERMANS WERE PUSHED BACK FROM THE great mountains and still Bronya had not spoken. By then, Sara had found a room in the Old Town in a dank basement apartment, close to Miriam and her family.

Bronya moved back and forth between the two households.

Misha didn't want her to leave him. He'd told Sara as much. "You can't have her all to yourself," he said. "She needs us too."

In the evenings Sara took to sitting in the courtyard brushing Bronya's hair for hours, until it was so dark they couldn't see one another. "This is all I need," she said to Bronya.

Then, one temperate evening, Bronya looked up and said, "Remember when we went to say goodbye to Mama?"

Sara, startled, nodded slowly, careful not to upset the delicate balance between the end of one state and the beginning of another. "I remember."

"Now she's gone and I can't forgive myself. I can't forgive myself for any of them."

"My brave girl, we didn't cause their deaths—we simply did what we did. We couldn't have known we could never go back." Sara twisted Bronya's hair into a knot at the nape of her neck. "Maybe we can forgive ourselves if we forgive them."

A FEW NIGHTS LATER, BRONYA WOKE SARA, SHOOK HER SHOULDER, and waited patiently while Sara collected herself and lit a lamp. "I don't know what to do with this." She held out the birch box.

"What is it?" Sara took the box from Bronya's hands.

"Avsey's treasure."

"Where did it come from?"

Bronya didn't answer.

She sat down under the lamp and spilled the contents out onto the rug. "Oh, hooligan, where did you get all this?"

"Nazim told me Avsey was a thief."

Sara smiled. "And what a beautiful thief he was." She plucked the silver cigarette case from the pile and handed it to Bronya. "Your father's initials."

Bronya took it and ran her index finger over the letters.

"Your mother's wedding ring and her necklace." Sara's voice wavered with emotion. "I can't believe it." She picked up a photograph. "Sergei."

"Mama's friend from childhood, Sergei?"

"Yes. And my friend too."

Sara held the birth certificate in her hand and studied the hole. She looked up at Bronya and wondered how much to tell. But then, there on the rug, was the sapphire. Sara couldn't catch her breath.

She picked up the stone between her thumb and index finger and held it up to the lamp. "Do you know what this is?"

"A jewel?"

Sara laughed. "Yes, a sapphire. A beautiful sapphire."

"Avsey stole a sapphire? Who did he steal it from?" Bronya's tone was incredulous.

"Your father."

"What? That's ridiculous. Why would Papa have a sapphire?"

Sara sighed. "Honestly, I don't know where to begin." She looked at the sapphire, then placed it in the palm of her hand. "Your father helped a woman, a long time ago, when you were little—a former person. This former person gave Papa the sapphire as payment for saving her life."

Bronya said, "That's odd. Did she live upstairs with Madame Alexandra? I saw her once at my piano lesson. She pinned her silver hair into a bun at the back with a beautiful comb. She told me I was very talented. Madame

Alexandra scolded her for talking to me and then gave me a doll."

Sara smiled. " I always thought you knew everything."

Bronya asked, "What about Sergei?"

"That, my love, is more complicated. But you are no longer a child." Sara looked at the ceiling before she began. "Your mother loved someone other than your father. She loved Sergei."

Bronya didn't know why, but she wasn't surprised. "Did we ever see him?"

"I don't know, but—and this is difficult—your mother had a child with Sergei, before you were born, before she married your father." Sara held up the birth certificate with the hole in it. "This is his, Kuzma's. She must have cut his patronymic and family name from his birth certificate. Your mother hid many things."

"Where was this child? Why didn't we know him?"

"He lived with his grandmother in Proletarsky. I'm not sure how much your mother saw him. He was unusual, never spoke."

"Where is he now?"

"He died at the same place, on the same day your mother died."

Bronya was silent for a long time. "Is that why the voices came? Because she loved Sergei?"

Sara swallowed and looked at the floor. When she raised her head, she brushed away a tear, her hand trembling "I don't know. My love, she was secretive, able to hide in plain sight. I wish I understood more. I loved her and I couldn't help her."

SARA SAT UP ALL NIGHT AS BRONYA SLEPT, SIFTING THROUGH THE contents of Avsey's box, contemplating each object. She could only wonder at his tenacity, his small boy courage. She knew some of his story from Bronya, that he'd kept the box and its contents when he'd been lost and alone and then with his father on the front lines, a feat so remarkable as to be preposterous. She held up the slingshot Bronya said was his, the item that held more grief for her than anything. She'd taught him to be David against Goliath, but for all his bravery, he'd lost. It was unbearable.

In the morning, after tea, Sara said, "Let's talk about the future, hooligan. For a change."

Bronya let her back relax against the chair. "All right. Will we stay in Tbilisi?"

"I will stay here. Do what I am doing now, for a little while. I have no desire to return to Rostov, even when the war ends. Have you thought about going back? After the fighting passes, as it will."

Bronya shrugged. "I sometimes want to be where they were, the places I remember them. At the same time, I don't."

Sara opened Avsey's box, tilted it, and reached in. She pulled out the sapphire and handed it to Bronya. "This will buy you a ticket out."

Bronya stared at Sara. "*Out?*"

"You don't need to stay here. The soil, the air you breathe, will always be blood-soaked. You can leave. Fanny can help. She's helped others. Through Istanbul, you can go anywhere."

"I won't leave you. Ever. You are everything, all I have."

"That's just the thing. I want you to have more. The sapphire can give you a new beginning. You'll buy yourself another violin, go to school, meet a boy. I have no idea what will happen here, but it won't be right for a long time. You'll waste half your life, your talent. Maybe one day I'll follow you."

"You don't want me to stay with you?"

"I want you to go, because I love you. The best thing you could do for me is live."

Bronya looked at the sapphire in her palm. "When Papa made the box, he told Avsey to choose carefully how he used it, that he would have to decide what was important and what was not." Bronya stared into the small interior of the box. "He couldn't have known."

"He was a wise little boy, that brother of yours. And he left you a life."

Bronya, still looking into the box, gasped. She pulled a small, folded piece of paper from its depths, smoothed it open over her knee, then held it up for Sara to see.

Written in Avsey's innocent cursive was:

Nothing changes, everything changes.

EPILOGUE
TEL AVIV 1970

BRONYA WATCHED THROUGH THE TERMINAL WINDOW, PAST THE expanse of pale-yellow sand and ineffable blue sky, as the El Al flight from Vienna touched down and then, propellers slowing, moved closer to the tower. She'd planned to mount the steps to the veranda to watch the plane land, had dreams of waving and calling out to Sara from above, but the veranda had been closed a month earlier.

Bronya hadn't seen Sara since they'd held one another on the Turkish border twenty-seven years earlier. In that expanse of time, some of Sara's predictions about life outside the Soviet Union had come to pass. Others had not.

Bronya's departure had not been a harbinger of peace and tranquility as Sara promised. The years had in fact seen wars and rumors of wars, conflicts large and small. Everywhere was blood-soaked: all of Europe with the stories of a seismic shattering, the proportions of which, impossible to grasp, were slowly revealed to the world. The land had had its share of tragedy and consequence, and so had Bronya. She'd married, lost her husband, secured a music career, and fashioned a life from hardscrabble realities.

On that dusty border all those years ago, they had vowed to

live lives unhampered by secrets, to strive for—if not happiness —satisfaction. Bronya, insofar as she was able, had honored her commitment. She spoke openly of everything, her experience of the Soviet Union, the war. The only secret she could never relinquish had to do with Avsey. His death had been her fault. She'd abandoned him. He died because she'd made the wrong choice. She never shared Avsey's story with anyone, made a point of recreating her past to exclude him, all the while plagued by nightmares of his last moments.

Sara had been right about the sapphire. In the intervening years, Bronya bought a beautiful Guarneri violin and an education with the finest teachers. And when in 1969, Babushka's violin made its way to Tel Aviv in search of its mistress, she acquired it without asking questions, its provenance and price meaningless compared to the joy of reunification, the star with its owner.

Bronya looked up. Sara walked into the terminal, as beautiful as ever, her long white hair pulled back elegantly, her fine fingers clutching a small satchel. Bronya was overcome. She wrapped her arms around her aunt and did not let go.

"Oh, hooligan, here we are together. Can you believe it?"

Sara broke loose and turned to look behind her as more passengers squinted on the tarmac and made their way into the small terminal. "I've brought surprises," she said.

A thin, dark-haired man walked through the doors and stopped next to Sara. His crooked smile was reminiscent of something or someone, but Bronya, staring at him, couldn't find the connection.

"You don't know me?" He moved closer and smiled again.

What a gentle soul. And then she recognized him. "Misha?"

Misha laughed.

Bronya hugged him. All she could think to say was, "You look exactly the same, only bigger."

"We are going to be neighbors, like in Tbilisi."

Bronya turned to Sara. "You've brought me a family."

Sara didn't appear to hear. She was craning her neck to see the passengers walking through the doors.

Misha looked up at the ceiling, "Isn't life funny? Not in my wildest dreams, standing here all together..."

Sara turned, smiling as another stranger put his small leather suitcase on the floor at her feet. Bronya, just for a second, felt that Avsey was there, whispering to her, trying to tell her something.

The man lifted his head. His white hair contrasted with his dark eyebrows. Who was this man standing so close to Sara? Was he lost? Misha was smiling now, watching her.

Bronya, confused, heard Avsey's voice again but couldn't make out the words. "Nazim?"

Nazim held his arms out. "They let us go, so here I am."

AT THE APARTMENT BRONYA SAT WITH SARA AND MISHA ON THE balcony drinking tea. Nazim stood looking out on the street. This edge of Tel Aviv was dusty, but villas had sprung up in recent years and with them, small gardens.

Bronya liked the balcony. It reminded her of Rostov. Passersby said hello as they walked past, children waved on their way to the small park on the other side of the building, and neighbors posted small announcements on the cement pillar at the entrance—births and deaths, occasionally a lost item. This was a community, a brotherhood of sorts, a recognition that they belonged to one another.

Sara took another date from the platter of dried fruit on the table. "When can we come to a concert? We want to hear the famous orchestra and its star violinist."

Bronya smiled. "I'm hardly a star, Aunt Sara."

Misha, who had been quiet for most of the afternoon, said, "You are a star for me. And not because of the violin."

Bronya laughed. "I'm not a star in any way."

Misha reached into his pocket and held out a small object. "You saved my life."

The green pocketknife. Bronya had forgotten about it.

"You gave it to me, remember? It has helped me through hard times, just knowing you risked your life for mine."

Bronya took the knife, turned it over in her hand. "You kept it?"

"You should have it now."

Bronya remembered the kitchen in Rostov, the first day of the war. The pocketknife, Babushka's omens, and Avsey in his undershirt. Like yesterday. Yet here she was with Sara and Misha and Nazim in a place they could never have imagined then. She felt the stone in her heart loosen and rise, break away from its moorings, its sharp edges no longer taut against the soft tissue of her soul. Nazim had turned his back to the street and was looking at her.

Bronya swallowed hard and nodded her thanks. She took Sara's hand. "Every time I play, they are there. The music conjures their voices. You'll all come to the concerts, sit in the front row, and listen together."

AUTHOR'S STORY

I heard about the Ravine of Snakes in the modest apartment of a woman from Vitebsk, Belorussia. Tamara, was my Russian tutor. Long out of graduate school at Oxford and raising four children in rural North Carolina, I craved conversation and intellectual companionship. So in between school runs, music lessons and sporting events, I stole away once a week to practice Russian and converse with Tamara. Little did I know that at her dining room table, set with declension charts, cookies and verb conjugations, I would imbibe a chapter of Soviet history I didn't learn at Oxford.

Tamara was a Holocaust survivor. Her stories were fascinating, brave, sad. As a child, her father at the front, she'd fled the German advances with her mother and little brother, hunted by men with guns and ill will. Her tales of digging frozen potatoes with her bare feet, of the shame she felt begging from strangers and the terror she endured living in ditches, vulnerable to the elements and German aircraft, remain with me all these years later.

One day Tamara asked me if I'd heard of Zmievskaya Balka, the Ravine of Snakes in Rostov-on-Don, where 27,000 Jews were murdered by Einsatzgruppe D in 1942-1943. I shook my head. I had never linked the southern portion of the Soviet Union to the massacre of Jews during the Second World War.

The Holocaust had not been a part of my M.Phil coursework in Russian, Soviet and Eastern European Studies, though I had been an amateur historian of the Holocaust for as long as I could remember. In the summer of 1990, I drove through the newly liberated eastern European countries, walked the killing sites of Auschwitz-Birkenau and then as I drove the rural roads and urban thoroughfares of Poland, Czechoslovakia, Hungary and Yugoslavia, tried to imagine how one might escape as a Jew, where one might find refuge, where one might hide. I followed the post-Soviet effort to memorialize the victims of Babi Yar, the killing site in Ukraine where, beginning in 1941, close to 100,000 souls, Jews and non-Jews alike, were murdered by the Germans and their Ukrainian sympathizers. I read Yevtushenko, the poet of Babi Yar and Vassily Grossman who detailed not only the battle of Stalingrad but the murder of his Jewish grandmother by the Germans.

My interest in Eastern Europe never abated— When my children were small, I completed an MA in Health Education with a thesis documenting the lives of Bosnian Moslem women and their experience of genocide during the Bosnian war of the 1990s. Later, when my children were older, I embarked on an odyssey of sorts, the contours of which took me years to define. I wanted to return to Russia.

As it happened, I had friends in Rostov-on-Don. Rabbi Chaim Danziger and his wife Kaila welcomed me with open arms and introduced me to the elderly Holocaust survivors in their community. I interviewed them without knowing what I might do with their stories or how I might communicate them with the world.

On my last afternoon in Rostov, I interviewed a survivor whose escape story surprised and intrigued me. She had survived because she'd walked thousands of kilometers as a 14-year-old girl, alone. On the Lufthansa flight home the next evening, I knew I wanted to write the story of this woman and the other survivors from Rostov, a fictional account of the Holocaust in the Caucasus based on true events. A fictional account, my thinking went, would be the best way to offer these stories to the world and make them accessible. I am glad I didn't know then how long the process would take.

I returned to Rostov again the next year, welcomed once again by the Danzigers. I collected sensory data; photos, smells, images of everyday life and continued interviewing survivors. I walked the Jewish neighborhood and visited the synagogues. I visited other killing sites in the area; Taganrog, Proletarsky and again, Zmievskaya Balka. The facts were often overwhelming and I struggled with the nature of what I was learning and how to write it. I returned home to life in Raleigh, North Carolina to let the information percolate and to do more research.

I read Father Patrick Desbois' *The Holocaust by Bullets: A Priest's Journey to Uncover the Murder of 1.5 Million Jews*, in which he reminds readers that before the Wannsee Conference in 1942, when the fate of European Jewry was decided and before the full-throated operation of the camps, hundreds of thousands of Jews had already been murdered throughout the German Occupied Soviet Union by the Einsatzcommandos, often with the help of locals. Father Desbois' careful research (only possible because of the opening up of the archives in the former Soviet Union after the fall of Communism) and field documentation, specifically his interviews with non-Jewish witnesses, gave me a larger context and a way to triangulate the data from my own interviews. His organization, Yahad-in Unum, provided maps of what were the very beginnings of the destruction of large swathes of world Jewry.

And then on a family trip to Israel I found another element in the emerging story. During a visit with my mother-in-law in a nursing home, I met another survivor. I am not proud to say I have forgotten her name. I was a casual visitor, our conversation in smatterings of Hebrew, Russian and English, off-handed. She had an enormous photograph of her younger self on the wall of her small bedroom. She'd been beautiful. I did not record her or write anything she said in my notebook, except for one thing— She had escaped the Germans on the Georgian Military Highway in 1942. Now I needed to go to Georgia.

The next winter my husband and I spent ten days in Georgia with a driver called Vitaly who shepherded us around his country in a battered truck equipped with a cd player and a collection of Russian rock and roll. We spent days on the road awed by the beauty of the mountains, the hospitality of Georgians and the history of the region. We visited the places where there were still Jews and synagogues; Tbilisi, Kutaisi and Gori. We visited Borjomi and explored the ruins of a Romanov palace left to decay in the forest. Then we drove east and found an abandoned Soviet air force base inhabited by armed refugees from Abkhazia. We climbed the steep and poorly marked path at the 6th century cave monastery, David Gareja overlooking the Azerbaijani plain. Most importantly, we drove the entire Georgian Military Highway, to Vladikavkaz on the Russian-Georgian border and back. I now had almost every piece of my story. Or so I thought.

One afternoon in Tbilisi, Vitaly took us to a Mountain Jewish synagogue. We spent several hours speaking with a few of the congregants and I knew immediately that my story had to include their experience. While the Germans had looted and murdered Mountain Jews who inhabited the collective farms in the Caucasus (in Menzhinskoe and Bogdanovka, for example) the Mountain Jews in Mozdok and Nalchik, with the help of their Muslim neighbors, managed to stay alive by lying to the Germans, casting doubt on their Jewish ethnicity. The Germans investigated, eventually deciding the Mountain Jews belonged to a different ethnic group and the Einsatzgruppen tasked with destroying them, left them alone. I wanted to know more about the Mountain Jewish community and we returned to the Caucasus the next winter, this time to Azerbaijan.

In Azerbaijan our guide, an Azeri journalist named Arzu drove us to Krasnaya Svoboda (Red Village), a once vibrant Mountain Jewish town nestled in the foothills of the high mountains, 10 kilometers from the Russian-Dagestani border. Mountain Jews are remnants of the Persian empire's Jewish population and speak Judeo-Tat—A dialect of Persian. In Krasnaya Svoboda they also speak Hebrew, Russian and Azeri. We joined men playing backgammon in a tea house, their attention wavering between the game and a Turkish soap opera on the television above their heads. My husband, born in Turkey, was delighted to converse in Hebrew and Turkish as we watched small boys on their way home from school in the afternoon wearing the kippot religious Jews wear all over the world.

Arzu ferried us to other places too. He drove us up into the high mountains one day and to an ancient Zoroastrian site where fire surged from the ground, the next. We visited prehistoric petroglyphs, astonishing for their detail and beauty and the absence of other visitors. By the time we boarded a British Airways plane full of British oil workers and took off over the Caspian Sea, I had a tiny window into Mountain Jewish culture. Over the years, I would meet other Mountain Jews around the world, always learning more, each encounter a sign that in some small way I was giving voice to a few of the many untold stories of the World War II in the Caucasus.

Gradually, and over many years I wrote the story of Bronya and Avsey and their ill-fated quest through the Soviet landscape of war. Researching and writing *You, With Your Waiting* has been an excruciatingly satisfying endeavour. It is my great privilege to share the Abramov family story now as a way to memorialize the lives of innocents so easily forgotten in the grand narratives of history.

ACKNOWLEDGMENTS

I want to express my gratitude and admiration for the courage and tenacity with which Holocaust survivors told me their stories over the years. That they were willing to offer a stranger an accounting of the most difficult chapters of their lives, is a testament to human resilience. It has been my honor to listen and attempt to imbue their stories with the dignity they deserve. I hope I have succeeded, at least partially, in giving voice to the lives they lived.

Then there are the writers, readers, editors and artists who have read drafts of my manuscript in whole or in part and helped to make it better. To those who taught me the elements of story-telling, helped me to refine my modest skills and encouraged and supported the long writing process—Thank you. My fondness and gratitude are immeasurable and never-ending. Any and all mistakes are my own.

To my friends, to my guides in far-away places and to the others who accompanied me, willingly or unwillingly on this journey—Thank you. To the people at cocktail parties and Friday night dinners around the world who have put up with my incessant enthusiasm for this work—my heartfelt thanks.

To my children whose love and patience buoy me always, I hope to repay the favor!

Lastly, to my travel companion and polyglot, adventurer husband–without your strong Turkish tea, your organizational skills and your love, I would never have finished this work. I love you.

ABOUT THE AUTHOR

Leslie Lacin is an emerging author of historical fiction. She is currently working on her second novel about Jewish life in the south of France after the Second World War. She lives in Raleigh, North Carolina with her husband and two terriers where they welcome friends, family and stray travelers.